THE KISSING NUMBER

LOUISE FURLEY

The Kissing Number

ISBN- 978-1-7349807-8-3 (Paperback)
ISBN- 978-1-7349807-7-6 (eBook)

Cover design by Pixel Mischief Design

Books by Louise Furley

Solitar

Halo Valley

Isle of Orainn

Anastasia

Distilled Duplicity

The Poser

Wrath of Wolf

Devil's Prince

Devil's Seed

Jungle Treasure

Jancarlo Mercury

THE KISSING NUMBER

CHAPTER ONE

Her heartbeats kicked up, she crowed, "Aha! I knew they were hiding something down here!" Piles of boxes lined two walls. Lifting a box to see behind the pile, Kandy-Marie Birchfield grinned with excited triumph at the crates stacked behind the boxes.

She couldn't wait to tell Rex about her find. Her smile softened, she thought of him with the fond affection of a puppy. A sexy puppy.

He was such a hippy, high on weed all the time, it was a wonder he was able to keep the gallery out of the red, and that was by the skin of his teeth. He may be goofy mellow, but he'll surely be pissed to find out someone's been hiding stuff in the basement!

There was really no reason for her to be in the dank old storage basement. It was her job to catalogue the artwork that arrived at the D'Faience Artinquity Gallery. "Huh," she snorted at the pretentious name.

Examining the box, she mumbled, "Faience, just tin-glazed earthenware. Other than the freaky Egyptian statue standing outside of the gallery there isn't another doggone piece of faience inside. Not much turnover with the paintings either."

Shaking the box in her hands, she tossed it and picked up another one, shook it. "Well, well, well, they're all empty. Just a screen to hide the real stuff."

Shoving the empty boxes aside to get to the crates, Kandy-Marie muttered under her breath, "I tell Rex the art is crap, but because the talentless artist is his friend, he never listens to me. You'd think he'd, *ow-* dammit." Trying to lift the lid up on a crate a nail tore off, it bounced off the wood and skittered across the floor.

Cursing, she glanced around to find something to get the lid open. Spotting a screwdriver on a dusty shelf, she grabbed it and proceeded to pry the lid off the crate. "Yeah," she murmured with

1

distain, "how they get away with putting a ten-foot tall, blue statue of a naked Egyptian lady with the ugly head of a bird by the entrance- ho-*lee* shit!"

Her eyes bugged out at the sight she unveiled. The dismayed grin widened as visions of blackmail thousands pinged in her head. "Oh yeah, all I need to do is catch- *ugh-*"

Wham! The crowbar slammed into the back of Kandy-Marie's head and she dropped like a sack of mud.

Two people stood over her. One of them sank to one knee, felt for a pulse, finding none and seeing her eyes open and blank, he tutted, "Damn, you killed her. I wanted to question the bitch, find out if she told anyone else about her suspicions." Wiping his hand on his pants he stood up.

"Whatever. Now her mouth is shut permanently, she won't be telling anyone anything. A dimwitted skank hired part time to keep things looking copasetic, she didn't blab to anyone. She didn't even know what she'd find until just now. We've been between the sheets with her enough times to learn other than her suspicions, there was nothing else going on upstairs." He tapped his head with a finger.

Bending over the girl he grasped her ankles and said, "Grab her arms, let's get her out of here before her blood gets ingrained. It's Monday night, there won't be anyone around to see us. Remember to destroy her phone."

"Okay, wait." The other man looked around then snagged a cloth covering a busted lamp. Crouching next to her, he wrapped the cloth around Kandy-Marie's crushed skull to keep the leaking crimson fluid from staining the cement floor. The pair lifted the body and hauled it up the stairs.

CHAPTER TWO

Digging his fingers angrily into his scalp then dragging them through his light brown hair disturbing the normal stiff neatness, Ellery Delian cursed then said into the phone, "You told me that on his deathbed in Singapore, Thorne Arabat, one of our leading smugglers informed Jang Jie that he was leaving his estate to his daughter." His querulous huffs spurted as his anger grew. "On that info I seduced that damned girl so I-"

A voice from the receiver cut him off, "You'd better worry more about Vitale Palumbo when he hears one of our major lines is expunged."

Shaking his head in disgust, Ellery's lips clamped in ire. He groused, "I got my own worries here dealing with my middle man. Right now, my problem is you, you screwed the pooch, my man, now I have to-" He broke off as his fiancée slipped daintily into the room. Abruptly hanging up, he slammed the landline down then scraped his fingers down his face to rake in his anger.

Her shy voice barely above a whisper, Coli Cassidy slowed her pace as she approached Delian. Holding her hand out, with a small timid smile she said, "Here, Ellery," and handed him the glass of amber liquid. "It's almost five, here's the cocktail you prefer in the later afternoon. I left the bottle out, I know you'll want more-"

Coli's head snapped to the side from Ellery's slap. Ignoring her cry out at the sting, the ice clunked and sloshed when he impatiently snatched the glass out of her hand.

Voice grinding, he threatened, "Don't you tell me I drink too much, woman. Do it again, Colipatra, and you'll get worse than a little slap." His elegant sip of the liquor an obscene contrast to his roughness with the slight girl, he said coldly, "Go wash your face, your sister and her mother don't need to see your sorry ass tears," and he headed to the door leaving her standing with her hand to her red cheek, lips trembling, angst smoldering.

Twenty minutes later, Ellery enthused, "Goldie." Greeting her, he smiling broadly at the woman entering the lavish parlor saying, "You are as ravishing as always. A feat of phenomenon, I do believe you look younger every time I see you." His custom-made grey suit fit his substantial shoulders nicely, the slacks almost too tight on his strong legs. He wore spit-polished, dark grey leathers with tassels.

He nodded to Goldie's daughter beside her, his tone dropped to a husky purr. "And my dear Silina, you, well," he took her hand, lifted it to his lips, kissed her knuckles gently. He allowed his cylinder-shaped brown eyes to stroll down her figure and back up, the smile tugged his lids down. "You are loveliness in a va-va-voom sexy package, eh?"

The butler who ushered the women in made his exit. The three ignored Coli standing off to the side silently observing her fiancé greet her half-sister Silina, and Silina's mother, Goldie.

"Oh you are too much, Ellery," Goldie Arabat gushed with a vain simper and a faux slap to his arm. "You exaggerate just the tiniest bit," her giggle twittered girlishly coy.

Silina sidled close to Ellery and slid her arm through his.

Goldie gazed down her long nose at Coli hovering in the corner. "Coli you lazy snail, get us drinks, what are you waiting for?" Her sigh belabored, she turned her smile to Ellery. "That girl, as useless as tits on a fish, I don't know how you bear her obtuseness." Her snide nose went up at Coli's simple flowered sundress. Goldie and Silina's slinkier dresses showed off their figures, leaving little to the imagination.

Not sparing a glance in his fiancée's direction, Ellery replied with a shrug, "Ah, she has her uses." His grin sharpened at Silina's snicker.

Hiding the hurt of their remarks, Coli tried to not let it get to her as she watched the women simper and snigger together, and sneer at her while they pawed her fiancé.

Goldie's crown of golden hair swirled around her face. At 53, she would still be pretty with her deep-set hazel eyes and enhanced figure if her expression wasn't etched in perpetual cynicism, and her nose was a tad too long, almost pointed.

Silina was a younger replica of her mother. She had the same manufactured bosom and cosmetically white teeth, dark blonde hair, although neither had to augment their buttocks.

When he'd been around, Goldie's husband Thorne made endless jokes about their wide bums, like, "I could toss a bridle on their backs and have them plow fields instead of the donkeys. Or," he'd laugh at their chagrin, "we'd only need just the two of them to fill up the bleachers to cheer on the teams!"

Goldie snapped her fingers at Coli, ordered, "Get to it girl, I need to wet my whistle."

Coli blinked out of her stupor and quickly moved to the bar set against one wall and prepared the drinks. The circular parlor was richly resplendent in peach and blue hues, the settee and chair cushions in a floral pattern, the rug silky, ivory Persian. Coli handed a Van Gogh vodka martini to Goldie.

The older woman's lip curled in derision, she shoved the glass back at Coli. Uncaring the liquor splashed over Coli's hand she snipped, "A twist? You know damned well I want olives. Take it back and do it right." She rolled her eyes at Ellery as Coli, her cheeks tinted pink with humiliation returned to the bar.

An hour later at dinner, her elbows on the table, waving her fork in the air, Silina said, "I still can't figure out how my mousey little sister hooked such a great stud, uh," her fingertips coquettishly covered her mouth. She cocked her head at Ellery, said with brazen solicitation, "I mean, you are so handsome, so wealthy, I can't see you," blatantly scavenging his well-shaped body in the expensive

suit, her eyes flit with disgust to Coli, "with my sister," she sighed in heavy resignation, "well, as I said, such a dull mouse."

At her mother's laugh, Silina grinned at her, cut a piece of blood-red prime rib and chewed it with gusto, her chomps gushy on the juicy meat.

"Ah, well," Ellery mused, appraising his fiancée. "Colipatra needs a strong man to keep her…" his lids lowered over the debased glint in the thin brown eyes, "on track. She knows as I have a good sixteen years on her I have the experience and wisdom to guide her. She knows her duties, when she doesn't keep in line as I demand, well," one shoulder lifted, "she is aware of the consequences, eh my flower?" His mealy eyes dared Coli to complain.

A loud sigh trilled from Silina, her eyes simmering with unconcealed lust at her sister's fiancé. "Oh, Ellery, I do love a…dominant man."

Her mother rolled her eyes at her daughter's cheeky words, then went on to deride Coli. "That ridiculous name," Goldie sneered, "what was her mother thinking?" They continued talking about Coli as if she wasn't present, or too dumb to speak. "She couldn't even spell Cleopatra correctly. Then she shortens it to Coli, what is she, Lassie? A collie dog?"

With a mild smile, Ellery lightly scolded her, "Now Goldie…"

"Vixie Cassidy was likely drunk or high or both when she squatted and pooped her out then signed the birth certificate," Silina offered.

"I mean, the slut produced my half-sister after a cheap one-night stand with my father. She gets her plainness from her mother. Anyway," she leaned closer to Ellery. He sat at the head of the long table with her at his right and her mother at his left. Coli sat beside her sister.

"Considering the evil little convict is sneaky and oh so dangerous," Silina said, grinning at Coli's sharp intake of breath, "you are a brave, strong man to take her in and keep her on the straight and narrow. I bet you don't let her get away with a thing, am I right?"

"Well," Ellery said, while stabbing an asparagus spear, "I make sure my young felon works 10-11 hours every day at Beaker's Laundromat, keeps her out of trouble and trim with that hard work, eh, my flower?"

Bending his head so he could see her, he winked at the shame spreading over Coli's pearly complexion. "With her record, she couldn't get hired anywhere without my connections."

Pupils enlarging, his mouth curled up on one side at the pink that flowed into Coli's high round cheeks. "She isn't near as beautiful as you by any measure, my lovely Silina." He shot her an admiring smile, then back to Coli where he paused, intently studying her.

"But, her features are quite remarkable, those huge blue eyes, plush lips, small tilted nose, put together on that smooth face shaped like an ivy leaf, flaxen hair spun into shiny fat curls, and that delicately stacked body of soft curves, well," he grunted, shifting in his seat, his own face warmed. "She's the kind of girl that makes it a struggle for a man to tear his sensibilities away."

"So," Goldie interjected, bored with the attention on Coli, she asked Ellery, "are you coming to Texas for Thorne's funeral?"

Silina eagerly tossed in, "Don't forget the reading of the will." She bragged, "Papa would have left everything to me, you know. I mean, I haven't seen him in years, living way out there in Singapore, he hasn't been home to Builu in what, Mama, fifteen years at least, right?"

Dollar signs dancing in her hazel eyes, Goldie's smile broadly avaricious she acknowledged, "At least, baby. Long enough to amass a fortune."

The greedy eyes slid to her daughter then to Ellery, she remarked, "A fortune he undoubtedly left to me and Silina. Only to us, he wouldn't shame us by leaving a dime to his bastard daughter." All three pairs of eyes latched onto Coli.

If only her misery could drill a hole in the floor for her to disappear into. Drawing a weighty breath, Coli looked straight at her sister and said, "And Kip? When you are wealthy beyond all means and can afford the best care, will you finally bring him home?"

CHAPTER THREE

Although he knew his name wouldn't be mentioned in the will, Silina's grandfather, the very regal, debonair Auston Augustine sat at the table next to the attorney, Baxter Wickerson. Auston's stacked palms cupped the top of the silver lion's head of his cane, the tip of the cane digging into the carpet.

Entering the room, Coli tossed her long light hair back off slender shoulders and consciously straightened her spine. Keeping her face averted from Auston, she slipped onto a chair as far from him as she could get. Nonetheless, she caught the knowing palpation in his hooded eyes tracking her movements.

Silina and Goldie were already present. Their golden heads together, they rudely whispered, ignoring Mr. Wickerson's reproving frown. When Coli was seated, the barrister cleared his throat and gathered the sheaves of papers in front of him laid out on the vintage cherry wood table. Standing the papers up on end, he tapped them on the table, evening the edges.

They were ensconced in his conference room inside the stately building with austere yet tastefully refined rooms. Burgundy walls trimmed with high white borders and floor moldings, overlarge, dark brown leather chairs with gold studding filled the room with luxurious comfort. Three narrow but long windows let in the midday sun.

Wickerson gazed kindly on Coli. "Welcome, my dear. I hope your trip here was uneventful yet pleasant?" He adjusted wire-rimmed glasses on his nose, grey turning white hair plastered precisely to one side. In his late sixties, his suit was an impeccable dark blue. Tapping the papers again, he smiled at the flush staining the young woman's cheeks at his attention. *Shy little thing*, he thought.

Her eyes shifted around the table avoiding looking directly at anyone, she finally raised them shyly to the attorney. "Yes, it was fine," she murmured. "Ellery went on ahead while I closed up the apartment."

"A long way from Ohio to Texas right?" he asked her politely.

"For frig's sake, let off the pleasantries Wickerson, and get on with it," Goldie snapped. "We aren't here to make BFF's, just read the damned will."

Silina grinned with an insolent snicker. Auston's posture remained rigid, his face a brusque mask.

The barrister's eyes cut over to the middle-aged woman, and narrowed.

Her head tipped back, Goldie looked down her nose at him and sniffed. Identical coifs of stiff, blonde, shoulder length bobs, mother and daughter were dressed almost like twin southern belles in white dresses with red polka dots, both décolletages so low cut the reserved attorney almost blushed himself in discomfiture at the doubly abundant cleavage.

Wickerson cleared his throat again and shuffled the papers in his hands before settling them back on the table. "As you wish, Ms. Arabat."

"That's Mrs. Arabat, old man, *Mrs*. I was married to Thorne Arabat, unlike that girl's whore of a mother who seduced him while he was away from home and..." she managed a moist eye and a sniff, "desperate with loneliness. She took advantage of my sweet, sweet husband."

"Huh," Silina snorted. "He was so sweet he stayed away from us for fifteen years. If he was so lonely he could have come home."

Her lips dragged down bitterly, "Not a card or present on my birthdays, Christmas, nothing."

"He paid the bills, honey, that's what was important," Goldie soothed her.

Glaring icepicks at her sister, Silina sneered with jealous resentment, "Yeah, you sued him for the money. But, he sent letters to her," she flicked her head at Coli.

"Now, now, honey," commiserating, Goldie patted her daughter's hand. "He only felt sorry for her. First prison, then stuck with that slutty junkie of a mother, he-"

"*Mrs.* Arabat," Wickerson interrupted her. Coughing into his hand, he drummed his knuckles on the papers. "As you said, let's get on with this." A shudder of distaste rippled across his shoulders. Smoothing his red tie with age-spotted fingers, he cleared his throat and began reading, "Ahem, well, 'With sound mind and-'"

Slapping her hand on the table, Goldie demanded, "Skip all that legal crap, Wickerson, just tell us what he left us."

With a heavy sigh, the lawyer flipped through a dozen pages to one of the last. Skimming down the page, he told them briefly that the bulk of Thorne's monetary estate would go to Silina, a small fund to Goldie, while the house he had grown up in, in Texas was left to Coli.

He advised the group, "The house passed from Thorne's longtime sickly grandmother to him when she died years ago. The building has been vacant for, oh, at least five years." He didn't mention that around 600 wooded acres came with the house.

"What?" Silina shrieked. Pointing a finger at Coli, she accused with sour contempt, "Why did he leave her a house?" Slamming both fists on the table, she shouted, "It should be mine! It should all belong to me!"

"Baby," Goldie cooed, "it's just a nasty ancient money pit. The land it's on is scrappy rock, it's not worth a tarnished penny. Even if she manages to sell that monstrosity that Thorne's grandmother was trying to turn into a B&B before she grew so sickly, Coli won't get a thin nickel from it. Heaven knows, the old woman was always

screwy with some kind of mental illness she could barely take care of herself.

"It's just a burden, honey, you should feel sorry for her that he unloaded that dump on her. She'll have to try to sell it just to pay the taxes, and likely have to cough up her own bucks to satisfy Mr. IRS. Now," eyes glowing, she gushed, "let's start making a list of what we can buy with your inheritance!"

The paperwork signed and sorted and notarized, Wickerson handed copies to the ladies, and keys and directions to the old house in Mal Tierre, Texas to Coli. With stiff politeness, the barrister thanked them all, said if they had questions to feel free to contact him.

Brushing a finger along his white moustache, Auston stood up, said, curtly, "Thank you, Wickerson. Ladies." He nodded to Goldie and Silina. "You can figuratively count your cash in the auto on the way home."

Leaning on his cane, he turned to Coli. The girl sat stiffly staring blankly at the table with anxious eyes. "We'll meet you at home, Colipatra, if that trashed car makes it. It got you from Ohio to here, should be good. Come along, girls," he held his hand out to sweep his daughter and granddaughter out of the room.

The old car rattled and wheezed along the highway, Coli clutched the wheel tightly with both hands. She hadn't expected anything from her father. Last she saw him was before she'd been dispatched to the juvenile penitentiary, and he had only sent a smattering of letters to her over the years, with no return address.

How Silina knew about them, oh, that's right, she would have snooped through Coli's things in Ohio as well as here in Texas.

A fitful sigh rolling through her, she headed not to her half-sister's grandfather's house, but to the monstrosity that her dad left her on Wisteria Road in Mal Tierre.

A warm hint of happiness sifted proudly through her, bringing a slight smile to Coli's wan face, still pallid from the wretched, stressful afternoon she'd spent with her family.

Her dad had left her something, she wasn't just a nobody, a nothing, maybe he had loved her the tiniest little bit. She kept to herself that the attorney had told her Silina's inheritance would likely be snatched from her by the government as it was likely income from illegal activities.

Also, she kept quiet that Wickerson said the house sat on 600 plus acres, most of it thick forest. That cheerful thought stayed with her until she pulled into the driveway of her inheritance.

Parking the car she groaned, "Oh Lordy." Goldie was right, it was a monstrosity. Coli exited the car and stood on the gravel driveway, taking in the house. Not house, Victorian mansion. It was enormous, three stories of magnificence in peeling white paint. "My goodness," she murmured with awe, "those are real turrets."

Eyes huge, she started up the drive to the house. She could see at least six white-bricked chimneys, and over one corner of the house was a small A-framed roof, a balcony perched over another section. Abutments, some square, some rounded, jutted around the immense building like a quaint castle.

She reached the entrance and gazed up. Several stone steps led up to a wide verandah with a thick brick overhang. White columns soldiered the doorway and wrought-iron fencing topped the roof, like a widow's walk.

The veranda wrapped around more than half of the first floor. Just perfect, Coli thought, for guests to visit in rocking chairs, play checkers maybe while sipping lemonade.

To the right of the driveway was a circle of grouped wrought-iron benches, across from those Coli could see another structure, it matched the house yet on a smaller scale. Giant oaks and ancient elms strutted the vast grounds. Weeping willows draped over numerous stone pathways that led from the mausoleum in all directions.

"Wow." Coli's eyes darted everywhere like flies on honey drops, it was a lot to take in. "I can see why Grandma would want to make this into a bed-and-breakfast. Good thing I love to cook." She slowly wandered up the steps thinking about the grandmother that had died before Coli got to know her.

Tugging a set of keys out of her pocket, she found the correct one and opened the big door. It creaked, dust wafted as she pushed it open. Her heart sunk with dismay. The outside needed a coat of paint, the inside, well, it needed everything.

The wallpaper peeled off in shreds, the tile and wood-planked floors and borders were chipped and worn, the wood was discolored and tatted in many spaces. The high ceilings were strung from corner to corner with cobwebs. Furniture covered in dusty white sheets scattered the main gallery.

She trudged around the house, making mental notes of what needed to be done. Upstairs, the tower room was the best. Round and romantic with several bow windows and a fireplace.

When she grew weary of touring, she sat in her car and stared up at the mansion, her jaw set with resolve. "I can do this, the house is paid for, I only need to take care of the taxes, electricity, water, all that stuff, and the supplies to fix it up. Once the B&B is up and running, I'll make money hand over fist." Her shoulders slumped as she turned the ignition on. "I hope."

The drive back to her mockery of a family's home in a different town seemed to take forever, yet it also sped by in a dreadful flash. Last thing Coli wanted was to go inside the big plantation-styled house and have to be with Silina, Goldie, and worse of all, Goldie's father, Auston Augustine who was Salina's grandfather but not a blood relation to Coli.

The days she'd been staying with them had been horrid. Silina's bitching, Goldie's sniping and ridiculing, and the creepy, sick feelings, blurred memories that crawled repulsively up her spine at the frightening sight of the austere, dapper grandfather. Under black wings and low lids, his ebony eyes tracked her every move. Of course there was also Ellery's brutal bullying.

CHAPTER FOUR

Sheriff Brogan Dillon zoomed down the serpentine rural road on his Hog. The air rushed through his dark hair, shades protected his green eyes, he hunched over the handles, the wind rippling over the leather jacket. He slowed to take a sharp corner, when a car raced towards him from up ahead.

The impatient driver overcompensated the hairpin turn causing him to enter Brogan's lane, his bumper struck Brogan's bike sending it spiraling.

"*Ahh*," the groan hurt scraping from his smashed lungs. Brogan lay on his back on the asphalt, his entire body screaming in pain. Still stunned, he couldn't push his eyes open.

"Shh," a whisper near his ear said, "don't move. You're injured, just lie still, the ambulance is on the way." The voice soothed Brogan's agony, his head tilted towards it. It was so soft, gentle, tone as sweet as sugar with a sultry hush to it. He wanted to hear more. Small, delicate fingers lightly brushed his hair off his forehead, he groaned.

Gently petting him, she continued her soft whispers. "Just relax, I won't leave you alone, everything will be just fine. Your motorcycle is scarcely damaged, you were able to gain enough control to let it skid into the grass before you were thrown off." She held his hand, murmuring quiet words of support.

Brogan fought to peel his lids up, he had to see where the entrancing melodic voice came from. Her soft words pierced his throbbing brain, passing through the dizziness and nausea that indicated he had a concussion. He could only make out a blurred face, it was shrouded with haze. The eyes were the only things he could see and they were a sea of blue mist.

"Hell," he groaned, feeling road rash burning his face, his arms. He was dying and God had sent him His prettiest angel. *Thank you*, he said in his mind.

Her eyes were certainly of an angel. Brilliant and gentle, twin blue skies gazed softly vibrant down at him, he could just make out small yet plush lips, he felt his loins tighten. Good, he wasn't dead, or broken too badly.

"Angel," he croaked, and reached up to touch her face. He needed to clear the haze from her face so he could see the rest of her. Straining, blinking, his eyes watered, he could make out those gorgeous lips, then a tiny nose, but the shroud refused to reveal all her features at once, it just moved around.

All he could perceive was a blurred figure kneeling, bent over him. A halo of gilded hair fell forward, tickling his damaged face.

At the sounds of sirens, she bent and kissed his forehead, then leaned back, gently setting his hand on his stomach, she patted it.

"They're here, they'll help you, you'll be fine now."

He could hear her shifting to her feet. "No-" he cried in a panic, throwing his hand out to grasp her. "Don't go, wait-" The sirens drowned out his pleas.

His body was too injured to let him rise up and go after her. His vision too cloudy to make her out, through wounded pinholes he watched her faint, watery form disappear into the tawny mist. "*Angel*," the word drained out of him in a wounded sigh as he passed out.

Twelve weeks later, Brogan reluctantly slammed the door of his pickup truck and tramped around the back of the house to where loud boisterous sounds rippled on the crisp, early spring breeze. Hitching his belt up his lean hips, he rounded the corner.

The back yard and patio were teeming with gleeful people, eating, drinking, laughing, a few kids skipped and chased each other around the grassy lawn.

Brogan was sure that along with the clambake abounding with corn on the cob, potato salad and such, there would be barbequed ribs, burgers, and enough food to feed the entire Lone Star State.

Most were dressed like him, jeans, boots, flannel or thermal shirts, many with cowboy hats, the girls, braving the still coolish air in shorts and fancy sweaters.

A few gave him waved greetings as he made his way to one of the grills. He bent at the cooler by the grill and took out a cold beer. Snapping the tab, he put the can to his mouth and guzzled half of it.

"Hey, Brog, didn't expect to see you here, you usually stay clear of parties, but I'm glad you showed." One of his deputies clapped him on the back with a grin. "After that nasty crash it's good to see you up on your feet. Those enforced couple weeks in the hospital gave you a well-needed rest."

Brogan turned to the brawny blond wearing a brown Stetson that matched his own black one, only the deputy's was cleaner and less worn. "Rocky," he nodded to his friend, swigged the rest of his beer, then wiped his mouth with the back of his hand.

Rolling his sleeves up his hard forearms, Brogan crushed the can in his hand, tossed it in the trashcan and got himself another and handed one to Rocky, AKA Deputy Elvin Narocki.

"Hey, pard, get me one too," Detective Kurt Vantarzani said, as he joined them.

Both men turned, Rocky commented, "Didn't think you were gonna make it, Tarzan. What happened to your plans to go to the lake?"

The detective wrinkled his tanned nose, scratched at the neat beard. Eyes as dark as his chocolate hair twinkled. "Boat's in the shop. It was leaking diesel."

"So? You were taking Sherleen fishing, you couldn't think of something else to do with her?" Rocky's grin implied he'd have thought of something.

Tarzan accepted the beer Brogan handed him. "We already did that something. When not getting laid, she's tedious as hell. Drones on and on about nail polish and shit. That's why I was taking her fishing. She made me feel bad when I snuck out of her room the other night after wham bam, I mean," he rolled his eyes.

"She cried, guilt-tripped me, begged me to take her out. I thought fishing, hell, there's no talking then, right? So I wouldn't have to struggle making conversation with a wall. A stacked wall, yeah, but still, nothing but wood and plaster inside that pretty head."

"So you ditched her anyway," Rocky said.

The detective had the grace to look abashed. "Yeah, well, we shagged and I couldn't take her inanity anymore, I had to hoof. Sex is great but sometimes I'd actually like to have an interesting conversation with a woman too. What about you, Brog? What are you doing here?"

Slugging down the rest of his beer, Brogan told him, "Tamy Lee cornered me at a bodega, pestered me until to get her off my back I said I'd come. I've made my appearance, I'll pop a few clams, gnaw a rib, suck down some beers and I'm outta here."

Rocky frowned. "Shit, Brog, everyone knows you're a cold, brooding son of a bitch, but you can act a little friendly once in a while. Been a raccoon's age since I've seen you with a broad. I mean, if you don't want Tamy Lee," he crooked his head to the left pointing out the brunette bombshell in question that fortunately hadn't seen Brogan yet.

"There's plenty of hot skirts here. Aisha and Tandy would give their favorite stilettoes for a night with you." Chuckling, Rocky grinned at Brogan's twisted lips.

"You know I don't hit the talent in Shire's Cross, Rock. I don't want sticko fingers clingin' to me, showin' up on my doorstep. Besides," Brogan said, glancing around, "ain't nothin' here stokin' my fire, not worth the effort."

"Huh," Rocky grunted. "Hasn't been a broad around for quite a pack of time since you've bothered to make the effort. Admit it, you're just a cold, hard bastard with hate and pain buried so deep in

your heart it's turned into a red glacier. Except for a few of us close to you, you don't give two shits about anyone else."

Brogan bumped a shoulder. "So what. I take care of this town, its residents. I do my job."

The edge of his lip pulling in, Tarzan said, "Everyone knows you'd throw your life down for every single body in Builu County and Shire's Cross, and all the other surrounding towns, but bro, it's time you lightened up. Grab yourself a girl, or two, or three, there's plenty here willing, and have a good time. Let that dark shit inside you go.

You can't go back, you can't un-ring the bell. It was atrocious what happened to you, to us. The hell of it has dug its talons deep inside your gut and is holding on, relentlessly destroying you. You have to try to let it go, man."

Squinting green eyes at his friend, Brogan grunted. "I don't recall writing a check for psychiatric services, Doctor Tarzan. Lay off, I don't need a bang right now. When I do, I'll hitch on out to Heuco."

Rolling his eyes, Tarzan sipped his beer watching the women, even the married ones, scarcely trying to hide their surreptitious observance of the three lawmen with steamy interest in their eyes. He and Brogan and Rocky, although different as night and day, garnered way more than their share of heated, inviting looks.

With a Master's in Police Science, Tarzan was a detective with classically chiseled model looks, but scars marred his tanned beauty, toughening his masculinity with an edge of danger.

Rocky, a deputy, with his blond hair and friendly blue eyes, was the opposite of Sheriff Brogan's angry, brooding darkness.

Face as harsh as a ragged mountain, meaner than a junkyard dog, green eyes shaded with hell and hate, restrained violence clung to Brogan like a rough coat. Yet, women were still drawn to the fiercely private, tough lawman, melting in his virility like papyrus in a raging fire.

Rocky said, "Listen, Brog, the twins, Patty and Hattie have hot pants for both of us, why don't we-"

"I gotta go." Brogan tossed the empty beer can into the trash, spun on his heel and stalked away leaving his friends frowning sadly at his broad back.

Muttering profanities under his breath, Brogan strode through the heavy partying throng and around the side of the house heading for his truck. As he passed the front, he saw a ladder propped up against the house.

Curious, he followed the rungs up until, he groaned, "Have mercy, *hola mamacita*, hello little mama." Feeling his jeans tighten, he looked up at the juiciest, roundest ass he'd ever seen. Small, but plump globes of lush flesh that would fit perfectly in his big calloused hands.

Moving closer, his gaze traveled slim but shapely legs up to the shorts that hugged that incredible behind, up to the curved indention of her tiny waist. Was the front as amazing as the back? No way, impossible. Gotta be ugly as sin. Long, fluffy saffron curls bounced around her back as she reached over- the ladder tipped-

"Shit, girl!" he barked. Jumping forward, he grabbed the side of the tumbling ladder and shoved a hand under that hot ass keeping her from falling.

Letting out a shriek, one hand clinging madly to the ladder, the other clutched a hammer that she had been desperately trying to bash into the wall.

When Brogan slapped his palm under her butt she dropped the hammer with a yelp. Gasping in shock, she gripped both sides of the ladder now, holding her body close to the rungs. Sucking in fast breaths, she glared down at him.

He had leveled the ladder, his hand still firmly under her bottom. She shouted down to him, "What do you think you're doing? You scared me half to death!"

With a sly grin, he raised his hat, gave a short bow and said, "You're welcome."

"What are you talking about? Why should I thank you?" Her chest hitched with startled breaths.

The grin widened. "I saved your beautiful neck, sweetheart." Then he frowned. "What the hell are you doin' up there, anyway?"

She huffed, catching her bearings, pointed at a sign resting on a rung. It said, 'Clambake by O'Riordan's.'

His lips pursed at the sign, then back up to her. "Again, what the hell are you doin' up there? You're fixin' to fall and break aforesaid neck."

"Harrumph," she huffed again. "I was just fine until you came along and startled me. Can you please hand me that hammer?" She pointed to the ground. Then she said coolly, "And remove your hand from my, uh, behind."

Brogan looked down at the hammer, then to his hand still webbing her butt, and smirked. "That's a man's job, sweetheart," to himself he thought, *both, hammering and butt squeezing, definitely a man's job, and he was a man.* The smirk lowered to a frown. "Again, why the hell are *you* doin' it?"

He effectively had her pinned to the ladder. Twisting awkwardly on the step she demanded, "You remove your hand from my- bottom you perv, before I start screaming."

"Yeah, okay, if you insist." He forced himself not to squeeze that fine hunk of flesh before he dropped his hand.

"Now, can you please hand me the," with another huff, she muttered, "never mind, I'll get it myself." She started down the ladder that he still held. When she reached near the bottom, Brogan didn't move. That round derriere pressed into his pelvis, she couldn't step down to the ground or her body would be flush against his.

Feeling his appreciation of the situation hardening against her butt, a blush curled up her neck and warmed her cheeks. She half-turned to see his cocky grin. A day's worth of whiskers darkened his hard jaw. Quickly looking away, she said coldly, "Step back, or I swear I'll scream the house down."

"Okay, feisty tiger cub, don't get your panties in a bind, I was just makin' sure you didn't fall." He released the ladder and moved back so she could step down.

Shooting him a glare, the girl shoved fat blonde curls off her shoulders and turned quickly so he couldn't see her embarrassed face stained pink. She stepped to retrieve the hammer but he bent

and snatched it up before she could. "Hey," she frowned then ordered, "give me that."

Quickly bounding up the ladder, Brogan laughed. "No, little tiger cubbie, I got it." He took the sign and pounded a couple of nails that were in a cup attached to the rung into the wall.

Leaning back, he studied it to make sure it was straight and grinned down at her. She was standing with her hands set angrily on her small hips. He jumped down the last few rungs and held the hammer out to her.

Angrily grabbing the hammer, she snapped, "How dare you! You're ridiculous with your, 'It's man's work.'"

Crossing big arms over a strapping chest, he smirked drily at her. His gaze swarmed over her body. Big handfuls of plump breasts pushed angrily against her blouse, his pupils expanded making the green eyes darken. *Oh yeah, the front totally rivaled the back, fuckin' totally.*

At her near accident, he sobered, stowing the grin. "Little girl, you were about to take a nasty spill when I came along and prevented it. You didn't know shit from shinola what the hell you were doin'." Brows lowered displaying his irritation. "What asshole handed you that hammer and told you to do this?"

She turned to the ladder, snipped, "That's none of your business." Wrapping her fingers around the sides of the ladder she tugged to close it. It didn't budge. She fought with the steel to fold it up, but the ladder wasn't cooperating.

"I'm guessin' a man hauled that ladder out and put it up for you. Even if you could close it, it'd fall on you and crush you when you tried to set it on the ground, much less carry it." Spouting his lecture he went on, "You're a tiny thing, what the hell were you and that asshole thinkin'?"

Blinking huge blue eyes up at him, a scowl thinning her pretty lips she told him, "I had a job to do, Mister, and I was quite capable of doing it without your interference," and pulled hard at the infuriating ladder. It staggered, started to tip.

"Aw, woman, get the hell out of the way." Brogan nudged her aside and caught the ladder. Burly muscles bunching, with ease he

calmly closed it together and let it slide to the ground, then picked it up with his big hand with no trouble. Her eyes rounded at his bulging biceps, she quickly stepped back, the color fled her face.

His brows dropped. "What's the matter? You're not afraid of me? Listen-"

She pivoted and strode, almost jogged to a van parked in the driveway. In confusion he watched her flee, that fine little bum twitching in those jean shorts. What had he done to scare her off?

When she opened the door to the van, Brogan shrugged, perplexed, and stalked around the house to the garage to put the ladder up. Once he'd done that, he thought maybe he could use another cold beer, no, he knew what he really wanted.

The hottest thing to hit his senses in forever, and for some inexplicable reason, she was afraid of him. "What the hell," he growled and strode out of the garage. They were going to have a talk, the fierce little tiger cub and him. Straighten things out. Get her number.

His face relaxed with a scant smile, maybe he could take her out tonight. *Yeah, that's it.* Her body was hot as hell and there's no denying he wants her under him, but, there was also something intriguing about the girl that made him want to get to know her, to actually talk to her.

It'd been years since he'd gone out on a real date, didn't have the time or inclination, but now the idea perked up not only his brain, but his manhood as well. Feeling invigorated, the best he'd had in a long, long time, he quickened his pace.

Out at the driveway, he was relieved to see the van with O'Riordan's painted across the side was still there but it was empty. She must be in the house.

Brogan hurried inside the large building. Rushing past doors and hallways, he found no sign of her. He heard voices laughing nearby, coming from the kitchen. As he strode in that direction, he saw her approaching a closed swing door with her back to him. Carrying a big box, her shoulders slumped with the strain of the heavy carton.

Striding quickly to her, he reached in front of her with one hand to push the door open, the other to take the box from her. But, with her body already in motion, preparing to push the door open with her shoulder, when it wasn't there, she stumbled forward, trying to catch her balance and scrabbled to hold the box. It tumbled out of her hands.

Brogan only had a few fingers on it, he couldn't catch it, he could only grab her, prevent her from falling. The sound of a lot of glass breaking stunned him when the box hit the floor. Judging by her horrified expression, it was expensive glass.

"Uh, was, uh, that glass in there?" He held her upper arm, steadying her.

She stood with her mouth open, staring in horror at the box on the floor. Liquid was oozing from the bottom. Then she spun and yelled at him, "Glass? You imbecile!"

Her hands fisted at her sides, she snarled, "Yes, it was glass. Liquor bottles, a case of very expensive liquor!" Her skin blanched, a hand went to her forehead, she shook her head, tears welled.

Still clutching her arm, he said quickly, "Shit, girl, don't panic, I'll clean it up," he looked towards the kitchen. Her tiny strained voice stopped him.

"You've probably gotten me fired." Blinking the tears back, she said in a small tight voice, "Thanks." Wrenching her arm from his grasp she turned quickly and ran out of the house.

He'd only frighten her more if he gave chase like a creepy stalker, he could only stand like an idiot and gawk after her. Hell, he didn't even know her name.

CHAPTER FIVE

After cleaning up the mess, Brogan stood for the longest time outside, staring blankly down the road she'd fled. A fight brewed in his gut. He'd look the fool to go out back and ask people, find out who she was, but, on the other hand, he couldn't let it go.

He couldn't make his feet move to his truck, to shuck it and go home, cap a six-pack on the way to clear her from his mind.

It didn't matter, his feet had a mind of their own. He trod back through the house to the backyard where the party was going strong, in full buzzed swing.

He hated to, but he headed over to where Tamy Lee held court. Last thing he wanted was that horny bitch hanging on him like a koala in a tree, but, he sighed and kept walking towards the blowsy woman.

Tamy Lee knew half of everyone in Builu County, and most everyone in Shire's Cross, the Barriga, and surrounding villages. A few males hovering around her split when they saw him approach. He may be in jeans and flannel, but he still carried a badge, and that unnerved even some of the innocents.

A remaining blonde female nudged Tamy Lee, motioned to Brogan. Tamy Lee turned, and a huge avaricious smile raised her voluminous, fuchsia glossed lips. Dark brown eyes glowed under lined lids suddenly leaden with lust; they traveled his powerful body as he neared, his long legs eating up the polished pavers.

"Bless my heart, here's our handsome sheriff, Brogan Dillon. Baby, you came, you've made my dreams come true." She stood on tiptoes, grasped his thick arms and tried to kiss him. He turned his head and her big lips brushed his rough cheek.

"Hardly handsome." The blonde standing next to Tamy Lee commented, although interest was flagrant in her droll voice.

Cunning hazel eyes roved the big man, slender lips rose in baiting appeal. "No, he's way too tough and rugged with that harsh face and cold eyes." She moved closer, tipped her head back to look up at him. "Not handsome, but," her smile curved in a designing arch, she said, "damned hot in a brutish kind of way."

Brogan winched Tamy Lee's claws from his arms and set her back from him, and took an unconscious step from the blonde as well. Turning his back to the blonde, he stuffed his hands in his jean's pockets. No point in beating around the bush, he jumped right to it. "Tamy Lee, there was a young woman here earlier, not a guest I don't think, I think she was workin'."

Penciled brown brows dipped down at his mentioning another woman. Tamy Lee's lips pushed out in a snoot. "Hmm, there's that sexy western accent of yours that comes and goes. What about her?"

"She was about this high, like petite." He held his hand out lower than both females. "Long curly blonde hair," his gaze flitted to the blonde. "Much lighter, softer than yours, hers looked natural."

Ignoring her mouth firming at the insult, he went on, "Gorgeous with huge, babydoll blue eyes, bright like the sky. Her figure," he took an obvious breath of desire, "uh, curves with no end." He held his hands curved over his pecs and said, "Tits like-" realizing his coarse words, he broke off, red tinged the tips of his ears.

"Anyway, you know who she is? She came in a van with O'Riordan's on it."

The two women shared a look and curled lip. The blonde said, "O'Riordan's is a fancy, yet sleazy saloon in the Barriga." Barriga meaning belly, was the hotspot, the epicenter of the county of Builu.

"I mean, I've been there, music's good, atmosphere is cool, dark, throbbing." She grinned at Tamy Lee's snicker. "They do catering on the side next door. It's nice and all, but the chicks that work there dress like sluts."

At Tamy Lee's louder snigger, the blonde smiled, said snidely, "Who am I kidding, they are sluts, am I right, Tams?" The pair giggled wickedly together.

"Ain't that the truth, Silina." Tamy Lee nudged her with her elbow.

"Listen," their obnoxious talk annoying him, Brogan said, "about the girl, do you know who she is?"

Then the blonde started, frowned. "Hey, my sister works there. She kinda matches your description. Although," she snorted crudely, "gorgeous?" Her laugh abrasive. "Hardly. A bug on the hairy ball-sac of a mule is prettier than that sow. She used to be engaged to my fiancé, but he totally dumped her for me."

She held her left hand out and wriggled her fingers, the sunlight dazzled off the sparkler on her ring finger. "Thankfully she split to go live in her gothic necropolis and got out of my fiancé's and my hair."

Tamy Lee's brown eyes jacked at her words. "Your sister? I didn't know you had a sister. You've never mentioned her."

Silina's tanned leathery skin darkened, her lips already thin as a red slash in her sun spoilt face flattened further. "She recently moved here from Ohio. She's my half-sister. We have different mothers, thank God. Our father passed eight months ago and left her that big old Victorian out in Mal Tierre, the badlands." Her hazel eyes zapped to Brogan. "We don't talk about her because she's a jailbird."

"What?" Tamy Lee's false lashes flew up. "Your sister's been in jail?"

Salina's expression flashed an emotion Brogan couldn't read, then her jaw compressed, face hardened. Brogan couldn't picture the soft, delicate female he'd had his hands on earlier, in jail. No way. At his shaking head, Silina spoke up.

"Yes, she spent most of her childhood in juvenile detention, prison."

Tamy Lee and Brogan gaped at her. "No way," Brogan spat.

Silina's hard eyes swung to him, her lids fell to hide her feelings. "Yes. She...deliberately pushed, threw...our...uh, baby brother out of our tree house when she was seven. He fell, and..." She shrugged. "His brain was damaged in the fall. He will never be...normal. He has the mind of a...I don't know, a seven, maybe an eight-year-old?" She didn't look either of them in the eye.

"Holy hell, girl, you never mentioned him either," Tamy Lee said with surprise.

Sighing her embarrassment, Silina replied quietly, "He's been in an institution, a group home or something out near Cleveland. The State pays for his care. There's not much point in talking about him. It was fifteen years ago, I was thirteen when it happened, I'm over it."

Tamy Lee burbled, "Wow, a sister in prison and a retarded brother, you sure hit the jackpot, huh?"

Brogan couldn't believe his ears. "No fuckin' way that pretty little thing hurt anyone, not on purpose anyway. I don't believe it."

Silina cocked her head up at him. "Well, you're wrong. My mother was afraid of her so she pushed for incarceration even though they rarely lock up a person that young. She was a cold-hearted murdering convict, and now she's a whore working at that sordid joint O'Riordan's.

"I hear the girls make more money in the back rooms on their backs and their knees than they do on the bar floor slinging drinks. What are you looking for her for? She commit another felony?" Her face brightened. "You gonna arrest the bitch? What's she done now? Kill a little old lady?"

Brogan felt gutted. The feisty cub he'd felt an incredible attraction to, the only woman that caught his interest in forever was a convicted felon. Attempted murder. Her own flesh and blood. Fuck. A bolt suddenly struck his head, remembrance exploded, that voice, those blue eyes, hell, the girl was his angel that day he lay broken in the street.

He covered his eyes, rubbed them, dragged his hands down his face. Just his luck, his angel was an ex-con, a fucking criminal. And a slut. She wasn't real. Boy, he could sure pick them.

He turned and started walking away in a disappointed daze. Then, he stopped, looked back, both women were staring at his butt, their jealous faces wreathed in satisfaction.

He asked gruffly, "What's her name?"

The girls looked at each other, Silina shrugged. "Colipatra, Colipatra Cassidy. Coli for short, you know, like the dog. Apropos doncha think?"

"Colipatra?" Tamy sneered. "What the hell kind of name is that?"

Silina chuckled and explained, "Her mother was a real mess. A drunk, hardcore junkie, Coli got her whoring criminal ways directly from her skanky mother." Silina's resentment of her younger half-sister infected her words and stained her face, she clearly reviled Coli with a festering hatred.

Tuning out their cackling, Brogan traipsed across the lawn ignoring people trying to greet him. Hopping in his truck, he needed that beer, no, bourbon. This kind of news needed drowning out with the hard stuff.

He swung by the liquor store on the way home. Strong drink will keep her out of his thoughts, he'd be damned if he wasted another thought on the beautiful felon again.

CHAPTER SIX

He didn't make it one day. He could have sent the box of booze over to O'Riordan's with one of his deputies. But he didn't. It was on the seat next to him. Brogan pulled up in front of the bar. It was a large, two-story structure, chicly rustic with varnished light wood. It looked like a nice pub or restaurant except for the neon beer and wine blinking signs above the windows.

Inside, the lighting was dim amber, a giant freaking stuffed bear stood in one corner with its arms raised, claws out, teeth bared. To the right, a mounted cougar, huge curved incisors glistening, prowled in a half lunge. Patrons sat hunched at the extensive L-shaped bar, mostly men, the few women wore cropped t-shirts and skintight jeans.

Stairs to the left of the bar led up to a fully packed loft. Over the top of the stairs were mounted buffalo horns. Downstairs, a small band played honky-tonk in the back. A few couples danced in languid drunkenness in front of the band.

Bowl shaped lights around the top of the bar illuminated the darker oak pillars and colorful bottles of alcohol stacked behind them. More neon lights flashed inside the tavern, partial brick walls broke up the wood paneling. Pictures of boats and hunting hung crookedly, knocked askew by clumsy drunks and brawls.

Red and white-checkered tablecloths covered the crowded wooden tables scattered throughout the enormous room. Customers spoke loudly over the band, laughter rang with sporadic shouts.

Holding the box of liquor, Brogan stood near the entrance, letting his eyes adjust, he scoped out the place.

He had told himself he was just going to drop the booze off with the manager and be on his way. It was his fault she'd dropped the bottles, and the distressed way she said she'd be fired told she obviously couldn't afford to replace them. He had called to find out what bottles were destroyed.

Brogan sauntered over to an open space at the bar and set the box on the counter. The bartender saw him, and came right over.

"Hey pal, what's up?" The bartender nodded at the carton. Because he was dressed in jeans, cowboy boots, black leather jacket, and a light-beige thermal, the bartender didn't know Brogan was the sheriff.

"Ah, well, I understand O'Riordan's catered a party over at Tad Brownie's place this weekend." At the bartender's nod, toning down his country accent, Brogan went on, "Yes, so, this girl, I think her name is Colleen, or Collie or something?" Another nod of acknowledgement.

Brogan's attention lowered to a barmaid that nuzzled in next to him. His brows rose at her attire. Her top was barely a black lacey fringe, and very tiny, tight black shorts peeked flashes of the bottoms of her butt cheeks when she moved.

Black nylons and black booties completed the barely there uniform. The girl was slightly pudgy, a small muffin top skirted the top of the tight shorts. Thick thighs bulged from the hems of the shorts.

"Bennie, two Bud drafts," she ordered, sparing Brogan a long approving glance.

Jerking his faintly repulsed gaze from her exposed pudgy skin and heavily made up face, Brogan turned back to the bartender. "Anyway, this Colleen or something dropped a box of liquor and all the bottles broke. I've brought replacements."

Looking at the carton, the bartender smiled. "Yeah, that was Coli," he spelled her name. "Coli Cassidy. She was sent to nail up our sign on the house and bring extra cases of booze for the party. She came back in tears. Bossman ripped her a new one, said the cost

was coming out of her pay. Of course," his voice dropped with disgust, "he said she could work if off in other ways, like, you know," he said with a shrug, "the other girls do."

Feeling his stomach cringe, Brogan asked, "Uh, so did she? Work it off like that, I mean? Does she usually do stuff like that?" He wiped his palms on the front of his thermal shirt then forked agitated fingers through his hair. Place sounded more like a brothel than a bar.

Bennie glanced across the dim room then back to Brogan. Spoke over the noise, "Na, she got all upset, in a tizzy, face all red, she ran off. Bossman was *pissed*."

"Hmm." Brogan turned partially to view the room. He did his duty and now he should leave. But his mouth kept talking. "So, the girl, Coli, she working tonight?"

Bennie squinted through the dusky room. "I don't see her. She was here a minute ago. Bossman said he was going to have a…private word with her, if ya know what I mean, eh?" At Brogan's frown, he shrugged and motioned his head to the back of the room. "I think they're down at his office, down the hall to the right of the band. Can I get you something to drink, uh, Mister, uh?"

Brogan turned on his heel and strode across the rowdy room. Threading his way through the crowd, here and there he saw people making out, and then some.

If he wasn't on a mission he'd slap his badge between the couples writhing against the walls and haul in a few of them for indecent behavior. Mission. Right. What the hell was he doing? He'd dropped off the booze, his duty was done. His boots kept marching along the planked floor until he reached the hallway the bartender pointed out.

There were other hallways and several doors. He paused, listened, he heard talking. The parties sounded upset, one male, one female. The male sounded angry, the female sounded very upset and scared. Brogan followed the voices down the hall.

He turned a corner and saw them. Saw her. And she was more. More than he'd remembered, more of everything. Tingles pricked up his body.

The man had her pressed up against the wall. A foot taller than her, he looked in his forties, mop of dark unruly hair, bull-shouldered and barrel chested. He had a large thick hand curled around the front of her throat, and his grip must not be gentle because her eyes bulged, face white as a sheet, tears glistened with her tangible fear, she gripped his wrist with both small hands trying to pull his hand off.

His other huge paw was on her midriff and was shoving up, the crescent of his hand pushed against the underside of her breast causing the plump flesh to mold up and even further out of the low, flimsy top. "Coli girl," he growled, his face close to hers.

She tried to turn away but his tight grip forced her to face forward. His breath misted her pale skin; his mouth hovered over her trembling lips.

He snarled, coarse and low, "Maybe I hadn't made it clear enough when I hired you. I expected you to put out, to me. And you haven't. Now you owe me for the booze you destroyed and you won't even let me cop a measly feel?" His hand shoved up further, pressing her soft breast up and out, over the low bodice, another inch and she'd be half topless.

A whimper shook out of her, she pleaded, "M- Mr. Luzzini, please, I- I, I'll pay you back for it, I'll work extra, please let me go-" she struggled to push away from him, he slammed her back against the wall. Her breath oofed out sharply when the air snapped out of her lungs.

"Fuck no, girl, I warned you. Right now I'm gonna have myself a good feel of those pretty titties, and that sweet honeypot between those fine legs, then later tonight," he leaned in closer, his spit dampened her face, "you're givin' it to me. All the damned way. I'm gonna split those skinny legs and I'm gonna fu-"

"Get your fucking hands off her," Brogan snarled as he stalked down the hall towards them. The pair froze, both turned at his belligerent voice.

Keeping his hands where they were on Coli's body, Luzzini leaned back slightly, scowled at Brogan. "Listen son, this ain't none of your bizness. Me and my employee are having a little us time, so

butt out. Take off." He turned back to Coli. Her eyes like wide terrified saucers goggled at Brogan.

Brogan stomped closer. "I said," his voice dropped, lethal and dark, "get your motherfucking hands off the girl. *Now*."

Luzzini's head rolled back, he looked up at the ceiling. Lowering his head with a hard exhale, he said to Brogan, "I won't tell you again, boy, me and the girl got bizness that don't involve you. Now take-"

Blam-

Brogan's fist connected with Luzzini's jaw, snapping his head, saliva and blood flew out spattering the wall. The manager staggered backwards, his hand to his jaw that hung open in shock.

Coli's palms flattened against the wall, frightened eyes on Brogan as if he was going to hit her next. She inched away, her back scraping the wall.

Massaging his jaw, Luzzini straightened up, enraged, he pulled his fist back- and Brogan hit him again before the manager could even throw his fist forward. The blow launched the bar owner into the wall. A grunt burst when he hit the paneling then he slid down the wall to his butt.

Brogan warned, "Move again and I'll wipe the floor with your face, after I rip it off your head."

A busted lip and nose bleeding like a faucet, the man stayed where he was. Dragging the back of his hand across his nose with a wince, he blustered, "I'll have you arrested for assault, boy."

"No problem," Brogan told him. "Call Builu County Sheriff's Office and ask for the sheriff. That would be me. Brogan Dillon. You need me to spell that for ya?" At the man's grunt, Brogan said to Coli, "Come here."

The whites of her eyes shone clear around the blue irises she was so afraid of him, she mutely shook her head.

Dark brows daggered down, Brogan moved to her and snatched up her arm as she flinched from him. "Where's your shit?"

At her confused look, he said with irritation, "Your purse," his disgusted gaze slew down the front of her risqué top, "and jacket. You ain't goin' outside in that."

Blinking in fear and bewilderment, Coli's trembling lips clamped closed.

Sitting propped against the wall, the manager muttered, "Her shit's in the employees' lockers. Turn right at that first corridor. Get it and get the hell out of here." A purple bruise was already forming on his jaw, his bleeding nose swelled.

He snuffled crudely then said, "You be back here tomorrow night for your shift, girl, without the white knight," he glanced at Brogan then flicked away at the wrath in the sheriff's hooded eyes. "We got unfinished bizness. You don't show you can forget your job. Ain't no one else gonna hire your felon ass."

Brogan wrapped his long fingers around her thin arm and dragged her away from the bleeding pig. She glanced from Brogan to the manager to Brogan as if undecided which was the more dangerous.

Made no difference, Brogan wasn't giving her a chance to choose, or refuse. Practically lifting her off her heels, he pulled her with him to the corridor.

Under his stoic glare, Coli collected her purse and removed her jacket from the locker. Brogan took the jacket from her quaking hands and held it open. She hesitated, mistrusting he wasn't going to suddenly pounce on her.

He nodded wordlessly at the jacket. Silently she allowed him to help her into it, and he took her arm again and led her back down the corridor and through the main body of the tavern and out the front door.

"Which one's yours?" He gestured to the parking lot.

Her voice was quiet, shaken, she murmured, "In the back." Tugging at her arm, she said, "Uh, th- thank you for- for your help. I'll be- be on my way." She started for the back of the lot, but he stopped her.

"No, you're shakin' like a leaf, you're in no condition to drive. I'll take you home." Without waiting for her acquiescence, he swerved her around and walked her to his truck. Opening the passenger side, he motioned, "Get in."

Digging her heels in the gravel, Coli tried to push away from him, yanking at her trapped arm. "N- no. I'm not going anywhere with- with you. Let go of me."

"Get in the goddamned truck, Ms. Cassidy."

Shaking her head she pulled at her arm. "No, let me go, I- I'll scream," she threatened like she had before at the barbeque, he had let go of her that time.

A dry smile turned up half his mouth. "Go ahead little doll-cub. I'm the sheriff, I'll just tell folks I'm arresting you, and you're resistin'. That sound familiar?" He got no satisfaction at the mortified blanch that struck her at his taunt, throwing her past in her face.

Her lower lip thrust out. "How dare you, you release me right this minute or I'll-"

"You'll do nothing, honey." His country boy accent gone along with his patience, he grasped her arm, bent, stuffed his arm under her knees and lifted her off the ground and about tossed her into his truck.

He bit back the grin at her affronted face when he slammed the door in it. Locking her door with his remote, he trod around to the driver's side and climbed in.

Face red as a wasp sting, she rounded on him. "You can't do this, this is kidnapping! I'll have you arrested!"

Now he did grin at her, lifted his jacket to show her the badge at his hip. "Sheriff, remember? I can do what I please with you. Now sit back and buckle up. If you don't do it," a smirk tipped his mouth, "I'll get my handcuffs out and do it myself, only it'll be much more restrictive. Feel me?"

Her lips flapped aghast at his brash behavior. "I- I, *oh*," she huffed with resignation and slammed her back against the seat. Buckling her seatbelt, she crossed her arms rigidly over her chest and sat fuming, glaring out the front window.

Smothering his grin, he put the truck in gear and took off down the road. They drove in silence, her in anger at being kidnapped, he in amusement at her ire, the night cloaking the buildings as they left the downtown area and headed for her village of Mal Tierre, Spanish

for badlands. So named as the ground was so rocky, poor soil, too hard to farm, too expensive to dig foundations to build on. It was useless land. Homes out there were few and far apart.

They hit the country, the road flush with fields and pastures on both sides, cows grazing looked up with dumb curious eyes, tails swishing. Brogan marginally missed an armadillo strolling along the roadside. Colie perked up when they neared meadows and they could see a ranch in the distance.

Forgetting her anger, she told him gleefully, "This is my favorite part of this drive, Sheriff. There's this big horse farm and the horses are usually trotting around the meadow. They have a training area where I think they give riding lessons and," she wriggled in her seat, her voice grew more excited, "I've seen them jumping fences. The people wear these funny little hats, or helmets and they seem to be all one movement, horse and rider together as they leap so gracefully over the fences."

Brogan slowed way down as they passed the equine ranch so Coli could look her fill. Sighing as they passed it, Coli said wistfully, "Someday when I have time I'd like to learn how to ride."

He tilted his head to her. "Oh yeah? I have stables nearby where I keep my steed. Riding is great, it relaxes and energizes you, clears the cobwebs. Galloping out in nature, riding trails just empties your mind." It appeared he was going to say more, but he didn't, just faced forward.

They didn't pass many other cars along the way, the area was quite rural. The truck bumped and rocked over the uneven antiquated road, grass and wildflowers encroached on the worn tar.

Coli went on, "There is another horse farm down further, but I don't care as much for that one. I think they train the horses to race, like thoroughbred racing. Poor things, they run around and around in circles getting kicked in the stomach and caned to go faster and faster, I think it's kind of...abusive."

Her nose wrinkled and she squinted at the large barn and enormous ranch. A huge spread, the workout tracks and rails, training arenas were just past the sprawling hacienda, an adobe chateau at the heart of the farmstead.

The rest of the ride was just grass and dirt, scattered with short and tall cacti waiting to bloom. As they went by a grove of hickories, Brogan said quickly, "Look, there," he pointed. "A roadrunner."

Black and brown with white streaks, the bird had a long tail, long legs and long beak. A smudge of red flashed behind his ears as he sped across the road then disappeared into the tall grass.

Coli shrieked with joy, "Oh! Oh! Oh my gosh! A roadrunner! A real live roadrunner!" Her head twisted, nose pressed against the glass as she tried to spot it again.

A few more miles of prairie, and Coli realized Brogan had turned down Cornflower Lane, the last long road that led to her street. Like its namesake, Cornflower, startling blue-flowered weeds littered the fields along the way.

It dawned on her he hadn't asked her for directions to her home. Turning quizzically to him she asked, "How do you know where I live?"

His face was as hard and uncompromising as always, he said nothing. "Oh," she slumped back, said with sarcasm, "that's right. You're the sheriff. All knowing, all seeing, all judging."

He skewed a glance in her direction, then turned back to face the motorway. Many open miles separated scant clusters of homes. He drove for some distance down the tar road.

When he turned onto Wisteria Road, the Victorian came in view. Huge and magnificent, looming in the dark, reminiscent of an opaline castle on the cliffs overlooking a boundless vale.

Brogan pulled into the gravel driveway and parked up by the house. By the time she'd unbuckled her belt and fumbled at the locked door, he'd gotten around the truck and opened her door himself. Surprised, she said with a mix of fear and anger, "What are you doing? Are you expecting something from me for helping me out? Or am I under arrest?"

His lips bunched at that. "That would be familiar for you, yeah?" He watched her skin pale, eyes sadden, plush mouth droop. He put his hands around her waist and ignoring her objections, lifted her out and set her on her feet.

They walked up the path to the steps, and up to the front door. "No, I don't want anything from you, Miss Cassidy, and of course you are not under arrest. Give me your keys." He held his hand out, palm up.

"What? No." She clutched her purse to her chest.

His hand flew out and he snagged the purse right out of her hands. Ignoring her gasp, he rifled through the small bag, took out her keys and handed the purse back to her.

"Wh- where on earth do you think you're going?" She didn't move as he shoved the door open and took a step inside.

"Like a brainless ninny, you live way the hell out here, a young defenseless woman alone. You think after the episode that still has you shakin' in your shoes, that I would just drop you off on your isolated doorstep without checkin' things out first?"

Shaking her head, she said, "No, no, this is ridiculous. There's no danger out here, I'm not defenseless. I resent that you-"

Disregarding her protests, Brogan clasped her arm again and pulled her inside and closed the door. "I am the sheriff, and I ain't leavin' you alone until I check out this ancient hull." He craned his neck, looking around the vestibule. "You stay here," he ordered and took off before she could object.

He searched every room, parlor, sunroom, bathrooms, closets, porches, kitchen, and returned to find she'd moved to the broad, grand staircase that curved up to the second floor.

Shiny mahogany bannisters bracketed royal blue carpeted stairs, over it draped a stunning chandelier replete with all the normal sparkling crystals dangling that one would see on such a beauty. He approached her with a frown. "I told you to stay put."

She returned his frown. "You are not my boss, I don't have to do what you say."

"Yeah, if I were your boss, apparently you'd be on your back right now, naked as a jaybird with those legs spread wide and welcoming."

"Oh!" She hauled off and slapped him, then scowled at the pain in her hand and the smirk on his face. "How dare you talk to me as if I'm- I'm a tramp!"

His hooded eyes grazed on her body like they were feasting on sweet and savory bits and pieces. "If it dresses like a whore, acts like a-" He threw his hand up to catch the slap. "Uh, uh, you only get one sweetheart."

Jerking at her wrist, she snapped, "You have no right to talk to me like that."

"Listen babe, you dress in that," his gaze skimmed again over her half-naked body under the open jacket. "You deserve to be spoken to and treated like a whore." He stood stoically watching her struggle to get out of his grip. "See," holding her without effort, he said with that cocky smirk, "defenseless. Helpless."

A weird sound sputtered from under a round marble table in the center of the foyer. A tan lump slumped under the table on diamond shaped black and white tiles, the strange sounds were emanating from the lump.

Brogan squinted at the lump. "What the hell is that?"

Coli yanked her wrist free and hurried over to it. She bent and picked it up. Holding it in her arms, she cooed at it while carrying it over to him. "This is Douggie."

"Doggy?" His brows knit, he stared warily at the lump that snorted and snarled and snored in her small arms.

"No, Douggie, sort of a cross between Doug and Doggie I suppose," she said with a shrug and nuzzled her nose in its fur.

"That's a dog?" he muttered with some disbelief. Brogan studied the short-furred lump.

It looked like a puppy, a French bulldog. So ugly it was cute. Its nose was all smushed and flat, thankfully he didn't have the big drawing, drooling mouth with huge fangs poking up. One short ear twitched with a reflexive stretch.

"You see," she told him, smiling tenderly at the dog, "I have protection, I'm not defenseless."

"Yeah, sure." His eyes rolled. "What's he gonna do to intruders, slump them to death?"

Cuddling the dog to her bountiful chest, she scolded, "That's not nice. I'm sure if there was the need, he'd jump right in and take

down the burglars. Wouldn't you, Douggie?" She snuggled her face in his fur.

Rolling his eyes again, he mumbled, "Uh huh." Looking around with a nod, Brogan complimented, "You've done a helluva job on this…place. I saw it a year ago when checking it out for fire hazards and squatters, vagrants. It was in quite disrepair."

She chuckled delightfully. "It's okay, you can call it a monstrosity, my sister does." Her smile vanished.

"I can believe that." He still gazed around the circular room. "I met her today, your sister."

Her blues flipped up to him, then lowered with shame. "I see. That's why you alluded to my…criminal past. She loves to tell anyone and everyone we meet about it. That's why I moved to Ohio. Well, one of the reasons."

He made an acknowledging sound then said, "And what were the other reasons you moved there?"

She blinked at him realizing he listens very carefully, picks up every word, every nuance. "Uh, they're not important. Well, thank you for seeing me home, and for…you know, the other thing." Her cheeks flushed with embarrassment at what happened in that hall. Her boss was all over her, his hands groping, mouth seeking hers, slobbering and threatening.

She was well aware if the sheriff hadn't come along she would have been unable to prevent Mr. Luzzini from assaulting her. And with her criminal record, even if anyone believed her they would say she should expect it, deserve it, that she asked for it. Men had been hitting on her, some being downright ruthless and forceful since she'd moved to Texas.

"Last time I saw this place it was dusty and webby, furniture covered with sheets, walls peeling, that bannister," he motioned with his head to the staircase. "Was as worn and scratched up as the floor. You've done a lot of work, did a really nice job, Miss. Cassidy."

Embarrassed yet pleased at his compliment, she said, "Yes well, I have plans for it."

"They are?" he prompted.

She strolled away a few paces, cuddling the dog. "Years ago, she was always so ill, but nevertheless, great-grandma was working on turning this place into a bed-and-breakfast. I find I like that idea. I like to cook, don't mind cleaning. Next door is a large structure, like a carriage house. I'm thinking of turning it into a…kind of shop. I'm hoping to fill it with local art. You know, paintings, jewelry, sculpture, clothes maybe."

He was impressed. "Wow, ambitious."

She buried her face in the fur, then looked up at him with stars in her eyes. Then they disappeared, the glow left. "Yes. As you have been informed, I was in…penitentiary during my youth. Even though my juvenile record should be sealed, with people blabbing my business from all corners of the earth, well," she shrugged ruefully.

"There's been little opportunity for me to find work. Colleges refuse me entrance, not that I could afford it anyway. No," she twirled slightly smiling at the house. "This will work. With my job and a small loan I pleaded for, plus a ton of elbow grease I've already got most of the rooms done."

"Yeah, I saw the dining room. You've even put chinaware on the table. I guess you finished the woodwork yourself?"

She smiled at the image. "Yes, I sanded and used tung oil on all the wood including the maple table. The lace tablecloth, china and glassware were my great-grandmother's. I found them tucked away in boxes in the attic. I love the crystal with a hint of transparent dark pink, the china with tiny red flowers. Candelabras and candle sconces were treasures to find and bring back to their former beauty."

Relaxing, Brogan slid back into county talk. "Polishin' up that chandelier thing over the table must have been a heckuva job, yeah? Looks kind of gothic with the drapin' gold arms and diamond chains."

"Oh yes, it was difficult because it's up so high. I had to stand on the table. It's an eight candle, vintage, Italian gilded chandelier with gold scrolling arms. The delicate chains hanging around the arms are gold, and the drooping pendants are crystal. Fortunately

Grandma left a quite detailed notebook on all the antiques she had here. Some were heirlooms, some she purchased from antique shops."

Brogan watched her eyes beam, skin glow with her enthusiasm. "Uh huh, you do like to climb up perilous things to do work. Well, you've done a great job so far. I guess I can understand why you're workin' at that fu- uh, joint."

"Yes." She lowered her head demurely. "Mr. Luzzini was the only person to hire me. I need the money. I need it to pay the taxes, the electric, buy supplies and furnishings, the loan wasn't that much. And, well," she bumped one shoulder self-consciously, "I need food, gas for my car, which, oh dear, I have no way back to the, oh, I'll have to call a taxi." The cost of the taxi obviously worried her.

"Why are you livin' way out here, roughin' it in this unfinished castle when you can be residin' in comfort with your sister and your mother?"

"Half-sister," Coli said absently. Staring blindly at the floor, she sighed, raised her eyes to his. "Goldie is her mother, not mine. I was engaged." Her shoulders quivered when she said that, her eyes lowered in what appeared to be fear to Brogan.

"He uh, came with me for the reading of the will. I think he thought I was going to inherit a bundle. I didn't. We moved here from Ohio and were staying at Goldie's. I came home from the reading much later than they did because I stopped off here first. And, well," her voice drifted off.

"And?" Brogan prompted, studying her pained expression, the tightness around her lush mouth.

"Ahh…" She tacked on a false smile. "When I got home I found them in bed. Together. In my bed. I moved out here that night. Slept on the floor for weeks. It was for the best anyway," she shrugged, "they weren't really very…nice to me."

Recalling the resentful vitriol that spewed from her sister's mouth regarding Coli, Brogan could easily see it. His brows dropped with suspicion. "Did he hit you?" His question was confirmed by the swift intake of her breath and then sudden shift of her eyes away from him. Her face paled at the same time as her cheeks flushed.

"He…was, is a big man, powerful." She looked up at the sheriff then quickly away.

Her fear of Brogan and his muscles became clear. It wasn't just him, it was all big strong men. "Coli, tell me the bastard's name and I'll-"

"No," she said quickly with a shake of her head. Blonde curls danced across her back. She moved to the door, set her hand on the knob, held the dog against her chest with her other arm. "It's water under the bridge. It all is. I just want to move on, make a life for me and-" she broke off awkwardly.

"And who?" he asked, his boots akimbo, arms crossed over his big chest. He'd never considered she had a current boyfriend. Hadn't even thought about it, he had seen her and instantly wanted her, wanted to own her, like a mindless caveman.

"Um, you know," she said, lifting the dog. "Me and Douggie. Listen, I'm kind of bushed. I need to get to the bar early tomorrow, my shift starts at 7:30 a.m." The entire time the dog never lifted nary a lid, just snored away, huddled against her soft body. Brogan felt a pang of envy.

"Seven thirty?" His brows arched. "The bar opens that early in the morning?"

"Uh, not exactly. I help next door prepare the food for catering, and do some cleaning." She turned the knob, opened the door, clearly it was time for him to go.

"Okay. I'll be round about 6:40, that enough time to get to O'Riordan's?"

Her forehead knit. "No, I mean yes. I mean, I'll call a cab, you don't need to-"

He stepped over the threshold, straightened his hat and smiled. "It'd cost a fortune, little cub, to have a taxi come way the hell out here and then back to the Barriga. Just sit tight, I'll pick you up at 6:40. Lock the door. I checked all the other doors and windows. First thing you need to spend your pay on are new locks for everything. I could pop them all easily myself with just a butter knife. They're as ancient as the house."

"Sheriff, I can't-"

"Lock the door, little doll-cub," he ordered and closed it in her face. It took her a second, he pictured the annoyance pushing those puffy lips out in a pout.

Hearing the lock set, he smiled and hopped down the steps and headed for his truck.

CHAPTER SEVEN

They didn't talk much on the way to the city in the morning. "You have breakfast?" he asked her, glancing quickly then away.

"Sure. Fruity Pebbles with chocolate milk."

He glanced at her again with a short smile. "A bit of a sugary start for the day, doncha think?"

A shoulder bumped in dismissal. She said blithely, "Cereal is a lot cheaper than eggs, Sheriff."

"Hmm. Coffee?"

Shaking her head. "No, I'll grab some at the pub."

"Hmm." He swung the big truck down the main street. "This job, Coli," he paused, "you can't get something else? Something better than…"

Her mouth pressed in a line. "Better than what? I told you. No one in Builu County will hire an ex-convict. Trust me, I hit the pavement until my shoes wore out. My reputation managed to proceed me to every town I went to."

"Yeah, I know, but, shit, girl, the outfit, you know…" he glanced over, his gaze striping down then up her body. She was wearing jeans and a sweatshirt.

"Know what?" she asked absently staring out the window at the buildings they passed.

"Hell girl, that uniform you wore yesterday, you're practically nekked. Tits hangin' all out, ass cheeks, men hangin' all over you-"

"Sheriff!" she squawked, "stop it!" Her face tinting pink, she said quietly, "You don't have to be so vulgar. I have no choice in what I do to earn my keep. When I get the B&B up and running, and it starts paying the bills, then," she turned to the window with a shrug, "I can quit the bar. But," she sighed, "until then, I have to do what I have to do."

She turned back to him with a rebuke, "And it's none of your business or concern where I work, what I wear."

The truck slowed then stopped in front of the saloon. She didn't wait for him to put the truck in park, just yanked up the handle and slid out, and down, way down. She hadn't realized since he helped her in and out of the truck how high up it was. She went down with a squeal.

"Shit," Brogan cursed, jammed the truck in park, shut it off, hopped out and ran around to her. She was sitting on the ground rubbing her ankle. Tears of pain spotted her cheeks.

He barked, "Hell, girl, what have you done? You shoulda waited for me. Let me see." He crouched in front of her and wrapped his fingers around her calf and lifted it gently so he could see the ankle she rubbed.

"It- it's okay, Sheriff, I think I just landed too hard on it." She tried to pull her leg from his grasp but he ignored her and inspected her ankle.

He pushed her jean leg up then stroked the pads of his fingertips down her ankle then up to her calf and back down, he circled her anklebone with his fingers and pressed.

"Ow, oh, that hurt," she cried.

"Can you move it?"

She wriggled it. "It hurts."

"I don't think it's broken. Just a small sprain. I'm gonna take you to the hospital." He slid his hands under her and stood up with her in his arms.

"No! Stop! I'm fine, really. I don't want to go to the hospital, put me down." She kicked her legs for him to set her down.

"Coli, listen-"

"No," she grated, "I'm fine. I have to go to work. I don't have insur- I mean, I need to go to work, I don't work I don't get paid, put me down."

He hesitated, looked down at those clear blue eyes, pouty lips, the determined set of her pointed chin. "That manager, what's his name," he scowled.

"Mr. Luzzini, Winston Luzzini."

"Yeah, the asshole. You gonna be safe around that prick?"

She flinched at his crude language, then smiled. "Yes, of course. I just, he just managed to get me cornered last night. He was wrong about my shift today. I don't work the bar tonight, and tomorrow he's leaving for a trip to see relatives out in Oklahoma. So, I'll be perfectly safe."

"Uh huh." He shifted her in his arms. "I'm sending Chase out to change those locks of yours, so don't freak when he knocks at your door."

"You can't-"

"Not talkin' about it. It's a done deal. My job is to keep the residents of Builu County safe, and that includes you. If somethin' happened it would be my fault because I knew your locks sucked and did nothin' about them."

"Sheriff," she said softly, "please put me down."

Brogan looked from her to the bar, his forehead wrinkled with his grimace. He said, "If you need the money for medical care because you don't have insurance, I can-"

"I said no," she snapped. "Put me down."

Her glare didn't bother him, but she had the right to refuse to go to the hospital. A harsh breath blew out. "Fine," he grit then started for the tavern.

She protested, "What are you doing?"

"You need to stay off that ankle for a few hours. They can find you a job to do sittin' down." At her shaking head and parted lips to object further, he said, "That's it or the hospital, your choice," he kept walking knowing what her decision would be. When she said nothing, he traipsed into the building next door she directed him to.

When she opened the door, he carried her in. The workers inside stopped what they were doing and gawked at them.

Brogan walked over and set her on a stool. He asked her, "Who's in charge?"

A woman in her late thirties with a short cap of black hair set down a roll of cellophane and came over to them with a smile. "Hi, I'm Annie," she smiled at Coli, then frowned. "What's going on, hon, are you hurt?"

"No, I-"

"Yes, she sprained her ankle. She needs to be off it for a while. Can I trust you to ensure that happens?"

Annie took in the tan uniform he wore, the gun at his hip, the badge on his chest, and the smile widened. "Sure thing. You're Sheriff Dillon, right? I've seen you around. I thought you and Tamy Lee-"

"I have to go, see that she stays off her feet, yeah?" Brogan nodded to Annie, then Coli, then he left.

Brogan jumped in his truck and headed off to the station. He figured that stubborn little girl would last about twenty minutes and she'd be up and around. Shaking his head with a wry grin, he tried to put her out of his mind and went to work.

"Hey, Brogan," Minnie Willow greeted him. She sat in the bullpen at the desk closest to the door. The police station was located outside of the Barriga, in Lupo, more in the scrublands near the Coyote Lake Marina. There were satellite stations scattered throughout the county, in the grasslands, the foothills, up in the mountains and out in the plains.

Builu County resembled a honeycomb. The Barriga is the center where the money and more elegant shopping and restaurants and activities are. The tallest building is only five stories, most were no higher than two.

The Barriga is a giant square of mostly brick, some stucco structures surrounding the central park where outside concerts and festivals are held. Streets layer around the main square. Scattered between streets feature expansive avenues and alleys loaded with

specialty shops that jumble with colorful patio restaurants on terrazzo and mosaic.

The Barriga was the busy, buzzing, hub of the honeycomb with other towns like metaphorical compartments spread out around it all the way to the mountains. Some towns more rustic, others residential, there are vast farmlands, and there are always pockets of the ultra-wealthy that keep their gated mansions closed off from the peasants, the cowboys, the degenerates. Coli's Victorian was quite far out in her rural town of Mal Tierre.

Only one-story, the police station was flat-roofed and mostly red brick. Brogan didn't even get his hat off and Minnie said, "There's a call out in Vacià. Miller Pakan called, someone broke into his barn again. Andy Caper called in a complaint as well. Someone let his horses out of his stable. Mike and Duff, Rocky, everyone else are all out on calls, that leaves you, hon."

"Okay, I'm on it. Forward any calls or catch me on the radio." He tracked back out to his truck. While he drove, he wondered if Coli was behaving herself. Hell, he shook his head. He had to get her out of his brain. She was a convicted felon for heaven's sake. Tossed her baby brother out of a tree house.

Of course she had been only seven. A child that young could hardly have conceived the direness of the act, the permanence of death. That's pretty young for incarceration; he wondered why they imprisoned such a young child. Apparently the baby's mother pushed for it. Still…Before he could start feeling sorry for her, he turned the radio on to drown out his thoughts.

A few hours and Coli got her work done, her shift ended. She cashed her paycheck and had enough to go buy the paint she'd been yearning for. Her ankle was a mite sore, but it'd be fine after she warmed it up some. She hobbled to her car and headed for Pete's Paint Store in the Barriga.

Inside the shop that smelled of paint and sawdust, Coli was dickering with Pete Polito the storeowner over the particular cream color she wanted.

Pete was a nice looking man in his early thirties with sandy hair that hung over his shirt color, and intense chestnut brown eyes. Coli was unaware that a man passed by the front window and saw her inside. The bell over the door tinkled as it opened.

Pete left to get her order and she was running her fingers down a raised, embossed cream and rose print wallpaper thinking it would be perfect for the morning room where she'd serve tea and finger sandwiches to the guests.

"Colipatra," a low voice spoke behind her.

She twirled around, only one person called her that, Ellery Delian. Her ex-fiancé. When she'd caught him in bed with Silina, she'd yanked the diamond ring off her finger and threw it at him. It missed him and plunked off the wall by the bed.

Then she ran before he could punish her. She had stayed at the Victorian ever since. Next thing she heard was her half-sister Silina and her ex-fiancé were engaged. He hadn't even bought Silina a new ring, just gave her Coli's.

"Ellery," she said stiffly and turned back to the wallpaper.

"Hey, that's rude, no way to treat the man you were engaged to. We might be broken up, doesn't mean we can't still get together for some fun time, eh?" He paused, she ignored him.

Moving so he was in her line of sight, he went on, "We were good together, Colipatra, you have to admit the sex was great. Loose hole and an ass like a hippo, your sister hasn't got half of what you got going on, you know? I miss it. I miss us. Don't you?" He waited, she kept her back to him.

His voice lowered, tone darkened. "Colipatra, I'm talking to you. You ignore me and I'll-"

Recalling their sex-life more as nightmarish brutal assaults, red-faced with anger, she twisted around and snapped, "Or you'll what? We are no longer involved, you can't tell me what to do. Now, take your gold-digging cheating self and go home to my man-stealing duplicitous sister and go screw yourselves." She flipped her back to him.

His enraged gasp should have warned her. Ellery grabbed her shoulder with a painful grip and shoved her to turn around and face

him. His face scarlet with fury he demanded, "You apologize for speaking to me like that, right now. You don't and I'll beat that disrespectful shit right out of you like I have before!"

Her eyes narrowed at the fingers on her shoulder that were digging into her flesh like a serrated vice and then up to his angry face, brown eyes spitting ire. "You get your filthy hands off me right now, Ellery Delian. You have nerve, you have no right to touch me, talk to me. You went after me because you thought I was going to get a big inheritance. When you found out it was Silina that was getting it, you dropped me like a hot potato and jumped on her. Well, as far as I'm concerned you're nothing but gum stuck under my shoe."

This time his gasp was more a choke, and he slapped her, and again.

At her cry, Pete raced over and pushed between them, yelling, "Hey, hey, what the hell is this? You can't hit her, you bastard!" He put a hand on Ellery's shoulder and shoved him. At Pete's shout, two employees ran up and grabbed Ellery's arms holding him back.

The enraged ex-fiancé huffed and struggled, tried to get at Coli roaring threats at her and cursing at the men holding him back.

Pete looked at Coli. Her hand was pressed to her cheek, blue eyes blurred with tears of the sudden pain and shock. Humiliation soon followed.

Pete said gently to Coli, "Hey, honey, it's okay," then turned and shouted, "get that asshole outta here!" The two male employees dragged a blustering cursing Ellery out the door.

Glaring lances of hatred at Coli, Ellery threatened, "I'll get you back, you bitch, you'll see, you can't treat me like this!" Seconds later they heard tires squealing fiercely down the road.

"There, there, there now, he's gone sugar," Pete patted her back, handed her a handkerchief. She dabbed at her eyes, sniffed back her mortified tears. Handing him his hanky, she squeaked, "I have to go, excuse me," she hurried to the door.

"What about your paint? Hey, Miss Cassidy! What about the-" aw, heck, he'd bring it over to her tomorrow. Give him an excuse to see her, talk her into a date.

Coli ran red lights racing home. How mortifying! Wiping at her leaking eyes, she sped down street after street until the buildings became more and more sparse, the grass turned to dirt, the dirt to rock, until, her held breath eased. The Victorian was there. Immense and strong, bracing and welcoming. And her sanctuary. Parking quickly on the gravel drive, she ran up the steps, hurried inside. Closing the door, she breathed easier.

It still smelled musty, she should leave the windows open to air it out. "Douggie!" she called out, tossing her keys on a square marble table by the entrance. Her booties clacked across the beautiful tiled floor she's restored.

She felt pride in renovating the diamond-shaped black and white tile, and refurbishing all the natural wood. Now, their sheen of maple hickory and honey glowed warmly. She'd spent long hard hours on her hands and knees, but it was worth it. It would all be worth it.

She couldn't wait to get the B&B up and running. A few more months and it would be ready. She needed to start advertising.

Ambling through the house, she searched for her lumpy lazy dog. "Douggie!" she called out again. No responding heavy panting, or clickety nails pattering on the floor. Normally, somehow, with her never seeing him move, he always seemed to be in a lump right near her.

She went into the kitchen and put the kettle on to boil. She felt like hell. Embarrassed, tired, achy from her ankle. Hungry. At work she had nibbled on some pickles but they'd had a party to prepare for and it was busy work. She hadn't had time for a real meal.

She grabbed the bread and the peanut butter, got a plate and knife and made a sandwich. By that time the kettle had boiled. She poured it over the teabag, and sighed as she waited for it to steep.

A faint noise broke the silence of the great house. Curious, she took a bite of the sandwich, set it down, then went to the hall. She heard it again. It was coming from the unfinished morning room. The sun shone into it most of the day and it was the warmest room in the house.

Peeking into the room darkening from the lowering sun, she smiled. There he was. The sound she'd heard was Douggie snoring. "You are the laziest," she grinned, stooped and picked him up. She carried him to the kitchen, he didn't stir when she laid him on a pad by the refrigerator.

The commercial kitchen was immense, and thankfully, fairly modern. Her grandmother had replaced most of the appliances with stainless steel. A wide, long butcher block strode down the center of the kitchen.

Pots and pans hung over the block, their copper bottoms gleaming from her polishing. After scouring the kitchen clean, she had hung ruffled curtains with roses on the two windows. A row of herbs in terra cotta pots strung along the sills.

Coli took out a can of dog food, using a can opener she undid the top and dumped the food into Douggie's food bowl. She filled his water bowl also and set them both in front of the sleeping dog.

His nose wrinkled with a sniff. Then another. One brow rose, without opening his eyes, or moving much, he shuffled on his belly until his mouth plopped into the food dish, and he guzzled noisily without lifting his head.

Giggling at his lazy antics, Coli sat on a stool, poured cream and dropped in a cube of sugar then stirred her tea. Taking a sip, she sat back, relaxed, and sipped the horrible day away.

She'd been at the mercy of Ellery's anger before. Too many times. She allowed herself to become engaged to him because he, and Silina, and Silina's mother Goldie had told her over and over and over, that she was no good. Ruined goods, they said. No one would ever want her. Told her she was lucky Ellery gave her the time of day.

Goldie had pounded it into her that he was Coli's only chance. She'd never have a decent life. No one would hire her. She was nothing but a worthless criminal. Not quite eighteen when she'd completed her sentence, she'd gone from the juvenile prison to her mama's house. Her great-grandma had been moved to a nursing home so Coli had nowhere else to go.

Coli's mother, Vixie was not pleased to have another mouth to feed. Not that Vixie ate a lot herself, the drugs gave her the fuel she needed to get through the day. Drugs and her latest man. Both were interchangeable and as quickly used and forgotten, just like her daughter.

Vixie hadn't been a mother to Coli when she was a child before the incident, afterwards she never visited her once in prison, and she wasn't a mother now. One night Coli had walked in overhearing Vixie selling Coli to one of her male friends for the night for drugs.

Coli slept in the fields that night. And many nights after. Then she'd hitched to Ohio. Occasionally, Silina's grandfather sent her tickets to visit them in Texas, heaven knows why. Where was the money when she'd needed it for food, lodging, huh? He never sent cash, just the tickets. And, she thought with a sick feeling squeezing her belly, she'd hated every single visit.

Between Silina and Goldie, and…Grandfather Auston, an icky shiver spiraled through her, she pushed the memories aside, they were too awful to recollect. Obtaining her GED in jail then finding work for cash cleaning houses and picking fruit with migrants, Coli lived in a boarding house while trying to get into college when she met Ellery on a campus.

To this day she didn't know why he was there. At mid-thirties he was past normal college age. A girl she knew suggested he'd been there on purpose, had orchestrated running into her. Goldie said he was acquainted with their father, Thorne Arabat. It made no sense to her then, but now...

Her father had been very ill for a couple years she'd heard, then he died. It was well known in Texas that he was wealthy with ill-gotten ways, and it was assumed that Coli would likely inherit when he passed. Which as it turned out, she wasn't bequeathed any money.

When she inherited the house she moved back to Texas. That day, after returning home where she was staying with her family a few hours after the will was read, Coli found Silina and Ellery in bed together, and last time she'd seen her, Silina had showed off

Coli's engagement ring on *her* finger. She and Ellery were now engaged.

As soon as it was learned that it was Silina that had inherited the bulk of the estate, and Coli only the money pit, it would appear that Ellery was after the inheritance all along. If only Coli had known that two years ago, it would have saved her countless beatings, violent rapes, and heartbreaking misery. Prison was hideous and savage; Ellery was the beastly icing on the horrific cake that was her life.

At the time, though, not knowing any better, feeling the dregs of the earth, no good to herself or anyone, she had let Ellery sweep her off her feet. He was so much older than she, everyone convinced her that he was her savior; he would be the iron fist that would help her stay on the straight and narrow.

After a whirlwind engagement, once the ring was on her finger he showed his true colors and became cruel. He was rough, sadistic really with his love making, huh, she snorted, took a sip of hot tea. More like rape. He never asked her if she wanted to, he just grabbed her, threw her down and jumped on her.

Those were the good times, better than when he got his rocks off torturing her before taking her. She had the burns and cuts and whip marks to remind her.

What did she know? She'd never been with another man. She hadn't wanted to have sex that first time, she wasn't ready, they hadn't known each other long enough. But, he took what he wanted, when and how he wanted, told her she was tainted, lucky he touched her, no other man would.

It took her a week to recover from that first night losing her virginity. And the beatings, Coli flinched at the memories. He'd told her if she left him he'd kill her.

She knew he was involved in something nefarious. He was a broker at the Exchange in the Barriga, but she'd overheard enough phone calls, his trips out in the middle of the night. But, she'd kept her eyes and mouth shut. He would only hurt her if he thought she knew anything about his dealings that were undoubtedly illegal.

Why she stayed so long, took so much, suffered the pain and abuse, the degradation from Ellery and Silina and Goldie whenever they were together, she shuddered at her weakness and fear. Ellery was a big, strong man, she became conditioned to fear men like him. Like the sheriff. She had been so beaten down, crushed.

But now, gosh. A heavenly sigh of relief eased the tension from her shoulders. She was free. She was her own person, her own boss, in charge of her life, her destiny.

Ellery and Silina deserved each other. Coli had dodged a bullet, thank God he ditched her before she married him. It was the best thing that ever happened to her. Her voice scraping raw with emotion of relief and blessed gratefulness, she raised her teacup in salute. "He's all yours, dear sister, good luck. You'll need it."

She smiled down at Douggie. He'd fallen back to sleep with his nose in his dish. Yes, it's all good now. She had her dog and her B&B, and she'd be a success. She just needed to be careful, steer clear of the Arabats and Ellery. She needed to keep her eyes open, watch her back. She would not let him take her by surprise again.

With her new resolution, and full warm tummy, Coli finally felt safe, at peace for the first time in her life.

CHAPTER EIGHT

Brogan prowled the Pakan farm. The barn was never locked. Miller Pakan said he hadn't found anything missing, but things were in disarray. Bales of hay had been disturbed, tools tossed around. The sheriff saw some cigarette butts and a roach clip in a corner messy with broken straw.

Down on his haunches, he examined the barn wall, fresh initials and hearts were carved in the old weathered wood, he found a used condom shoved under some hay. He finished his investigation and went out to talk with Miller.

"It's nothin' Pakan," he told the farmer, his western drawl coming and going. "Just kids foolin' around and such. You might want to put a lock on the door. I don't think they plan any thievery or vandalism, but you want to protect yourself from them hurtin' themselves with some kinda foolishness like fallin' off the loft or accidentally settin' the place on fire."

Miller grunted his thanks, and Brogan tipped his hat and climbed in his truck. Before going on to the next complaint, he stopped to grab a burger at Flossie's Diner.

Sitting at the counter, pouring ketchup on his burger and fries, he was about to take a huge bite, when someone slid onto the stool beside him.

"Sheriff Dillon?"

Holding his burger with both hands, Brogan closed his mouth. Then turned to the man beside him.

He took in a stiff black suit, grey and white striped tie, wraparound shades up on his head pushing back the slicked black hair, stoic expression giving nothing away. The man looked around in his late twenties, and he had the cool calculating eyes of a lawman.

Taking a huge bite, then setting the burger down, Brogan licked ketchup off his thumb, talked through the wad of meat against the inside of his cheek, "Yeah, that's me. You FBI, CIA?" His gaze rolled over the suit. He said, "Don't look like a Texas Ranger."

The man held out his hand with a half-grin. "Yes, you're good, as I was informed. I'm Jackson Navarro with the FBI."

Brogan looked down at his hand, then up to a hard, implacable face, then back to the hand. He wiped his hand on a napkin and shook it. "What's the FBI doin' around these parts?" While he waited for the man to reply, he forked some fries and stuffed them in his mouth, washed them down with a slug of coffee.

Navarro watched him for a minute, then picked up his own coffee cup the waitress just set down and took a sip of the black brew. "Ah, I normally wouldn't let local law enforcement know what I was up to, but," he took another sip, set the cup in the saucer. "I need to poke around, ask questions. I don't want my head blown off. People in these more rural parts tend to shoot first, ask questions later. Or not at all. I supposed I could use your help with the locals."

"You ain't told me what your business here is yet." Brogan hunched over his plate and picked up the burger, took a big bite.

The agent studied Brogan. He found him interesting. The sheriff had the good 'ol country boy act down perfect. It appeared part natural and part put on, but it made people underestimate him. He didn't get excited, or loud, or demanding. Stayed cool, calm, professional. He wasn't going to punch holes in the agent with questions.

Not what Jackson was used to in these small towns. Normally he got belligerence and resistance, and sometimes downright stupidity. He felt an unusual trust of the sheriff.

"We've been tracking gun traffickers from overseas, lately Singapore to this general corner of Texas." Brogan kept eating, didn't look at him, but Navarro saw his brows twitch. When Brogan remained silent, the agent chuckled. "You're a cool man, Sheriff, don't let things ruffle you. Don't push fast, hard, you wait for shit to come to you."

Brogan downed a gulp of coffee, turned to Navarro, taking in the suit, polished black dress boots, slicked hair, and the intelligent glint with a stab of humor in the secretive dark eyes. "Hmm," he grunted and went back to his meal. The agent wouldn't have spoken up if he wasn't going to tell him everything, Brogan had patience. Had to in these parts.

Navarro chuckled again. "Okay. We got an undercover in Singapore. He was kept in the dark about most of the operation and the players involved, but he was able to put tracers in a bunch of the shotguns ready for shipment, then had to back off. One of the smugglers was growing suspicious of him.

"Anyway, as I said, we traced the guns to this general section of Texas, but we think maybe the tracers' cell batteries died before we could pinpoint them. Or, the guns might be buried under lead-lined and we can't detect their signal through the lead."

Done with his meal, Brogan tossed his napkin on his plate, drained his coffee, and dropped some bills on the counter. Then he turned on his stool to face the agent. "What is it you need from me?"

Navarro smiled. "Nothing at the moment. But I'll be poking around as I said, and I don't want to get shot or arrested. I just need you to run interference for me if it becomes necessary. Also, keep your eyes and ears open to anything suspicious that might have something to do with the weapons. What do you say?"

"You got a card?"

The agent blinked. "Uh, sure." He pulled one out of the inside of his coat pocket and handed it to Brogan. Brogan gave him one of his.

"Okay." Brogan slid off the stool, tapped two fingers to the brim of his hat to Navarro and strode out of the diner with the agent's surprised and comical eyes on his back.

Brogan drove out to the village of Pastizales to address the second complaint of a farmer that had come in. The rural town was made up of mostly farms and grasslands. Teeming forests banked Andy Caper's farm. Brogan parked in front of the farmhouse and turned as Andy Caper ambled from one of his barns, a weathered hand raised in greeting.

Same thing, the farmer said nothing was missing, but his animals had been let out to pasture in the middle of the night. Caper had already retrieved them, penned them in a fenced area. He led Brogan to the barn.

Standing in the doorway, "Uh huh," Brogan mumbled, doing a quick visual search of the inside of the barn. "You go on about your business, I'm gonna take a look around." In the air was the pungent smell of freshly mown hay mingled with the musty dry straw that was strewn over the hard packed, earthy soil. The wooden interior of the barn was weathered but well kept.

"Sure," Caper said. He had seed to plant, his boots clomped and shuffled over the loose straw on the floor as he traipsed out of the barn.

Brogan wandered the barn, carefully perusing every inch, every corner. There seemed to be nothing amiss. There were no butts, weed roaches, condoms or graffiti like at Pakan's place. A few tiny spots of what looked like dried blood caught his eye, but it was a barn filled with animals, there would be injuries from rustling about and fighting.

He made his way outside and did the same diligent search of the perimeter. He was about to pack it in, when he saw a dark clump a few feet into the grass. Likely just cow puck, he went over, crouched down.

Clotted in the blades of grass, the clump was brown with a hue of red. It looked like blood. About a small hand-sized clod of blood. He pulled out his cell and called Caper.

"Yeah?" The farmer sounded rushed.

"Anyone injured around here lately? Enough for a good glob of blood to fall?" He was met with silence as the farmer thought.

Then, "Uh, no sir. Can't say I recall anyone hurt lately. No animals neither. What-"

Brogan disconnected and noticed a few feet from the blood some of the grass was mashed down, looked like footprints, more than one set off to the side of the barn. He tramped over to the crushed grass, and saw another couple drops of blood. Moving further into the taller grass he followed the prints heading towards the woods nearby. Squinting, he could see something lying amidst the blades.

Down on his haunches, Brogan took out a pen and lifted it. It was a plain cloth, color indistinguishable as it appeared to be saturated in blood. There was nothing in or under it. He set it back down where he found it and moved on avoiding both the footprints and drops of blood.

Every few feet Brogan noticed more blood drops. Entering the woods, he saw the blood increased, the grass flattened. He followed the flattened grass, until, *what the hell-* there was a mound of fresh dirt. The blood led right to the mound.

Could just be a dead pet or something someone buried, but, his gut pinched. Down on his knees, he drew plastic gloves from his back pocket and donned them. Using his hands, he carefully scooped dirt away, until he saw something white.

Very gently, slowly, he brushed at the dirt, when, sure enough, there was an arm. A human arm. "Aw shit," he cursed. Pulling off his hat, he wiped his forehead with his jacket sleeve and took out his cell. He called it in, requested backup, the medical examiner, and ordered forensic techs to the scene.

Hours later, the body had been dug up and taken away. It was female, no ID on her, no purse. Her clothes were intact, didn't look like sexual assault. The medical examiner had pointed out a huge gaping gash in the back of her head.

"Some blood around, Sheriff," forensic pathologist, Dr. Harlon Martone told him. "But not enough. Lividity showed she died face down. When we dug her up, she was on her back. She was killed somewhere else. It appears that at first someone tried to ditch the

body in the barn foolishly thinking the farm animals might eat at the body making the ID as well as mode of death hard to determine. Then, seeing that the horses and goats and others only got agitated at the blood and smell and tried to get away, they changed their minds and buried her out back here. They maybe let the horses out to keep them quiet so no one would wake and catch them in the act."

When the medical examiner left, there were only CSI's still searching for evidence in the barn, around it, and between it and the perimeter of the body's location.

Brogan made his report then climbed in his truck and drove into town. He called Agent Navarro to tell him about the murder, maybe it was connected to the smuggling ring. Navarro said he appreciated the call and he'd meet him tomorrow at the morgue.

The next day, after the autopsy was completed, Dr. Martone preliminarily advised that the victim had died from a mighty blow to the head. He informed Brogan and Agent Navarro, "There were miniscule traces of iron in her hair, the wound was cylindrical. I think you're looking for maybe a tire iron or the like as the weapon, boys. The bar went deep, almost dang clear through the poor girl's head. Crushed her skull like a damned ripe melon."

The trio's attention focused on the body, a head block under her shoulders, her brunet hair combed of particles, the deceased female lay cold and greyish-white, sutures crisscrossing her exposed chest.

Snapping the plastic gloves off, the doctor dumped them in a closed container, clicked off the ultraviolet light above the table and said, "I was correct about the murder site not being where you found her. There was some blood there even after she'd already died, but that's because head wounds bleed so heavily. It would leak out as they jostled her about."

The distinct odor of strong disinfectant and formaldehyde lingered in the room made up of cold steel sinks, gurneys, freezers. Rust colored tile concealed inadvertent stains.

Brogan was wearing his brown uniform shirt but with jeans. He and Navarro were given gloves, goggles, face masks and scrubs. Crossing his arms, the sheriff said, "There's nothing yet from

Missing Person's, we still don't know who she is. My people have entered the prints into the system, pictures referenced with DMV facial recognition, DNA of course will take a while. But, as a young woman, dressed fairly professionally, probably not a hooker." He nodded to the nude corpse lying on the dissection table. "It's highly doubtful a match will come back from the prints or DNA, best hope is the DMV with facial recognition. There's nothing else to do here, I'll be in touch."

The doctor, somewhere in his late sixties wore a pale green paper cap covering his greying hair, dragged glasses with thick layered, microscopic lenses off his head, and drew a white sheet over the body covering it entirely. "I have more things to test, I'm waiting on the tox screen, and I want to make a mold of her teeth for when we get dental records to match. I'll contact you if anything comes up."

When the two lawmen exited the building, Navarro shook Brogan's hand. "Thanks for calling me, and allowing me observe, Sheriff."

"Sure." Brogan gave him a nod as the agent hopped in his vehicle and drove towards Shire's Cross.

Brogan left the morgue and took off to handle some other calls.

Hours later, Brogan headed back to the Barriga and to a paint store. He needed some nails for his mailbox, it was hanging by a thread.

He lived between a suburban town and the Barriga. With a lot of open space between the towns, for entertainment the kids shot at any signs they came across, and played chicken in ATV's with the mailboxes. The bell over the door chimed as he pushed through.

"Hey Sheriff," the owner, Pete Polito greeted Brogan with a friendly grin. "How're they hanging?"

Brogan grunted his response and chose a few nails from one of the baskets.

Pete followed him to the register. Brogan pulled out his wallet, took out a twenty. Pete went behind the counter to the register. He

rang him up, handed Brogan his change and receipt. "You need a bag?"

Brogan looked down at the six nails in his palm. "Na, don't think so." He dropped the nails in his front pocket, said, "See ya around, Pete," and strode to the door.

"Uh, hey, Sheriff, Brogan, uh, I, uh…"

Sighing, Brogan turned around. "Spit it out Pete, what's up?"

Pete came out from behind the counter and moved closer to the sheriff. "Ah, well, you know that new girl down at O'Riordan's, that hot piece from Ohio?"

Brogan stopped moving, bristled with a frown. "You talking about Coli Cassidy?"

Nodding, Pete smoothed back his long sandy hair with both hands, gave a leer as he said, "Yeah. Got a fine little ass, huh? Wouldn't mind getting that on all fours-"

Narrowing his eyes at the store owner, Brogan interrupted him with a surly, "What about her?"

Shifting his feet nervously under Brogan's mean stare, Pete said, "Well, she was here yesterday to pick up some paint."

Crossing his arms over his chest, boots planted a foot apart, Brogan's voice lowered impatiently. "So?"

"Well," Pete gossiped, "this guy come in. Don't know him, like in his thirties mebbe, but, he charged up on that little girl, and, uh…"

Brogan took an angry step towards Pete. "And what? Pete? Spit it the hell out. Did he hurt her?" Brogan could feel his brain start to burn.

"I, uh, not really, well yeah. He- he hit her." Pete had started out gossiping. But seeing Brogan's face darken, red creeping up his neck, his square jaw clenched, when the sheriff rolled his big hands into tight fists and took a hard step closer, Pete said quickly, "I mean, they had words. Could tell the guy terrified her, but she spoke up anyway, told him to back off. He told her to respect him, she told him he couldn't boss her around anymore, and well, and he slapped her."

Brogan's jaw jutted out, lids lowered to mean slits, Pete cringed fearing he was going to take a swing at him!

"Then what, Pete, what the fuck happened next? Spit it," Brogan growled, his arms curled up almost in fighter mode.

"Uh- uh, he slapped her again. She cried out, I rushed over. Joe Stamms and Rolly Brown came over too. They grabbed up the bastard, hauled him right out the door kicking and cursing and threatening he was going to get her and make her pay."

Brogan pushed his hat back, hair on his forehead tufted up. "Hell, Pete, she didn't call in a complaint. How bad was she hurt? "

"Hell if I know, Sheriff, I tried to talk to her, but she got all flustered, ran out before I could see if she was okay. I think-" he was talking to air.

Brogan was already out the door and the bell was tinkling as the door closed behind him.

"Well, shit," Pete muttered. "Dude sure takes his job protecting the town residents seriously."

CHAPTER NINE

Brogan sped out of the Barriga traveling the populated land until the road grew bumpier and buildings changed to fields, farms, scrubby prairies, then rock with burgeoning forests. He turned onto Wisteria Road, and knew when he reached the Victorian she wasn't there. That piece of crap car she drove wasn't in the driveway.

He stopped anyway and peered into the garage out back and in a few windows to confirm the place was empty. He did note with satisfaction the shiny new locks on the doors.

Chase had done his job. He'd told Brogan the girl became ruffled and angry when he wouldn't give her a bill. Reluctantly, Brogan drew his phone out and called Tamy Lee Crawford.

She answered with a piercing excited, "Hi handsome! You finally called me, I've been waiting and waiting and-"

He cut her off with a gruff, "Yeah. Listen, I need, uh, the name of a bloke."

There was silence, then she said with irritated laced sarcasm, "What am I now, your phone book? You need to-"

"Yeah," he cut her off again. "That girl, Coli, the sister of your friend Sabrina, she was seeing some dude that Sabrina stole away and is now fucking. I need the dude's name."

He was again met with silence. Longer this time. He could practically hear her gurgling with annoyance, and probably jealousy. He'd turned Tamy Lee down again and again, and here it was the second time he was asking about Coli. "Tamy-"

"Her name is Silina," she snapped, spelling it, "not Sabrina, and she didn't steal the whore convict's fiancé, *he* went after *her*. He does like having a harem of women. Even Silina's mom is enamored with him." A half chuckle and sly sounding grin she went on, "Girls of all ages seem to dig the bad boys, those that have that shade of danger. Right? Anyway, why do you want his name?"

Scrubbing his nails over the scruff on his chin, Brogan took a calming breath. Bitches, catty back-stabbers the lot of them. All country boy left his accent. "You don't need the details, Tamy Lee. Just give me the dude's name." He could hear the wheels squeaking as her scheming mind worked out what was in it for her to help him.

"Oo-kay. I want a deal for the information."

Biting back his curse, he growled, "Yeah, what kinda deal?"

Her coarse laugh trebled the lines then her voice softened to a sultry purr. "You agree to take me out, on a real date, and I'll be your white pages."

He had to struggle to swallow his curses, damned bitch. He was going to tell her where she could shove her deal when an image of Coli crying with a bruise on her pretty face, worse maybe happening later, blew in front of his eyes.

Letting out a hard breath, he said tersely, "Yeah, yeah, you got it. Whatever the fuck you want. Now, tell me the asshole's name, and number and address if you have them." Her triumphant hoot made his ears bleed.

"Okay, you got yourself a deal. I'll tell you where and when I want my date. I promise you, honey, one date and you'll get hooked. You're going to want more of me, you-"

"The goddamned name, Tamy Lee," he cursed through grit teeth.

With a huff, she said, "All right, all right. He's Ellery Delian. His number is," she paused while rifling through her phone, then rattled off a phone number. "He lives with Silina, I thought you'd figure that shit out yourself, Brogan. They live in Silina's granddad's mansion, the gaudy blue with white brick one in Beyth Aven. It's south, just outside the Barriga, you know the one.

Anyway, Ellery works at the Exchange on Main Street in the Barriga."

Her voice lowered in a sexy tease. "Plus he has a secret little hideaway. I know because he likes his variety in women. I took him from his latest side piece, Camille Blanca. Silina would have a *stroke* if she knew about us. Anyway, you think you can erase his particular brand of screwing from my memory with your own? You're both big men..." A husky chuckle, "I think we-"

He disconnected. So angry at his stupidity, he slammed his fist into the side of his truck. Of course, Coli's sister stole the crud from her. The pair of them, Silina and Delian, right on bedswervers, Shakespeare's disparaging coinage for adulterers. Coli had told him Delian was shacking up with her sister.

He could have discovered Silina's address on his own, and gone out there- he'd let the panic of Coli being harmed scramble his brains.

Hell. Now he was stuck with a date with Tamy Lee 'Horny Claws' Crawford. Just effin' great. Still, he hadn't known Silina's last name, cripes, he'd even gotten her first name wrong.

He headed out to Silina's home. Appropriate for sure, Beyth Aven. Beth Aven in the Bible, means the house of vanity, or iniquity. Wickedness, they all suit. Right.

An older woman answered his rough knock. Appearing in her fifties, she was the kind of woman that refused to let go of her sex appeal. Her makeup was heavy, dark blonde hair with big stiff curls flopped on her shoulders, she wore tight jeans, a tighter blouse, long red nails that matched her thin lips.

Brogan could smell the tequila and the leaf of mint in the glass she held in her hand.

"Hello, I am Sheriff Dillon, I'd like to-"

"Hah thay-arh," her Texas accent accentuated, making two syllables out of 'there.' She said, "Aham Goldie Arabat, pleased to meet ya'll, aham sure."

Her survey of Brogan started with his green eyes barely visible under the brim of his Stetson pulled down low over his brow. She moved over his harsh face and down to the thick chest in his

uniform, the sheriff's star partially showing under a leather jacket. Her gaze slinked further down to the V of his hips, and lower, where it stayed.

Her tongue slipped out and slid around her skinny lips. Leaning against the doorframe, the invitation in her leer clear as a smoke signal, she simpered, "So, what brings the big bad sheriff out here? You come for little 'ol me?"

She held her arms out, wrists together like she wanted him to cuff her. "Aham all yours, sugarbear. Ah dig bondage, hon."

Rudely, he didn't even remove or tip his hat respectfully to her. According to Coli the woman had degraded her and made her life miserable, he didn't owe her any respect. "No," he said curtly. "I want to speak with Ellery Delian." He waited while her eyes traveled up and down and around his body, settling back on his crotch.

"You packin' son, or just happy to see me?" She burst out in ribald laughter at her lame joke. Her braless blouse was open halfway down her chest, slipping her index finger inside it, she drew it seductively up and down her enhanced cleavage, her tongue sculling the thin lips.

Brogan knew if he pushed his way inside and without another word, she'd drop to the floor tearing off her clothes and stick her ass up high for him. The blouse tucked into the tightest jeans Brogan had ever seen. She had the same tanned leathery skin and figure as her daughter, fake tits, wide waist and a gigantic butt.

His stomach revolted at the thought of pounding that heifer from behind. Be like being out in the pasture with one of Andy Caper's cows. Moo, gag.

Today was a trial on his temper. "Ma'am, I want to speak with Ellery Delian, please retrieve him."

Hearing the edge in his voice, she prickled. "Listen-"

He got in her face. "No, *you* listen, *ma'am*, you produce that bastard right the fuck now or I'll haul you in for obstruction."

Goldie took a step back from his fury. Snapping her blouse closed, she glared at him, all traces of the accent gone, she retorted, "Ellery is not home. You might find him at his job, Oshident Exchange on Main, or somewhere-" virulence pitching her voice

high and strident, she shrieked, "fucking some random ho off the street!"

Unaffected by her wrath, he said, "Uh huh. What's he drive?"

Her eyes narrowed, she seethed, "You-" then grimaced and sneered, "Black BMW," and slammed the door in his face.

"Whoa," Brogan heaved a breath, "scorned much?" Seeing only a pink Audi TT and a red Mazda Miata in the garage, Brogan believed only Goldie and Silina were home, then he saw a Lincoln parked off to the side he figured the grandfather was there too.

He drove back to the Barriga and to the Exchange. It was after five by now and the place appeared closed. The lights were off, but Brogan located a black BMW parked in the lot next door.

Rounding the front of the building he parked then hoofed to the door of the Exchange and found it surprisingly unlocked. The building was quiet except for landlines ringing in all directions. He wandered the building looking at names on doors until on the second floor he found Ellery Delian's nameplate. The office door was slightly ajar.

He knocked lightly. No response. He gave the door a little push calling out, "Builu County Sheriff, anyone here?" Nothing. The lights were off, he pushed the door open and entered, stood to let his eyes adjust to the dark. In the large office there was a smell, not heavy, but not pleasant, metallic. Across the brown carpet obscured in the dark was a large glass-topped desk.

Behind the desk, a large window overlooked the center of the Barriga square; facing from the east the lowering sun was cloaked, offering less than meager light. He could just barely make out in the gloom a figure in a chair at the desk.

"Ellery Delian? I'm Sheriff Dillon, I want a word with you." More like a few seriously hard punches and an arrest for assault. Silence.

Brogan looked around, found a light switch by the door. He pushed it up with his elbow. The room lit with fluorescent light from the ceiling. Brogan presumed it was Ellery Delian at his desk. He was hunched over, his forehead flat on the desk.

"Delian?" Brogan moved slowly to the desk. Was the guy asleep? The angle was awkward, something didn't look right. The man didn't move as Brogan neared him. One hand on his gun, reaching out two fingers, the sheriff touched the side of his face. He was stone cold. "Shit." Brogan moved his fingers to the vein on his neck to check for a pulse, nothing.

He slid a hand under the guy's shoulder and lifted him slightly, and then saw the pearl-handled knife sticking out of his chest. Now he could see the blood soaked shirt and the trail of blood running down the front of him and pooling on the floor.

Brogan carefully lowered him back the way he was. Delian's forehead rested on the desk, and a few tiny light brown hairs fluttered on the glass top.

There were two cocktail glasses on the desk, almost empty. Brogan leaned over and sniffed, smelled like brandy. Straightening, careful not to touch anything, he fished out his phone and called the station. When dispatch answered, he said, "Got another cold one, 211." He gave the address and called Agent Navarro.

"Holy cow, Sheriff, this lazy little city hardly seemed the hotbed of murder, but bro, you got some shit going on here, a real crime wave." His chuckle turned serious. "I'd like to be at the autopsy. And I'm going to call in a gunpowder sniffing dog from Georgia."

Brogan gave him a few details then hung up. When the crime scene techs and the medical examiner arrived, he said to the doctor, "I lifted him up about six inches. Check for miniscule hairs on the desk. They dislodged off the body when I moved it, they're light brown and the deceased has black hair." Staying back by the door, he observed the investigators until they were ready to move the body.

When Dr. Martone snapped his gloves off, Brogan mumbled, "Talk with you later," and went to his truck where he wrote up his report.

He drove back to Coli's place. When he arrived, the sun was shifting way down the sky but there was enough dim light to see Coli on her porch, with her arms around a man.

His heart clenched and his stomach twisted, he climbed out and slammed the door. His boots crunching on the gravel, the couple stood in the low light, and held hands as they turned to face him.

Country accent nonexistent, "Hope I'm not interrupting anything…important," he ground with disgruntled sarcasm. Sure, he didn't want her because she was an ex-con and he was a cop, but, still…it tore possessively at his gut to see another man's hands on her, and vice versa. Jealousy creased the lines around his grit mouth.

"Sheriff." Her soft voice always sprinkled shivers up his spine. Her exquisite face made his groin scream. It grated that she still called him Sheriff when she probably called the man she was holding hands with Lover. He shouldn't feel such a sense of loss, but still…

Coli moved towards Brogan bringing the man with her. "What are you doing here?"

It was hard to not glare daggers at the guy, Brogan kept his eyes on her, which wasn't hard. "I came to see how you're doin', I need to talk to you," he shot a glower at the man, "alone."

"Oh, um…" she hesitated.

"Ms. Cassidy," his voice lowered, harsh with annoyance, "you can separate from your…boyfriend, for a moment." He couldn't tell if her sharp inhale was in anger or resistance. If she was his he'd never leave her side, but this asshole was for sure stepping away.

"Sheriff," she said softly, "this is my nephew."

"Huh?" His eyes darted to the male she held hands with, they narrowed. He could see now, he wasn't a man, he was a boy, no, a teenager. His hair was dark, not sunny saffron like hers. He was taller than Coli, and his face…there was something off.

The teen grinned at him, but Brogan could see the stairs didn't go all the way to the top. Brogan's eyes flit to Coli who was smiling, yet her mouth hovered in uncertainty of how Brogan was going to react.

"Kippie," she pulled the teen forward and introduced him, "this is Sheriff Dillon. What do you say?"

The grin was happy and totally without guile. Sounding like a young child but with a slightly deeper voice, Kip said cheerfully,

"I'm Kip," his brow furrowed as he fought for the words. Holding his hand out, he said very seriously, "I am p- pleased to meet you, Sher-iff Bamillon." The child-like grin rose right back.

Brogan paused, then shook his hand. The teen's hand was firm, maybe a bit too hard as if he didn't know his own strength. "Pleasure, uh, Kip Cassidy." His gaze swung back to Coli who was watching Kip with big warm eyes.

She gently remonstrated the boy, "That's Dillon, Kip, Sheriff Dillon. You know, like on the cowboy shows you like. Try again, k?"

Kip grinned, then his face grew very serious and he said, "K. Sheriff Dil-lon." He looked to Coli, asked anxiously, "Is that right, Cotty? Did I say it right?"

Nodding with an adoring smile, Coli tenderly brushed back a lock of dark hair off his forehead. "Yes, you did very well, Kip." She turned to Brogan with a gentle smile. "His full name is Kipley Thorne Arabat, Sheriff, not Cassidy."

Silina's horrible words dashed into his head. Studying the teen with grim intent, Brogan frowned, said, "Your sister told me about him. She said he was your brother. Both of yours."

Coli shook her head. "No, Kip is her-"

"Sleena my mama," Kip said loudly, his head bobbing in adamant affirmation. He looked from one to the other, grinning.

Then with a great big smile, he said, "But Cotty's my auntie, she takes care of me. She loves me. She said I can live with her now. Mama and Gram Goldie doesn't want me."

"*Don't* want-" Coli bit the correction off her tongue. "Kippie, honey, I think Douggie might be ready for his dinner. Do you think you can get it for him?"

Face glowing at being asked to do a task, Kip nodded hard. "Yeah, yeah, I can fee 'im." He turned towards the house and shouted, "I'm coming, Douggie, I'm gonna fee you!"

Without another word, he raced back up the solid stone steps, his feet clomping quickly across the wide verandah and into the house, the screen door banged shut behind him.

Brogan stared thoughtfully after the boy. Then he tipped his head to Coli. "You were saying, Kip is Silina's what?"

Her eyes still on the house, she clasped her hands with a fidget then shrugged. "He's her son."

Even though the boy had just said it, he couldn't stop the gasp. "Her son? But, he's gotta be 15, 16, she's too young. She's what?"

"Twenty-eight." At his surprised affect she said, "Silina had him when she was thirteen. She never revealed Kip's father's name. Everyone figured it was so he wouldn't get in trouble. He was probably eighteen or over, she was only twelve when she got pregnant, and he would have been arrested for statutory rape."

"Her mother hadn't a clue as to who he was?" His voice held a hint of disbelief.

Coli replied, "Maybe. But no one ever saw Silina around any boys, so, I don't know."

Confusion slanting his eyes, he asked, "If she's his mother, why is he here with you?"

Sadness filled her gentle blues. Clasping her hands loosely in front of her, she explained, "Silina and her mother Goldie, and Goldie's father Auston had put Kip in a group home far away, out in Ohio. Said he'd be better off. I think they were, ah…" she took a breath, "ashamed of him. And didn't want the trouble of raising a mentally challenged child. They never visited him."

She shrugged as if it was of no matter and said, "When I left my…own mother's home here in Texas, I hitched across the country to Ohio."

Picturing what could have happened to the young, vulnerable female traveling the road alone tensed lines of horror in his already hard face, of.

Seeing it, she said quickly, "Yes, it was foolish, reckless, but I was lucky. For once in my life someone didn't try to hurt me. I had no money, it was the only way I could get…there."

Brogan's face cleared as the light dawned on him. "That's why you lived in Ohio, to be close to him?"

Nodding, she said quietly, "Yes. I love him. You see, he's sweet and happy, all the time. He has the brain of a maybe a six or seven

74

sometimes an eight-year-old. He can read some and take care of himself and do easy tasks. He just can't live on his own. Silina is soon to receive her inheritance, I talked her into bringing him here. Plus, now that she'll be getting riches, the State would start taking funds from her for his support.

"She finally, albeit quite reluctantly and resentfully, acquiesced, but only because it would cost her to keep him in the home. He was going to end up in a sterile, indigent institution because Silina refused to bring him home with her, and she wouldn't pay for a good group home where he could live a relatively normal, pleasant life.

"I asked her to let me take care of him, she wouldn't have to pay a penny. So, I was more than thrilled to have him here with me. He'll be around regular folks, and I can love him and give him tasks to do that will make him feel useful, needed." Her voice held melancholy and determination.

Brogan carefully said, "Silina said it was because of you that he was…hurt?" One dark brow arched in question.

Her cheeks paled, eyes dropped. She raised them with a deep breath, stared levelly at him. "Yes. That's what I was told."

"What do you mean, *told*?"

Slender shoulders bumped. "Silina said she saw me deliberately pick up Kip, and," she sucked in a shuddered breath, "throw him, or push him, I'm not sure. Her story changes. He was just a baby; I don't know why he was even up there with us. Silina detested spending any time with either of us. I was just the bastard lovechild of the slut who stole her father's affections, and she hated having a baby. I'm the one that fed him and took care of him with help from the maids, neither Goldie nor Silina acknowledged his existence.

"It was so hard, I was only seven, but he had no one else. My sister hated having me around, and she was so young herself at thirteen, she didn't want the responsibilities of raising a child, even if Goldie would help. Silina was embarrassed about having an infant, was afraid she'd be shunned, made fun of. Said no boy would date a slutty teenaged mother. So they told people he was Goldie's."

Having met both Silina and Goldie, Brogan could see the truth in Coli's story.

"The only reason I lived there was because Silina's and my father, Thorne Arabat, said Goldie had to house me or he wouldn't pay a dime of support to her and Silina. My mother was…incapable of caring for me."

Brogan's heart had been encased in ice for a long time, but her life as a child just kicked like a mule at the ice. He could imagine how, as a product of an affair, she had been treated by her father's wife and the half-sister who burned with jealousy over her existence. "Uh huh. So, you were all playing together that day?"

"Um, well, like I said, Silina never wanted to hang with us, but that day she said 'Let's go up and play dolls in the tree-house.' I asked her why she was bringing Kip, he was a baby, he couldn't play. She said since he was a real baby, he could be like a real live doll. Goldie had just brought us up a plate of cookies, and we were having fun, for a little while, I thought, anyway, suddenly I hear Silina screaming at me, 'Why! Why!' Then she shouted, 'Why did you do that, Coli? Why did you push Kip off the ledge?'

"I thought she was still playing. I was picking up a doll we'd put in the corner in pretend time out, I turned around laughing, asking her what she was talking about. I thought she'd thrown one of my dolls out of the house.

"When I saw her looking down, I ran over, and-" Coli covered her face with her hands, closed her eyes, reliving the horror of seeing her baby nephew lying on the grass under the tree, not moving, not crying. She struggled to stem her rising sobs.

"Okay, Cubbie girl, it's okay now." Brogan rolled an arm around her, pulled her to him. She muffled her face into his thick chest, hiccupping back the tears. He stroked her back, they stood silently for a moment; for her to compose her grief, he to digest her description of that fateful day.

Wiping at her eyes, Coli took a few deep, shuddering breaths, expelled them. Moving from his embrace, she pushed her hair back and sighed. "It happened so fast. An ambulance came for Kip and the police came for me. I never went home again. I don't recall much

of the hearing, there was no trial. Goldie insisted to the mediator in the case that I was a born sociopath, a danger to society and needed to be locked away. We took a plea. I mean, I understand all of this now, but back then..." she swiped at her eyes to catch the new tears.

"I was so young, all I wanted to do was go home. Even as terrible as it was, it was all I knew. But," she gave him a sad, teary quivering smile. "I couldn't. They locked me away, but by law, I had to be released when I was no longer a juvenile. They let me out before I'd actually turned eighteen. Of course I had nowhere to go. As still a juvenile, they basically forced my mother to take me in."

Her lips hardened, eyes darkened. "From one nightmare to another. For two years my mother, Vixie, drank, drugged and screwed. I had to fight off her male friends, she couldn't bother to feed me, I literally had to steal food from the neighbors.

"She refused to buy me clothes. With my criminal history broadcasted I couldn't get hired for a real job so I had to mow lawns, rake leaves, collect recyclables, harvest vegetables, anything and every labor heavy job I could find just to stay alive. I worked 16-18 hours a day.

"It was hell, I had been better off in prison. It was cutthroat and abominable, I was hit and groped and stuff but I was fed and clothed, and was able to obtain my GED there."

His heart bled for her horrible past, things weren't all that much better now. "Tell me about the guy, Delian. He doesn't sound the greatest of boyfriends."

She crossed her arms as if to ward of a frightening chill, took a deep breath, exhaled slowly. "The night I overheard Vixie selling me for drugs I left and never went back. That's when I took off for Ohio. I was trying to enroll in a college there, not," her mouth twisted bitterly, "that they would take a penniless, convicted felon, of attempted murder no less.

"How everyone got ahold of my supposedly sealed juvenile record I have no idea. Anyway, that's where I went from the frying pan to the fire and met Ellery. He intimidated the few friends I had until, afraid of him they stayed away. He isolated me."

"Huh," Brogan grunted with disgust. "Typical abusive male. Like in the animal kingdom, that creep is like the lion that wants to mate the female but she's busy caring for her young, so he mauls the pups to death then violently rapes the female to show her who's boss and takes over."

Her eyes crinkled with a half laugh half appalled choke. "Boy, you hit the nail on the head. It was so hard for me to earn a living, and with no car and there was no one to help me learn to drive. Ellery got me a job and taught me how to drive, but all with the agreement that I couldn't see Kip. Ellery didn't maul him to death, but he did prevent me from visiting him. I figured down the road I would somehow manage to get to Kip. But yes, Ellery beat me, sexually assaulted me, kept me from the only person in the world who meant something to me.

"Once he had me in his claws, I wasn't able to free myself until he realized I wasn't getting the big money inheritance he had expected and he dumped me and latched onto Silina. Thank God." She stuck her tongue out in loathing. "I don't know which one is a worse human being."

A calm smile eased the distress from her face pinched in remembered torment. "Anyway, at least Silina gave me Kip. He flew in late last night." Her lip curled wryly. "I guess Silina and Goldie too, probably brought him by early this morning when I wasn't home. And, just like her, let herself in with the key I put under the flowerpot and just left him here all alone.

"By the time I got home, he was in tears, scared out of his mind. I found him hiding in a closet with Douggie squeezed in his arms. He was crying so loud I heard him the second I walked inside."

Brogan scrutinized her. She was his angel, the soft beauty that consoled him, a stranger that stayed with him while he lay broken on the road that day. The young woman, still a girl really, went across country to be close to her damaged nephew, and is now housing him on her own indigent dime, caring for him, loving him. Her heart breaking at the sight of Kip in terror.

Abandoned by her family, Coli suffered the abuse of a battering bully because her self-esteem had hit rock bottom, and she'd had

scarce way to support herself. Most of her youth she spent in prison, the pain of her past etched grotesque memories onto her gorgeous face. The anguish drained the light from her angelic eyes.

He agreed that the treacherous pair deserved one another, then, he remembered what brought him there. Hearing a snuffle, he looked down. That lump she called a dog was next to her foot, sound asleep. "Where'd he come from?" He hadn't noticed or heard the puppy approach.

Coli stooped and picked the dog up, cradled him in her arms, smiled lovingly down at him. "He does that. I never see him coming either, he mostly just, appears."

Brogan stroked one short ear, the thing purred like a kitten. Chuckling, he said, "Kinda like a ghost, he's too lazy to walk so he just pops in."

"Like Samantha on Bewitched? Twitches his nose and he materializes where he pleases?" They laughed together, she said, "He's a scobberlotcher." At Brogan's arched brows she explained, "That's someone who avoids work like it's their job."

He laughed. "That perfectly describes the little guy, yeah?" He gave the pooch's head a scratch.

Coli rubbed the side of her face on the dog's fur. "But I don't mind, he doesn't have to do anything except accept my unconditional love." A laugh burbled out, she said, "Kip's going to go crazy looking for him."

There was something else he hadn't noticed before on the ground by their feet. "What's that?"

She looked down with a short laugh. "That's his favorite chew toy." She nudged the stuffed rabbit with rubber feet with the toe of her shoe. "I never see him carry it or chew on it, but somehow, it's always right next to him. And, it has teeth marks all over it, the rabbit's red plaid suit is half gone so he does actually chew it, you just don't see him doing it, just like you don't see him moving."

Brogan smiled at the mysterious pup, then he sobered. "Ah, Coli, there's something I need to, ah, ask you. Where were you the last couple of hours?"

Nuzzling the dog that slept on, she answered, "I did a lot of running around. Searching antique and thrift stores for things for the house. This rustic land is rife with antique shops. Earlier today I checked several stores in the Barriga for wallpaper, paint, things like that." Her expression paled.

"I, uh, heard about what happened at the paint store," he said with concern in his voice. He lifted a hand to caress her face, then dropped it. "Are you okay? Did he hurt you?"

She shook her head, cheeks tinted pink in her pale face. "Just my pride. I was mortified, he…hit me in…public. Kind of…scared me." Angry resolution dragged her blonde brows down. "It will never happen again. I…refuse to allow it."

"What can you do to prevent it?"

"I…can get a restraining order. If he persists, I'll have him arrested."

"Would you…hurt him? Physically attack him?"

Her lashes flew up in surprise. "No, of course not. How could I? He's so big, strong," she shuddered at old memories. "I'd need a gun to stop him, and I abhor them. They frighten me. I sure wouldn't have a gun around Kip. No, I would go to the law if he did it again."

"What about a knife? Would you use a knife to protect yourself from him?"

She shook her head harder, lips rippled in revulsion. "Ew, no. Slasher movies gross me out. I could never," her tongue stuck out again, "no, ick." She buried her face in tan fur. The dog grumbled then settled back down.

He watched her for a moment. Then said quietly, "Coli, tonight Ellery Delian was found…dead, murdered."

Her head popped up, mouth dropped open. She studied him to see if he was speaking truthfully. Seeing his stoic demeanor, she exclaimed, "Oh my gosh, what? Are- are you serious? Are you sure? It can't be-"

"I found him myself. I matched his face with his DMV picture. The medical examiner will need to confirm it, but it's him."

"H-how? You said…murdered? Was he shot? Is that why you asked me-"

"He was stabbed."

Her lips compressed, eyes lowered trying to take in what he said. Then her lips pushed out, angry eyes rose then narrowed in contention. "You asked me those questions, where I was, and a-about knives. You came here not to see if I was okay, but to accuse me. You- you think I killed Ellery?" Aghast, she shouted, "You came here because you think I'm a suspect in his- his murder?"

Her rage huffed as her face reddened. "I get it, because I've tried to kill before I'm game to do it again?"

He held his palms up. "Now wait, simmer down, Coli. I was originally coming to check on you after Delian's assault and got waylaid when I stopped at his office. But, I'm a cop, for the record I had to ask. I don't think you-"

"Get. Out." She said it calmly, quietly, with barely a quiver to her voice, but her eyes shrieked betrayed fury.

"Listen, Coli, I-"

"Get out," her voice rose, louder, the fury turned the betrayal to hurt.

Brogan kept his hands up as he protested, "Come on, Coli, we need to talk-"

She screamed so loud Douggie's head jerked up. "Get out! Get out!" Her voice strident in hysteria she cried, "Get out!"

"Aw, shit." She was too distraught to reason with. Her face beet red, eyes bulging in apoplexy, he feared she'd hurt herself if he stayed. He spun and strode to his truck.

As he opened the door, he looked back. Her face was hidden in the dog's fur, but her shoulders shook with wracking sobs.

CHAPTER TEN

Brogan's head banged around inside his aching skull, his brain reeled with the hangover. It'd been several days, every night he'd put away a ton of bourbon but it did nothing to wipe out the picture of Coli's stricken face. He couldn't erase from his mind how hurt she had been, and he'd been the cause of it.

He stumbled into the shower, nicked himself shaving, twice, cursed while he pulled a white tee over his pounding head. He wore his uniform shirt buttoned over the tee, but instead of the brown uniform slacks he put on jeans.

Nibbling a slice of dry toast, he gagged down a glass of OJ and poured a thermos of coffee to drink in the truck. Buckling his weapon to his side, he plopped the Stetson on his head, grabbed his keys and jacket, and took off for the station.

Still early spring, tiny puffy clouds idled in the vivid blue sky, the air was cool but the sun made it tolerable. On the drive in to the station he thought about when he had driven Coli home and she'd shared her joyful enchantment of the horse farm, and they experienced the rare sighting of the roadrunner, her squeals of delight still rang pleasurably in his ears.

Old crumbly leaves scattered and tossed in the breeze, and he could think of nothing but spending that time with her again, and more. Brogan had to admit to himself, he was enamored, smitten by his angel. He could argue and deny it all he wanted, try to keep her convict status between them, but, it meant nothing, really.

He didn't believe she was guilty of attempted murder on her beloved nephew, and, truth be told, didn't care. She had been too young then to have a clue to injury or death of a child, besides, Silina's story was majorly suspect. His body and mind and heart wanted Coli, and he couldn't fight it. His severe jealous reaction to her nephew was evidence he was besotted.

Inside the station, he joined his lead deputies and detectives. FBI agent Jackson Navarro was present. Brogan flopped down on a chair at the long table. They were in the station's conference room, the table was wood with its shares of stains and scratches, the chairs on wheels were old but the cushions comfortable.

Besides the table, and a smaller one in the back, there were two-dozen chairs, shelves with books and DVD's on the walls, standing poster boards, and a screen for PowerPoint presentations.

While chit-chatting, everyone pulled out notebooks and pens. Some used their phones for notes as well.

Brogan interrupted the rumble of conversation. "All right, y'all know each other, but you brothers," he winked at the lone female deputy, "and sister, don't know our guest." He motioned to the man in a suit sitting across from him and grinned at Navarro's pragmatic dip of his head in acknowledgement.

"Jackson Navarro is with the FBI. Now," the sheriff held his hands up as protests emerged. "He has his own project goin' on down here, but we are workin' together. The two murders might be connected with his mission. You will treat him with due respect. Anyone doesn't," he speared a deputy who was scowling with a steely glare at the agent, "can go find themselves another job, yeah?" Back to Navarro, he said calmly, "Let me introduce the team."

His voice laidback and with only a hint of his western drawl, he started with a man in black jeans and a black shirt, the sleeves rolled up. A laptop was open and on in front of him. "That scoundrel there is Lóránt Debar. We call him Lo, or, Pirate."

At Navarro's pointed brows, Brogan chuckled. "Yes, his name sounds familiar, you'll find a lot of things, towns, people here, names come right outta the Bible. Lo Debar means basically, no communication. It's funny really because I recruited Lo because

he's a white hat/black hat hacker. We were in the military together, same as Rocky and Tarzan."

Navarro hid his surprise. He stared stone-faced at the hacker. Pirate had short black hair, longer on top, a trimmed black beard and black-framed glasses that you'd see on geeks. The cold emptiness in his dark eyes as he stared blankly back, and the tattoos pocking his neck and covering his muscular forearms conveyed the complete opposite of geekiness. An air of deep-rooted anger and distrust permeated the young man's hard features.

Brogan smiled at the way the two strong men coolly studied each other. "The IT civilians at the station do adequate work," he told Navarro, "but they've never dealt with serious crimes before. Pirate works for himself as a subcontractor for investigations. When he works for the government, he's a white hat hacker. When he works under the radar as it were, needing to search the dark web, he becomes the black hat hacker. Personally, I give two shits which he is, as long as he produces."

The two men still stared at each other, one side of Pirate's mouth curled up in a cold non-smile.

"You can call me Jacks," Navarro said with his own icy smile.

The female deputy asked, "Jacks? Like the game with the ball and little metal pronged pieces? Or Jax with an X?"

Navarro kept his eyes on Lo, but he replied to the woman, "Like the game. But I don't play."

Leaving that comment open to interpretation, Brogan said, "Movin' on. That is Deputy Elvin 'Rocky' Narocki," Brogan gestured to the blond with twinkling mischievous blue eyes that was silently laughing at his friend, Pirate.

"And next to him is Detective Kurt Vantarzani, we call him Tarzan," he nodded at the man with the dark tan, neat scruff and dark chocolate eyes. He too was grinning at Brogan.

"Pirate, Rocky and Tarzan?" Navarro said with humor tendering his disbelief. "What, do we also have Bullwinkle and Jane, and, what was the monkey's name?"

"Cheetah," Brogan said to a round of laughter. "But, no, that's the extent of our cartoon characters."

"Speak for yourself, *Brogan*," Tarzan rumbled with pretend irritation. "Now there's a common name for ya."

"Movin' on." Brogan motioned to another male. "Bo Buckhorn, we call 'im Bucky," he said with a provoking grin. Buck was the oldest of the team at 39 and it stuck in his craw that he had to answer to the sheriff who was more than 10 years his junior.

The sandy-haired deputy with round brown eyes growled disrespectfully, "It's Buck, you asshole." He nodded to Navarro, scratched at a sandy patch under his lower lip, muttered, "Welcome, Fibber."

Letting the asshole comment slide, Brogan kind of deserved it, he said, "Over there is Daminico DeCarlo, yep, we call him Dam." There was humor in the sheriff's tone, but his eyes were stern. Dam had been the one protesting the FBI's presence. Silky dark Italian hair and midnight eyes, the deputy was also the Casanova of the station.

"And," Brogan smiled at the lone female, "last but of course not least, we have Lenita Pupatelli. Call her Pup at your own peril."

Navarro's mouth listed in a semi smile. "I knew this damned backwoods town was lazy, but you're even too lazy to call each other by your full names."

Everyone chuckled. Brogan thought about Douggie, the slothful dog fit right in. A pang pinched his heart at the thought of Coli. He pushed the sentiment aside. He never thought in his life he'd ever crave to see a woman, miss her, ache to touch her. He musta hit his head harder than he thought when he crashed his bike.

Lenita settled lusting brown eyes on Navarro while primping the side of her brunette hair pinned back in a bun. Sizeable lips showed big pretty teeth, she purred, "Please to meet you, Agent Jacks, welcome. Anything I can do for you, show you around, take you-"

"Okay then," Brogan broke in and ignored her scowl because Jacks turned his attention from admiring her admirable rack to face Brogan. "Rocky, you met with Dr. Martone this morning; did he have anything to add on our male vic?"

The blond shrugged his massive shoulders. "Not much. Said good move on your part noticing the almost invisible hairs on the desk of the male DB, uh," he glanced at Navarro, and explained, "means dead body."

"Hmm." Navarro smiled faintly, gracefully not offering a snide remark, he was after all a lawman as well and knew all the lingo.

Realizing this, Rocky cleared his throat and went on, "CSI's mighta missed them. Dr. Martone thinks they might be animal hairs. He sent them to the lab for confirmation. The knife had a seven-inch blade and a pearl handle. Pearl part had gold flecks. It was expensive, Martone said, he had thought it's likely a steak knife and assuredly part of a set."

He shrugged. "I've been online to see if I can identify the maker. Then I can go on from there with footwork. Check stores where it might have been sold. But," he shrugged again, even under the uniform those shoulders were impressive. "Martone says it looks old, it might be hard to locate where it came from."

Nodding, Brogan said, "Okay Rocky, good, keep on it. Tarzan?"

The dark-haired detective glanced at his notes. He had a dark tan making him appear even more his nickname. He'd heard every joke about loincloths and would punch out the next person that said one. Unless it was a chick, then he'd consider wearing one, for her. "I took the cocktail glasses to the lab. Only prints on one, and those were Delian's."

"So the other was deliberately wiped clean?"

"Seems like. The glasses matched, but there were no others like them in the building. Lab said really good crystal, gold rimmed, also expensive. You were right, they'd held brandy. Cognac to be exact. The brand unknown. Rocky and I got a search warrant and went to the Arabats' house to look for the rest of the set, and kept an eye out for the matching knife set too."

Brogan's grin crooked, he said wryly, "I bet that was a treat."

Tarzan chuffed, rolled his eyes. "At first they were flirtatious as alley cats, then we showed 'em the search warrant. The two bitches, sorry Lenita," he nodded to the deputy. "I mean the *ladies*, went

wild, both were beyond livid. Screeched and cursed, not like ladies, carried on some such. *Prostitutas,* hookers in lace, ya know? Said they felt violated, the police rummaging through their things. We only searched the kitchen and curio cabinets type things. It's not like we went in their panty drawers." That drew male chuckles.

"They didn't give us permission to search Delian's room or things." Rocky added, making a dour face, "There was this austere old guy present, black suit and tie starched, perfect to a T. Had black hair streaked at the temples with silver, white moustache.

"He just stood in the background leaning on a silver topped cane, watching. Reminded me of those old-timey movies of vampires, you know, *Dracula.*" He drew the name out with the Romanian accent. "Gotta tell you, he gave me the willies."

Brogan hummed, sat back, set an ankle over his knee, rested one forearm along the chair arm, he tapped his pen on his open notebook. "Sounds like the older female's father. Okay, anyone else got anything?"

"Sorta," Pirate muttered. "I pulled video surveillance tapes from the vicinity of the Oshident Exchange."

"Tell me you got a good clear shot of our male's killer," Brogan said eagerly, leaning forward.

"Na. No such luck. I stayed up most the night reviewing all the tapes. Best I got was this, it was an hour before you showed up. I gotta tell you Brog, you're not very photogenic. The camera does nothing for that harsh face of yours. Maybe if you smiled."

"Jokes from you, Lo? Gotta be a first. Show me."

Pirate turned the laptop so Brogan could view it. The others shifted their chairs so they could see the tape.

It was dark with spare illumination from outside lights and street lamps. A very hazy video showed a fuzzy figure at the front entrance of the Exchange.

Pirate said quietly, "See the big tote over the shoulder, could have had the liquor and glasses in it. The glasses had been at the scene but forensics found no sign of the liquor bottle, and employees questioned said alcohol wasn't allowed in the building." They watched the person wearing gloves unlock the door and slip inside.

"Apparently no one gave Delian the memo about the liquor ban," Rocky said drily. He squinted at the screen, commented, "It was after hours, most staff probably gone for the day. But it's undoubtedly an employee, they have a key."

The group was silent as they continued viewing the tape.

"One light in a window turns on for a bit," Pirate murmured, "appears to be Delian's office. Thirteen minutes later, the light goes out and the same figure comes a-runnin' out the door and scurries down the street, out of view of any cameras. That's why the door was unlocked when you got there.

"Unfortunately, the person was covered in a boxy trench coat, a ball cap concealed the hair and face. Slacks hid the shoes. That was the only unidentifiable person that entered the building that day. The rest I put names to with the help of the receptionist."

"Oh, ho," Rocky snickered, "that must have been fun. Since you don't leave the station or your home unless forced to, much less have to *speak* with another human, much less of the female kind." He leaned forward towards the hacker and asked with a leer, "Tell us, Lo bro, she hot? Or was she a hundred?"

"How 'bout you shut the fuck up," Pirate's words were tough, but a telltale red slunk up his neck confirming the female was young, and hot.

Rocky opened his mouth to further torment the hacker, Brogan cut off the ensuing battle with a raised hand. Rocky would tease and annoy the normally stone mute man until Pirate would have enough. He'd remove the black-framed glasses and the men would jump up and start throwing fists. All in masculine fun.

"Can't tell if it's male or female, Lo," Brogan studied the film. "Can't you get it clearer or find a shot of the face on one of the other cameras on the building or the street?"

"No. There was one camera that would have caught the front of the person, it was actually on the Exchange's building over the entrance. But, I spoke with the manager dude, it wasn't working. Been out of order for a week. I measured the door, due to the high and odd angles of the cameras, it's hard to be precise, but it appears to be either a shorter male, or a woman. Whichever, they were

shorter than you, like most of the population. With the outer clothes and hat, I can't tell the weight, or figure. I'll keep pruning the tapes, then I'll hoof it back to the scene and review the neighborhood for cameras to see if I mighta missed anything."

Disappointment at not having a clear shot of the suspect lowered his voice, Brogan nodded, "Okay. You did good, carry on."

Rocky snickered, "Hey, bro, then you can go see your hottie receptionist. Maybe a little smooching-"

Brogan broke in as Pirate started rising out of his seat, "Sit down, Lo, clamp it, Rocky, what are you, 9? Anyone else got anything?" He looked around the table.

"Yep." Dam DeCarlo spoke up with a grin. "Got an ID on the female vic." All eyes went to the handsome Italian.

He bent his head to his notebook and read, "Miss Kandy-Marie Birchfield. A Missing Person was finally filed and the lab matched the dentals. She is, was, 26, dropped out of high school in the twelfth grade to run off to California with some surfer bum.

"Came home six months later with her tail between her legs. I mean, I got that info off the social media site Chat-Wi'me. She's a brunette with blue eyes, five feet six, 115, and, according to her site page, she loves, loves, loves men, dancing, men, drinking, shopping, and men!"

A few groans tempered the room, Brogan glanced around shutting them up. "What else?"

"Uh," he looked down and said, "she works a couple hours a week at the D'Faience Artinquity Gallery down from Main at the corner there at Quimera."

Her brows knit, Lenita asked, "That the place with the giant blue Egyptian statue out front?" Dam nodded. "Oo," she pursed her lips then said, "it's so ugly. A glossy naked woman with a bird's head."

"She ain't fully nekked," Rocky laughed, "some of her bottom half is covered with a veil."

Lenita grunted. "An almost transparent glazed veil, and her breasts are exposed. I mean, kids go in that neighborhood, there're shops and restaurants, it's disgusting."

"Come on, Pup, it's art. Just a big glossy statue with a bird's head and boobs, don't be such a prude," Dam cajoled with a grin.

Lenita turned on him, snarled at his full-lipped mocking grin, "I am not a prude, and don't call me Pup-"

"Okay, okay, settle down folks. We have serious work to do." Brogan glanced at Navarro who, although his face was hard and implacable as usual, mirth glimmered in his dark eyes.

Dam took the floor again. "Not that it helps, but I spoke with the forensic pathologist. He checked Kandy-Marie's stomach contents to see if he could determine what she ate last, maybe we could have tracked her steps, but he said she was pretty much empty. Enamel worn on her teeth and scarring on her esophagus indicated she was bulimic."

"Shit, women," Rocky groused.

"Hey." Lenita scowled at him. He winked at her.

Brogan sighed, slapped his pen down on the notebook in front of him. "All right. Tarzan, you and Rocky head on over to the Birchfield's house, talk to the parents, ask about friends, boyfriends, you know the drill. Ask why they didn't do a Missing Person's right off the bat."

The pair bunched their lips, but they bowed slightly to the sheriff. No one relished death-duty calls.

"Dam, I want you to do the work up on the knife, and Buck, you trace the glasses. Get the info Tarzan and Rocky already have, then do the digging."

Lenita said, "I heard the deceased male was a player. Might have a love-nest or such, maybe a honey on the side with a jealous husband. I can check that stuff out. Co-workers talk."

"Very good," Brogan complimented her idea. "I should have mentioned it, I had word he did have a secret place he took women. Talk with Tamy Lee Crawford, she knows where it is, and question her whereabouts when he was killed, she was one of his side women. I'll get you her number."

Buck interjected, "Speaking of his babes, his write-up file indicated a broken engagement. I can go interview the ex-fiancée, her name and address would be in the file. There's an additional

journal note that when she was buying paint downtown the other day that Delian came in and slapped her, and threatened her. Pete and his guys had to pull the freak away. She's as likely a suspect as anyone."

Brogan said quickly, "No. I've already interviewed her." He didn't say what the outcome was or if he had any suspicions about Coli.

Lenita asked, "What about Delian's current woman? Didn't I read that he got engaged to the last one's sister?"

Rocky answered that one, "Silina Arabat. Engaged to both sisters, guy was a tool, huh? We questioned the newest fiancée when we went to look for the glasses and knives. She claimed she was home all night and would never harm a hair on her beloved's head. Her family is her weak alibi."

Tarzan added, "Silina Arabat is a shrew with a pointy face, the first fiancée must have been *really* hellacious if he dumped her for the pointy shrew."

Brogan wasn't about to tell them anything of what Coli had gone through. The Arabats were on his list to check out further. He believed Silina Arabat only wanted Ellery Delian because he had been her sister's fiancé.

Once she would find out Coli wants nothing to do with the abusive bastard she'd drop him like a prickly cactus. Especially if she realizes he was only interested in the sisters because of the inheritance. He had a healthy bank account himself, but he liked to live high on the hog at top dollar. A flush of big income would keep him living at the style he wanted to stay accustomed to.

The sheriff instructed the detective, "Okay, Tarz, you guys hit your assignments. I'm gonna check out the gallery."

"You just want to see the nekked lady," Navarro teased, mimicking Rocky's accent.

"Yeah, that's it." Brogan's lip tugged in. He stood up. The rest followed suit.

"I'd like to go with you, Sheriff," Navarro said, treading to stand near him.

Brogan laughed. "You wanna see the nekked lady too, you deviant?"

"Ain't no deviant if it's a male's attraction is for a female, son. It's not like she's all fowl, a total beastie. Listen to me," the agent shook his head, "I've only been here a few days and I'm already starting to sound like you country folks. My ma would wash my mouth out with soap if she heard me say ain't."

Buck interrupted them with irritation, "Where's that Scottish lad, MacBaird, and fatso Gillan? Why aren't they here doin' their share of the work? That Scotty cop needs a haircut, all those long red waves, gettin' to look like that guy on Outlander."

Raised blond brows, Rocky smirked at him. "Aren't you the romantic into chick flicks."

Scowling at the deputy, Buck retorted, "I'm just saying those two need to pull their weight too."

Not that Brogan owed him, or any of them an explanation on how he ran the county's law enforcement, he said, "Not that it's any of your business, but Lachlainn is out hikin' the Alto Colinas, the high hills. He told me he's a senderista, a mountain walker. Said he used to walk the cliffs and the moors for days on end when he lived in Scotland and tragedy had struck. He's not over his loss yet. He needs time. Duff Gillan is off today."

Brogan's eyes narrowed at Buck, but he bit back his rebuke and turned to talk with Navarro. He should chastise the deputy for calling Deputy Duff Gillan fatso, but Brogan could barely stomach Gillan himself. He had a belly and was slovenly. Talk about lazy.

The deputy was a recent transfer in. Brogan hadn't caught him yet, but he was pretty sure Gillan was working below the law, accepting bribes, maybe pocketing drugs he confiscated from dealers. He needed to keep a close eye on the man. He ended the meeting.

The group chatted as they exited the room to proceed onto their tasks.

Brogan said to Navarro, "You want to ride with me in my truck?"

Navarro shook his head. "No, when we're done I'm going to pick up that gun sniffing dog I told you about. I'd like to go to the dead guy, Delian's house, let the dog sniff around, the Exchange office too, and the love-nest if they find it. See if there's any trace of gunpowder. Could be why the guy was killed, mixed up in the gun smuggling."

CHAPTER ELEVEN

Brogan called ahead to ensure the gallery owner was available. It was a bit of a drive from the station to the gallery and he didn't want to waste the trip if the owner wasn't there. There was a lot of sprawling open space between towns in Builu County.

Ranches, farm fields, prairies, woodlands, the lake and marina, residential and wealthy gated communities stretched in all directions from the main belly of the Barriga. The city's real name was Shire's Cross, the Barriga was the center of it.

After they parked, the pair stood looking at the statue standing to the side of the main door of the gallery. On the other side of the door was a window taped with flyers advertising upcoming events in it. But it wasn't the flyers that held the men's interest.

"She's nekked alright," Brogan commented.

"Sure is," Navarro replied. "And anatomically correct, sort of." Their heads lowered as they moved their gazes from the top of the strange head and down the mostly nude female body.

"Kinda disturbing. You know, with the bird head and all."

Navarro agreed, "Sort of ruins the whole naked lady thing."

"Uh huh," Brogan concurred. "Could always throw a bag over her head." Navarro laughed and they went inside.

The gallery was red brick on the outside, stonewashed walls on the inside. Paintings scattered the walls, padded benches were placed strategically for viewing with a few tables around to set purses and drinks on. The gallery advertised periodic art events.

Two connecting rooms were widely spaced and open, the only adornments were the paintings, the interior was pretty plain.

A rather tall, lithe, that is, she hadn't much of a figure, woman came to greet them. "Hello gentlemen," she said coolly, taking her time inspecting both strapping men, and smiled her appreciation.

Her brassy red hair was pulled up at the sides and held with barrettes, the long red curls and waves streamed down her back almost to her waist. Her eyes, a bright unnatural green, her thick red lips didn't look natural either. The green dress clung like a second skin down just past her knees outlining her sinuous figure. Her body was a rail, but she worked it.

She had a deep, husky voice, sexy if you liked that kind of smoky sound. "How may I help you?"

Brogan and Navarro both pulled out ID's, flashed them and put them back away in the blink of an eye. "I'm Sheriff Dillon with Builu County, this is Special Agent Navarro with the FBI. We called earlier; we would like to speak with the owner of the gallery."

"And we'd like to speak with you as well," Navarro's tone held flirtation. His dark eyes swept her lean body as if it heated him.

Brogan firmed his grin and didn't look at him or he'd break out in laughter. He'd seen the agent checking Lenita Pupatelli out, dude was definitely a breast man. And this redhead lacked in that department. Navarro was working her.

The woman shuffled up closer to Navarro, she was tall but she had to crane her willowy neck to look up at him. "I'm the owner's assistant, Petra Peerina. I'd love to answer any questions you have, Agent Navarro."

Navarro wore a suit and tie. He pushed back the sides of his unbuttoned jacket and tucked one hand in his trouser pocket, using the other hand he lifted a curl off her shoulder. "Well, that's right friendly of you, Red. You can call me Jacks." His mouth ticked at Brogan's choke that he quickly turned into a cough.

Petra frowned at Brogan, then smiled at Navarro. "I'll go get Mr. Reno. BRB." Her high heels clicked across the tiled floor, she glanced back over her shoulder at Navarro, gave the agent a grin and wink, then disappeared behind a door.

"Right friendly, Red?" Brogan teased, parroting Navarro. "You're sounding more and more like a native, *Jacks*."

Navarro patted his tie, grinned at the sheriff. "Flies with jelly, son, catch more flies, you know?"

"I think that's honey-" Brogan broke off as the door opened.

First person out was a tall, broad-shouldered man with dirty-blond hair tied back in a ponytail. A dark yellow beard covered half his face, dark blue eyes warily regarded the two men waiting. He wore loose, sloppy faded jeans, flip-flops and a white button-down with the top buttons undone exposing dark blond chest hair.

Brogan's attention shifted to a second man that came out behind him.

Long, shaggy brown hair and a thick beard, he appeared in his early thirties like the first man.

A third person followed the men out. Young, maybe even in her late teens, she was small with delicate bone structure, fair skin and long, light strawberry blonde hair. Big blue eyes gaped at the lawmen standing there looking stern. The dark-haired man tucked her possessively under his arm.

Both men had a hippy vibe with their hair and attire. Blond guy in worn jeans and flips, the dark haired man wore brown corduroys and a flannel shirt, scuffed boots.

The blond man came forward, his voice soft and low, he said unhurriedly, "I'm Rex Reno, the owner of the D'Faience Artinquity Gallery. Petra tells me you have some…ah, questions for me?" He shot a sideways glance at his male friend.

Brogan and Navarro's gazes crossed to the friend. A hawk nose that made him look dangerous and daring at the same time, he shoved a flop of brown hair back off his brow revealing bold golden eyes that coolly assessed the men.

Brogan noticed both men's eyes were red and their lids were low and puffy. They each sported a slack Mona Lisa smile. *High as kites*, he thought to himself. Well, he was here today for murder, he didn't have the time to hassle them about a bit of marijuana.

His limp smile turning dour, "Dane Zachary," the brown-haired man introduced himself. Stepping forward, he held out his hand and shook both lawmen's hands.

Rex Reno's smile expanded. "He's my main artist. These are all his works." He proudly waved his arm to denote the paintings. Brogan and Navarro politely looked at the paintings closest to them. Most were bland western scenes of prairies, cacti, horses. Brogan's gaze returned to land on the girl tucked under Dane Zachary's arm.

"Um." The artist patted her shoulder. "This is Poppy Mikola," he said, a chuckle brightened his dour face. "Her folks must have seen the color of her hair when she was born and named her after the perky California flower. She's just arrived here to study painting techniques from me."

"Pleasure, ma'am." Brogan lifted his hat slightly. "Mr. Reno, do you employ a Kandy-Marie Birchfield?"

Petra hovered off to the side. Reno glanced at her then sighed with an edge of anger. "Yeah. She only ever did show up once in a blue moon, hasn't been in for over a week. She shows her face she's fired."

Her eyes on Navarro, Petra shimmied across the room, high heels rapping over the white tiles, she pressed up to Reno's side, slipped an arm around his waist.

Brogan and Navarro avoided exchanging a look. Brogan asked, "When was the last time you saw her?"

Reno blinked a few times, his eyes lowered, one shoulder hitched. "Like I said. It's been at least a week. Maybe last week Saturday?" He glanced at Petra and Zachary, they both shrugged.

"I guess there about," Zachary supplied. "You were out at the Silver Cactus Bar with her, remember, Rex?"

Petra's face scrunched, she narrowed her eyes in pique at Reno, Zachary's comment appeared to upset her. "You told me you were done with her, Rex, you told me that *I* was the only-"

"Petra." Rex didn't snap, his downy voice stayed unflustered. "The officers are not interested in our...personal lives." He said to Brogan, "Sheriff, what is this about? Is Kandy-Marie in some kind of trouble? Does she need my help?" Beside him Petra made a

grumbled snarl. Reno gave her a squeeze, a signal to be quiet. "Sheriff?"

Keeping his stance firm, face blank, Brogan replied stoically, "I regret to inform you that Miss Kandy-Marie Birchfield is...dead."

A gasp eeked from the girl, Poppy. All color drained from her fresh-faced prettiness. A sprinkle of freckles across her small nose stood out in her complexion that had turned white. She squeaked, "Dead?" Zachary gave her a pat and said quietly, "Hush now, Poppy."

Reno asked, "An accident? Was she in a car accident?"

Brogan shook his head. "No. She was murdered."

"Murdered!" Petra and Poppy squealed.

"Any of you know where Pastizales is? Town way out in the flats of Builu, mostly farmland." Brogan and Navarro were carefully watching all four of their faces, scrutinizing their expressions.

The women looked horrified, the men vaguely disturbed. But then again, Brogan surmised they were both stoned. He could smell the marijuana reeking from them. He detected a Boston accent from Reno, Zachary he couldn't quite tell. All four appeared to be searching their minds for the town Brogan asked about.

"I've heard of it," Petra said, a slight shake to her voice, her hand was at her throat. "I- I've never been there."

Zachary shook his head, and Reno said, "I've only lived here less than a year, I'm not really familiar with the towns surrounding the Barriga. I live in a loft apartment in Liso Piedra, it's just on the outskirts of the Barriga. They tell me it means smooth stone." His grin boyish, he said, "I can't attest to the truth of that as I'm not much of a walker, you know?"

"You, Miss?" Brogan centered his attention on the younger woman. She looked so pale he thought she might pass out. She'd shifted from the artist, she was now a foot away from the group. Her strawberry lashes shot up at Brogan speaking to her.

"Me?" Her throat rolled with several swallows, voice trembling roughly she cried, "What about me? What are you asking me? I don't know, I hardly knew Kandy-Marie, she barely said two words

to me. Mostly. I didn't have brunch with her and that woman last Sunday, I mean, I mean-"

Brogan halted her rambling. "That the last time you saw her? Sunday? Where'd you have brunch?"

Poppy blinked and swallowed, her panicked gaze galloped from Brogan to Navarro, it slid to Rex then skidded to a stop at Zachary. If possible, her skin paled further. "I- I- we ate at the Purple Majesty Tearoom," she inched towards the door.

"The woman with Ms. Birchfield at lunch, who was she?"

Half-turned to face the door, her words tumbled out in a rush of breath, she stammered, "I- I don't know, her neighbor, her mother, girlfriend, she didn't eat with us, she left when I- sat down. I need to get my sweater, I- I left it in my car, I'll be right back."

Mouth quirked with absurdity at the younger girl, Petra remarked, "Uh, hello, what are you, a flake? You don't have a car." Like a trapped animal about to chew its foot off to get away, Poppy's skin blanched, her hand set on the doorknob.

Observing the girl becoming unglued, her strange behavior, Brogan told them, "I'm gonna need all four of you to stop by the station so we can gather more information." Poppy's face blew up with terror, Petra smiled at Navarro as if this was going to be a date.

Rex Reno and Dane Zachary showed zero emotion, or interest. "Yeah, sure, we'll be there. You girls can ride with us," Rex said. Before he completed his sentence Poppy was gone, the door still swinging closed behind her.

A few minutes later, out by their cars, Brogan asked Navarro, "What was your take?"

Jackson grinned, tucked his hands in his trouser pockets. "Petra has town tramp written across her forehead, she's slept with both men and is already grooming her bedroom for my visit. The way she checked out your ass when you turned around likely you're on the list as well," the men shook their heads with a chuckle. "Reno, the owner, looks harmless enough. Can't tell if that's the weed, the truth, or a façade. We need to check into his background, he's only been here a year."

"The other two?" Brogan asked. He leaned against his truck, bent a knee and propped a foot against the side.

Navarro widened his stance, shook some change in his pocket. "The girl, Poppy, is scared out of her mind. Can't tell if that's because she knows something, or because she may have been one of the last people to have seen Kandy-Marie alive."

"Or," Brogan offered, "she's in love with Dane Zachary and fears his ire for opening her mouth and involving herself in the investigation. I don't think painting is the kind of tutoring Zachary has in mind for her, and she seems totally innocently blind to his lust. She looked at him like he was a protective big brother or some such, not as a lover. He watched her from under his low brows like she was on the dessert menu. We need to know where she came from and how she hooked up with the artist."

"Uh huh," Navarro nodded in agreement. "We didn't tell them the vic was killed sometime Monday night. None of them admitted to seeing her on Monday. However, what was talked about when they did last see her could be important. Then again, one of them might have been holding her against her will until they did the deed on Monday. So, what about Zachary?"

"Cool fish, secretive eyes. He acts all hippy artist and open and forthright, but…"

"Yeah, I got the same vibe. He gives me gooseflesh, makes me feel uneasy, but not exactly why, I can't put my finger on it."

Brogan opened his door. "I'm with you on that. Spooky fellow, peers hawkishly through those shaggy bangs with those weird golden eyes, don't trust him one speck. And, he's one helluva crappy artist."

Navarro agreed with a mocking nod, and said, "We'll get more when we go into his background, and question him at the station. You putting that hacker on him?"

Laughing, Brogan slid into his truck. "Yeah. Lo. Pirate. He's the best of the best. I'm lucky he's a friend. He's always been a major help. You noticed both the males have beards? Maybe it's fashion, maybe sluggish grooming, maybe hiding their faces." He stuck his key in the ignition. "I gotta go."

"Right. Dog's not coming in until tomorrow. I'll pick him up at the airport then head over to Delian's business. I'm starting there because the description that deputy gave of those two women he lived with, hell, I'm not eager to experience them."

Turning the truck on, Brogan muttered drily, "You have no idea."

CHAPTER TWELVE

For the hundredth time Brogan berated himself. Tamy Lee had phoned earlier and said she was calling in her chip. She wanted their date to be tonight. There wasn't much going on with both murder cases so Brogan had no excuse to get out of it. Last thing he wanted was to be locked in a car with her, stuck in a restaurant booth, on a dance floor, or worse, fending her off after he takes her home.

That was the last thing, the first thing he wanted was, hell, he wanted to see Coli. He wanted to- he pulled into Tamy Lee's driveway, her door flung open before he got his truck in park.

As he expected, he had to fight to get her out of her house and into his truck. She'd met him at the door in her underwear. Scarlet thong and some matching see-through half-bra that did nothing to hide her mammoth breasts.

Giggling with a drink in her hand, already tipsy she told him, "I'm not ready. Why don't we have a drink while I decide what to wear."

He'd stalked into her room, ripped clothes out of her closet and threw them on the bed. "You have fifteen minutes to get dressed or I'm out that door without you," and he went and stood by the front door.

They followed the hostess to the table. The young African American hostess swung her hips in an oscillating rhythm. Every other man watched her pass by. Then they watched Tamy Lee behind her. Both women wore tiny skirts, the hostess' skirt was

molded to her hips, Tamy Lee's flounced. Every other flounce revealed she was now commando. Brogan looked at his watch trying to configure how much time he had to spend with Tamy Lee before he could dump her home.

The hostess had stopped at a table, which Brogan had requested, specifically not a booth. Then his mouth dropped. Several tables away, Coli Cassidy was sitting in a booth with the paint store owner, Pete Polito.

Brogan's breath hurt, his stomach plummeted. He'd blown his chance with her, marching out to her place and just about accusing her of being a killer. Right. Soft, darlin' bundle of sweetness. It seemed to be her fate to be accused of terrible crimes. First her baby nephew, and now... Still, he was the sheriff, he had to do his job.

Telling the hostess, "Thanks," he quickly pulled out Tamy Lee's chair and hastily seating her, he said, "Order a drink. I'll be right there." He turned too fast to see her angry pique, not that he cared anyway.

He stepped over to Coli's booth; his shadow fell across the white tablecloth. In the middle of the table a romantic candle flickered in a crystal bowl, on the wall behind the booths were paintings of flamboyant pheasants and vineyards in France.

Coli was pressed against the wall, Pete faced her, lurking over her. His arm was around her shoulders and his hand on her thigh. Coli was holding the wrist of the hand on her thigh, her arm was rigid as if she was trying to push him off.

"Coli," Brogan said. Their heads turned to him. At first, a warmth spread through his chest at her sudden smile, true joy at seeing him. Then, the remembrance of the other day infiltrated, and the smile fell to a pucker of sadness, then anger.

"Yo, Sheriff," Pete greeted him with mild confusion. "What brings you here?"

Brogan frowned at Pete's hand on her thigh. "Here for dinner. Saw you, thought I'd stop and say hi."

Coli averted her eyes from him. Pete nodded and said, "Nice to see you." He glanced at Coli then back to Brogan. "We're ah, busy. Catch you around, okay?"

Ignoring him, Brogan said, "You doin' okay, Coli?"

Getting annoyed at Brogan's intrusion, Pete said, "You want something, Sheriff? You're not on the job." He indicated Brogan's suit coat and black slacks, white shirt with open collar. Pete wore a suit as well but he had a tie knotted around his neck.

Brogan had the urge to wrap his fist around that tie and twist-Snubbing the shop owner, he leaned over to get a better look at Coli. He asked, "Cubbie, can I have a word with you?"

Pete grouched, "We're on a date, Sheriff, you want to talk to her call her tomorrow. Now if you don't mind," he curled his arm more tightly around Coli's small shoulders, not seeing her wince. But Brogan saw it.

"Not talkin' to you, Polito, I'm talkin' to her. Let her out, I want to talk to her. Come on Coli, just for a minute," he motioned to her to leave the booth. Pete didn't move.

Huge eyes filled with dejection and anger, Coli said, "You had plenty to say the other night, Sheriff. Unless I'm under arrest-"

"Under arrest!" Pete squawked, his mouth dropped in incredulity. "You fucking kidding me right now? Arrest for what?" He tightened his arm even more as if he could keep Brogan from taking her away.

"Come on, Coli," the good ol' boy drawl gone. "I told you, I originally came out to see how you were doing. I was also doing my job when I asked you where you were earlier. Your fiancé was found dead after you two had an altercation in which he hit and threatened you. It's only natural I'd ask-"

"Dead? That ass that slapped you is dead?" Pete blanched. His skin darkened, he crowed angrily to Brogan, "You think this little girl could hurt a fly? That guy was twice her size and mean as a rattler."

He choked out a laugh. "You overdo your position, Sheriff. You're so lame to prove yourself you go after a young woman to close a case quickly? Huh," he sat back, shaking his head.

Ignoring Pete again, Brogan persisted, "Coli, please, just for a minute, just give me a minute." His brows wrinkled in supplication,

lips pulled in, he held a hand out to her. He was a dog for hitting on a guy's date but he didn't care.

She blinked at him, he seemed so sincere, apologetic. Coli cleared her throat, put her hand on the tabletop. "Pete, let me slide out, I'll only be a-"

"Broggie, baby, what are you doing over here?" Tamy Lee whined. "I've been waiting for you. I've already ordered a drink, come to our table." She rolled her hand around his waist and set a breast on his arm. Brogan ignored her, Pete and Coli's gazes flashed to the woman pawing him.

Her dark brunette hair was one long curl over one shoulder, the top pouffed high. Cat eyeliner streaked heavily from the corners of her dark brown eyes, her lips dark red to match her blouse. If Tamy Lee moved the wrong way, her blouse was open so far she would be cited for indecent exposure. Six-inch heels brought her closer to Brogan's height and made her legs miles long.

Coli slumped back against the wall, turned away. "We have nothing to talk about, Sheriff," she murmured, "clearly you're quite busy at the moment."

Trying to pluck Tamy Lee's talons off his arm, Brogan rasped with irritation, "I'm just asking for a minute, Coli."

His chin in the air, Pete said smugly, "You heard her, Sheriff; she doesn't want to talk to you. Now, why don't you go take care of your date, while I take care of mine?" He snuggled Coli into his broad-chested embrace.

Brogan still tried, "Coli," but she turned her head from him. Tamy Lee tugged on his arm. "Come on Broggie baby, leave the lovers to their date, we have our own thing going on."

Seeing the brick wall Coli put up, Brogan's jaw clenched, he had no choice but to leave their table. He'd look like a stalker if he persisted.

He spent the rest of the night brushing Tamy Lee's fingers off his thighs, shrugging her groping hands off his ass when she insisted on going dancing after dinner. When he drove her home he had to pry her off him, drag her out of his truck and push her to her door.

"You gonna come inside and have another drinkie with me, Broggie?" she slurred. After a bottle of wine then a martini, and several more at the dance club she was unsteady on her heels. She bent a knee and plucked one heel off then the other. She dangled them over one shoulder coyly, then dropped them on the ground and reached for him.

Sighing wearily with heavy aggravation, Brogan took her purse, fished her keys out and opened her door. Snatching her hands from their journey under his belt and down his pants, he gripped her upper arm and carted her inside, leaving the door open.

He half carried her to the sofa. When he released her to have her to sit down, with a grin and shrill bawdy laughter, Tamy Lee whipped her blouse off over her head and tossed it. The transparent bra covered nothing. "Look what I got for you, Broggie," and she lifted her skirt.

"Aw hell." He really hated being called Broggie. He gave her a slight push. Already off-balance, she toppled backwards flopping on the couch landing with her legs open and gales of giggles.

"You wait there, Tamy Lee," Brogan took a deep breath. "I'm gonna get my jacket in my truck, I'll be right back." He pivoted and hurried to the door.

"Hey," she called out with a slurred giggle, "you're wearing your jacket!"

He quickly pressed the lock and closed the door to her cackling, and bolted to his truck.

Speeding down the street, he left Tamy Lee's suburban town of Bamah, raced to his house, oblivious to fields spotted with bluebonnets, groves of hickories and elms.

He turned at the old Evangelical church not seeing the prancing coyote stealing through the bluestem grass, and drove down his street to his house and parked. Hurrying inside, he grabbed something up, hopped back in his truck and headed to Mal Tierre.

It was well after midnight when he pulled down Wisteria Road to the Victorian. He was praying the lights would be on which would mean she was home, and Polito's car wouldn't be in the driveway. And the shop owner not in her bed.

The tight breath he held eased out as he saw the lights on in the front room, and, he scanned the driveway and over to the garage and the carriage house, and let out the rest of the breath. No car except her rundown thing in the driveway. He parked behind it. Grabbing up the fussing critter perched on the seat next to him, he climbed out.

He'd calculatingly brought the beast hoping it'd make him look like a nice guy, perhaps soften her heart towards him some. She must have heard the car because the light over the door to the verandah came on.

Before he reached the porch the screen door was opening, and, it wasn't Coli who stepped out. It was Kip who stomped across the wood planks and to the porch steps, and the sweet faced kid looked royally pissed. It was the baseball bat he held raised as if he planned on using Brogan's head for baseball practice that gave the sheriff pause.

Brogan tried for the casual approach. "Hey there, Kip, how's it goin?"

"You go and get out of here, Mr. Polito, Im'a gonna hit you this time you don't go," the teenager marched down the steps with the bat high and threatening.

Brogan slowed. "Ah, Kip, I'm not-"

"Kip!" Coli shouted, hurtling out of the house, across the verandah, and up to her nephew.

"Honey," catching her fast breath she said, "that isn't Mr. Polito, that's the sheriff, Mr. Dillon, you remember him? He won't hurt us, it's okay, unless," her eyes narrowed at Brogan. "Unless you're here to arrest me?" She didn't notice Kip had stomped all over the big yellow flowers by the flat stones that led to the side door.

"No! Everyone stop hurting Cotty!" Kip started towards Brogan swinging the bat.

Coli caught his arm. "No, Kip, don't hit him, he won't hurt us, will you, Sheriff?" He was still dressed in the suit coat and black slacks, no gun at his hip. Her eyes fell to the white puff he held in his arms. "What is that?"

107

It was starting to dawn on Brogan that something had happened tonight that made a sweet teenager enraged and wielding a bat about ready to take Brogan's head off. He looked at Coli, there was a scratch on her cheek. He commanded, "Son, you put that bat down, Coli, you tell me what the hell is going on here."

Kip hesitated and looked to his aunt in confusion. She smiled and touched the arm holding the bat. "It's okay, Kip, why don't you take Douggie," in fact, the pup was lying at her feet, snoring, his chew toy by his side. No one had seen him coming. "Uh, into the house and give him one of his doggie treats, okay?"

His lips firmed, Kip looked from Coli to the sheriff to the dog to Coli, confusion, wanting to please, and yet not wanting to leave Coli in danger warred on his young face.

Coli said softly, "Go on, it's fine, go on now." She gave him a little nudge and nodded down at Douggie.

"Uh, okay. Here," he handed the bat to Coli and bent and scooped the dog up, grabbing his chew toy. Although thoroughly chewed, the red and blue plaid suit was still clinging to the rabbit's body. Kip glared hard at Brogan, "You do not hurt my Cotty. I come out and kick your ass."

"Kip!" Coli spouted, "Where did you learn that word?"

Kip grinned, snuggling the dog. "Mr. Gregory. Mrs. Gregory makes him put a quarter in a jar when he says it and other bad words." He shot another warning glare at Brogan then hurried up the steps to the house.

When the screen door slammed, Brogan moved close to Coli and brushed the pad of his finger over the scratch on her cheek. "Do I need to go put a hurtin' on Pete Polito?"

Shaking her head with a glum smile, she said, "No, I think he got the picture. Who have we here?" She held her arms out for the enormous feline curled up against Brogan's big chest.

Brogan handed the cat to her, then took her elbow and brought her to the verandah steps and helped her sit down, then sat beside her. "All right, enough stalling, what the hell happened here?"

A frown tugged her brows down as she petted the cat and watched it squiggle on her lap, getting comfortable. "What are you

doing here, Sheriff? Where's your date?" She craned her neck to see if there was anyone waiting in his truck.

Growing impatient, Brogan replied crankily, "I dropped Tamy Lee at her home and came straight here." He curled his fingers under her chin to lift it so she was forced to look at him.

"Hell, Coli, I didn't want to go out with her in the first place. She made me trade a date for information I needed from her." Coli didn't need to know that the information was about Ellery Delian hitting her and Brogan's plan to *talk* to him about it. "I am not here right now as a sheriff, Coli, I'm here because, uh…"

Long saffron lashes swept down making feathery shadows on her apple cheeks then rose to blink in puzzlement at Brogan.

She prompted, "Because why?"

CHAPTER THIRTEEN

Dragging a hand through his dark hair, the tips of Brogan's ears turned red. He'd never been in this position before. He didn't date generally, the women he saw didn't want a relationship any more than he did, they each got their needs met and that was it.

But, the little heart-shaped face that beamed up at him tugged at his heart, it had since he was lying wrecked on that street and his very own angel was there petting him. When he ran into her at the clambake the nail hammered in his coffin. He knew then he wanted her, wanted her body, yeah, but he wanted more. How much, he didn't know.

What he did know was no other woman had held him wrapped around her little finger so tightly he could hardly sleep, barely keep his mind on his job for thoughts of her, the need for her, the hunger and the desire to hold her in his arms.

Seeing Coli with Pete tonight about killed him, he had wanted to grab the storeowner and bodily throw him out the door of the restaurant, get him as far away from *his* Coli as he could toss him. Words weren't exactly his forte, but this beauty was the kind of woman that needed to, should hear his feelings.

"I, uh…" While the cat snuggled on her lap, Brogan picked up Coli's hand and held it. "I want to see you. I mean, like a date. Like a lot of dates. What do you say?" God, he sounded like a dorky tongue-tied schoolboy.

Coli stared wide-eyed at him, glanced down at their twined hands then back up to his dark green eyes. She studied him like she was trying to judge his sincerity. "You want us to...date? Each other?"

A chuckle drawled out. "Yeah, girl, us." His eyes firmed intently he said firmly, "Just us. No Pete, no Tamy Lee, no one else for either of us. Unless," he wavered, "you and Polito got somethin' heavy goin' on. Are you and he-"

She shook her head, blonde curls fluttered over the cat that wrinkled its nose and he batted at the ticklish strands then settled back down. "No," she snorted.

"He kind of pushed me to go out with him, I wasn't really all that interested. The man I was interested in," she peered shyly up at Brogan through those long yellow lashes, "thinks I like to go around killing people. So," she shrugged one shoulder, "I figured I might as well go out with Pete. I could use some friends, and he seemed nice enough, but..." she turned her head away from Brogan.

His jaw stiffening, he cupped her chin and turned her back to him, ire flared like heated emeralds in his eyes. "Did he hurt you? Tell me right now, Coli, I don't want to pussyfoot around with this, I haven't the patience for it. Too many men have thought it okay to manhandle you, I'm fixin' to end that. Answer me," his angry sight was aimed at the scratch on her face.

A soft smile curved her lips, she told him, "When Pete brought me home, he wouldn't leave. Kept hanging on me, trying to kiss me. I told him I wasn't interested. He didn't want to accept my no and he started getting too persistent, then a...bit...rough."

At the rage that started burning in his eyes, she said quickly, "I didn't know Kip was home. I enrolled him in that school, Raising Minds, for special kids like him." The smile broadened tenderly.

"He met another boy there, Markie. They hit it off and Markie asked his parents, that would be the Mr. Gregory of the curse words, if Kip could hang at their house tonight. They live in Beyth Aven, and since Kit had left a few things at Silina's place, afterwards the Gregorys were kind enough to take him there, then, Silina brought him here. She said Goldie was interested in seeing the place so

they're planning a visit. Anyway, it all worked perfect since I had this date..."

Brogan's expression was heading towards thunderous. "That cut, Coli, did he-"

Playing with the cat's soft ear, shaking her head, she declared, "No, no. Actually, Kip heard me, um, kind of trying to fight Pete off and he ran out of the house so fast, when he reached us he tripped, fell into us and knocked all three of us to the ground."

An amused laugh, she said, "Pete hopped right to his feet, stood flustered, then reached down I think to help me up, and Kip, well, he's very protective of me. He stuck his chest against Pete's and literally pushed him with it until he got to his car. Kip told him to get out and don't come back. He thought you were Pete when he saw you, he thought Pete had returned to hurt me, so, ergo the baseball bat."

"The cut," Brogan reminded her, stroking his fingertips above it.

"Oh," she laughed lightly, "that happened when Kip knocked us down. I don't know how, I didn't feel it at the time. So, you see, Pete didn't hurt me, and, well, even if I wanted to go out with him again, I don't think Kip would cotton to it too much, right?"

For the first time that day, Brogan's harsh face relaxed into a smile. "Good. I think Kip and I'll get along great. Hey," something rubbed against his leg. Somehow Douggie had materialized again, he'd laid his muzzle on Brogan's boot, and appeared to be fast asleep. "Hell, that dog..." He leaned over and scratched Douggie's head. "Where'd you get this little guy, anyway?"

Smiling down at her pet, she explained, "Right after I moved here I found him on the verandah. He had no collar, and he wouldn't leave. I called the local Humane Society and said if anyone was looking for him where to find him. He didn't seem to want to leave me, like I said, every time I turned around, he was at my feet. I was pretty lonely when I first moved in, so he was a perfect present.

"I hear people that don't want their pets anymore drive out here to the boondocks wilderness and drop them like the animal will be thrilled to be living outside and roughing it. Trying to get food,

water, stay out of coyotes' mouths." Petting the soft white fur of the large cat, she said, "What about this huge guy?"

Brogan lifted the cat from her arms and set it down by the dog, to see how they got along. "Pretty much the same thing. He showed up on my doorstep. I didn't want to feed him 'cause you know then he'd never leave, just like your pup. But," he smiled fondly at the big ball of fur. Appearing not to have moved, yet somehow now both animals were nose-to-nose.

"I did feed him, and I took him to the pound. Felt bad about that. I called them a week later, see if his owners came or someone had adopted him. They said they were going to euthanize him in a few weeks if no one came for him. They had too many cats to take care of. So," he shrugged.

"What's his name? He's so big, like, a giant cat, if he was yellow he could pass for a fat, furry baby cougar or something," she smiled in admiration at the feline at their feet. "How old is he do you think?"

"He's not fat, Cubbie, he's husky, has big bones. According to the Vet he's still a kitten." At her barked snort of disbelief, he laughed. "Yeah, I know, he's huge, could put a dang saddle on him. But the vet said he's less than a year. He gets any bigger and I'll need a bigger house." They chuckled together. "His name is Felipé. I know, odd, but it kinda just came to me."

"Hmm, I would have named him Snowball or something like that, leave it to a man to come up with that name," she teased.

"Uh huh." His eyes on her lips, he nodded, mumbled, "Gotta get him a little sombrero." He leaned closer to her and cupped her chin again. Sliding his hand along the side of her face hoping his callouses weren't hurting her delicate skin, Brogan bent slowly, giving her time to back away, say no. She didn't, her lids lowered, she was looking at his mouth, and her lips parted.

Brogan took that as a yes, and settled his mouth on hers, and took her. Gentle, exploring, tasting at first, then, the kiss burgeoned hot, fast, *hallelujah*. His palm splayed on her back crushing her to his chest. Feeling the top of his head about to explode with the blazing heat of the kiss, damn the girl could kiss, *damn*…all thought

left his brain and he became all feeling. An entire body of searing sensation, like going from being cocooned in warm, sweet soft cotton candy and suddenly sticking his finger in a light socket.

Yeah, he was gonna go off like a freakin' missile if he didn't stop. He had to stop. Now. In a second. He licked her lips, went after her tongue and sucked it. One more second. He bit at those plush lips that tasted like silken sugar cubes, just one more second...

Coli's small fingers dug into his rocky biceps, she couldn't get her hands all the way around them, urgent mewing sounds blended with his deep rumbling growls. She was pulling him as close against her as hard as he was holding her to him. Then, her palms moved to his chest, and she was pushing him, turning her head, breaking the kiss.

It took a moment for her resistance to float into his now erotically charged brain. Both of them sucking in panting air, he moved his hand from clutching her face and the other from pressing against her back.

Blinking unfocused eyes, his chest heaving with the ravishing kiss, Brogan forced himself to grip her upper arms and set her slightly away from him. Yeah, another heartbeat and he'd have had her flat on her back on the ground and climbing on top of her. And probably have a baseball bat to the head.

He swiped his jacket sleeve across the beads of sweat trickling across his forehead. "I, uh," he huffed, couldn't help reaching out and brushing back a few strands of yellow hair that had caught in her lashes. "Coli, I know I should apologize for that, but, hell damnation girl, it was too good to try to erase." He noticed he wasn't the only one breathing rapidly or have heavy-lidded dazed eyes.

"It's, um, okay, Sheriff, I..." she trailed off as if she didn't know what to say.

Brogan frowned in hazy lust-laden irritation. "Coli, I just had my tongue down your throat, maybe you could call me by my given name. You call me Sheriff and that makes me feel like I just used my badge power to coerce you, making you afraid to resist my forcing myself on you." Her head was bowed, the long curls covered

her face, he couldn't read her expression. Had he pushed too far too fast?

"Hey, uh, Coli, I'd like us to be up front and honest with each other, please, look at me, talk to me. Tell me if I was out of line. I would never want you to do…things, with me if you didn't want to, yeah?"

He waited. She slowly lifted her head, and he groaned. The lips he'd been crushing and sucking and biting a second ago were red and puffy, as were the lids thick over the bright blue eyes gleaming with…it looked like passion, like he was looking into his own reflection. Sort of. She looked like how he felt.

Coli cautiously lifted her hand and laid her palm against his rough cheek, he leaned into it. "I'm not upset Sher- uh, Brogan." Her eyes lowered in shyness, but she caressed his cheek. Looking up at him, she said softly, "I liked it, the kiss. I just…" she started to turn from him again but he clasped her chin, holding her to face him, she dropped her hand.

"Just what?" he prompted, missing her soft hand on his rough cheek.

Her shoulders slumped slightly. She told him, "Ellery was the only man I've ever been…intimate with. I'm not sure what to do, how to act. He never…" a deep breath inflated her chest.

Brogan struggled to not look at it. He was already over-heated and ready to take her to bed, he didn't need anything like her swollen heaving breasts pressing against that blouse to put him over the edge. Stroking her face with his palm, he said, "He never what, Coli? Talk to me."

Swallowing a hard gulp, she explained in a quiet, strained voice, "He never asked me if I wanted to, ah, have sex or anything. I mean, he didn't do anything to- to, you know," a gorgeous blush rubbed pink in her cheeks.

Her eyes lowered, she coughed awkwardly then said, "Get me ready, or to enjoy the act. He just did it, took what he wanted even if it hurt, a lot, he was, um, kind of violent. When he got angry at me, anyone, anything, he…you know, took it out on me. I…don't think I can go through that again. I think we should leave all this at

that kiss, and forget it happened. You need to have a girl who can be…normal for you." She looked away at his gasp.

If the bastard wasn't already dead, Brogan would be on his way to his house. He cradled her face with both hands. "Baby, you are normal, you were abused, most relationships aren't like it was with that bully asshole. If, when we get together, it'll be mutual. Everything. I would never hurt you," *did light spanking count? Hell,* he thought, *it'll be a long time before she's ready for that kind of play.*

"If you give me half a chance, I can show you what real lovin' is like. I'll take care of you, Coli, always."

He slowly leaned into her and gently bussed her lips, inhaled her fresh scent then leaned back, but clasped one of her hands like he just needed to be touching her.

"How about I take you on a proper date and we get a bit more comfortable together? We'll take our time, get to know one another. If we go further than kissin' that will be when you say so, when you're ready. Okay?"

Because there was no way they weren't gonna kiss again, the way their lips and bodies had crushed together will be playing all night in his brain like a hot and heavy tune. He'll be lucky if he gets any winks of sleep.

Shoulders that spanned doorways, his chest slabs of thick hard muscle, huge biceps bulged when he moved, but he touched her like she was the finest, daintiest china. Hearing the sincerity in his voice, the way he looked at her like she was a precious jewel to be cherished and beheld, and desired, she murmured, "I'd like that." The tenuous smile lifting her lips to a pretty bow soothed the tension in her face.

The tight breath he held flushed out. "Good. Now, it's late." He stood up and effortlessly pulled her to her feet. "I'll call you tomorrow and we can plan something. Let me just grab that gigantic furball-" he glanced down then swiveled, looked around in the dark night surrounding them. "Where'd Felipé go?" The dog and the cat had vanished.

"Uh oh." Coli giggled. "I think my dog has corrupted your cat."

"Say it ain't so." He scratched the top of his head, muttered, "Juvenile delinquents." he called out, "Felipé!" Behind him came a yawned, "Meow."

Brogan swung around, looked down. "What the-"

Douggie lay on his belly on the ground, asleep. The cat sat beside him calmly licking its white paw.

"How the hell did they-" shaking his head he grinned at Coli. "Okay, that's just too weird."

She laughed. "Yeah, you get used to it. Someday I may even figure out how he gets in and out of the house." They both turned in the direction of the verandah. The floor was blue painted wooden planks, a white slatted railing encircled the porch, and Coli had decorated with white wicker chairs and rockers. Flower baskets hung over the railing adding cheerful flowing colors of red and yellow bouquets.

Brogan bent and lifted the big cat into his arms. Instantly it purred and rubbed its paws on his shirt. He set the feline in his truck, then moved close to Coli. Slowly, he cradled her chin, lowered to her, slanted his head and kissed her, sweet, tender, with care and caring. Her arms lifted and she wrapped her hands around his neck, pressed her curvy body against his and the kiss deepened, and he hardened.

This time Brogan pulled back. "Any more of that and I won't be leavin'. I'll call you tomorrow, yeah?" He gently chucked her chin and slipped behind the wheel.

Driving out to the street, he stuck his hand out the window and gave her a wave.

CHAPTER FOURTEEN

Early the next morning, Brogan sipped his coffee while ambling into the station. Minnie Willow was at her usual station, she manned the main switchboard. They had all the modern conveniences but the switchboard kept everyone in contact with…everyone.

Around 45, Minnie Willow was just like her last name, long and slender. With her willowy figure, short cap of dark curls and a thin nose, she'd had to endure Olive Oil comments her entire life. It didn't bother her, though, or she'd grow her hair long and dye it red. "Howdy, Sheriff," she greeted him, "Tarzan and Rocky are in the conference room waiting on you."

"Hey, thanks, Winnie. I'm expectin' the FBI guy, Jackson Navarro. Will you direct him when he gets here?"

"You bet, hon." Winnie watched the tall lawman walk away, nodding and saying a few words to people on his way to the meeting room. Winnie smiled, something was finally easing that boy. The hardness in his eyes was warming, the jaw not quite so tight.

He wasn't exactly friendly, but she'd seen him almost smile today, and that was rare. He'd had a hurting, she didn't know what, the men kept their secrets, but something now was bringing a lift to the sheriff.

Brogan removed his hat and jacket when he entered the room. Hanging both on the coat rack near the door, he trod around to the rectangle table that Detective Kurt 'Tarzan' Vantarzani and Deputy Elvin 'Rocky' Narocki were already sitting at. They were dressed as he was in jeans. That's where the similarities ended.

As a detective, Tarzan wore a long sleeved, brown button-down shirt and black tie with black jeans, he had black hair and dark eyes, tanned skin.

Rocky wore the short-sleeved, brown deputy uniform top, he was fair-haired, blue-eyed and tattoos raced up and down and around his exposed arms. The tats helped mitigate the boyish appearance. Both clearly hard, dangerous men, but bore relatively open expressions.

In a cream colored, long sleeved thermal, his badge hooked to his belt, Brogan's brooding, closed face was harshly haunted with old secrets, betrayal, loss. All three men's boots were weathered but polished, they kept their clothes clean and pressed.

"Boys," Brogan greeted them as he sat at the table.

Deputy Rocky squinted one rascally blue eye at his friend and boss and commented, "You're looking right chipper, my brother, which fine lady finally got you in her bed and worked off some of those hard edges?"

Detective Tarzan grinned with Rocky.

Relaxing back in the chair, Brogan took a sip of coffee then set the cup on the table. He stuck his long legs out and crossed his ankles. Paper cups of coffee were in front of the men, a box of two baker's dozen doughnuts sat in the center with paper plates and napkins.

Brogan smirked at Rocky's fingers white with powdered sugar that he was licking. He teased, "You look like Felipé lickin' yourself, son." The *son* was country talk; the three friends were all the same age.

Rocky's lower lip thrust out in pretended affront. "You comparing me to your cat?"

Lifting a shoulder negligently, Brogan said matter-of-factly, "Your hands are all white and you're lickin' them like the puss does, make sure you do the rest of your lickin' in private, not somethin' I wanna see."

Tarzan spat out coffee with his barked laugh. "Hell, Brog, nasty picture you just painted." Wiping his mouth with a napkin, he chuckled, "That aughta put off the ladies, Rocky sitting on the table buck-ass naked licking his-"

"Okay, forget I said anything." Brogan reached for a chocolate doughnut. Taking a huge bite of half the doughnut, he laid the rest on a paper plate.

"Really, guys?" Rocky reached for another pastry. "Get your minds outta the gutter, you're disgusting." Taking a big bite of the strawberry frosted doughnut, he licked the icing that caught on the corner of his lip. "Besides, Brogan, your cat is the fattest feline I've ever seen. And as you can see," he drew a hand down the front of his torso, "I am quite svelte."

"Huh," Brogan grunted, "you won't be if you keep eating this crap. I thought we decided no more doughnuts. Besides being such a cliché, they aren't good for us."

Rocky grinned as Brogan shoved in the rest of his chocolate pastry. "Ain't stoppin' you any. I have a naturally fast metabolism, I can eat anything, it all goes to muscle." He lifted an arm, squeezed it up displaying a healthy bulging bicep.

Two raps came from the doorframe, the trio looked over. Jackson Navarro stood taking up the doorway with his large form, tough face. He may be in a suit but it didn't hide the body of a strong physique.

He said, "I'm good with clichés, especially tasty ones." Entering the room and unbuttoning his coat he bee-lined to the pastry box. He already had one out and stuffed in his mouth while shrugging out of his coat.

"Sure, Fibber, since you asked so politely, you may have one," Tarzan heckled, laughing as the agent chewed on the doughnut hands free as he removed his coat and dropped it on the coat rack. By the time he joined the men he'd gobbled the pastry and was reaching for another.

Rocky commented, "Dude, you act like you haven't eaten in a week."

Nodding while chewing, Navarro mumbled around the cream-filled dough, "About right, been racing around, I need the sugar burst."

"Whacha been up to?" Brogan inquired with a lopsided grin, watching the agent chomp down a third doughnut. Seeing Navarro

would be busy for a minute before he could talk, Brogan turned to the deputy and detective and asked, "What's to report?"

Rocky sat back with his hand on his full belly, his other wrapped around his coffee cup. "We went and met Kandy-Marie's parents, Ramona and Randall Birchfield."

"Musta been a bitch," Brogan commiserated, "tellin' folks their kid is gone."

Both males' faces pinched. Rocky rubbed his jaw. "Yeah, that's an understatement." He glanced at Tarzan who had a matching grim expression.

Brogan asked, "They have anything that could help us?"

Rocky swung his blue gaze from his partner to the agent. His expression lightened a hair watching Navarro slug down yet another pastry and lick his fingers. "No, they didn't even know she was missing for a while."

"But her DL has their address on it. Wasn't she living with them?"

"Yeah," Rocky replied, "but apparently, Kandy-Marie was a bit of a...a..."

"Slut," Tarzan filled in flatly.

Rocky frowned at him, then shrugged. "I mean, they didn't come out and say that, but, they said she spent so many nights out, sometimes not returning for days. They didn't miss her because they were used to her staying away without calling. We interviewed a couple of her girlfriends."

"Any special men in her life?" Brogan asked.

Tarzan answered him, "That's where the slut part comes in. Apparently she has a lot of beaus and isn't very particular about who they are. They let us search her room, which offered nothing. Her phone and computer are in our IT lab."

Brogan said, "After they examine them I want them sent to Pirate."

"Okay." Tarzan went on, "Her mom gave us a list of her friends, and we interviewed them. They said Kandy-Marie lived on the wild side. Thought nothing of picking up guys at bars and going home with them. Her parents supported her financially; she worked

here and there at the gallery but nothing to earn a steady income. Sometimes the men she *dated* gave her money, her friend Camille frowned on that. Said it made her more than just a lay."

"Did her friend have anything helpful, like any dangerous types the vic picked up?"

The deputy and the detective shook their heads. Tarzan told him, "She just flit from man to man like a bee on the stamen of a blossom."

There was silence for a moment as the men pictured a girlie bee having sex with the flower's stamen, then Brogan said, "She worked at the gallery, we thought she was doing either or both the owner and the painter."

"Yep." His mouth quirked, Rocky replied, "Her friend Camille told us she'd been with both of them. Said the painter could be rough, cold, not really very nice. The owner, Reno, was more laid back. When he was done with her he liked to smoke weed and sprawl out on a chair and watch her and Dane Zachary go at it like rutting dogs."

Navarro stopped chewing, looked up at that. "She did them both at the same time?"

Tarzan looked half revolted, half aroused. "She told her friends although Reno was a bull in bed, he liked to watch too. Especially when Zachary got really rough. Apparently Kandy-Marie dug the really rough stuff, whereas one walk on the vicious side was way more than enough for her friend."

Navarro's black brows spiked. "Rough? How rough?"

Glancing around, Tarzan half-grinned. "Good thing we're not in mixed company. According the girlfriend, who also was boned by Reno and Zachary, she fled after their first encounter never to return. The men liked to take turns holding the woman down while the other, ah," a streak of red crept up the back of his neck. He rubbed his palm on it.

He coughed then went on, "She said, Reno wasn't as bad, he just liked to slap her breasts, and, uh, other body parts. Some whipping with a belt, a little biting, pinching and twisting, hard. She said most of that was okay until they'd start really getting into it,

and no amount of 'No, please stop, don't,' would stop them. After Reno drew enough blood to satisfy his bloodlust, he tied the girl down, then sat back and watched Zachary go to town."

"Uh, I hate to ask," Navarro said with a wince, "go to town?"

Nodding with bunched lips, Tarzan scraped his nails up and down one of his tanned arms in agitation. "Biting, like heavy duty biting, blood-letting vicious whipping, strangulation, ballgags, nipple clamps, using objects to impale-"

"Okay," Brogan broke in, shuddering at the thought of the artist getting his hands on that little girl that was at the gallery, the strawberry blonde. "I think we get the picture. Who saw Kandy-Marie last? That would be Monday, maybe Sunday night?"

Scanning his notes, Rocky said, "Everyone we interviewed said they hadn't seen her for a couple of weeks. The last anyone saw her that we could get was she and her girlfriend, Camille went shopping on the 10th."

All of the men flipped pages, reviewing their notes, each jotted down a few words.

Stroking his chin, Brogan set his palm on the table. "No, wait, that girl at the gallery," he glanced at Navarro who wrinkled his brow. Brogan said, "You remember, Poppy, the young woman with the strawberry blonde hair, she said she'd had brunch with Kandy-Marie."

Remembrance lit in his eyes, Navarro replied, "Yes, you're right. Cute little thing, she said they had brunch at a purple place on Sunday."

Brogan closed his eyes, thinking, then opened them. "Yeah, the Purple Majesty Tearoom. Her full name," he pulled out his own small notebook and leafed through it. Tapped the page, "Poppy Mikola. Barely looked twenty, if that. Was scared to death. At the time I thought it was just because we were cops. But now…"

"They had lunch, Kandy-Marie might have told her something. Something like she was afraid of the sex with the violent men, or she heard something, saw something," Navarro commented, as he pushed the box of doughnuts away, but didn't stop looking at them.

Brogan turned to Tarzan and Rocky. "The gallery people were on their way in for further questioning. I want to see their transcripts, and I want the Mikola girl brought back in. And I want all their stats."

"That was Dam's job, I'll call him." Rocky stood up, moved a few feet away from the table, slipped out his cell and pushed buttons. He could have called him on the radio attached to his shoulder but then everyone else wearing one would hear too, and Brogan had wanted to keep the main investigation exclusive to the team.

Tucking the phone between ear and shoulder, Rocky wrote notes. Moving back to the table, he sat down, said into the phone, "Okay, call him, tell him we're in the conference room." Ending the call he slid the cell in his pocket, Rocky told Brogan, "Dam didn't interview them, Deputy LaRoyce Darkan did."

Frowning at his disobeyed order, Brogan asked, "What the hell? Why?"

"Dam said he'd been called home for a family emergency."

"What about Buck or Lenita? Why go outside the team?" Brogan tried to lock down the anger that bubbled at his orders being screwed with.

"Buck was way out in Meseta where there's a string of antique shops just outside the town before the ranches start, looking for the cocktail glasses angle. And, Lenita," Rocky inclined his head to Navarro who had just stuffed his fifth, or was it the sixth doughnut in his mouth, almost whole.

"She said she was going to take Jacks and his powder sniffing dog to Delian's job, home, and the hideaway Tamy Lee told you about. Besides, LaRoyce is good people, he's a great deputy. He's bringing over the transcripts."

"By the way, he prefers just Royce, without the La," Tarzan told him. "Says the minute he calls people and says his name they assume he's black, which of course he is, but it puts preconceptions in their minds, good, bad, or indifferent. He'd rather be taken as indistinctive."

Rocky grunted, "Huh. I thought it was because he thought the La made him sound gay, not," he held his hand up quickly, "that there's anything wrong with that, yo?"

"What-the-fuck-ever, who cares." Brogan's voice low with irritation. "What about the knife and cocktail glasses from the scene of Delian's murder?"

Referring to his notes, Rocky said, "Dam talked with Buck, got his research. Dead ends, Boss. Knife that killed Delian was an antique, turn of the century, George V with a mother-of-pearl handle, real flecks of gold in it, and stainless steel. Didn't even know they had that then.

"Anyway, Dam went to a few specialty stores, spoke with an expert, and went online. The knife could have come from a collection, or just by itself passed down through family, or garage sales. You can buy the knives on the internet. A collection of 12 costs about four grand. There's no way to trace it."

Tarzan whistled. "Four thousand? For a freakin' knife?"

"Twelve knives," Rocky told him then went on. "Same with the glasses. Leaf etched, gold rimmed, good quality crystal. No way to trace 'em. Sold on eBay, auctions, garage sales. Unless we come across a collection with two missing, they're a no go. Lab says no prints other than the vic's on the glasses and none on the knife. Only Delian's blood on the knife."

Brogan had expected as much. His attention went to Navarro who was licking his fingers. "You done yet or should we order another dozen for you?"

Navarro shrugged a heavy shoulder. "Man's got to eat, my brother."

"Yeah. So, you got the dog, you and Deputy Pupatelli checked out Delian's places?"

A smile crooked across the agent's rugged face. "Yup. Picked up Pompeii and we inspected the buildings."

"Pompeii? And you made fun of our names?" Tarzan snorted.

The agent grinned. "Pompeii because of the ashes over the buried city. Pomp sniffs out gunpowder, soot, ash, things like that. But he's mostly trained for the gunpowder."

Impatience making his voice brusque, Brogan groused, "Just give me facts, people, I don't need extraneous crap about names and shit. What did you find out?"

Navarro's grin went all the way up to his dark eyes. "Nothing in the house he lived in with the Arabats, and the office was clear, but," his brows wriggled with success, "it was present in his love shack nestled between businesses on Butter Beat Street in the Barriga." He chuffed a laugh out. "Butter Beat? What does that even mean?"

Brogan sighed. "Again, enough with the names, just the facts, please."

Still grinning, Navarro said, "Delian kept more than babes in his nest. Ol' Pomp went nuts as soon as the manager opened the door. Unfortunately, there weren't any weapons there. They must have been brought there then moved. The place was pretty small."

Thinking on his words, Brogan remembered, "Tamy Lee told me that Delian had a boat docked at the marina. You might want to check it out. He might have brought the guns in from somewhere else and put them temporarily at his nest. When he got a stockpile, maybe he moved 'em someplace bigger."

"Could be," the agent concurred. "Must be why we were able to detect the guns were here in Builu County but not specifically where. The first location was likely Delian's nest or boat then they were transported to some place that was probably lead-lined. The cells on our tracers should have lasted longer than they did. It's more feasible the building was lined with lead than the batteries expired. That's why I have the dog; he can smell through, or around the lead."

Navarro said to Brogan, "It appears your murder and my smuggling are tied together. It's too coincidental that Delian was trafficking in weapons and murdered."

"Uh huh," Brogan concurred. "What about Kandy-Marie? Is she involved or was her murder a separate incident?"

Everyone shrugged but no one gave him an answer.

Navarro glanced around at the men and said, "Anyway, I need to find the main receptacle. The guns were passed from place to

place likely to keep them moving, so no one would get suspicious before they were dispersed further up the chain to be sold."

Brogan said to Tarzan and Rocky, "I want Delian's phones dumped, should have already been done. Pirate's gone through his computer and found nothing of interest. But, a co-worker said they'd seen him with a different laptop besides that one we took from his home, and his one at work.

"Run his associates' records and backgrounds and question them, including girlfriends, employees, family, anyone he came in contact with. Put Lenita, Buck and Dam on it with you. Find a connection between Delian and Kandy-Marie. Both of them might have been killed because of the gun smuggling."

There was a brief knock at the door before a deputy strode through. "Hey Boss," he nodded at Brogan, "boys," he said to Tarzan and Rocky. His unsmiling gaze drifted over Navarro.

Brogan made the introduction, "Deputy LaRoyce Darkan, this is Special Agent Jackson Navarro with the FBI." The deputy and the agent exchanged slight head bows. "Grab a chair, Deputy, doughnut," he gestured to the box.

Mid-thirties, with cocoa skin with a touch of cream, Royce was at least as tall as the other men present. Bulky shoulders indicated regular iron pumping. The hair on his head and face was trimmed neat and short, jaw strong and squared. He proudly wore the full Builu County Sheriff's Office uniform.

Royce grabbed a chair from near the wall, brought it over and sat down. He laid a leather notebook on the table. When he had wolfed down a doughnut and held another in his hand, Brogan said to him, "Tell us about your interviews with the gallery people."

Munching, Royce opened the folder, swallowed and replied, "None of them knew nothin', saw nothin'. Last they'd seen Kandy-Marie Birchfield was well over a week ago. As far as background," he lowered his head to the papers. "There's nothing on them. According to him, Rex Reno is 28 years old, born in the Appalachians, in rural Tennessee. Nothing remarkable. No criminal record, was home-schooled, worked in coal mines before apparently moving here and buying the gallery."

He took a breath. "Dane Zachary, even less info. I wasn't able to track him before his showing up in Builu. I asked about that. Reno spoke for the dude, said he'd been an ill child, orphaned and also, coincidentally home-schooled by a relative. Didn't mention the name and avoided answering when I asked.

"Reno said Zachary was juggled between relatives all over Alaska. Reno said the pair ran into each other in a bar when Reno had traveled to Alaska. Zachary showed him his work, and Reno brought him and his paintings here to his gallery."

"Reno said? Zachary didn't speak?" Brogan asked.

Shaking his head with a grim humorless smile Royce replied, "Very little. As if he or Reno thought he'd give something away. I tried to separate them, but Reno said he was afraid we'd lead one of them into saying something screwy and hold it against them. Said any more questions and they wanted a lawyer. I couldn't find any indication either man had living relatives. Neither of their names lead anywhere, there's just no paper trail, not even DL's on the DMV site."

"If we knew that when we were there the first time we could have watched them then taken them in for driving without a license, got more info outta them." Brogan scratched the side of his head and looked down at his coffee cup, muttered, "Wished I'da gotten another cup."

Looking up, he said, "Okay, I want you to keep delving, digging into their pasts. I want to know how they both really came to be here in Builu. What did Reno sell in the gallery before he brought Zachary in?"

Palming basketball sized hands over his short hair, Royce answered, "According to Reno, he had only just purchased the gallery in the Barriga. It was an empty building. He said it was damned good luck he'd run into Zachary."

"Huh." Brogan's eyes shifted towards the window that let in a modicum of light. The group sat quietly thoughtful.

Rocky said with troublemaking grin, "Ya know, Royce, we all say the Barriga wrong. It's Spanish so it should be La Barriga for *the belly*. So, does that make you rethink the La part of your name?

You would be The Royce." He chuckled, the other grinned slightly at his joking jibe.

Brogan lowered his head and shook it. Not giving into Rocky's foolishness, he said, "What about the women?"

Royce leaned back in his chair and looked down at Rocky with hooded lids but didn't say anything to him. When Rocky smirked at him, Royce said to Brogan, "Ah, let me see," he bent to his file.

"Petra Peerina, thirty-two. Born in Dallas. Again, unremarkable but I had better papers on her. She did almost a year here in Builu at the County College, dropped out before the end of the year. She admitted also meeting Reno in a bar. Lotta drinking going on around here. I saw her high school yearbooks from ninth through twelfth online, a few pictures easily traced her."

One shoulder bumped. "Nothing stands out. Her parents still alive, divorced, two sisters. She moved here with a fellow who dumped her right as they crossed the city border."

Brogan waited, when the deputy didn't continue, he asked, "The other female. Poppy. What about her?"

Royce's forehead crinkled. "Only one female showed. The tall pipe cleaner with the red hair." His lips twisted. "Damn, horny woman, was all over me while I interviewed her."

"Get on the horn, Royce, call that Poppy girl, get her in here. We need to know who the woman was that was at the tea place with her and Kandy-Marie. You can't reach her, find where she lives, her family. I want her like yesterday, yeah?" Brogan stood up.

"Somethin's not right there. That Reno fella's got a Boston accent, not rural Tennessean. I don't like that the painter's background can't be traced. Everyone has a paper trail. Find it."

Tossing his empty cup in the trash by the door, he said, "It mighta been a female we saw enter Delian's building, we need to explore Peerina and Poppy. We'll meet back at, say six and debrief." Dropping his hat on his head, he put his jacket on, and started out the door, then, paused.

Brow knotted, he stuck his finger in the corner of one eye, thumb in the other pinched then rubbed, something he was missing.

"Sheriff?" Navarro rose, grabbed one last doughnut.

Shaking his head, Brogan blinked, then snapped his fingers. "Yeah, the girl," he pointed at Rocky. "Kandy-Marie's friend."

Rocky got up. "You mean the other ménage-a-bonee? Camille Blanca?"

"Deputy," the country lessened in his accent, Brogan said curtly, "clean it up. There're no ladies present but you're a lawman, don't need to get in the habit of talking about women like that. Yeah, her." He quieted, said thoughtfully, "Tamy Lee said she and a Camille were both sleeping with Delian."

"And he was apparently bopping every other female in town, young or old, I hear he wasn't picky. Camille is not that common of a name, but still," Navarro shoved the rest of the doughnut in his mouth and slipped his coat on over his suit. "Camille could be the connection between Delian and Kandy-Marie. Camille slept with both Ellery Delian and Rex Reno."

Rocky added, "And Dane Zachary. Could be a coincidence." He cringed when everyone looked at him, then rolled his eyes. "I know, I know, in murder there are no coincidences."

"Okay, everyone has their assignments, Tarzan text me this Camille's number and address. Then dig into her background. I'm gonna look her up and then chat with Reno. Ya'll be back here at six."

"Hey, Sheriff, wait up." Navarro followed him out the door. Walking beside Brogan as he strode down one hall to another, the agent said, "Let me go with you and bring Pompeii."

Brogan glanced at him.

Navarro said soberly, "I don't want to miss any chance to examine any structure, never know what I could find."

CHAPTER FIFTEEN

In Liso Piedra, Brogan hit a dead end with Camille Blanco. She wasn't at her apartment, didn't answer her phone. They checked her job. She worked as a bank teller, but wasn't scheduled to work today.

He and Navarro headed over to the D'Faience Artinquity Gallery to speak with Rex Reno.

After parking, as Brogan stepped from the truck, Navarro opened up the back door and a golden Dutch shepherd jumped out.

The crisp air had warmed and the wind lightened to a mellow breeze. Brogan held his hand out. The dog didn't move until Navarro gave him a nod.

Tongue hanging, tail wagging, the dog's ears and nose and some mottling were a darker brown on the amber coat, came right to Brogan, sniffed his hand, then licked it. Smiling, Brogan patted the dog's head.

"Pomp, stay," Navarro commanded and hooked a leash on the dog's collar.

"I don't think anyone is here, there are no lights on, and-" Brogan gripped the door handle, it was locked. "Let's go around back."

The gallery was flanked on both sides by rows of shops, flower, books, clothing, a pharmacy, restaurants and a couple of saloons. The pair trod down the walk, Brogan nodded politely or tipped his hat slightly as passersby greeted him.

At the end of the block, they followed the sidewalk around the last building before another street bisected, and they started traipsing behind the shops.

Behind Main Street, more stores backed the front buildings. Mexican designs of adobe and wood with a lot of reds and yellows, signs hanging in front advertising food, alcohol, art, jewelry, the scent of fresh bread wafted as they passed a bakery. More shops, antiques, a store boasting unusual goods, trees interspersed with ornamental wrought-iron fences.

At the end of the street, a sea of brick and sienna orange pavers opened to a huge, wide-open square.

A few bricked steps led up to a circle of more buildings, mostly open-air, pastel hued restaurants and cafés. Between two of the tallest buildings Brogan could see the faint bluish silhouette of the mountains in the very far distance.

People mingled, threading their way in and between numerous patios that held a variety of decorative shops clustered with tables and cropped by colorful umbrellas. In the center was a fountain. Water spurted from a monument in the middle.

The atmosphere was fiesta festive with the smorgasbord of colors, food and people. "This is nice." Navarro sounded impressed. He held tight to Pompeii's leash. The dog was well trained, but there was a lot of food, and other people with their dogs. He didn't want Pomp to lose his mind over some sassy poodle and run off.

"It is," Brogan agreed. "I think I'll bring Coli here for lunch."

The agent's head swiveled to him with a sly grin. "Got yourself a filly, do you?"

Brogan erupted with a loud laugh. "Filly? I think you've been here too long, Agent."

Navarro was going to retort, but then Pompeii suddenly tugged hard on his leash.

"He got something?" Brogan watched the dog pull at the leash.

"Dunno, could be a hotdog beckoning or something, I'll let him have his head and see where he leads." The men followed the dog.

His nose to the ground, Pompeii passed a collection of round tables with guests laughing and chowing, and went past the buildings that abutted some of the front shops on Main Street.

The canine sniffed the ground until he reached the brick back walls the front stores, one of which was the gallery. Then, his nose on the ground, it never raised more than a few inches, the dog trotted up one end and down the other. He did this several times, until, he sat down, appearing confused.

"What is it, Navarro?"

The agent patted the dog's head. "I'm not sure. Either he can't pinpoint what he's smelling or, maybe there's a gun store around here?"

"No, there's no gun stores in this location. Maybe because people are carrying, everyone in these parts has a permit to carry, he's smelling the bullets."

Navarro's lips pulled in, he shook his head. "No. He's trained to seek out what I tell him. He knows the difference when people have guns or there's a large amount of powder, we're not interested in the single carries."

The men and dog remained still for a while. Then, Navarro said, "He's done. The buildings might be too thick, or, like I said, lead-lined. He can detect through, or more like around the lead, but there are too many buildings, walls, we'd have to get inside to let him hunt further."

Brogan would dearly love to get inside Reno's gallery with the dog. "We don't have enough to get a warrant to search. Let's go." On their way to Brogan's truck, his cell rang. After answering, he listened, said, "All right, thanks."

"What?" Navarro asked striding alongside him, both men's long legs rapidly eating up the walk.

Unlocking the truck, Brogan answered, "That was Tarzan. Camille Blanca was dating Vitale Palumbo's son."

"Chick gets around." Letting the dog hop in the back, then climbing in the passenger's side, Navarro asked, "And that's notable because?"

Brogan started the truck. "Vitale Palumbo is our representation of the Mafia here. He's been suspected of gun trafficking. Never been caught. He runs the strip clubs, a few bars and restaurants, probably laundering money and running prostitution, drugs for sure, but, he always manages to slip out of our nooses when we plan raids."

"You ever thought maybe you have a dirty cop in your league feeding him information?"

The corner of Brogan's mouth nicked in with anger tightening his jaw. "Of course. But he's a right sneaky careful bastard, or she. Haven't been able to catch him, or her, yet." Driving down Main, the men took a quick look at the gallery, but the lights were still off.

"Anyway," Brogan said, scanning the rest of the street, "this Camille was sleeping with Vitale's son, Tonto Palumbo, and Ellery Delian, as well as doing that threesome with Reno and Zachary. Your dog's sniffin' the building like crazy, nope, the county is too big for that to all be a coincidence. I need to talk to that Poppy girl. Palumbo could have ordered hits on Delian and Kandy-Marie."

He called Coli on the way and asked her if she would go for lunch. She agreed but said she'd drive out and meet him so he wouldn't have to take up police time driving back and forth to Mal Tierre. He dropped Navarro and the dog off to his own rented car then went inside the station to quickly clean up.

Brogan didn't like making a date and then not picking her up himself. It wasn't chivalrous. And if it was nighttime, he would not have allowed it. But he was so happy she agreed to go out with him he wasn't about to stir the waters.

An hour later he drove to one of the open piazzas in the Barriga down a few streets from where he and Navarro had been. He'd told her to meet him by the gazebo with the cowboy on the horse carved in brass.

The stallion reared back on two legs, the cowboy was tossing a lasso in the air. In the very middle of the park was a great white gazebo. In the winter, the snow would dust it and the holiday colored lights strung around it would glow through the snow. The buildings

surrounding the park would also be decorated with lights making the whole area Santa's fairyland.

Brogan's heart lifted when he saw she was there.

Coli was already in her car when she'd spoken to Brogan. She had left earlier and driven to the Barriga to pick up a book-bag and supplies that Kip would need for his school.

Standing by the fountain with the cowboy statue, she was wearing a yellow summer dress and a light sweater, sandals with white flower blossoms on the tops.

Good enough to eat, Brogan thought as he approached Coli with a rare smile on his hard face. "Hey," he said when he reached her.

She ducked her head and shyly parroted, "Hey."

He found her split of shyness and strong backbone irresistibly alluring. She was sweet as honey syrup but stubborn as a runaway mule. Everything and every part of her aroused his mind, and body.

Brogan kept his eyes above her neck. His first glance of her in the saucy little dress, shapely legs, the way the bodice was not too tight to outline her breasts, but not too loose she was bouncing all over the place, and she had plenty to bounce. His jeans felt like they were shrinking, *keep your eyes on her face, you tomcat, or it's gonna be an uncomfortable lunch.*

He moved in close, but not so close to make her uneasy, but close enough he could smell her fresh scent, honeysuckle. "You hungry, Cubbie-doll?"

Coli's laugh at the nickname was a pretty tinkle. "Yes. I've been running around all day, I'm famished."

"Good." He grasped her hand, twined their fingers and started to lead her to an outside patio restaurant that had caught his eye earlier.

The restaurant struck him as romantic with a three quarter adobe wall bedecked with flower baskets springing with pretty blossoms, as well as colorful blooms in barrels scattered around the patio. The outside patio had terrazzo flooring and designs on the wall were a montage of blues. The tabletops were blue and black mosaic tiles, the chairs black wrought-iron. Each table was set with white

stoneware place settings, and a pop of color from a single red gerbera daisy. A star-leaved sweetgum tree anchored a corner.

The hostess seated them, handed them menus and said, "Your server, Verity will be right with you." A busboy set down glasses of water and a basket of tortilla chips with bowls of guacamole and salsa. They nibbled on the tortillas while waiting for their food.

They made small talk about the weather and the beautiful plaza until the meal was served.

Devouring cheesy chicken tamale pies, grilled steak burritos with avocado pico de gallo, and corn chilaquiles with rice, they chatted about their pets, and Coli told him how Kip was settling in.

Brogan asked her about her family, her cheerful smile diminished. "I really have as little contact with them as possible," she told him, "but lately, they've been coming around. Goldie said she wants her and Silina and Silina's grandfather, Auston to come and stay overnight. They supposedly want to see how the B&B is fashioning up, and look for misfires."

"Misfires?"

She sighed, scooped up some rice but didn't eat it. Staring at the rice on her fork she said, "Yes. Goldie claims she just wants to stop mistakes I'm making before they…happen. I guess she wants to be helpful." Coli didn't sound like she fully believed that was possible. She took a bite and absently chewed the rice.

"She ever run a bed-and-breakfast before?"

Coli about choked on the rice. A short sarcastic laugh, she said, "No, she has a cook and maids, Grandfather Auston is wealthy. I've never seen her make a grocery list much less bake raspberry scones with clotted cream. She sure wouldn't know about a business license, or city and county licenses and permits, Federal and State tax ID's, merchant accounts to process credit cards, DBA registration, zoning, forget bookkeeping, seller's permits."

Brogan cocked a smile at her knowledge.

She took a breath and continued, "She wouldn't have researched the going rates in this region, she sure wouldn't have heard of Professional Association of Innkeepers International."

Realizing she was going on and on, Coli suddenly grabbed her limeade and sucked the straw.

"Hells bells, girl, I am impressed." Brogan sat back admiring not only Coli's spunk, but her intelligence and diligent research on running a B&B. "You aren't just playin' at this, you're daggone serious. I can see you're gonna be quite the successful innkeeper." He smiled his admiration, a dimple in one cheek played peek-a-boo.

Her eyes on that dimple, Coli told him, "Well, as soon as I learned about the house I jumped into research with both feet. I managed to get a small business loan from a friend of the family that works in the bank, which was amazing since I have zero collateral. I think Mr. White assumed Grandfather Auston would step in if I got in over my head. Huh," she snorted.

"Little does he know, none of them have ever offered me any kind of assistance. They only allowed me to stay with them here in Builu because I brought Ellery with me." Her eyes rolled with the funny sound she made, "See how well that worked out!"

Brogan's lip cut in, he nodded in commiseration with her, but he said nothing. They were her family, sort of, he didn't want to disparage them even if everything he'd heard about them was nasty. Plus, he'd experienced Goldie and Silina first hand- an ugly shiver rolled across his shoulders at the remembrance of the she-bitches.

"Anyway, I've already applied for the licensing and permits, and I have most of them back. I really want this, Sheriff, with all my heart. I believe I can make a nice living doing something I enjoy, and make a happy, productive home for Kip. He'll have privacy but there will be people around if he wants company.

"And, I hope to spruce up people's pride in this community, and income in Builu by putting their arts and crafts for sale in the carriage house." She took a breath, her eagerness diminished. "But, the Arabats, they're just..."

"You don't want them there?"

Her lips pushed out, eyes lowered, hiding the angst in the blue depths. Embarrassment made her words almost inaudible, "No. I mean, that's selfish of me, right? Not wanting my own family in my new home? I mean, I had at least planned on going to Ellery's

137

funeral, but Silina said that when the morgue releases his body that his family is having him flown to Bangor, Maine where he's from.

"I would have somehow managed to pay for the funeral if he had no family because Silina said she'd be damned if she...uh, still. I'm relieved that he's going without my having to deal with it all, having to see him again... I just wish my family would go away. I know," she sighed her guilt, "it's horrid of me to feel that way..."

Brogan set his burrito down and covered her hand. "No, it's not horrid of you, Coli. First of all, they aren't entirely your family. You have no relation to Goldie or the grandfather, and Silina is only your half-sister. They're treated you abominably. Why don't you just say no? It's your home, you have the right to say no."

Coli chewed on the end of the straw in her limeade, looked down then up at him. "I don't want to be a doormat, Sheriff, but they did put me up for the first few months when I moved back here."

Her mouth twisted ruefully. "Even though Goldie claimed that when I was seven that she was terrified of me, said I'd kill them all in their sleep." A shoulder rose slightly. "Plus, I don't want to do anything that might jeopardize them getting mad and maybe taking Kip from me."

Brogan's laugh was a snort. "Sweetheart, you have no worries in that respect. Those selfish self-centered ass- uh, jerks, well, you don't need to fear they'll take Kip away. Hell, for what, fifteen years he'd been livin' in a group home out of state and they never went to see him? Ever? Even once?"

Her mouth pulled in with a morose shake of her head, Coli flipped a thick flaxen curl off her shoulder to her back, took a bite of tamale pie. After swallowing she said, "No. Never. Not once. I called and begged them until I was blue in the face, but they had written him off. Acted like they didn't even know he existed." A small laugh lifted some of the tension from her shoulders. "You're right, I don't need to fear they'll take him away."

He nodded. "Yeah, they do not want that burden that you so tenderly took in."

"But," she sighed, "they still are sort of my family. My dad left the house to me and not Silina or Goldie, I kind of feel like I owe

them, I don't know, at least to spend a night there if that's what they want. Moreover, I'd hate to take away any chance that Silina might step up and be the mother she should be to Kip. Maybe them hanging around together might foster a bit of...maternal love." Her words were hopeful but her tone held doubt.

Finishing his burrito, Brogan spooned up the last of the corn chilaquiles. He patted her hand and said, "You have to do what you feel is right. But," he face grew grim, "I don't trust any of them. Don't turn your back on them for a second. If you feel in any...danger, or anything, you call me immediately, day or night."

He curled a finger under her chin raising it and leaned in. "I mean it, day or night. And, remember, it's Brogan, yeah?" He gave her a stern smile then leaned over to her and kissed the tip of her nose bringing a smile to her tense face.

Coli dabbed at her lips with the linen napkin.

He smiled watching her, so ladylike, dainty, never thought he'd see the day he was content to just sit and stare at a woman. Aware of his intense scrutiny, a hint of pink crayoned her cheeks. Only made him smile more.

His old squad wouldn't recognize him now, smilin' and grinnin' like a lovesick puppy. Then the familiar pain and rage rose, strangling his throat, threatening to ruin his good mood. He forced it down, shoved it back behind the steel walls he'd built to protect his pride, his deep hurt.

Pushing her plate away, Coli rested her arms on the table and wove her fingers together. "Have you lived in Builu your whole life?"

His expression turned pensive. "Actually, no. I was born in Clarefork, a small town outside Abilene. I've only been sheriff here for two years."

When he wasn't more forthcoming, Coli prodded, "So, were you a policeman in Clarefork?"

Feeling his jaw harden, lips pinch, Brogan took a deep breath, tried to exorcise his bad memories with it. "Ah, no, I left Clarefork to join the Marines. After, ah..." he stared off, eyes filled with pain.

Blinking several times, he composed himself, smiled weakly at the concern on Coli's face.

"After a few years I... left the Marines and lived in Dallas where I went to the police academy. I had a jump on rank from the military training, I was a beat cop for a year before I started studying for Detective. In the meantime, this position came to my...attention, and I applied for it. I wanted to get away from the big city, I need the open space around me, to breathe."

Coli started to ask another question but Brogan finished his Coke and asked her, "Would you like dessert? Ice cream goes good with spicy food."

Rubbing her stomach, her head shaking with mirth she declined, "Oh, heaven's no, I'm stuffed. I don't think I'll eat for a week!" She looked at their table. They'd only eaten about half of the food. Actually, Brogan ate about three fourths to her one quarter. But there was still so much left. "Brogan, I'd like to hear more about your life. Do you have siblings?"

"I have to go back to work," he told her. "How about we get doggy bags for Kip and that sloth you call a dog? Does Douggie do Mexican?"

A sweet laugh rippled. "Huh, Douggie does anything that even remotely resembles food, and then some! Kip will probably be thrilled, at the group home they served mostly institutional type food. I've been teaching him a few basic things to cook. I managed to get my shift moved to days doing mostly catering prep so I have time to be with him when he's home from school." She let him divert the conversation, obviously something in his past upset him and he didn't want to talk about it.

Relieved to hear she wasn't working the night shift in that skimpy outfit, he bit his tongue to keep his opinion to himself. If she ever found out he'd had a rotation of deputies trolling the saloon to check up on her, she'd have a fit. "Oh yeah? How's he doin' with the cooking lessons?"

Her smile brightened the slight gloom talk of her family had brought. "Actually, he's really good. Taking to it like a duck to water. He might be some help to me when I have guests. He's

excited about it, he can't wait until we get our first guest. We've been going over housekeeping, how to present high tea, greeting and waiting on people, etiquette, manners. Oh, Brogan, I think this B&B will be the best thing for both of us."

Brogan signaled for the check then grinned at her. "I think you're right. You're smart and a hard worker, and a fantastic aunt to Kip, and," he leaned over to her, "so gorgeous you make my eyes burn," and he kissed her. His lips on hers, it was all he could do to remember they were in public, and he was a lawman, a role model, he reluctantly drew back from her.

Tossing a few bills on the check, he said, "Okay, Cubbie-doll, let's go." When she opened her purse to help pay for the bill, he grasped her elbow and pulled her out of her chair and away from the table.

He walked her to her car. She unlocked the door, Brogan turned her and gently pushed her back against the car. "I need just one more, sweetheart, a bit more sugar to hold me."

He wrapped his burly arms around her and kissed her until the heat boiled from his groin and started burning a trail up. In a second he was going to be tearing her clothes off, he grudgingly broke the kiss.

When she climbed in her car, Brogan said, "I'll call you later. I wish we could do dinner together, but I think I'll be havin' a late night." He leaned in and kissed her again, then stood back watching her drive off in her tiny, beat-up red relic.

CHAPTER SIXTEEN

Brogan drove to the other side of the Barriga and parked in front of an Italian restaurant. Tossing on a leather jacket, he locked the truck and read the sign above the entrance, *Luccesi's*. Ivy crawled over the red brick, the frame of the brown double doors, and some of the white window shutters.

When he approached the doors, two men suddenly appeared and blocked them. Brogan wondered how they found pinstripes and wingtips in the size of WrestleManias. They were such Italian Mafioso stereotypes Brogan had to swallow his smirk.

"Howdy boys," Brogan said, right friendly, tipping his hat. "I'd like a word with Vitale Palumbo. I heard he's always here at his restaurant."

One of the muscle-bounds said, "How 'bout you take off, Cowboy, before you get hurt."

Standing steady, boots akimbo, Brogan crossed his arms, and said nothing. His eyes hooded, he stared with implacable silence so long, the thugs started shifting their feet. One jiggled coins in his pants pocket; the other crossed then uncrossed his arms.

Brogan lowered a hand and pushed back one side of his jacket and rested his hand on his hip.

Simultaneously the *soldatos* saw the sheriff badge on his belt, and the gun at his hip. Brogan said coolly, "Sheriff Brogan Dillon. I want to speak with Vitale Palumbo. Now. Or I bring in the health

board, OSHA, and a drug-sniffing dog. That'll be after I haul ya'll down to the station and charge you with obstruction."

The pair blinked at him, then looked to each other, mutual shrugs and one pulled open one of the double doors and stood back for Brogan to enter.

The stereotype carried on. It was dim inside, murals on the walls depicting Italian scenes, vineyards, ancient hamlets dotting the mountains. Within the dark cedar walls, several men hunched over cocktails at the bar, the tables covered with white tablecloths with the predictable melted candle in the Chianti bottle flickering in the center.

Brogan suspected the typecast was deliberate. Old man Palumbo most likely enjoyed having the typical movie mafia scene around him.

Brogan didn't need an escort, he assumed Palumbo would be holding court in the interior of the lowly lit room, chowing away on spaghetti and meatballs and slugging back red wine.

He spotted the mobster stuffing his face in a large, half-moon, corner booth. Just as he thought, the man sat like a king, a woman in slinky attire on either side of him. Standing guard next to the table were carbon copies of the hoods outside. Brogan was right about everything, except the man was eating sushi and drinking a white wine.

Late fifties, his combed back hair still mostly dark but his brows were going grey, Palumbo wore a blazer with a white button-down.

Brogan resisted rolling his eyes. The shirt was open almost to his belly and corny gold chains were visible in the salt and pepper chest hair. Gold rings loaded with diamonds glinted on several fingers, the gold Rolex sparkled when he moved his arm.

Not heavy yet, but on his way with a large nose and thick face, the man set down his chopsticks, glanced at the men who had escorted the sheriff in, then he looked passively at Brogan.

"Vitale Palumbo?" Brogan asked.

The middle-aged man's gaze flicked back to the two thugs that had walked him in then roved over Brogan. "Who's asking?" His

fleshy face showed too many years of imbibing, his nose puffing with the red veins starting to become visible on it.

Brogan pulled back his jacket like he'd done outside exposing his badge and gun. "Sheriff Brogan Dillon. I have a few questions to ask you."

The man blinked at him like he couldn't believe Brogan's audacity. Then he sat back and smiled. He patted both women's thighs and said, "Go get yourselves a drink."

Sliding out of the booth, one African American, the other Asian, eyed Brogan's strong build and hard face, slight smiles revealed they liked what they saw.

He glanced at them, he liked knowing who was in his vicinity, and who was hanging with a known criminal. He'd file away the women to look into later.

"*Avere un posto*, have a seat, Sheriff." Palumbo motioned to the booth seat. Brogan obliged.

After he slid in, Palumbo asked him in Italian, "*Vuoi un*, um, that is, would you like a drink?"

"No, thank you." Brogan folded his hands together on the table and ignored all the sentries now gathering around them.

Palumbo took a sip of wine then carefully set the glass on the table. A fat, half-smoked stogie lay in an ashtray beside it. "What are your questions, Lawman? I will cooperate, you know I don't want the pigs hassling me. Although you look a bit on the young side for a sheriff. Must have relatives in the commission, eh?"

Brogan let the nepotism insult go, he asked, "Do you know a Rex Reno?"

Twisting the stem of the wine glass with his middle finger and thumb, Palumbo's heavy lips pushed out, he said calmly, "No. Next."

Not expecting anything different, Brogan went on, "Dane Zachary?" At the man's shake of his head, he said, "Kandy-Marie Birchfield?" Negative shake. "Ellery Delian?" Not a twitch of recognition. "Petra Peerina, Poppy Mikola?" Nothing.

When Brogan said, "Camille Blanco?" Palumbo's eyes flickered several rapid blinks. Thick fingers tapping the wine glass,

he said, "No. *Io non so nulla*, I know nothing. I have nothing to do with these people. Is that all, Sheriff? I am quite busy as you can see."

"One more, sir, is, or was your son, Tonto dating Camille Blanco?"

His face didn't express emotion, but he blinked again rapidly, Palumbo muttered, "No."

"I need his number and address."

Palumbo snorted with sarcasm. "Sure. And I think you can go fuck yourself. Now, is that all?"

Brogan mutely contemplated the restaurant owner for so long, that Palumbo started fiddling with the chopsticks then his napkin.

When Brogan slapped his hand on the table Palumbo and all the sentries jumped. "Yep," Brogan said calmly and slid to his feet. He tipped his hat to the soldiers that now squirmed uncomfortably, he said nothing to Palumbo.

As he strode to the door, Palumbo called out, "*Addio Sceriffo*, goodbye Lawman." Then muttered under his sneering breath, "*Ragazzo*, boy."

Brogan drove back to Camille Blanco's home. Loose asphalt crunching under his tires, he parked in the chipped lot, litter blew across the weedy grass.

The apartment manager told Brogan he hadn't seen her for a few days and her roommate was in Brazil doing a fashion shoot but was expected to return home any moment. "Odd thing though…"

At the manager's words, Brogan paused at the entrance to the complex and arched one brow. "Yeah, Axel?" He'd made the man provide ID when he knocked on the manager's door.

Lew Axel's jeans were faded and dusty, he wiped sweaty hands on his stained undershirt, he didn't wear anything over it. Somewhere between 40 and 50, hard to pin down with the dissolution dragging his flaccid, pallid skin down, his fingers were yellow from years of cigarette use. Tats poked up through the sparse hair on his forearms. Forking five fingers through a mess of brown hair, he could also use a shave. He muttered, "Her car is here."

"Which one is it?"

Lew nudged a shoulder in the direction of the door. "The white Accord over on the side. She has a lot of boyfriends, is probably off with one'a them."

Brogan's impulse was to have the manager unlock her door, but he had no probable cause and would get in a pile woe if he did it. He peered in the Accord's windows before hitting his truck. There was a sweater and some magazines on the seats but nothing indicating foul play.

He left his card with Lew asking him to have the girls call him if either Camille or her roommate returned.

Brogan stopped at the bank where Camille worked and got the same response, she hadn't shown for her shift today, and no, they didn't know anything about her family for contact info. He left a card there too, but no one seemed too interested that the girl appeared to be missing.

Minnie Willow texted him Poppy Mikola's phone number and address that Petra provided. Brogan called the number. Voice Mail in a female's voice came on asking him to leave a message. It didn't sound at all like the young woman Poppy. She rented a single room in the cheaper, seedier side of the Barriga. He stopped by the boarding house and spoke with the owner.

Short and stout with a head full of grey curls, in a flowered dress with a lacey collar Mrs. Parker, many years past sixty still gave Brogan a flirty eye. "Call me, Rue, honey. I haven't seen young Poppy in the last two days. I don't really know the girl very well, she's only just moved to town a few weeks ago. She has no phone or car, she takes the bus everywhere. She didn't include any relatives on her rental application."

"Tell me, ah, Rue, have you ever gone to the Purple Majesty Tearoom?"

Her hand fluttered at her chest and she laughed, "Oh dear me no, I've heard those tearooms serve sweets and tiny sandwiches with no crusts." Shaking her head the curls bounced, she gestured to her tubby belly with a down-to-earth grin. "I like my potatoes and red meat, none of that prissy tea stuff."

Brogan smiled. "I'm with you there, Rue. Do you recall seeing anyone with Poppy? Male or female?"

Grey curls springing with her head shake, she said, "No. She hadn't been here long, didn't have any friends that I know of."

"What about family, maybe her mother or aunt, sister?"

"Nope. Girl was a loner. She told me she was trying to get a job at this fancy shmancy art gallery in town." Chuckling, she twiddled with the lace on her collar. "Don't even ask me what it was called, some kind of highfalutin swanky thing like a Frenchy name."

Nodding, Brogan said, "I know the place. Did Poppy mention anything about painting lessons?"

Rue's face rumpled as she thought back. "Ah," her head rocked back and forth, "not that I can recall. We didn't really talk all that much."

"Did she mention any names to you? Maybe people at the gallery? Any of them come to visit her, maybe give her a ride home?"

She hated to deny the gruff man with the handsome yet harsh face, Rue told him, "No. Like I said, she hadn't been here long. I never saw her with anybody. She had no phone, she used my landline."

Making a mental note to have Parker's phone dumped, the sheriff gave her his card, asked her to contact him as soon as she saw or heard from Poppy.

Recalling how terrified the girl had been at the gallery, at the time Brogan assumed it was because the police were there and had just informed them that a person she'd been the last to see had been murdered. Now, he wondered if she had something else to fear, something nefarious, secret, maybe something to do with Kandy-Marie's death. Or gun smuggling.

He called Dam, told the deputy to put BOLO's out on both women, Camille and Poppy, and have Pirate access Mrs. Parker's phone records.

He went back to the gallery. The lights were on but the door was locked. He rang the bell and in a minute he saw the long lean

legs of Petra Peerina approaching. Well, at least one of the females was still around and kicking.

She bent and peeked through the window and then opened the door. Her smile broadened with sexy cheer, "Sheriff, to what do I owe this pleasure? You've come to see me?"

Brogan nudged past her inside, stepping aside as she closed the door. He glanced around, all the same paintings were still there. "Ah, actually I'd like to speak with Reno and Zachary. Do they sell many paintings?"

Petra started at the sudden question. "Um, well, I haven't seen much of a turnover since I've been here. But that's only been a few months. I'm sorry but neither Rex nor Dane are here." Her voice sounded odd.

Brogan asked, "When's the last time you saw them?"

Nibbling her lower lip, she appeared vaguely unsettled. "Um, that would be when one of your men interviewed us."

"Is that unusual for them to not be around?"

Her eyes flit back and forth. "Uh, well, yes. To tell you the truth, I've been getting a little worried. They haven't called, and I haven't been able to reach them. My calls go to voice mail." She tried to discreetly slide a damp palm down her thin sweater that hugged her narrow figure, and nervously poked at a few red curls that fell over one eye.

"Hmm. What about Poppy Mikola? She been in contact since that day?"

She shook her head, her expression grew more worried. "No. I was off yesterday, and when I came in today it appeared that no one has been in."

Brogan didn't like to use notebooks, witnesses tended to give less information if they thought they were being held to their words. "What was Ms. Mikola's position here?"

The side of Petra's mouth pulled in then up. "Well, I'm not sure exactly. I think she came to see if she could get a job. I got the impression she'd left her home quickly, like she was running away from something, something bad. She's only lived here a few weeks

or so, she was very quiet and kept to herself. I believe Rex told her Dane would take her under his wing and teach her to assist him."

"Assist him with what?"

Petra's mouth tipped in a sardonic mock. "To be honest, Sheriff, if I had to guess I'd say assist him with his hard-on." She grinned at Brogan's baleful expression at her crudeness. "I haven't seen them together much, really. The girl tries to avoid being alone with him. I really don't know that much about her."

"What exactly do you do here, Ms. Peerina?"

The mock morphed into flirtation. She batted her eyes. "Please, call me Petra." At Brogan's steely glare, she sighed, and told him, "I'm Mr. Reno's assistant. I schedule events, his travels, painting classes for Mr. Zachary, I keep the books, but," her nose wrinkled self-effacingly, "mostly I do the cleaning."

"How many painting classes has Zachary conducted?"

She picked at one of the several open buttons on her very tight scarlet sweater to draw his attention to her rather slender bosom. The sweater matched the red swirls in the short white skirt that exposed her long, thin, but shapely legs. "Well, now that you mention it, I've advertised for them, set up a few, but he cancels. Offers one excuse or another."

"How many paintings has he sold?"

Petra's fidgeting quickened; she patted her red curls, then dragged her fingers through them scraping her scalp. "Well, you know, it is hard to get established as an artist, he-"

"None?"

Her face fell, arms dropped to her sides. "None."

"Are, were you intimate with Reno or Zachary?"

She looked about to refute it, then pink stitched up her neck. Sighing with a hint of discomfiture she admitted, "Heck, Sheriff, they were both hot guys. Girls flocked in and out of here like a revolving door. I mean, yes, I slept with Dane, but the last time Reno and I got together, he told me we were exclusive."

Her lips warped in a sullen moue, she made a snit sound. "Yeah, you were there, you heard him, he had been with Kandy-Marie the night after we hit it. Asshole." Her dejection didn't stop her from

snaking closer to him and lifting a hand presumably to set on his chest.

The woman was less than useless. He pulled out a small notebook, flipped to a blank page and handed her a pen. "Write down Reno and Zachary's addresses and phone numbers."

"Um," she mumbled, started writing, "I don't have either of their addresses, just their phone numbers."

Brogan's lips bunched. "I've heard the men have...private parties, where do they hold them?"

Looking unhappy, Petra responded, "There's a room way in the back with a bed. Their...equipment, ah, that would be whips and sex toys, they keep in their car trunks." She sidled close to him again.

"Listen, Ms. Peerina." Brogan stepped out of her reach and slapped his card in the hand grasping for him. "The main number for the station on it. "You hear from any of those people, Reno, Zachary, Miss Mikola, or you hear anything at all about them, you call me."

Holding the card, she read it, then opened the top of her sweater and tucked it in her bra. She rolled her head back to look up at him with sultry invitation. "How about I just call you, handsome, maybe for cocktails, or something else-"

He was already striding to the door. The thick door wafted closed behind him.

Climbing in his truck his lips twisted, ick. She made him feel dirty. Here he was trying to keep more people from dying and find a damned killer and she's all hot and bothering.

Call him sexist and old fashioned, possibly it was the preying male animal in him, but Brogan preferred to do his own choosing, his own hunting, chasing, seducing. And there was only one pretty little filly as Jacks had called her, he was dying to seduce.

Huh, he just got through in his mind censuring Petra for hitting on him when all he could think about was getting Coli under him. In his bed, her bed, over the front of his truck, up against a tree, on a picnic blanket, he wasn't particular.

On the way, he called Pirate and gave him Reno and Zachary's phone numbers to trace. When he got back to the station he called

Rocky and told him to have the systems officer of their NCIC, the national criminal database that can be accessed by any law enforcement in the country, to put wants on Rex Reno, Dane Zachary, Poppy Mikola and Camille Blanco.

As he was putting it away, his cell rang. At Brogan's answered, "Dillon," Pirate said, "Neither Rex Reno nor Dane Zachary have driver's licenses, and they hadn't filed taxes, ever. Reno bought the gallery from a third party in New York City, I'm trying to track him down, but I think they used a shell, either a single person or a business.

"It appears Reno got the business license transferred from this third party. The gallery is under a year old so there haven't been any taxes filed in regards to it yet so I can't locate them that way. I'm still searching for their addresses but so far both men are ghosts. Oh, and the numbers you gave me go nowhere, burners."

"Okay, keep-"

Pirate clicked off without a goodbye. Brogan's half-smile held benevolence. Pirate didn't do it to offend, the guy's genius brain just kept buzzing and useless things like pleasantries didn't fit in. He was tucking his phone away and maneuvering towards his office when Tarzan came out of a hallway.

Tarzan had his phone to his ear while shrugging on his coat. When he spotted Brogan he jutted his chin to him. The bantering from the other day was gone, his mouth was drawn down in serious absorption to whomever was on the other end of the phone.

At the detective's indication that something was up and he was heading out, Brogan kept his hat and jacket on and trod alongside him.

CHAPTER SEVENTEEN

The cool air coursed their faces as they stepped outside. The unusual warmth of the early spring had waffled back to the crisper more normal temperature of the season. Brogan and Tarzan made their way to Brogan's cruiser. "Okay," Brogan said when they reached it and climbed in.

Tarzan put his phone up and said, "Camille Blanco has been found."

"Oh yeah? She at home? I was just there an hour ago, manager was supposed to have her call me." Brogan pulled out of the parking space and started back towards where the young woman lived. "You look a shade past grim, brother, what's goin' on?"

"Uh huh." Tarzan nodded. The sun was halfway down the horizon, through the window the yellow light glinted off the detective's black hair. His dark eyes darted around, glancing out his side window, the windshield, then to Brogan. "Camille Blanco is dead." He waited while Brogan's head whipped in his direction before facing front again.

"What the fu- how could that be? I was just at her apartment." Recalling peering in her car, he asked, "Was she found in her car trunk? How?"

Tarzan held up a hand. "Slow down, bro, let me tell you. Blanco has a roommate who is a model and has been out of the country."

"I know," Brogan said impatiently heading back to Liso Piedra.

"Geesh, give me a break, let me spit it out." Tarzan rolled his eyes but grinned at his boss and good friend. They'd known each other in the military. Brogan had come to Builu first and then brought Tarzan and Rocky in.

His tone deepened gravely, he said, "The roommate found Camille lying on the floor in the living room."

"Bullet? Knife? Beating? What'd she say?"

"That's all I have, Brog. It was called into the local 911. When the cops saw the body, and determined she was deceased, they grabbed the manager who freaked and gave them your card with the dispatch number on it. Minnie had the call transferred to me because you were on another task away from the station. The local coroner was sent right out, they haven't taken the body to the morgue yet. They want the doctor to see the site."

With thoughtful inquiry, Brogan said, "I wonder if it's just a fluke that Reno and this girl live in the same town."

The detective replied, "Maybe, maybe not. Everyone has to live somewhere. This county is like the kissing number, you know, the technical term for like when spheres are arranged so they each touch another sphere but don't over-lap. Each town surrounded by other towns extending out until the mountains stop them on one side and another county on the others."

Turning onto the interstate freeway that speared like a crooked blade through the lattice of towns, Brogan grunted. "When I moved here, they told me Builu was like a honeycomb. That's easier to understand than a, what'd you call it? Kissing number?" Peripherally, he caught the detective's grin.

Bypassing exit ramps to towns branching like veins from a main artery they cruised through vast stretches of sweeping land. Brown swaying fields of barley and green corn crops, groves of pecan trees, farm spreads, pastures dappled with cows feeding in tall grass, all paraded by with the fir topped mountains always cresting in the background. It took 50 minutes to get to Liso Piedra, for the second time today for Brogan.

Liso Piedra was a small yet bustling town with suburbs encircling it. Camille Blanco's apartment was just inside the city limits on the poorer side.

As he turned into the Peachclub Apartments complex, Brogan commented, "Although Reno said he lived in Liso Piedra but not where, we don't even know if what he said was true, because we don't know a damned thing about the phantom gallery owner. We found no full home address on him, any paperwork like electric bills were only in the gallery name and address."

Tarzan was wearing a suit, Brogan his regular cream colored, long-sleeved thermal, leather jacket and jeans, so they both had to show ID to the policeman at the door.

The victim's apartment was on the second floor. Taking the stairs, the men avoided trash cluttering the steps. When they reached the apartment, the door was open and they had to show their badges to another cop at the door. The local police of the town of Liso Piedra were the authority on scene.

Brogan and Tarzan were employed by the Builu County Sheriff's Office. The county sheriff is recognized as the chief law enforcement officer in the entire county. He has jurisdictional authority over local police departments.

CSI were already there and processing, one handed Brogan and Tarzan booties and gloves, and caps for their hair. Brogan handed his Stetson to the officer at the door.

Tarzan grinned at his friend. "That cap is so you, bro, you should ditch the cowboy hat and go with the powder blue paper, you look so pretty."

"You're a funny guy," Brogan grunted as they moved into the two-bedroom apartment. The front door opened into the living room, a woman in a white lab coat was crouched beside the body on the floor. They finally found Camille Blanco.

Brogan stepped forward. "Doctor?"

The woman swiveled her head to look up at him, grey brows peaked in triangles of question.

"I am Sheriff Dillon of Builu County and this is Detective Vantarzani, the victim is part of one of our ongoing cases. What can you tell me?"

When she appeared to be about to stand up, Brogan grasped her elbow and assisted her. She gave him a smile of thanks.

Holding a recorder in her hand, she nodded to both and said, "I am Doctor Cloris Woodward with the Liso Piedra Coroner's Office."

Turning back to observe the deceased girl, she said plainly, "Of course I'll know more and be more precise when I get her on the table, but, for now, she's a Hispanic female about 5'4" and around 138 pounds, I approximate late twenties. Her purse is here, the officers are verifying her identification." The trio studied the shell of Camille Blanco, her soul was long gone.

She lay curled fetal, eyes closed, even with the loosening of expiry, death caught her face seized in a grimace of such excruciating pain, it wasn't difficult to see the beauty that had attracted Ellery Delian, Rex Reno, Dane Zachery and Tonto Palumbo.

Thick dark hair waved on the carpet. Wearing a tight pink t-shirt and short skirt that was up around the tops of her thighs did reveal she had the full figure that would interest most men.

Doctor Woodward said, "Decomp hasn't started and there are signs of rigor so I'd say she died 3 to 6 hours ago."

"I'm not seeing any blood, Doctor, what do you think cause of death was?" Brogan crouched beside the body. Camille's skin color was yellowish, lips and fingertips had a blue hue.

Woodward replied, "You're going to find this hard to believe considering her youth, but it appears she died from a heart attack. There's no sign of foul play."

"Bullshit," Brogan grunted then glanced apologetically to the doctor. "Sorry." He stood up and crossed his arms. "We've got a couple of murders recently and this woman was at the very least peripheral to parties involved. No way she succumbed from a heart attack."

Tarzan stood silently scanning the typical apartment room of white walls and beige carpet. Along one wall was an entertainment center with TV and DVD systems, and four stereos. Two easy chairs in burgundy slightly worn, a pale green sofa with darker green throw pillows, an open square in the wall revealed a small kitchen beyond.

The hallway likely led to the bedrooms. There were posters of concerts but no other decorations or photos on the walls or tables.

Brogan noted Tarzan checking out the room, he asked the closest officer, "Where's the roommate?"

"She's downstairs in the manager's office," the officer answered.

"Okay." Giving her his card, Brogan said to the coroner, "Thank you Doc, you'll contact me as soon as you have answers?"

Woodward bent her knees to kneel back down by the body, already back into Doctor mode, she smiled vaguely at the sheriff. "Of course."

Brogan and Tarzan wound back down the stairs and looked for the manager's apartment. Reaching the bottom, they exited the filthy stairwell to an equally dirty hall.

When they found the manager's place, a female officer was standing just inside the open door. Brogan showed his ID and asked her, "What's the witness' name?"

The officer held a small notebook in her hand, she read the top page, "Uh, Miss Iataña Mão de Ferro." She said with a small chuckle, "I'm sure that's not near how you say it, I only speak some Portuguese."

Brogan stepped inside, Tarzan behind him. It wasn't actually an office, it was identical to Camille Blanco's apartment upstairs, only not as clean. Sitting on a ratty brown couch, the men saw a beautiful woman dabbing a wad of tissues at her leaking eyes, her chest hitched with sobs, she stared unblinking at the floor while sniffing loudly.

Brogan moved to her, said politely in his Texan accent, mangling her name, "Iataña Mão de Ferro?"

Squeezing her puffy lids shut for a second, she opened them, looked at Brogan and Tarzan with red weepy eyes. Sniffing, she

nodded, "*Sim*, uh, yes." Plucking at the tissues blackened from the mascara that streaked down her sharp featured face, caused pieces of tissue to dust her lap.

Brogan introduced them and asked, "You are Camille Blanco's roommate?" At her nod, he asked, "How long have you lived together?"

Wiping her eyes, she crushed the tissues in her hands. With a heavy Portuguese accent, she said sadly, "We met in communication's class at University." She shrugged ruefully. "Did not complete our degrees, either of us. She decided she wanted to be a bank manager, and I, well, why waste this beauty, *certo*?"

Cocking her head with a vain look, she drew a long fingered hand down the length of her uber-skinny body. "I will be super model, yes?" Iataña finally noticed both lawmen were attractive, the tears eased and her smile erupted into lots of big teeth.

Observing her sudden diminishing tears, Brogan inquired, "Do you know if Camille has any family?"

The woman wore yoga pants on long legs, and a thin cotton shirt that contoured her wafer-thin build and small breasts. Long blonde hair was twisted down her back in a French braid, she batted almond shaped, dark brown eyes at the men.

"*Sim*, but they are all in Brazil where we are both from." The smile crumbled, she wailed, "Oh, *meu deus*, her parents, how am I to tell them?" The tears spurted out again and ran down high sharp cheekbones.

Tarzan offered quietly, "You don't have to, we will take care of that. We'll need their names and addresses."

"Miss, can you think of anyone who would have wanted Camille dead?" Brogan kept his voice soft, low.

The woman raised a bony arm, let it drop to the couch. "*Não*. No one would want that beautiful girl to die."

"Do you think one of her boyfriends could have harmed her?" Brogan asked. His hands curved over his hips, boots grounded on the floor.

Tarzan stood with one hand tucked in his pocket, both men wanted to appear as innocuous as possible so the girl wouldn't be

frightened and clam up. But, instead of fear, an angry red infused her face and she jumped up.

Waving her skinny arms she shouted, "Ah! *Namorado? Não! Ele é um suína! Valentão!*"

From the front of the room the female officer interpreted, "She more or less said, 'Boyfriend? No! He is a swine! A bully!'" Iataña rattled on and on so fast, shrieking, that the officer gave up interpreting.

"Okay, Miss, um…" Brogan didn't try her name again, he'd only strangle the pronunciation. He allowed his country accent to slip in, it induces people to think he's harmless and thereby become more relaxed and open.

"Calm down, Miss, we need to ask you questions and you aren't helpin' Camille with your hysterics. Now, go on and have a seat, and tell us which boyfriend you're talkin' about, is it Rex Reno? Ellery Delian?"

The model flopped down on the couch with a gushed sigh. It took her a moment to calm herself down, stow the rage aside. Gulping air to cool off, she pushed her aquiline nose in the air and sniffed inelegantly. "I do not know this Rex Delian person. Her *boyfriend*," she sneered the word, "is the *bruta* she is," a sob caught in her throat, "*was* seeing, is Tonto Palumbo," his name slimed off her tongue like he was snot.

Tarzan subtly removed his phone from his pocket and made notes on it.

Brogan asked calmly, "Was he abusin' Camille?"

"Huh," she snorted and the tears resumed. "He did not break bones or punch her in front of me, but he slapped her, in the face, her back, head, breasts. Sometimes it took as little as a man giving her an admiring look for Tonto to be berserk with her."

Brogan and Tarzan exchanged a glance. "Do you consider him a dangerous man? I mean, do you think he could be responsible for her death?"

"Huh," she snorted again then wiped her nose with her palm. "What do you think? He shows off, waves those guns around, bragging, threatening."

"Guns?"

Nodding and wiping, she said, "*Sim*. Yes, every time I was home he was here showing off a different gun. Each one was bigger than the last."

"How big? Like shotguns?"

She lifted one shoulder. "*Sim*. Many. Oo," judging by the female officer's embarrassed look the model was rattling off a bundle of curses. "I hate him. If- if Cam was murdered, it was Tonto that did it."

Brogan asked, "Was she seein' any other men besides Palumbo?"

Another ugly snort. "No way, he would kill her." She took a breath, lifted one thin shoulder. "Maybe. She liked men and men liked her. But I do not think Tonto would know if she fucked other men. Cam would have been very, very careful he would not find out. If so," she shrugged, "he would kill her. He is dumb, stupid man, maybe did kill her." Iataña dissolved into sobs.

They weren't able to get much more out of the model. Armed with Camille's family's phone numbers, Brogan and Tarzan left her to her tears.

At the threshold, Brogan asked the young female officer what her name was.

"Officer Pressley Pine, sir."

"Okay, Officer Pine. I'm gonna send a deputy out here to bring Miss…uh…"

Pressley helped him with a friendly smile, "Iataña Mão de Ferro, sir."

"Uh, yeah. Can you see to it that she stays put until my guy gets here?"

With a bigger smile and a nod, she affirmed, "Yes, sir."

The men disposed of the paper booties, hat, and gloves, and Brogan retrieved his Stetson.

They were almost to the exit, when Brogan stopped. "Wait."

"What's up, Brog?"

Brogan clapped Tarzan's arm and said, "We need to go back upstairs." They took the elevator and when they reached Camille's

apartment, Brogan held up a hand. "Stop here. Look." He pointed to the linoleum floor.

"Footprints? Tarzan's lips pursed quizzically.

"Yeah, they seem to be only in front of the vic's door." Brogan studied the prints. "Because of all the grime in the hallway I didn't notice them." Camille's door was still open. He scanned the rest of the hallway.

"The prints stop outside her door." He pulled out his cell and took pictures of the prints then followed them. "I didn't come up here when I was questioning the manager earlier so I don't know if they were there then."

Tarzan was already tracing the prints when Brogan stalled in the doorway. "Brog, look at this." He gestured to a small pile of powder by the staircase at the far end of the hall, not where they had come up earlier.

"What is it?"

Squatting, Tarzan touched the red-brownish powder, held his fingers to his nose, shook his head. "Appears to be separate and apart from the rest of the trash and dirt. I don't know, but it matches the stuff with the prints."

"Looks like some powder spilled by the stairwell then a bit more in front of the apartment and the person stepped in it there and tracked it back to the stairs." Brogan stuck his head in the door and motioned for one of the forensic techs to come over.

"Yes, sir?" The young female investigator responded.

"See those prints." He pointed out the prints. "I need for you to take pictures, measurements, and make molds as best you can of these prints, and determine what the material is. Maybe sticky tape to lift the prints or that super glue trick."

The tech nodded. "Yes, sir."

He half-turned and pointed. "There's a pile of powder at the end of the hall by the stairs, check that out. Looks like it was spilled and someone walked in it. Scoop it all up. I'm going to want it examined for identification, its chemical makeup, what it is. I want the deceased and the model's shoes. As soon as you have everything

packed up, call this number." He handed her his card that had the main number of the Sheriff's Office on it.

"Yes, sir," The girl repeated and took his card. Glancing at it she stuck it in her pocket and turned away to get her forensic kit.

When they got in the truck, Brogan called Dam.

Without polite preamble, in his professional speak, he told him, "I need for you to find out if there are any cameras on or around Peachclub Apartments on McGinley Street out in Liso Piedra. Take Buck and anything you find bring it to Pirate. I want the last 24 hours.

"Bring in the manager of the complex, Lew Axel, to ID the people coming and going on the tapes, and also bring in Camille Blanco's roommate, uh, Tatiana or something. There's an Officer Pressley Pine with the roommate, she's holding her until you get there. And I want a canvas of the neighborhood, find out who saw who going in and out of the complex, cars, and if anyone noticed when Camille Blanco came home last. And, if she was alone when she did."

On the drive to the station, Brogan asked Tarzan, "What's your take on all that?"

Tarzan chuckled. "I wouldn't want to piss off the Brazilian beauty, she'd go right for the nuts and the eyes."

The edge of Brogan's mouth quirked. "You know what I meant."

Blocking a yawn, the detective answered, "Hard to believe the vic croaked of a heart attack. Camille was known for sleeping with at least Reno, Dane, Delian, and Tonto Palumbo and who knows how many others. We know all four were relatively violent men with women. The model said Tonto knocked the girl around for just an annoyance, if he was such an uber hothead what would he do to her if he caught her screwing another guy?"

He drummed his fingers on the door handle. "Maybe he just clocked her just right and one punch killed her."

"There was no evidence of bruising visible. He could have hit her in the back of the head like Kandy-Marie. The coroner will let

us know the COD. Still, with no blood, I'm bettin' dollars to doughnuts it was some kinda poison. What else could it be?"

"We don't even know if it's murder yet, Brog."

"Two dead already in this pokey county and now a third dead of unknown causes, all with ties to each other?" Resting one hand on the wheel, the other on the armrest, Brogan said, "Oh, it's for sure murder, brother."

At the station, Brogan stopped the truck but didn't park. He said, "Tarz, I want you to call the chief of police in Liso Piedra. The doctor that examined her was a coroner. In the more rural areas coroners are used and they don't have to be forensic pathologists. Before they cut into her I want the body brought here to our own medical examiner's office.

"Tell the chief we want whatever evidence they collected, especially the powder and the footprints, the shoes. Send a tech out to pick it up. That way we make sure we have a lasso on all the information."

"Someone's going to be peeved, Brog, either the cops or the doctor that we're taking their case, their evidence."

"Don't give two shits. I don't want them treating this as just a local homicide and not keeping us informed of the process. They'll have no choice to turn everything over to us. We have jurisdiction over them. They got a problem give 'em my number. I don't need to say I want everything expedited, right?"

Tarzan slid out of the truck. "Where you going?"

Brogan stifled his grin. "I have a dinner date. See ya."

"Oh yeah? Who captured the sheriff's cold, cold heart? You don't do dates." A frown dropped his brows, "Not that Tamy Lee chick. She's a ball bust-"

"It's nunya business." Brogan let his grin show and he started driving when Tarzan gave him a thumb's up and a go get 'em smirk and closed the door.

He had called Coli and said he'd be done earlier than he thought and could he take her to a late dinner. She surprised him by shyly inviting him to her place for a home-cooked meal. "Oh yeah, real

food," Brogan groaned happily. It's been years, he can't hardly remember the last home-cooked meal he had.

CHAPTER EIGHTEEN

It was seven thirty when he pulled into Coli's driveway. He'd swung past his place to grab Felipé. The cat and dog seemed to have enjoyed each other's company, although it had been hard to tell. They hadn't interacted in front of him and Coli. But, he figured Felipé could use a play-date.

Boots thudding across the planked verandah, before he could knock on the door, it opened, and Kip stood there glaring at him.

"Hey Kip, what's up?"

Kip crossed his arms in a blockade and said fiercely, "You not hurt my Cotty, I won't let you."

Taken aback, Brogan could see the teen was in protective mode. He deliberately softened his hard face, spoke casually, friendly, "No worries, Kip. Coli invited me. Look, I brought Felipé, you remember him." He held the large cat up.

The pudgy Persian draped boneless in his arms and yawned, his whiskers twitched, he let out a bored, 'meow.' Big blue eyes blinked at Kip then he wriggled trying to get back against Brogan's broad chest.

Kip's anger vanished, he forgot he was warning Brogan off and reached for the cat with a gleeful smile. "Ken I hold 'im, Mr. Sheriff?"

Brogan let the feline tumble into the teen's arms. He said, "You can call me Brogan, Kip, or just Brog like my friends do."

"Really? I can talk to you like I'ma adult?" He cuddled the white cat to his chest and both boy and cat seemed to purr in unison. Felipé's tail unfurled and stroked around Kip's neck.

"Sure, Kip, we're friends, right? You're almost a grown man." The kid was sweet, but he'll probably put a crimp in the kissing plans Brogan had thought about nonstop, all day. That said, Brogan was glad the boy was staying with Coli. He may have a child's mind, but he had a man's body and a strong protective streak.

"Cotty says someday we might get horses. That'd be great. I love animals." He hugged Felipé, smiled at the feline's purr. Speaking with his mouth against the fur he said, "We weren't allowed pets at the Home."

"Hi, Brogan," Coli's soft voice trickled from behind Kip.

Kip chortled excitedly, "Looky, Cotty, my friend Brog brought Felipé with him and he's letting me hold him!"

Coli stroked the cat's fluffy fur, she said with a smile, "That's because you are such a good guy, Kip, and you help me so much. Why don't you find Douggie so the three of you can-" she looked down at the slight weight on her foot. The dog was lying on his belly, his muzzle on her toes, closed eyes made him look bored.

Brogan wondered which critter taught the other that look. "How do you get used to that? That sudden materializing he does," he said in weird awe.

Kip giggled and carried the cat towards the house. He was only a few feet away when Douggie gruffed a short bark. Laughing, Kip came back out and scooped up the dog too and disappeared inside leaving Brogan and Coli alone.

"Heck, Coli, I thought Felipé was already lazy, he's learned a whole new ballgame from your pooch. Huh, those critters have your nephew trained."

Coli smiled shyly up at him, then clasped her hands in front of her and lowered her head suddenly timid and a bit apprehensive. The sheriff was so much bigger than her, taller, stronger, like Ellery, a shiver roiled through her and she stepped back from him. Her blue eyes flickered with fright as memories of Ellery's rapes and beatings slammed into her.

Brogan's smile wavered at her evident fear. "Hey, Cubbie-doll, it's me, Brogan, yeah? Not your ex-asshole. I won't hurt you, baby, never."

Keeping his big hands harmlessly in his pockets, he spoke gently, without moving, although he wanted badly to hold her in his arms and sooth her fear, nestle that fine body against his. But she was like a skittish colt, a filly, as Jacks had said, the agent was on the mark with that description. He relaxed his stance, and smiled at her. Smiling didn't come naturally to him, but she brought it out in him, and he was liking it.

Coli's breathing quickened, blinking rapidly she struggled to settle her nerves down. Brogan's face was harsh, his expression hard, she could see his attraction for her unmistakable in his smoldering dark eyes. Most men stared at her breasts while talking to her. Brogan did look at them; he was a red-blooded male after all.

The way she made his blood boil was palpable, and observable by his arousal growing substantially in his jeans when he looked at her, but he mostly kept his eyes respectfully on hers. He spoke slowly, calmly, endeavoring to dissipate her fear of him.

If he wanted to, he could have jumped her already, even with Kip playing guard dog, but he made it plain he wasn't going to harm her. She apologized. "Um, you're right, I'm sorry. I'm being ridiculous, I know, I shouldn't-"

"Cubbie-doll," his smile lopsided, he suggested, "how about you get me a drink, yeah?"

His easy question lessened her worry, gave her something to do to break the tension. Bestowing a tremulous smile on him, she said, "Sure, of course. Come in, Brogan, I'm sorry."

He stepped inside so she could close the door. Standing facing each other, he admonished her gently, "Stop, Coli, stop saying you're sorry. You have a form of PTSD from Delian's abuse. Believe me, I fully feel your suffering, I understand it. It'll take some time for you to work through it, learn to trust. I'm not gonna beat around the bush, Coli, I want you, it's plain as the sun in the sky, and I think you're worth the wait. I want way more than just a one-

night-stand with you. I'm feeling you are at least a little interested in me too? So we can take things slow, okay?"

Her smile brightened. "Okay. Come on, we can go to the kitchen and I can check on dinner and get you that drink." Then she turned with uncertainty. "I mean, if that's okay, no, maybe I, I should take you to the-"

Brogan caught her hand, twined their fingers, gave them a squeeze. "Coli, if you could just understand that all I want is to be with you. It can be on the porch, on a rock, doesn't matter, I don't care where, I just want to spend time with you. So, please, take a chill pill, I am not judging or needing anything other than your company. Okay?"

She was wearing a soft, pale yellow sweater and jeans, shoeless but in her socks. She squeezed his hand back. "Okay. That's what I want too. Except," she grinned up at him, "I also want to dazzle you with my cooking!"

He couldn't resist, Brogan tugged her hand and pulled her in close. Wrapping a big hand to hold the back of her head, he bent and laced their mouths, tenderly touching them together. At first she was stiff, then she softened against him and let him gently explore her mouth, lick her lips, suck her tongue.

When they heard Kip's laughter in the distance, Brogan smiled against her mouth, nipped her lips, tugging on the lower one, then separated from her. If he didn't, he'd be all over her like a swollen flooding river rushing a tiny canal, and that she was not ready for, yet.

Coli started to lead him from the foyer, breathlessly, she said, "What would you like to drink? I have a full bar supplied for my guests. I framed my brand new liquor license just today!"

Brogan swung their hands up and kissed her knuckles. "I'm partial to bourbon, with an ice cube."

On the way to the kitchen, Coli stopped in what she called the Tea Room. Against one wall was a polished teak bar with clusters of colorful liquor bottles and sparkling glasses of all kinds. Curio cabinets containing antique china, large, cream colored cushy chairs

and two divans filled the room. An elegant, intricately designed four-tiered tea stand was off center.

Two rectangle windows that went to the ceiling were bordered with blue stenciling, and surprisingly, the rug which covered most of the floor was a huge zebra print. A paddle fan for humid days hung from the ceiling, and large pictures of exotic birds decorated the pale peach walls. The room was comfy cream with a splash of the wild.

Coli went behind the bar and picked up a rock glass and bottle of bourbon. A miniature fridge contained ice. She made his drink and handed it him, then poured herself a glass of rosé.

When she joined him he took a sip of bourbon and admired the room. "This is one interesting room, Coli. It's like sleek modern meets elegant vintage, trendy and quaint yet casually comfortable. It's pretty cool, makes me look forward to high tea. You'll have to invite me to one. I always thought they were just for ladies, but I know you get little sandwiches and cookies and shit with the tea. And this room totally pulls me in. You have a helluva decorator's touch, girl."

She blushed at the accolade, murmured, "Thanks," and tipped her nose in her wineglass to hide her pink cheeks. They stood companionably silent while sipping their drinks and admiring the room.

Stirring from her musing, she said, "I need to check on dinner, you want to come with me or stay here?"

"Silly question, girl, I go where you go. Lead the way."

They passed through a wide hall with arched floor to ceiling windows that ran the length of the long hall. Small tables each with two simple chairs at them, along with benches lined the windows so guests could hang and visit, drink, catch up on email, net surf, play cards or just look out the windows and dream.

Recessed lighting in the ceiling gave gentle illumination, opposite the windows was another bar, this one had a lengthy counter with cushioned stools along it. Part of the bar was set up to provide snacks and sandwiches. The carpet was sapphire, everything

was trimmed with varnished wood, even the beams across the ceiling.

"Coli," Brogan said, looking all around, "this place is incredible. Stylish, yet it feels as comfortable as a worn-in baseball glove. It's peaceful but with an undercurrent of energy like whether you wanted to relax or play, the house is ready for you. I wanna live here."

Her laughter pretty and light, she moved them through the hall and onto the kitchen where mixed aromas drifted out and made Brogan's stomach growl.

She told him, "My grandma had the bones of the Victorian working towards setting up the B&B, but all the rooms needed remodeling and decorating. A lot of furniture was hers but with the loan I took out and my job at the tavern I was able to design everything the way I envisioned it. I pictured where I would like to stay if I was visiting a bed-and-breakfast and put it all here."

When they reached the kitchen, Brogan found himself sniffing the air like a dog. "Somethin' sure smells good in here."

Coli set her wineglass on the long wooden butcher block in the center island. "I'm making Hungarian Goulash. I think it's something you might never have had before, I wanted to give you something different. It's hearty and spicy, a man's meal."

"Oh yeah?" He sat down on one of the stools at the block. "I think I've heard of it but don't think I've ever had it before. What's in it?"

She went to the stove and lifted a lid off a large pot. Sliding a wooden spoon in she stirred and the aroma grew heavier, intoxicatingly savory. "It's big chunks of slowly stewed, chuck steak in gravy with pearl onions, sweet paprika, garlic, red peppers, and flat noodles, and I've added some potatoes for different texture."

Setting the spoon on the spoon rest, she replaced the lid and said, "There's roasted tomatoes in it too, and I made a side of sauerkraut. There's sour cream to dab on top of the goulash and sprigs of parsley. It's like a whole blend of spicy, sour, savory and sweet. I have fresh bread baking and I made a veggie-filled salad. In

the meadows near the woodlands I found some early strawberries. I hope you like strawberry pie with ice cream?"

"Hell, Coli," he moaned, rubbing his stomach, "you're making my mouth water. Between the smell of the baking bread and spicy meat I'm goin' crazy here. How soon will it be ready?"

She laughed. "Everything's done, I just need to dress the salad."

"Are we eating in here?"

It was a huge eat-in kitchen. The wall next to the oven was red brick and tiny red sparkly tiles made up the backsplash. The counters were white marble with blue veining. Pots hung over the butcher block island, behind one of the glass cabinet doors Brogan could see glass jars of preserved vegetables and other things, jams, pickles.

A rustic table held dark blue ceramic plates, antique salt and pepper shakers, blue denim linen napkins, a bowl of fruit sat in the middle.

On the block, Coli chopped up some cucumbers to add to the salad, she said, "Well, it's whatever you'd prefer. You've seen the dining room. It's fancy with shades of dark pink and rose, and crystal. The table can seat twelve without the extra panels. It can be romantic with low lights and candles, or cheery for families.

"I'm working on renovating the patio out back. I think guests would enjoy a few special grilling days and nights where they can enjoy burgers and mingle, get to know one another."

Mixing her own oil and vinegar and spices in a jar, she told him as she shook it to blend the ingredients, "Kip likes it in here. He spent most his time with huge groups of people and he likes the intimacy, the closeness in here where we can chat comfortably."

She gestured to the old weathered table in front of the large window that faced the back yard. "He enjoys the coziness in here. I think the elegance of the dining room intimidates him. So, do you want cozy or fancy?"

Brogan came up behind her and placed his hands on either side of her on the island. He lightly pressed his chest against her back, lifted her hair and bent to kiss her neck, her shoulder. He said softly in her ear, his voice low and rough, "I don't spend much time with families and such, so if it's okay with you, Cubbie-doll, I'd prefer to

eat in here where I can be closer to you." He didn't want a long stretch of dining table between them.

Coli turned in his arms to face him, she set her palms on his chest, but didn't push him away. The muscles in his pecs twitched under her touch, she shivered at the strength that moved against her palms. Tilting her head to look up at him, she smiled shyly and said, "Whatever makes you happy, Brogan."

"Uhhh, this makes me happy, sweetheart." He curled her closer in his arms then lifted his hand to cradle the side of her face, angled his head and cover her lips with his. Her tiny whimper meshed with his deep groan, and he pulled her in tighter, pressed their mouths together hard, and nudged her lips apart so he could taste her and party with her tongue.

Heady with smoking desire, clutching each other, mouths grinding, they didn't hear Kip come in.

"Hey, Cotty, what're you guys doing? Me and the pets are hungry." He marched right in carrying the kitten and pup.

Brogan and Coli reluctantly separated.

Her face bright red, Coli turned away quickly and tended to her salad. "Kip, honey, why don't you set the table. Most of the dishes are there. We need some cutlery, butter, a glass of milk for you. Brogan," she slightly tilted her head to him, "what would you like to drink?"

A chuckle rumbled. "That's a question baby, that I'll tell you later, in private, yeah?" Laughing at her face growing even brighter red, he said, "I'll help Kip here set the table. Do you have any beer?" His tone held doubt that she did.

"Sure." She ducked her head as her face blazed further. "I spoke with Detective Vantarzani at your work and asked him what you liked to drink."

She laughed. "I don't want to tell you what he first said. He teased me and told me to call him Tarzan, that's funny. Anyway, he said you favored the Lone Star beer. Go ahead and help yourself, it's in the fridge. There're glasses in the cabinet to the right of the sink."

Brogan stood without moving, his mouth slightly open in surprise. Then his Adam's apple bobbed with his hard swallow. No one had ever been that thoughtful of him before.

Kip set Douggie and Felipé on the floor and said guilelessly, "I think my auntie likes you 'cause her face gets all red when you guys smooch." Unaware Coli and Brogan gave him surprised looks, he set bowls of water for both animals near the table.

Mumbling, "I sure hope so," Brogan got himself a beer, sans glass. Silverware scraped metal on metal as he rummaged for the opener. Removing the top he took a healthy swig then set it on the table. Grinning at Kip, he announced, "Table won't set itself, boy," and he carried the finished bowl of salad and set it on the table.

Dinner was cheerful, filled with laughter as Kip told funny stories about other boys at the group home and antics they had gotten in trouble for. Brogan and Coli made moon eyes at each other over the goulash while Kip snuck food to both pets.

When they were through, all three carried the empty plates and dishes to the counter. Coli said, "I'll do them later. I made us some sweet tea we can have that and the strawberry pie on the verandah." She picked up the pie and a pie server and strolled out of the kitchen.

The males followed her out the door like puppies after a juicy bone, Brogan had the ice cream and scoop, and Kip brought the plates and spoons.

They set the food down on the glass-topped wicker table and settled on wicker chairs. Coli went back inside and brought out a tray with the iced tea with fresh mint leaves tucked in the ice.

They chatted and laughed some more as the moon tinted the black sky with its cool silver light and stars sprinkled around it. Kip was yawning, his lids drooping. Felipé was asleep on his lap, and Douggie's muzzle lay on his foot.

Brogan stood up, reluctance in the press of his lips. "It's getting late, I guess I should be headin' out."

Coli got up, her smile sweet and drowsily happy. "I'll walk you to your truck, okay?"

"Since my preference would be to stay here the night with you, Cubbie-doll," he grinned at her blush, "if I can't have that then I'd

truly like you to walk me to my truck." He held his hand out for her to take.

They trod across the dewy grass that sparkled in the twilight, the brisk wind shuffling their hair and jackets. "It's quiet as a butterfly still in its cocoon out here, ain't it, darlin'?" Brogan's deep voice rumbled into the dark open space. They reached his truck and he swung her around so her back was against the cool metal.

As his arms wrapped around her and his mouth descended, Coli whispered against his lips, "Brogan, Kip is right up there, I don't want him to-" His mouth captured hers and her gasp.

Swallowing her words, he swept her soaring into the black night with a sharply electric kiss that took them both by surprise. Scorching sensation seared their limbs, sending tingling prickles to their bellies and below. Chests heaving heavy against each other, breaths rushed, their brains fried out every conscious thought.

Erotic excitement firing through his body, Brogan leaned into her, his hard bulk pressing her into the truck. He maneuvered his hips between her legs, and thrust his surging arousal against her core.

Her hands stroked up his broad chest, curled around his thick biceps, then she moved them up to clutch handfuls of his hair. He could feel her rough tugs on his hair straight down below, it made his desire skyrocket even more fiercely. Their breathing grew louder, faster, Brogan cupped her face to devour her mouth, he hissed, "Coli, let's-"

"Cotty!" Kip called from the verandah. "Quit smoochin' with Mr. Sheriff, it's time for bed!"

The couple broke apart with laughter. Brogan took a shaky step back so Coli could scoot away from the truck. He caught her hand. "I'll call ya tomorrow, yeah?"

Under low lids, her eyes like glazed blue balls, she smiled and nodded as she composed herself. She looked as heated and turned on as he was. Her hair was tousled, chest still rising and falling with shallow rapid breaths. She licked her lips as if still tasting him there.

"Okay, Cubbie-doll, you keep doin' that and I won't be leavin'." He bent and gave her a quick kiss before he opened the

truck door. As he climbed in, a fluff of white streaked past him into the truck.

Shaking his head, Brogan smirked. "Hell, cat, I got so muddled I clear forgot about you. Sorry, fella."

Like he did the other night, as he drove off, he stuck his hand out the window with a raised wave.

CHAPTER NINETEEN

The next day Brogan plowed through boring paperwork that had been set aside when the murders started. It was hard to concentrate, a pretty little shy face kept wisping into his thoughts. He'd sent her a text thanking her for dinner and he'd get in touch with her later to set up another date.

The phone on his desk teased him. It chanted, 'call her, call her,' hell he was dying to hear that soft girly voice.

But, he sighed and shoved his laptop away, he knew the second he heard her voice he'd start burning, and would chuck the meeting due in five minutes and go to her. Hell, it had only taken one small female a couple of weeks to turn him into a whipped pussy.

Clearly he was smitten. He'd moved past all that 'I'm a lawman and you're a criminal' baloney. She'd been seven years old at the time and Brogan was pretty sure there had been some manipulating of events and people.

There's no doubt Coli loves Kip, no way would she have hurt him on purpose. Damn, he needed to stop thinking about her, he had things he needed to concentrate on.

"Yeah, like damned murders." He snatched up his phone and hooked it to his belt. "Ahh," with a groan he pushed his rolling chair back, the old leather crackled when he got up. The sheriff's station was kind of like Coli's Victorian, a mix of modern and rustic, make that just plain old.

They used the money budgeted to them by the County Commissioners for up-to-date, state of the art equipment and to pay for the best deputies they could hire. That left little left over for updating furniture and other non-essentials. A fresh slap of paint every couple years and weekly professional cleaning kept the place from looking downright derelict.

He'd called a briefing for everyone to catch up and provide any new data on the cases. Brogan didn't haul everyone in, just his basic core team. Their voices carried into the hall as he approached the smaller conference room. When he entered he saw Tarzan, Dam and Deputy LaRoyce Darken present.

Brogan had thought Darken had done good work when he filled in for Dam on a moment's notice so he decided to add him to the core team and put Bo Buckhorn more on the outer fringe of the investigations. Bucky lacked the drive and think-on-your-own that the others had.

"Boys," Brogan greeted the men with a nod. Rocky came in right behind him, they both grabbed chairs and sat just as Jacks Navarro strolled in. When everyone settled, Brogan started, "Okay, give me what you have. Royce?" He called on him first because he wanted the deputy to feel part of the team.

Blinking back his surprise at the honor, Royce cleared his throat. His notebook lay open on the table in front of him but he didn't refer to it.

That impressed Brogan even more, that the deputy had studied his information thoroughly, he knew it inside and out. Royce wore the full deputy brown uniform with gold markings, his was crisp, boots shined. He struck Brogan as the kind of man that would always wear expensive and highly cared for clothing. His hair and beard were trimmed short and neat, long square jaw firm in conscientious determination.

Royce glanced around respectfully at the other men, but he spoke to Brogan. "Rex Reno and Dane Zachary are in the wind. There is no trace of them. The cells they used were likely burners, there is no email or snail mail address to track them. It's like they didn't exist. Pirate hasn't been able to pull up any solid backgrounds

on either of them. He thinks they are using aliases as their identities can't be traced, or their addresses located.

"The assistant at the gallery gave me descriptions of their cars, but she didn't know the plate numbers. I put BOLO's out on their vehicles, but," he shrugged, "finding a medium sized silver something, and what looked like a small, dark blue SUV weren't the greatest descriptions. Especially if they've left the area, it'll be the needle in the haystack scene. I spoke with her an hour ago, she still hasn't seen or heard from them. Their phones don't even go to voicemail; the dial sound doesn't go on so they must have destroyed them.

"Ms. Peerina says she's getting nervous over the murder of Miss Birchfield and now people disappearing, she's going to go hide out at her sister's place in Albuquerque. She left contact info if we need her." He said to Brogan with a grin, "She made me promise to give you her phone number, asked that you keep in touch."

The men at the table snickered at the annoyed look on Brogan's face. Twining his fingers together, Brogan set them on the table in front of him. Ignoring the part about keeping in touch with Petra, he said, "I figured as much. As soon as we went back to question Reno and Zachary again they were already gone."

In his normal dark suit and today a silver tie, black hair combed straight back, "Sheriff," Navarro spoke. "We have probable cause now to search the gallery. I'd like to have Pompeii take a walk through."

Brogan nodded once. "Sure. We'll do that after the meeting." He said to Royce, "What about the girl, Poppy?"

Royce's head lifted from his notes, checking he hadn't missed anything. "Poppy Mikola. She does exist. Pirate dumped the boarding house's phone. The only calls in reference to Poppy were a couple of calls to the gallery, and to someone up in Oregon. Turns out she has kin there. She's only 18. We called, she has an aunt and a cousin out there. That's all that we could garner, and the aunt doesn't answer or call us back."

"You can-"

Grinning, Royce spoke over Brogan, "I obtained neighbors' numbers and questioned them. They told me that the girl had lived in an old raggedy, rusted trailer with her mother and father. Girl's father's been in prison for sexual assault on a minor, is looking at parole in less than six months, got dealt a really short sentence, get that shit, huh?" The deputy's grimace matched everyone else's at the table.

"Anyway, no one is sure if the victim was Poppy or not. But quite likely was. The father was a nasty abusive drunk that beat the girl's mama so badly she's deaf in one ear and is in an institution, no longer right in the head, she left Poppy alone with her father. But, according to the neighbors, the mother had never been *normal* to begin with.

"The girl, Poppy, sounds like her life was hell on trailer wheels. One neighbor said Poppy took off when she learned her father was being released from prison soon. The neighbor claimed Poppy was terrified of the old man and was sure when he gets out he'll be coming for her."

"Has anyone been in contact with her?" Brogan asked. The mood in the room had turned grim with Royce's report.

The deputy glanced down at the table briefly before answering, it sucked to have to supply that sordid information. "Yes. I finally reached the cousin, Melinda Price. This is the important part, Sheriff." The men at the table stilled.

"Poppy spoke with her when she moved here and then a week ago. Said that a girl she met at the gallery was gabbing at her that she was full of suspicions of things being smuggled in and out of the gallery."

Brogan and Navarro shared a look. Brogan's mouth bunched and Navarro cocked a brow.

"Poppy poo-pooed this, at first," Royce went on. "Then, apparently the last time Poppy saw the girl, Poppy told her cousin that the girl was hopped up and excited. The girl, the cousin didn't have the name, told Poppy she's pretty sure she's onto something. The next day, the girl was found murdered."

Gazes shot around the room then centered back on the deputy. Brogan grunted. He supplied, "Kandy-Marie. Then what?"

Royce replied coolly, "Poppy told the cousin she was supposedly the last one to see this girl alive. And now she was afraid that whoever killed the girl would think Poppy knew whatever it was she discovered, and she would be next. Poppy told the cousin she was leaving town. She didn't tell her where she was going."

The room was quiet as the men contemplated his information. But Royce wasn't done. "I set up facial recognition system software at the bus and train stations as the girl doesn't have a car and no bucks for a plane."

Brogan lifted a brow at the thin smile on the deputy's dark face. "Yeah? You got something, huh?"

Royce nodded with a not well hidden pleased grin. "Yes, sir. She left town the day you interviewed her. Her image popped up at the Fair Street Bus Station. I went on over there. Confirmed she purchased a ticket. It was only to Elk Ridge Utah. I've spoken with officers up there to see where see went next. Looks to be headed back to Oregon. That's it, that's all I have."

"Well, hell, Deputy, I think you did a shitload of work. Good work, good job, Darken, great self-motivating," Brogan praised him, glad he'd made the decision to switch him out with Bucky.

The other men murmured faint praise, they were after all guys, with egos, and real men don't gush. Brogan filled them in about his visit to Vitale Palumbo and the death of Camille Blanco.

"Holey moley," Rocky crowed. "It appears we have a serial killer in Builu County. Maybe we should call in the FBI?" He wore his regular attire of uniform top and jeans. "What?" he said at Tarzan's guffaw at his childlike terminology of holey moley.

Rocky retorted with a grin, "I've had a few complaints from the ladies so I'm working on cleaning up my cursing. So, about the FBI being brought-" he stopped at the way all the other men were staring at him like he'd flunked his nursery exam.

His gaze slew to Navarro's mouth curled in a derisive half grin. "Oh." Sheepish at the insult he inadvertently slung at the agent, Rocky muttered, "Sorry. Guess the FBI is already here."

"You know, Rock, they have these things they invented, called brains," Dam joked, ducking a swing from Rocky's hand.

A mild scold in his tone, Brogan said, "Okay, enough foolin' around. Who's next?"

Giving Rocky an exaggerated eye roll, Tarzan toyed with the phone he held in his hands. "The lab sent their report on that powder we found at Camille Blanco's apartment. I spoke with a forensic tech who told me the powder was only exactly where we saw it, nowhere else. So the tracks couldn't be followed. The prints are wide yet relatively small around a men's size eight. There was not a trace of powder on either Blanco's or the roommate's shoes, or inside the apartment. The shoe size print did not match Blanco or the roommate.

"The roommate and the manager said they knew nothing about the powder. They said no one noticed it because the place was filthy, and everyone takes the elevator. The prints head only from the opposite direction by the stairwell that we didn't use."

The detective held his notebook in one hand, his phone in the other. Today he wore a full suit and tie. He stuck a finger under the knot of the tie at his throat and pulled, loosening it. Flipping the notebook open in his palm, using his thumb he sifted through to get where he wanted. "They got a good print of the design." Tarzan nodded towards his friend. "Rocky?"

"Yep." Rocky grinned. "I took the print design to some local shoe stores and discount departments like Wal-Mart. Pattern wasn't worn so they were probably new. I found out they're Coleman's Workman's Work Boot."

Brogan nodded his approval. "That's great. Were you able to find buyers?"

Rocky's grin slipped. "Ah, well, no. They're too popular, sold everywhere, and a lot of sales were cash. No telling when or where they were bought therefore no surveillance tapes to check, so we're out of luck in that respect."

His shoulders hunched, fingers still looped together, Brogan asked, "What'd they say about the powder?"

Tarzan referred to his notes. "Ah, it was an ordinary white cement-"

"Crap," Rocky grunted, "another dead end."

Turning to face the deputy, Tarzan grinned at him. "Not so fast my fine little stone." He grinned larger at Rocky's throwing him the finger.

He read the notes on his phone, "It was ordinary white cement, but the kind that's more expensive and used for architectural purposes like terrazzo, and ornamental products, garden paths, pools, stuff like that. And," Tarzan paused, the grin even wider, "in this case, the powder wasn't pure white, it was a colored cement. You get that by mixing 5-10% mineral pigments with plain cement, used mostly for decorated floors, and the other things I said."

"Okay, great. Good work." The group waited while Brogan jotted down notes. Lifting his head, he looked at Dam. "What do you have?"

Attention swiveled to the handsome man pompously smoothing back his rich black hair with his palms. Dark chocolate eyes and his indolent grin and cheeky attitude were charismatic assets that had the ladies calling him Casanova. The grin deepening at the attention, he told Brogan, "You were on the dime, Sheriff. Camille Blanco was poisoned."

Everyone looked at Brogan, he shrugged mildly. "It was obvious. What was the poison?"

"Well," Dam's mouth curved up on one side in consternation, he replied, "they're leaning towards a varnish. The chemist's wife was having a baby, when he returns he'll be able to be specific."

"There isn't anyone else in the entire lab that can figure it out?" Irritation groused in Brogan's irascible voice. He leaned back in his chair, set both palms on the table, drumming his fingers in exasperation.

The smug expression and grin gone, Dam's mouth pursed in apology. "Yeah. Apparently the supervisor let a lot of people out on leave and he has only a few interns manning the fort."

"Great way to run a lab." Brogan twisted his neck until it cracked. His hands coiled into fists on the table, he said to Rocky

and Tarzan, "Go canvas Blanco's neighborhood, look for construction sites, check for work trucks in driveways. Find the person that spilled the cement. And," he paused reining in his annoyance, "as soon as the lab staff gets back to work and has something, I wanna know. And I wanna know where she ate last, let's get a timeline on the girl, find who she was seen with last."

The detective and the deputy immediately rose and murmuring together left the room. Brogan told Royce, "Keep on trying to find Poppy Mikola. Buzz Pirate; tell him to stay on Reno and Zachary. They couldn't have vanished into thin air, everyone leaves a trace of themselves somehow, somewhere."

Royce got to his feet, gave Brogan a clipped nod and he left. Dam stood up as well and said, "I'll go back to the stores Rocky hit and see if I can dig up people that purchased the boots." Tucking his notebook in a pocket he split.

Brogan called Lenita Pupatelli and told her to also go to Camille's complex and hit the neighbors for any security cameras. Dam had checked, but at that time a lot of people would have been at work or school. She could catch those home now.

CHAPTER TWENTY

Armed with a search warrant, Brogan had taken the time to send someone to Petra Peerina to borrow a key before he and Navarro entered the D'Faience Artinquity Gallery.

Both lawmen could have gotten the door open, but Brogan was going by the book and he wanted to leave minimal damage so no one could claim that vandals broke in and left evidence behind.

The first thing they noticed was the paintings were gone. "Aw hell, I wanted to put an undercover stashed outside in the shadows in case Reno or Zachary came back, but I would have needed two and we just don't have that extra manpower."

"Perhaps the redhead took them?" Jacks held Pompeii's leash. As soon as they were inside he released the leash from the dog's collar.

"I doubt it." Looking around Brogan rubbed his chin. "She sounded like she just wanted to get the heck out of Dodge. She wouldn't have taken the time to box up the artwork. Besides," a slight grin dented a dimple not normally noticeable on his rugged face, "everyone agreed the paintings were shit, including Petra. I think they used them and the gallery as a cover."

The dog took off sniffing along the baseboards and the men sauntered slowly through the two open rooms where the paintings had been on display. Other than the seats and tables the rooms were virtually empty.

Craning his neck to check out the upper walls and ceiling, Jacks said, "Cover for what?"

Brogan ran a palm along a wall tapping here and there to see if anything sounded hollow. "Ah, anything, money laundering, drugs, but I betcha it's most likely those guns you came hunting for."

Jacks agreed, "Uh huh, that's why I brought Pomp," he trailed after the dog.

Watching the dog sniff the baseboards, Brogan said, "Petra admitted that the paintings never sold. There was no turnover. Reno hosted a couple of wine and cheese events, but no one bought anything. I think he did that to divert suspicion, make the gallery appear real."

The men separated, Jacks followed the dog to a small hallway.

Brogan found what was apparently Reno's office. He diligently opened and checked the cupboards. The drawers of a desk were as empty as the cupboards and the top of the desk. There was absolutely nothing. No paperwork, not a paper clip or even a stapler.

Next to the office he found another room. There was an easel off to one side with a blank canvass sitting on it. A few tubes of paint and paintbrushes were scattered on a wooden work desk.

Brogan found nothing useful in that room either. It looked like someone had set it up to appear as if Dane Zachary was really painting, but nothing was used, the tubes were unopened. Just another ruse to deter suspicion.

Next, he made his way down a corridor to another chamber. Stepping inside, he glanced around. There was a bed, and, Brogan shook his head, iron cuffs and chains were bolted to the bed and walls. One was bolted to the ceiling. "Great," he muttered. Wandering in he checked the closet, under the bed, there was nothing else there.

Finding zero information, Brogan traipsed down the hall Jacks had strode into. He found him and the dog standing still.

"Whatsup?" Brogan said, joining them.

Navarro asked him, "You find anything?"

Shaking his head, he replied, "Naw, it didn't even seem like anyone was actually doing anything in the gallery. There is a

painting room with no painting being done in it. An office with no office work in it. I've got a feeling Reno hired the women just to showcase, make people think it was a working gallery. If the stories of sadistic violent sex occurring here were true, they spent most of their time cleaning up blood."

Navarro winced. Brogan went on, "According to Petra, she and Kandy-Marie really put in only a few hours a week, and Petra did more cleaning than anything. She said the girl, Poppy, had only been there a bit over a week. They were window dressing, nothing more. Before we leave I'll show you their...playroom."

Navarro's lip twitched up with interest. "As long as there's no blood, that sounds like something I wouldn't want to miss." The canine was standing stock still, nose pointed straight at a door.

Brogan asked, "What's going on with the dog?"

"He's on point. We need to open that door, I was waiting for you."

Brogan moved to it, turned the doorknob. "It's not locked." He opened the door and was met with total darkness.

Navarro hooked the leash back on Pompeii and let the dog lead the way.

"Wait-" Brogan said sharply. He snapped a penlight off his belt and clicked it on. He shone the light ahead. "There are stairs, it's a cellar. Here, I see a light switch." He flicked it and lights came on leading down the steps.

A bit breathy Jacks said, "Whoa, great, we just about took a header down those stairs. Too eager to find my guns, I need to be more alert. Not like me to leap before I look. Okay, I'll let Pompeii have his head. Go on, Pomp," he ordered.

The dog obliged, tail wagging, his nails clickety-clacked down the wooden steps. Jacks followed him, Brogan right behind.

At the bottom of the stairs, they saw it was just a regular basement. No frills, just crude concrete walls and floor, the floor was painted over in a commercial blue-grey.

Brogan went over to some cardboard boxes stacked near a wall. He lifted one, shook it, tossed it on the ground and repeated with them all. Opening a few he said, "Empty, all of 'em."

Pompeii pulled at his leash so Jacks let him go. He trotted over to a wall where there were more boxes, but those boxes appeared to have been tossed around. Like someone moved them in a hurry. Jacks kicked a few, lifted a couple, peered inside, dropped them. "Empty."

"Maybe they used them to bring the paintings in," Brogan suggested.

Shaking his head, Jacks replied, "No. they're too small for those paintings that were upstairs, and not sturdy enough for guns. And look," he lifted one, showed Brogan the inside. "It looks like there's never been anything in these. They are not scraped or dented, just neat squares. I think maybe they used them to hide other stuff behind them. Bigger things. Like crates of guns."

The dog had stopped. He was standing perfectly still, nose pointed straight ahead, tail stiff.

"Ah, yup, Pompeii is signaling gunpowder. The guns were here at one point. But," he glanced around the chamber and stated the obvious, "they're gone now."

"Uh huh." Brogan set his hands on his hips and studied the room. "I'll get forensics in here to scour the place, top to bottom." Disappointment tugged his mouth down. "There is absolutely nothing here now."

"It'll be impossible to prove there were weapons here, Sheriff, now that they're gone. But Pompeii is never wrong. There had been a lot of them stored here. If you have forensics check, I bet they'll find that ceiling, or the floor above is lined with lead. I think the best bet is to go back after Palumbo. Find the connection between Reno and him, and that other guy, the dead one, he had the love nest where Pompeii had indicated gun powder."

"Huh, Ellery Delian," Brogan exhaled the name with aversion. "But, I'm thinkin' it's the son, Tonto Palumbo. I'm positive that's why Kandy-Marie was killed. She must have overheard Tonto talking about the weapons. He had shown them to Camille and her roommate, he could have shown them to Kandy-Marie too. Seeing Tonto with a bunch of new shotguns all the time she grew

suspicious, and maybe Kandy-Marie started snoopin' around on her own.

"Well, we can't do anything more now, let's go-" he took a few steps and dropped to his haunches. Pulling a handkerchief from his pocket, he bent over and carefully picked something up.

"Whatcha got?" Jacks came over to see. Viewing it in Brogan's hanky covered palm he said, "It's a fingernail. One of those fake ones girls wear. Nice blue," he commented.

"Yeah." Folding it in the hanky, Brogan stuffed it in his pocket and pulled his phone out. When Minnie Willow answered, he said, "Get me Petra Peerina's number." He clicked off, waited a few seconds, then heard the chirp announcing a text. He dialed the number and waited for the rings.

Jacks stood patiently petting the dog's head and murmuring compliments to him.

Petra answered warily, she didn't recognize the number. Brogan said stiffly, "This is Sheriff Dillon here in Builu County. I gotta ask ya a question. Did-" Shaking his head, he forked his fingers through his hair in agitation. "No, Ms. Peerina, I'm am not calling for a date. This is police business. Can you tell me-"

Rolling his eyes he said more sharply, "No, I said it's not for a date." Shaking his head again he scowled at Jacks who was trying to hold a snicker in.

Sucking down his irritation, Brogan replied to something else Petra said, "Ah, no, we haven't found Reno or Zachary. Listen, would anyone, you or Kandy-Marie have any reason to go into the cellar at the gallery?" Jacks moved closer and Brogan put the phone on speaker.

Petra was quiet a second, then she responded with a sound like the basement was nasty. She had that deep husky voice Brogan remembered. Some men might find it sexy, the sheriff not so much.

"Heavens no, Sheriff. We had no reason to go down there. I peeked down from the stairs once, it was damp and dark, spiders lurking, nothing there but storage, stacks of boxes, couple of broken statues and a lot of dust. Rex never asked us to go down there. Why would-"

"Could you think of why Kandy-Marie would have gone to the basement? Maybe to collect a box to put something in?"

"No, of course not. I told you before, nothing actually went in or came out of the gallery. There would have been no use for boxes. Tell me-"

"One other question, Ms. Peerina," he paused while she went off on a tangent about dank cellars and disappearing men, dead bodies, sheriffs that didn't know a gift horse when it was kneeling in front of him ready to please him, and he finally cut in. "Last time you saw Kandy-Marie, do you recall if she had fake nails, and what color they were?"

"What on earth, why would you-"

Brogan's sigh was heavy and annoyed. "Just answer me, please." He repeated the question.

Petra huffed and responded with scorn, "Yes, Kandy-Marie's parents gave her a huge allowance. She spent it on clothes, shoes, mani's, pedi's and lunch." She snickered adding, "Oh yeah, and bars."

A hint of resentment stirred in her husky voice. "Yeah, the girl liked bars because that's where the men were, and at the gallery. She was poaching on my-"

"The nails, Petra" Brogan struggled to contain his frustration, and Jacks grinning at him like a jack-o'-lantern didn't help.

"Uh, yes. Her nails were long and as fake as the rest of her. Rex complimented her one day, said the blue dress she wore brought out the blue in her eyes. And, that was it. Wore blue every time she came in for the next week, including her acrylic nails. Fingers and toes. So, can-"

"Okay," he cut her off again, "Tonto Palumbo, you ever hear of him?"

Her displeasure came through the line. "Yeah. Kandy-Marie came around with him one day, said she wanted to show him the paintings."

"You ever hear Kandy or Tonto or Reno, or anyone talk about guns? I mean a lot of weapons, shotguns, rifles?"

"Guns!" she squeaked. "N- no, certainly not. They were all just harmless, sex partying, pot smoking ne're-do-wells."

Brogan said quickly, "Thank you very much, Ms. Peerina, you've been a big help," and he hung right up. Within a skinny minute his phone rang. He glanced at it, rolled his eyes and put it on silent then clipped it to his belt.

Amidst Jacks' chuckles, Brogan growled, "Okay, there's nothin' else here, let's get goin'." As he turned towards the door, he paused, took a few steps then stooped to look at something.

Jacks came to stand next to him, he crouched down.

"Someone's cleaned up, but I'm thinkin' that's blood," he showed Jacks the reddish-brown smear he found in a crease of the painted floor.

Sounding excited, Jacks offered, "If there is a little, there will be more."

Brogan nodded, said, "I think we found where Kandy-Marie Birchfield was killed."

****

Driving in separate vehicles, Tarzan headed east of Camille Blanco's complex, and Rocky went west. In an hour, they found themselves back at the complex. Tarzan parked but didn't get out.

Rocky slammed his door and strode over to him. He set a palm on the roof of the car and complained, "This area isn't all that attractive, not that much remodeling or restoration shit going on. I found only one work truck, it was lawn maintenance."

Aggravation pulled his brows down, through his open window, Tarzan said, "I know. I saw a plumber, and a construction crew over on Moffet Street. I checked with them, but they aren't using cement. All right. You want north or south?" Rocky chose south, so Tarzan went north.

The detective had only gone a few blocks when he found a yard with several trucks out front, and men looking like construction laborers tramping back and forth and around a house that looked under construction. Tarzan's heart sped up.

Parking in the street behind two trucks that had **Garfield Loom Construction** on the side, he walked up and asked the first man he reached who the supervisor was. The smallish man had tanned skin, black hair and a moustache on a round face, he pointed towards the back of the house. His jeans and boots were caked with dried muck and various shades of powder residue.

As Tarzan made his way back of the house, he noticed that the men working wore helmets, muddy boots and dusty jeans and were speaking Spanish. Mexican hires, Tarzan presumed. Most of them were short, huh, he grunted, good luck with that size eight, probably more than half of the laborers wore that size.

Around the back, he saw what they were working on. A new house was mostly completed, the laborers were scrambling around the foundation of a swimming pool. Tarzan stuffed his triumphant grin, crowing quietly, "Oh yeah, I found the location." He asked a man where the supervisor was.

The man gestured to a tall fellow who appeared to be the one giving orders. Tarzan went up to him, pulled out his ID and held it up. "Hello, I'm Detective Vantarzani with the Builu County Sheriff's Office."

The supervisor was the only one not wearing a tool belt, but he did have a protective helmet on covering what appeared to be a shaved head. Dark-skinned, he had a full black beard, the dark sunglasses gave him a mysterious dangerous presence. He bent to read Tarzan's ID. "Detective, ah," he let a dry chuckle rumble out with a flash of big white teeth. "I don't even want to try to repeat your name."

Tarzan found himself returning the laugh. "Yeah, Vantarzani, parents stuck me with a good one, huh?"

"I have an easy one, Joshua Brown. I'm the foreman, what can I help you with, Detective?" The smile was gone changing to mild curiosity, his body language was relaxed as if he had nothing to hide.

Tarzan replied, "I am working an investigation. First, what I need to know is if you are working with this material." He tugged a folded paper from the inside breast pocket of his suit coat, unfolded

it and handed it to Brown. The specifics of the cement were printed on it.

While the supervisor read the chemical components of the cement found in Camille Blanco's complex, Tarzan surreptitiously glanced around, and exhilaration tightened his gut. The foundation of the pool looked like the exact pinkish-brown color of the cement Brogan had photographed with his phone.

Brown handed the paper back with a negligible inquisitive shrug. "Yes. The ratio amounts of the chemical characteristics are exactly what we are using to construct that pool," he crossed his arms and nodded in the direction of the pool.

"Can I ask what this is about? What interest does the police have in our pool?" Then his eyes narrowed. "Are you with ICE? We don't want any trouble here." Already some of the workers were aiming curious and worried glances at them.

Tarzan folded the paper and tucked it back in his suit coat pocket. "I'm afraid I can't comment on it, Mr. Brown, but I can say I am not with Immigration. Can you tell me if your entire crew reported in today, anyone call in sick or on vacation, or just not showed up?"

Brow furrowing in deeper curiosity, Brown shook his head. "No, the entire crew reported in. Why-"

"Good," Tarzan said. "What I need now is for every single man, and woman, if there are any here, to line up."

"What the-"

"Please, sir. I can get a warrant and force it, but that would entail everyone coming to the station therefore taking up a lot of time, shutting down your operation, ID's and green cards checked, and I would really rather not do that."

Tarzan waited with a mildly pleasant expression. He watched the war raze inside the supervisor's head. He clearly wanted to balk, but he also had a rigid schedule to stick to. Tarzan knew he had given in when his shoulders lowered.

Without saying anything to Tarzan, Brown turned from him and called out in Spanish and then English, "I need everyone over here, now, pronto!"

The workers hesitated, brows knit in confusion, then slowly they dropped what they were doing and approached the supervisor. Several eyed the side of the building as if planning to flee.

Tarzan said politely with cool authority, "Can you line them up, please?"

Brown blinked at him, then shrugged. "Guys," he spoke in Spanish, telling them to line up, then repeated in English. A bit of grumbling and muttering, the staff maneuvered themselves into a crooked line.

Tarzan said to Brown, "Tell them they can refuse if they want to. If they refuse, we will write their names down and they can expect a trip to the station." He smiled coolly at the foreman.

Brown grimaced, then repeated what Tarzan said in Spanish.

Tarzan trod up to the first man, and said, "Show me the bottom of your boot." He could only assume these laborers would only wear one pair of work boots and not have a second pair at home. When the man didn't move, Tarzan raised a brow to the foreman.

Again, Brown repeated what he said in Spanish. The man turned around and bent his knee to show Tarzan the bottom of his shoe. Tarzan pulled out another paper and held it next to the sole of the boot. "Tell him he can go back to work. Next."

The next man also wasn't wearing boots resembling the ones Tarzan was looking for. He told Brown to tell him he was dismissed.

In all, out of twenty males and two females, Tarzan only checked out four of them. The others either weren't wearing the Coleman boot, or it was a different style, or too worn to be the one they were looking for, or clearly the wrong size. Even Brown wore a different brand.

When the detective reached the last man, his chest wrung with disappointment. The boot they were looking for was not there.

Scratching his forehead in consternation with a few fingers, Tarzan squinted at the foreman through a strand of stray black hair that had fallen over one eye. "Sir, are you sure no one called in sick, or didn't show to work today? Maybe quit or got fired recently?"

Brown rested his large hands on his hips and shook his head. "No, I told you, all present at sign-in at the office and accounted for. You didn't find what you were looking for?"

His lips pushed out in skeptical frustration, Tarzan had been so sure. The cement was the right quotient, the color was spot on, the site was in close proximity to the apartment complex just down the street, what the hell? He held his hand out. "Thanks for your time, I appreciate your and everyone's cooperation."

Brown shook his hand with a curious smirk. "Sure."

As Tarzan turned around to head back to his truck with disappointment leaden in his footsteps he heard the supervisor yell out, "All right, party's over, get your asses back to work!" Then repeated it in Spanish.

CHAPTER TWENTY-ONE

The new doorbell Coli had installed rang a catchy gay tune but not so loud it would disturb the guests she would have. When she had guests, the bell would only ring in certain rooms, her bedroom, the kitchen, laundry room, anyplace where her guests wouldn't hear it.

She'd read she could have the doorbell hook up to her phone, that would be perfect. That way if she was outside in the gardens or the patio she would know if someone was at the door.

The guests would have key cards that would fail to function once their stay was over.

She was upstairs putting the finishing touches on a bedroom. It was one of her favorite chambers because it was one of the turret rooms and it had a trio of bow windows that gave different views of the back grounds of the house and gardens.

Outside, velour grass spread like green butter for miles, hiking and bird watching would be enjoyable in the woods beyond.

The four-poster queen bed mooring the center of the room was covered with a quilted comforter and pillows branded in bold strokes of purple and red. She'd done the room in shades of blue and violet with blurry Impressionistic paintings to match.

Wallpaper swathed in stripes of blue and violet flowers was softened by white ruffled curtains, the plush carpet purple and white.

Folding fresh linen to put in the closet, Coli paused when she saw Kip out in the back yard.

Her tender smile curved in pleasure. She had discussed with him that when she had time she wanted to make a vegetable garden on the far south side to help sustain the bed-and-breakfast. Her plan was to use as much of her own gardens as possible, can and bottle food for the winter, and surplus that with livestock and food grown by the locals.

She had placed ads in travel magazines and on the web for guests, which reminded her, she needed to get ads in the local papers for residents to provide their own artwork to sell in the carriage house. Her desire was to immerse herself, Kip, and the Inn in the community. Finally belong somewhere, be a part of something.

To the right side of the house her grandmother had created the beginnings of a fine rose garden that had gone to weeds when she'd fallen ill. But it was what Kip was doing on the left side that plucked a tear from her eye. He had a shovel and was digging long straight lines in the hard earth.

Her heart just warmed to bursting. She'd been told the soil was no good for growing anything but Coli believed with enough hard work, patience, love, and really good fertilizer she could have a garden flourishing with every kind of vegetable and herb she could squeeze in.

She was so blessed and thrilled to have Kip with her. When he was at the group home they'd only allowed her to see him on Sundays. Now she got to enjoy him every single day.

The bell rang again several times, and Coli's heart went from warm to excited, maybe it was Brogan! Quickly setting the linens on the shelf, she hurried off hoping it was the sheriff. He'd called daily but they hadn't been able to get together the last few days because of his busyness with his cases, and her doing catering for the bar.

Her feet scurried down the grand sapphire staircase, palm skimming the smooth mahogany bannister; she skidded to a stop at the door. "Heavens," she scolded herself, "get a grip, he's just a man."

Pushing her fair hair back to tumble off her shoulders, Coli took a deep breath and smoothed the dark green, short-sleeved sweater

down over her jeans. Her hand on the door handle, a grin teased as she went to open it, murmuring to herself, "Yeah, but what a man! Tall as the sky, dark burnished hair, and eyes that held secrets and pain behind hooded lids, but warmed with affection and blazed with desire when he looked at her.

"Brogan, I'm so glad-" she swung the door open, and tried to mask her reaction at seeing her half-sister Silina, Silina's mother Goldie Arabat, and Silina's grandfather, Auston Augustine, and another man, standing on her verandah.

Silina glared at the door, Goldie's sneer looked bored, and Auston's face was austere and unreadable. He was leaning on the cane with the silver lion's head.

The stranger's eyes were enigmatic but Coli's stomach pinched in discomfort at the way he appeared to be blatantly undressing her. She felt the need to put on a big thick coat seeing his interest in her revealed in the wanton tilt of his full mouth.

Blinking in stunned surprise, Coli tried to hide the disappointment that it wasn't Brogan at her door, and the sickness that churned at having her abusive family ganged up on her doorstep.

"Well?" Goldie snapped with haughty irritation. "You gonna stand there and stare at us like a gaping fish out of water, or invite us in?" Not waiting for Coli to respond, she just pushed her aside and stalked into the house. With a sniff and her nose in the air, Silina followed her.

Coli stood with her hand on the door handle stiff and ill at ease when Auston thumped by with his cane, his lip curled up at a corner in an unpleasant smile of greeting. The stranger managed to brush against her as he passed through.

Once inside, the four stood in one spot and surveyed the atrium.

Coli had wanted the foyer to be elegant yet warm and friendly. The floor tiling was glossy blush, the walls soft pale blue.

Near the entrance was a lengthy wooden bench that guests could sit on and remove hiking boots, jackets and place them on the rack beside it if they didn't want to bring them to their rooms. As always,

Coli put in comfortable seating and a few tables for guests waiting for someone or a ride.

A huge archway opened to one hall that led to the right side of the Victorian containing the morning room, tearoom, and the reading room that had plentiful windows and a stone fireplace, she'd stacked the shiny pine bookcases with every kind of genre of book, and board games.

The center corridor opened to the kitchen, and the dining room was off another sitting chamber. A sun salon and den rounded out the downstairs. The sandwich bar ran along the back side of the foyer. She had wanted there to be plenty of places for people to tuck themselves away, or for a group to hang with just their people.

To the left of the foyer the grand staircase wound up to the guest rooms on the second floor, then a smaller staircase led to the third floor of rooms. Laundry facility was in the basement with more canned goods, freezers, and storage of extra linens, extra furniture, and other necessities.

The stranger moved before Coli could react and grasped her hand. He lifted it to his lips and kissed the backs of her fingers. Black velvet eyes filled with wickedness glittered at her over her hand.

Still holding it, his cool, silky deep voice oozed, "Silina did not tell me how extraordinarily beautiful you are, *mia bella*. I am Ricardo Bastile, it is my great pleasure to meet you." His self-possessed words were spoken leisurely, almost supine, smooth and thick with a Basque accent from northern Spain.

Snatching her hand back, Coli gaped in misgiving at him. Who was this guy?

Silina quickly pushed her body against the man, forcing him to move away from her sister. Pride dented with jealousy transparent in her voice as she proprietarily petted his arm, she announced, "Ricardo is my boyfriend."

The tall man's black lacquered hair combed straight back framed an olive-skinned, elegantly classical face. Tiny lines around his full lips and dark, sensuous eyes made him appear in his late-thirties. Dressed in a black suit with a neatly trimmed goatee he looked downright villainous.

Coli swung her aghast posture to her sister. "Boyfriend? But Ellery has only just-"

"Well?" Goldie snipped loudly with an irritated sneer. "Are we to hang around the front door like unwanted strays or are you going to show us around this monstrosity?"

Marching towards the hall to the right, Silina added, "And we're hungry. You do have food in this mausoleum, right?"

Coli could feel Auston's unnerving regard making her skin crawl, her palms itchy, she didn't look at him. She answered, "Uh, yes, of- of course. I'll take you on a quick tour and then I can prepare a lunch for you. You can hang your jackets on the rack over there and then come this way."

Feeling like a beleaguered Cinderella, she had to endure snipes, disparaging comments about her decorating skills, sarcastic renunciations that a pimple on a bald man's head has a better chance of sprouting hair than Coli has of making the B&B a success. They even made fun of the name she planned to call the Victorian, **Colipatra's Inn**.

Ricardo tagged along behind them in suave silence, Coli could feel his gaze burning on her butt.

After the tour, biting her tongue, she brought them to the dark pink dining room and told them she'd bring them lunch. As she scurried away, she heard Goldie say, "Would you look at these heirlooms? This bone china, these dark pink crystal goblets, I bet we could get a fat dollar out of these, eh?"

Oh lord, they want my things, Coli quailed, *I knew I should have slammed and locked the door when I saw their faces*. Resignation slumping her shoulders, she prepared a quick, savory pasta primavera loaded with garden vegetables, warm, freshly baked bread slathered in rich butter, salad, and gingerbread cake with whipped cream.

As they complained about the food she produced, they had her running back and forth for drinks. She glanced around as she hurried about keeping an eye out for Douggie. There was no sign of him. Smiling as she made Silina and Goldie cocktails and opened a bottle

of wine for Auston and Ricardo, the pup was smarter than he looked, smart enough to stay away from harridan troubles.

The third time she entered the room with a tray of drinks, Coli came up short. Kip was standing just inside the doorway, and everyone was glowering at each other.

Silina's face rotated red-white-red at the sight of her discarded son.

"Oh, Kip, honey-" Coli hurried in and set the tray down at the end of the long table. Her lips pulled in at the unsightly stains they'd managed to get on the lacy white tablecloth. "It's early for lunch, I was just coming to get you."

Well, not exactly. She was hoping the family would settle down and round off some of their nasty edges before she brought him in to meet with them.

Ricardo lounged back in his chair swirling the Merlo in his relaxed hand. He remarked drowsily, "Ah, is this the poor brain damaged brother you told me about?"

Silina blurted, "Yes, we don't pay any attention to him. Just pretend he isn't here."

Not one of them said a word to Kip. After the shock of seeing him suddenly standing there like an apparition, and Silina's instructions to ignore him, they resumed eating and conversing amongst themselves.

Coli's heart that had held such loving warmth a short while ago, now bled with the anguish Kip's family must be causing him, especially Silina's referring to her son as their brother.

Kip turned a cheerful grin to Coli. "It's okay, I wanna eat in the kitchen with Douggie. K?"

Coli's eyes flicked to the table, they slowed in their eating at the name they weren't familiar with. Silina stuffed a zucchini in her mouth and spoke through it, "Douggie?" Sounding instantly resentful, she asked, "You have a new boy toy?"

Kip ignored the family and grinned at Coli as he strode past her to go to the kitchen.

"No," Coli explained, "Douggie is my dog. I brought him with me when I came out to get Kip's GI Joe soldier he'd left behind.

You saw him in my car." Before she had to hear more vitriol lashings she spun and ran after Kip.

Kip was just finishing his lunch in the kitchen when Silina poked her head in. She said to Coli, "Huh, figured I find you in here," and didn't even glance at her son. "I want you to show me the grounds, Coli."

Washing a dish at the sink, Coli sent her a puzzled frown. "You don't need me to show you, Silina, you just walk out any door and wander around. But don't go into that wooded area way in the back, I haven't cleared and marked the trails yet. The land is rocky and dense with box elders, hollies, scrag brush, it's a menace to traverse right now."

Without looking in Kip's direction, Silina walked across the black and white diamond checkered floor to her sister. She'd put her light jacket on and it was zipped up almost to her neck. She cajoled with a tinny whine, "Come with me, Coli, let's spend some sister time together."

Both Coli and Kip wore skeptical expressions. Coli set the dish she rinsed down and wiped her hands on the apron she'd neatly tied around her waist. "How about Kip shows you around? You and he can spend some Mom and son time," she pretended she didn't see Kip's tongue stick out like he'd tasted something yucky, or hear Silina's gasp of repugnance.

Silina groused, "No, I want to go with you. You can have Kip bring our things in."

"Things?"

"Of course, our suitcases. We told you we were coming to stay in this fleabag for a few days."

Kip said eagerly, "I'll get 'em. Are they in the car?"

His mother rolled her eyes at the teen, answered him with her typical sarcasm, "Uh, yeah, duh. You don't see them lying around here do you?"

Coli set her hand affectionately on Kip's arm while gently scolding her sister, "Silina, please."

Kip jumped up, kissed Coli on the cheek and pedaled in a rush out of the kitchen.

Sighing her frustration, Coli didn't muffle her annoyance. "Silina, I've asked you not to talk to him like he's brainless. The more maturely and respectfully you speak to him the more he'll retain and build his self-esteem, his confidence."

Face scrunching in revilement, Silina snarled, "Like I give a shit, Coli. You should have left the retard in Ohio where we could have forgotten he ever existed. He's an embarrassment."

Anger rippled through Coli fisting her hands and tightening her shoulders. "I can't believe a mother would abandon her own child, but," she held up a hand warding off Silina's responding tirade, "how about you and Goldie, your boyfriend and Grandfather just leave.

"It's bad enough how you treat me, but this is Kip's home and I won't allow anyone to demean him. I had hoped if you were here, you and the family could build a relationship with Kip. But if nothing but abusive name calling is all that's going to happen, I think you all should leave."

Seeing her mother-bear sister's face harden with ire and rigid protectiveness, Silina sighed. Without looking Coli in the eyes, she said, "Okay, okay, calm down. Geesh." She casually patted the side of her hair and asked, "Can we just go take a walk around the grounds like I asked before you decided to make a big dramatic deal out of everything?"

Coli stood unmoving, fighting down the rage that choked her every time Silina or Goldie denigrated Kip. It was one thing to trash Coli, she deserved it, but Kip was an innocent child.

Dragging in deep breaths to calm her ire, Coli nodded. A walk would chase the burn out of her anger. Untying the apron, she folded it and set it on the counter. "All right. We can go out this door right here." She walked over to a door that led to a small mud porch, grabbed a jacket off a hook beside the door and opened it.

"Wait." Silina pointed at one of Coli's blouses lying folded atop a laundry basket. "I might take a few pictures, put that on so you'll look pretty. That t-shirt is ugly."

"What? Come on Silina, I don't-"

"Come on, please? If it's a good pic I'll frame it and keep it on our mantel at home. That way you'll always be part of our home, right?"

Eyeing her sister with suspicion, Silina had never pretended to want Coli anywhere near their house. But, things had to start somewhere. Maybe her sister was finally growing up, coming around. Coli's heart leapt, maybe she'd even come around to accepting Kip.

She picked up the blouse and slipped it on. With her t-shirt under it the blouse was tight, she only buttoned the bottom two buttons. She held her arms out and asked, "Happy now?"

Silina traipsed over to her with a champion's grin. "See? Now was that so hard?"

Shaking her head in tribulation, Coli stepped out to the mud porch and opened the screen door then the outer door, breathed in deeply. "The fresh country air always smells so good, it's unusually warm, we don't really need our jackets." She tossed hers on a chair on the porch.

Coli showed her the vegetable garden Kip was digging earlier, and the rose garden she planned on restoring. At the rear of the roses there was a rock garden with pebbled trails, and wood and wrought-iron benches to rest on.

"How about the woods, Coli? Show me the woods," Silina insisted.

The two stood in the grass, a heated breeze fluttered Coli's long hair, the soft wind chopped at Silina's stiff do sitting stagnant on her shoulders.

Spacious spring lawn spread to the crotchety woods where Coli planned to clean up and mark trails for her guests. Way down the road she hoped to be able to stable a few horses for riding. The girls approached the woods and Silina stepped over a small bush just inside the tree-line then quickly disappeared.

"Um, Silina, I told you, right now the forest is terribly unkempt and could be dangerous with hidden holes and ravines and stuff." Coli tramped after her sister calling her to come back, "Silina, where

are you, Silina!" Stepping over sharp scrub, her ankle twisted on a rock, and she stubbed her toe on a shallow root.

Shoving at a branch that scratched her cheek, Coli yelled in irritation, "Dammit!" Peering through the thick foliage, her foot cracked a twig, she pushed aside large shiny leaves and shouted, "Come on, Silina! I'm going back to the-"

"Hey!" Silina popped in front of her making her suck in a gasp. "What's all the yelling?"

Startled, Coli stumbled backwards. Rubbing her cheek, she scowled, "It's hot as heck out here, I'm going back, right now. You can come with me or not." The trees and bushes crowded them and blocked sunlight struggling to streak through baggy leaves making it more humid and dimmer in the woods.

"Okay geesh, what a sissy you turned out to be. Let me just take a sister selfie. Just one," she pleaded at Coli's unsmiling face. Pulling her cell from her jean's pocket. "Please," her gritty voice coaxed her sister. "Just one, okay?"

Coli's head fell back with a sighing groan. "Fine. One, then we go. It's buggy in here and injurious." She slapped at a mosquito lunching on her neck.

Silina grabbed her arm and pulled her several feet from where she'd been standing. "All right," she said, lifting her phone and raised her arm in front of them. They tilted their heads up and together with smiles, and Silina's finger clicked the button, the flash went off.

Smoothing her hair back off her sweating face with a palm, Coli said, "Okay, let's go now." But Silina held her arm. "Wait, just one more," click, "another one," click. The fourth picture and Coli was not smiling. She jerked her arm from Silina's grasp and stomped along an overgrown trail.

Coli had too much to do, she had guests she needed to prepare rooms for. Her sigh weary and anxious, she slapped at scratchy leaves on her way over the rocky ground out of the dimness and back to the sunlight.

Inside, she slid the blouse off and set it on the counter to wash and put away later.

CHAPTER TWENTY-TWO

Brogan and his team gathered in his office.

Tarzan lifted files off a chair and put them on the floor so he could sit on it. "Heck, Brog, you ever heard of a computer? Why all these files?" He waved his hand at stacks of files and papers on Brogan's sturdy but worn desk.

Rocky dragged a chair near the desk and flopped on it.

Jacks Navarro strolled in and leaned one shoulder against the doorframe; crossed his arms and a foot over an ankle. Face stony as ever but a hint of humor broached the side of the agent's mouth.

Reclining in his chair, tipping back on two legs with his long legs anchoring him, Brogan clasped his hands behind his head, his elbows winged out. "It is disappointing," he said to Tarzan, "findin' the exact components of the cement but not able to match it to any of the workers' boots. You guys couldn't find another construction site?"

Rocky answered, "No, we searched the entire three mile radius. None of the residents in the complex had a clue about how the cement got there, and anyone carrying a bucket or whatnot inside must have arrived by foot. It's like someone had been walking by carrying the bucket and on impulse entered the apartments. Located on the outskirts of the town, the complex is closer to the straggling Grasshopper Prairies than the burbs or businesses, it's a crumbling neighborhood, not a lot of rebuilding or renovating going on."

Tarzan tugged on his pushed out lips. "I just don't get it. It has to be someone from that site."

Brogan let his chair drop, folded his hands and set them on the desk, his thick shoulders hunched. "You need to go back, do a more thorough investigation. Determine if there isn't another place the cement could have come from-"

"That precise mixture? And the construction site within walking distance? No way. It was spilled and tracked in by one of those workers. The foreman said everyone was present, no one called out. Unless one of the four I checked out that wore a size eight had another set of boots at home." Tarzan stuffed his hands in his black trouser pockets, slouched and stuck his legs out.

Shaking his head he said, "I just don't think so. I got a good look at the laborers, more like migrants they seemed. Clothes were worn and holey, most of the boots were barely still holding together, no," he shook his head again, "I really doubt any of them had more than one pair."

"Well, you're gonna have to go back there. You need to go to their homes, ask to see all of their shoes." Brogan glanced from Tarzan to Rocky.

"Without a warrant?" Tarzan asked with a dubious chuff of frustration. Sitting up, his tie had slipped to the side. He flipped the dark blue tie back and straightened it.

Brogan gave him a slight shrug. "You said migrants. Most are probably not legal. You go in with your badge in your hand, assert you aren't Immigration and aren't going to arrest them if they cooperate. They'll want you to go away as quickly as possible, they'll let you in, trust me."

"I'll take half," Rocky told Tarzan getting to his feet, "it'll go faster with us splitting them."

"Good-" Brogan broke off when Pirate ambled into the office. They all looked expectantly to the tall man dressed in black, with black hair, trim beard, and black-framed glasses. Tattoos ringed under the black hair on his rugged forearms, one peeked beneath the collar of his shirt. The man was the epitome of a geek thug.

Fingers twined, tapping his thumbs together, Brogan lifted his chin to the genius who looked more like a motorcycle brute in neat clothes than a brilliant computer hacker. Except for the glasses. They should have made him look nerdy, but instead they sharpened his features into a leashed, dangerous street-fighter, the dark eyes behind them were frozen primitive cinders. A hard, treacherous history glinted now and then when he was pushed to fury.

"Whatcha got, Lo?" Brogan leaned forward, knowing the hacker wouldn't have come if he didn't have something important.

Pirate carried a laptop. He set it on Brogan's desk facing him and opened it. It was already powered on. He said to the sheriff, "Deputy Pupatelli and Dam went to every house in the victim Blanco's vicinity. Most people didn't want to talk to them. It's not a great neighborhood, people keep to themselves. But," he pushed a button on the computer.

"They did note cameras and brought me the addresses. There were only a few and most faced the wrong direction, and the only one shooting near the complex showed only one side of the complex, not the other."

A fuzzy video shimmered across the screen. It was hazy and grey and the wideness of the shot was limited but they could make out a figure carrying a bucket come into screenshot. He was wearing a blue flannel shirt, and raggedy jeans covered in something, maybe dried mud.

He hesitated in front of the building, then his head twisted all around as if he was making sure no one saw him. Then it appeared he quickly ran up the steps and into the building, except the actual steps and front door weren't visible in the video, just a slice of the top half of his body moving up indicated he was going up the steps.

Five minutes passed and his slice of body came back into view moving down, and he hurried off down the street out of camera range.

"Ya see the boots, bro?" Rocky bumped fists with Tarzan. Tarzan grinned.

"Yeah, Colemans," Rocky said gleefully. "He's our guy."

"Do you recognize him from the construction site, Tarzan?" Brogan asked, his eyes on the screen.

Tarzan leaned in, squinted. "The film is blurry, wiggles, but, no. That guy was not there. There's only a blurry shot of the side of his face, he's got exceptionally long sideburns, he wasn't there."

"Okay, Lo, give the guys a few prints of the fella." Brogan smiled, sitting back in his chair. "Go get 'em, boys."

The men jumped up, Tarzan grinned, declaring, "Oh yeah, we'll get the sonofabitch." He and Rocky disappeared through the doorway.

Jacks took Rocky's deserted seat. Unbuttoning his suit coat, he tugged at his tie and relaxed in the chair, knees out, boots placed wide apart.

"Whatsup, Navarro?" Brogan propped his hands behind his head again.

Crossing an ankle over a knee, Jacks rested a crooked elbow on the chair arm. "Well, we know the guns were brought in on Ellery Delian's boat. Pompeii went bananas when I brought him there. Thing is, the boat wasn't in his name, it was in a guy's named Thorne Arabat."

At Brogan's hiked brows, Jacks nodded, his face tough, dark eyes ruthless. "So we know the guns were on the boat, and at Delian's love shack and the art gallery. They have to be stored somewhere nearby. We need to connect them to Palumbo so I can get a warrant and have the place raided. The son, Tonto," he chuckled, "nice name, wasn't that a horse? Anyway, I think he's the link."

"Tonto was the Indian, and I don't think he's the link, Kemosabe." Jacks looked surprised at his denial.

Brogan explained, "Deputy Royce Darken checked out Tonto. Darken went in undercover, located him at a pool hall. He hung with him a few times.

"Royce said he's damned homely, porky, big mole on his cheek, dumb as a rock, drunk or high most of the time, he's able to get women because his old man's a gangster with power and big bucks.

Told Royce with relish how he likes knocking chicks around, makes him feel like a big man like his dad."

"A bully," Jacks commented with disparagement, disgust twisting his lips.

"I met old man Palumbo, he probably beats on the son, and you know," Brogan's mouth pulled in at a corner, "it rolls downhill. The son looks for someone weaker than him to push around, take his temper out on."

"Mafia's a tough life, it doesn't generally suffer fools nicely," Jacks commented.

"Yeah. So, I doubt Tonto has any big part in the business. He's too stupid, and if he's as high all the time as Royce said he was, Palumbo wouldn't have him involved in minute operations. He'd screw them up. Palumbo gives him a title so the others are forced to respect him, but he has no real, direct hands in the mechanisms. Royce said he bragged about guns he 'borrowed' from his father, but wouldn't bite when the deputy tried to get him to show them."

Jacks stated the obvious, "We need to get inside Palumbo's restaurant."

Brogan agreed. "You're right. I've had Bucky and Deputy Duff Gillan snooping around for warehouses Palumbo could be using to store the guns."

"Any luck?"

Brows dropping with his frown, Brogan answered, "There's only one where he stores supplies and things. Didn't Duff give you that information? I told him to."

His mouth wry, Jacks told him, "No. But, I did get the information about the one warehouse from Pirate. He has his fingers in everything to do with this case and he did his own warehouse search and told me. I took Pompeii there in the middle of the night when no one was around, I found nothing, the guns weren't, and hadn't been there."

"If no one was there to let you in…" Brogan mentioned with a raised brow and wry pull to his lips.

Jacks held his hands up, grinned. "How about I say I was lucky and the door was unlocked?"

"Huh," Brogan grunted.

Later in the day, Tarzan and Rocky finally located the foreman's office, which was actually a small trailer. A truck was parked near the door and a light was on inside.

Tarzan knocked firmly but not rudely harsh. Nothing happened. After the second, slightly louder knock they heard a chair scraping and footsteps approaching the door.

The door opened and Joshua Brown's dark eyes flicked from Rocky to Tarzan. Recognizing Tarzan, not angrily but still holding a trace of annoyance, he said, "Detective?"

Behind him lounged a frayed sofa, a recliner with stuffing perforating out of the arms, and a desk messy with papers, pencils, blueprints, and a plate with fried chicken and potato salad. A half empty glass of beer set next to a crunched beer can.

"Hate to bother you, Mr. Brown," Tarzan said politely. "This is Deputy Narocki. May we come in? Just for a moment."

Brown stood in the doorway like a blocking fullback, looked from one to the other then sighed. "Yeah, sure," he stepped back.

Entering the rickety trailer, the lawmen shuffled to the side, waiting for Brown to shift from the doorway to in front of them.

Brown offered with offhand politeness, "Get ya a beer?"

Tarzan shook his head with a smile. "No, thanks. I just need to show you a picture."

"Oh?" Dark eyebrows arched up to his bald head, the foreman scrubbed a few fingers over his dark beard.

Tarzan pulled the photo from the videos and held it out to Brown. Puzzled, he took it.

Rocky asked, "Do you know this man?"

Brown regarded the photo, one shoulder bumped in a mild shrug. "Sure." He handed the picture back.

Rocky and Tarzan traded a quick look. "Uh, well," Tarzan took the photo, "what's his name?"

Reaching for his beer, Brown took a sip, said evenly, "Pedro Lopez."

"Does he work for you?" Tarzan asked, tucking the photo in the inside breast pocket of his suit jacket.

"Sure," Brown said, took a bigger sip then set the almost drained glass back down on the table and crossed his arms.

Tarzan's forehead furrowed. "When I asked you if everyone was at work yesterday you said yes. But this Lopez wasn't there."

"He wasn't," Brown replied with another negligent shrug, "he was at a different site yesterday over in San Palos."

The lawmen made an effort not to share a glance. "Oo-kay." Tarzan reined in his irritation at wasted time. "Do you have his address?"

"Sure," Brown answered.

They all waited. Feeling Tarzan stiffening next to him, Rocky asked calmly, "Can you give it to us?"

Another shrug. "Sure." The foreman moved to the desk, pushed a few papers aside and picked up a book. Thumbing through it, he stopped at a page and read off Pedro Lopez's address.

Reining in his annoyance, Tarzan said, "You told me everyone was present at the site, but this Lopez was not. Why did you lie?"

"Didn't lie, Cop. I said everyone clocked in at the office, that would be here. The crew went on to the site but Pedro went to a different sit to drop off shit." He didn't look smug, but the hint of it was there.

Feeling Tarzan starting to burn, Rocky quickly said, "Thanks for your time."

Tarzan climbed in the truck, his temper simmering.

Rocky got in the passenger side and threw his friend a grin. "Like pulling damned teeth, huh? I think he acted obtuse on purpose, not solid if we were involving him in something, he was careful to not give more than exactly what we asked."

Heading off to the highway, Tarzan grunted, "Whatever. We got what we needed. Let's hope Lopez is our man."

Lopez's home wasn't far from the foreman's trailer. Shadows drew long and lean over roads and homes as the sun settled down the horizon. The house was small in a deteriorated neighborhood.

Tarzan knocked on the door. While they waited, the detective tugged at the knot in his tie, a few drops of sweat dribbled his temple. "Damn, it's growing hot, I should have left my jacket in the car."

A tiny, plump, Hispanic woman, black hair twisted in a knot on top of her head opened the door. Her ebony eyes scaled both men, wrinkles abundant and wisps of grey in her hair put her at about 60. She ground out a wary, "*Si, Policía?*"

Between Tarzan's suit and short hair, and Rocky's Marine styled body, posture, hair, people who were constantly hiding and running from the law easily recognized them as cops.

Smiling with professional courtesy, Tarzan held out his badge and said, "Good evening. I am Detective Kurt Vantarzani, and this is Deputy Elvin Narocki. Do you speak English?"

Her eyes rolled from his badge to his face, her nod cautious, she replied, "*Si, Oficial.*"

"Okay, good. We're looking for Pedro Lopez. Is he here?"

Backing away, blinking rapidly, she started to close the door. "No, no here."

Rocky stuck his boot in the doorway preventing her from closing it. Using his blond good looks, boyish grin, in his friendliest voice he said, "Please, *señora,* we are not Immigration." He held up Boy Scout fingers, "I promise. We only have a few quick questions to ask him and we'll leave your family alone."

He widened his baby blues, broadened his smile to show his pearlies, implored with sincerity, "I swear, *señora,* we are not here to arrest anyone." *Yet.*

She bought it and opened the door to let them in. They stepped into a living room. The beige rug was thin and shabby. Scattered around on the threadbare furniture, three women appearing to be in their twenties sat with small children at their feet and babies on their laps. They all stared at the men with rounded curious, frightened dark eyes.

The older woman motioned to the men to follow her. Obliging, Tarzan and Rocky traipsed after her. She passed a dining area, the table still held a few platters containing bits of food, and empty

glasses, the lingering scent of spicy enchiladas evidenced they'd just finished dinner. Rocky shot a covetous look at the dishes, his mouth watered like Pavlov's dog.

When they entered the kitchen they saw three young men reclining around a round kitchen table. Dirty pots and pans stacked on the counter behind them. A can of beer sat in front of each man. Their heads cocked up at the lawmen's entrance.

Voice low and casual, Tarzan asked, "Pedro Lopez?" He and Rocky scanned the faces of the men. All had black hair in different home-cut styles, and medium to dark skin, two of them turned round black-olive eyes to the male that sat between them. That man's brown skin blanched, his eyes shifted back and forth. He had exceptionally long sideburns.

Tarzan went up to him, said, "Pedro Lopez?" He waited, the man's gaze jerked around the room at everything except Tarzan and Rocky. His body turned rigid, eyes flitting to the doorway, he appeared about to bolt. On either side of him, chairs scraped the yellowed linoleum floor as the other men shifted a few inches away.

The detective held up the photo Pirate had given him, he said firmly, "This is you, Pedro Lopez." He gripped a chair, lifted it, set it next to Lopez and turned the seat sideways to him, he ordered coolly, "Put your leg up on this chair."

Pedro's fingers clutched the end of the table, his jaw clenched, he looked to his friends to help him. They froze. The scent of fear and desperate fleeing rose in the air.

"Put your leg up here, now," Tarzan's voice lost its casualness. Pointing at the chair, he commanded, "Now."

Silence pulsed through the kitchen, the sweat and smell of fear was now a living thing, beating against the walls, stomping on the floor. The women chattering in Spanish drifted from the living room. Beads of sweat popped then rolled down Pedro's face, his fingers clutching the table edge quivered.

Tarzan stared him down. Rocky stood a few feet behind the detective watching his back. He placed himself so his back was to the wall and he could see the living room and kitchen at the same time.

With tiny slow movements, Pedro pushed back from the table, and painstakingly slowly lifted his foot and set it on the chair. He curled his fingers over the edges of the seat he was sitting on, his head was down but his eyes turned up to peer at Tarzan through a hunk of black hair.

"*Bueno, gracias.*" Tarzan pulled out the picture of the print from the camera at Camille Blanco's apartment and unfolded it. He ordered Pedro, "Stretch your leg out."

The man stared in confusion at the detective. Tarzan bent, grasped his ankle and tugged until Pedro's leg was lying on the chair with his foot hanging off.

Tarzan squatted and held the picture next to the bottom of Pedro's boot. His expression revealed nothing. He stood up and handed the photo to Rocky.

They traded positions and Rocky crouched mirroring what Tarzan had done. He stood up with a tight smile and nod to Tarzan.

Tarzan said, "Okay, you can put your leg down, Lopez. Everyone but Pedro out, *por favor.*" No one moved at first, then Rocky held his arms out and hustled the occupants from the room. When they were gone, he came back and resumed his sentry in the doorway.

Tarzan brushed off the chair after Pedro removed his foot and sat down. "You speak English, Pedro? You understand what I'm saying?"

Lopez nodded quickly, his eyes bouncing from Tarzan to Rocky. Tightening his grip on the chair seat, he licked dry lips then looked at Tarzan.

The steel seriousness of the FBI in his tone, Tarzan said, "On Friday, you were working down the street from the Peachclub Apartments, correct?"

Pedro glanced at Rocky standing guard at the door then back to Tarzan. He replied, "*Si, señor,*" his gaze fell, his shoulders slumped.

Going right to the heart of the matter, Tarzan said, "A girl was found murdered in that complex." He observed a shudder run through Pedro's slender shoulders, his head hung.

"You see this picture." Tarzan flicked the side of the photo with his finger. "We have proof you were there. You had a bucket of dry cement, and you spilled it by the stairs, and your footprints were found in the cement that tracked to the dead girl, Camille Blanco's door."

The trembling started in his shoulders and rocked through his limbs, he pressed his lips to quell their trembling, and said nothing.

Tarzan leaned into Pedro and told him, "I am giving you one, Pedro, one chance to explain yourself. Tell me what were you doing at Camille Blanco's apartment?" He watched fear and anxiety flow through the young man's body, but his lips stayed compressed.

Tarzan sighed laboriously. "All right, Pedro," he made as if to move to stand up. "I guess we have to round up everyone here, your friends, the women, your grandma I'm thinking is out there," he motioned with his head to the living room, "and of course the children, the babies, and take everyone to the immigration detention compound up there in Houston.

"But don't worry," he let a mean chuckle in, "they'll probably stay there for years and years before they're deported. Rocky," he said, standing up and unhooked handcuffs from the back of his belt. "Let's gather them up," he turned towards the door.

"No! Wait," Pedro squawked through a throat tight with fear. "I- I tell you, *oficiales, por favor*, please, do not hurt my family, please!"

Tarzan paused but didn't turn around, Rocky rattled his cuffs in his hand. Voice shaking, Pedro's cheeks flooded with dark embarrassment, he wobbled out, "I, uh, *si*, I was there. A few days ago these *mujeres muy hermosas*, uh, very beautiful women walked past the job, the house we work on." He took a breath and held it when Tarzan moved back near him.

Re-clipping his cuffs to his belt, the detective shoved his jacket tails back and set his hands on his hips. He nodded to Pedro to continue.

A gulp rolled down Pedro's throat making his Adam's apple bob sharply. "Ah, so, I have break. The cement mixer is overheated, we have to stop. I," he looked down at his hands, "do not know why

214

I carried the bucket, it was, just in my hands when I thought to go, uh..."

Rocky leaned his back against the wall. Tarzan prompted Lopez, "Okay, so you had the cement bucket in your hand and you, what, followed the women home?"

Pedro's head dropped down in shame, he nodded without looking up. "*Si*." His sigh thick with embarrassment, he raised his head, wiped at an eye and said to Tarzan, "Very beautiful Brazilian girls. I, uh, followed them home. Few days later, I had the bucket, and uh, break time; I walked over to see if they were home. Sometimes they leave curtains open and you can see," the darkness flushed up his neck to his face.

"You peeked in their windows, Pedro?"

He nodded, ashamed. Quickly glancing at the door where the women were ensconced, he muttered, "The curtains were closed. I sort of, creep down the hall, maybe if I knock on the door and one of them would be in her...ah, you know, panties when she answer it."

"Uh huh, so what happened, Pedro? Did they open the door?"

He shook his head, regret and shame squeezing his eyes shut. "No, *señor*."

Rocky asked, "How did the cement get on the floor?"

Pedro glanced at Rocky, his stance falsely benign against the wall. He may appear boyish looking but unhesitant lethality flickered in the depths of his pretty blue eyes, and Pedro recognized the threat for what it was.

If Pedro ran, Rocky would give chase, if Pedro went after Tarzan, the deputy would use deadly force if he had to, to protect his partner. Not that the equally dangerous Tarzan couldn't take care of himself, his double black belt attested to that.

In a small voice, Pedro explained, "I come up the stairs and trip over the- the strip on the floor where the door closed, and the cement spilled. I was gonna clean it up, I started to, then I see I cannot pick up powder with my hands. So, I leave it and go to the girls' door. I want to knock, but I realize," his shoulders raised self-consciously, "they are beautiful, and models, they would not want to be with, me.

You know?" Indicating his old grungy clothes with dirty fingernails. Scratching his head, he shoved the hair back off his forehead.

Tarzan asked, "So, what did you do?"

Pedro bent forward and put his face in his hands, his elbows on his knees. Rubbing his eyes, he dragged his hand damp with sweat over his mouth then chin, then clasped his hands, resting his forearms on his knees.

"Ah…" Dispirited, Pedro raised and lowered his shoulders. "Nothing. I hear footsteps coming down the other hall and got…scared. I run to the elevator, and…went back to work."

Another swift glance towards the living room, his face scrunched in worry he asked, "They…did they make a complaint that I…what you call…peep Tommed them?" Brows down, he said quickly, "Cause, they lie if they did. I see nothing. Uh, that day. Curtains closed, no girl in panties open door." He raised his palms in surrender and said, "I swear."

Tarzan moved his head towards Rocky with an arched brow. Rocky stared back, the corners of his mouth nicked in, *what next?*

Tarzan said to Pedro, "Did you see anyone at all? Anyone in the hall, the stairwell, the elevator, going in or coming out of the building? Pass anyone on the street?"

Pedro shook his head. "No, *señor.*"

"Think for a minute, Pedro, picture yourself walking from the construction site to the complex, up the stairs, to the door, down on the elevator," he spoke slowly, watching Pedro's eyes roam back and forth as he recalled his journey from the site to his peeping place and back to work.

He closed his eyes and shook his head again. "No, *señor,* it was still early, people gone to work or school, roads light. That is why I," his shoulders hugged his ears in abashment, "go there then. I think the girls may be home, and few people to catch me…uh, looking."

"You didn't pass one other person on the street?" Rocky asked impatiently from the doorway. "Think, man." The set of the deputy's jaw suggested he believed the laborer's story, that he had never gotten into the apartment. He was too ashamed, embarrassed

at getting caught spying on the girls. And, it was likely one of the women in the other room was his, and he'd catch hell if she heard what he'd done.

Pedro repeated, "No, *señor,* I told you, I saw no-" he stopped, blinked. "Ah, well the other side from where I come from, the east side of the building, way, way down the street I saw a-a woman. I think."

Rocky pushed from the wall.

Tarzan's body stiffened, he asked, "What'd she look like?"

Again he shook his head in the negative. "She too far away. I only know she is female because she wear shorts. But too far to see shape of legs." His shoulder bumped. "Could be hairy, could be boy's, too far, I do not know."

Tarzan asked, "What color was her hair?"

Pedro sat back, his hands clasped in his lap. "*Señor,* I tell you, she wear a cap and long coat almost cover shorts."

"Age? Height?"

Sniffing back his nervousness, Pedro wiped his damp palms on his thighs. "No, too far, many blocks away. Maybe not even girl, just 'cause of shorts I…a… assume."

The detective sighed glumly, checked with Rocky. Rocky mimed concession. The Mexican didn't kill Camille Blanco, and he didn't witness anyone that could have.

"Okay," Tarzan grunted, "give me your boots."

Pedro didn't move for a second, then he bent and untied them, kicked them off and handed them to Tarzan. "I need for work, man," he complained.

"Yeah well, think about that next time you're peeping at girls through their windows." Carrying the boots, Tarzan traipsed out of the kitchen, gave the grandmother a slight nod, and the two lawmen left the house and drove back to the station in the twilight.

CHAPTER TWENTY-THREE

The next morning, Brogan was in his truck when he saw Tarzan's name come up on his phone, he answered, "Tarzan, yeah?" While he listened to the detective sounding very disappointed reporting their visit to Pedro Lopez's house, he noticed although it was early, the sky off to the southeast was dark with smoldering thunderclouds. Dry, oppressive heat had roiled in ahead of them.

Tarzan explained their interview of Pedro Lopez and their reactions to his answers. "We dropped the boots at the lab last night. This morning the tech verified the residue on them was the cement found near Camille Blanco's apartment."

His hand on the wheel, turning a corner Brogan asked, "You sure he didn't do Blanco in?" Hearing Tarzan's confirmation that both he and Rocky believed the guy was just horny, not a killer, he had to agree with their conclusion.

Tarzan relayed the part about a possible female in the vicinity. "But," his frown came through the phone, "it could mean absolutely nothing. And even it was the killer, Lopez could barely acknowledge it was female, or not, much less give any kind of description. The vic may have been poisoned somewhere else anyway, the CSI's didn't find any evidence inside the apartment. No dishes in the sink, the dishwasher was empty.

"Besides, why would Lopez poison the girl? Murder in a fit of rage, sure, but that guy wouldn't know poisons. And the way he

looked there's no way either of those Brazilian beauties would have opened the door to him or given him the time of day anywhere else."

Hearing the frustration and disappointment in Tarzan's voice, Brogan tried to keep the defeat he felt out of his tone. "Okay." He couldn't help grousing, "Three murders and we have nothing." He told Tarzan to continue working on finding a lead and hung up.

On his way to the station, Brogan answered his ringing phone again, "Dillon." At the information coming through the cell, Brogan groaned and combed his broad fingers through his dark hair causing tufts to spring up after them. His hat was beside him on the seat, he was too tall to wear it inside the truck.

He called Tarzan back. When the detective answered Brogan said, "The owner of a paint shop in the Barriga…" he took a breath, dread climbing up his throat. "Yeah, I don't know if you know him, Peter Polito, he's dead. Headin' over to the paint store now, call the others and tell them." When he hung up with the detective he dialed Jackson Navarro's number.

"We got another body, Agent, wanna meet me there? Bring the dog." Brogan gave Navarro directions and did a U-turn back to the main highway to an exit that would take him to the Barriga.

White cruisers with green striping took up all the parking spots on the street, their emergency lights swirling blue and red neon bursts over buildings, trees, across people standing on the street gawking with curiosity. Brogan parked up on the sidewalk in front of Pete's Paint Store.

The store perched in the center of a strip of Mom-and-Pop shops positioned in a maze of businesses just outside the main square of more upscale establishments. An officer was stringing yellow police tape between the stores that embraced Pete's, and to the walk, a deputy stood guard on either side of the open door.

Leaving his hat in the truck, waves of dry heat battered Brogan as he strode up to the store. Dressed in his uniform shirt, and jeans, badge and gun on his hip, he lifted his chin in greeting to the officers who nodded back in deference to the sheriff. When he stepped inside he saw Dr. Martone already at work.

"How'd you get here so fast, Doc?" Brogan asked as he slipped on booties.

The medical examiner twisted his head and looked up at Brogan with a smile. "As it happens, I was just about driving by here on my way to the bakery over on Lorandos when I got the call. Fortunately, I keep a forensic kit and apparel in my trunk, unfortunately, my bear claw will have to wait."

Rows of remodeling equipment, buckets of paint, tools, rolls of wallpaper stacked the walls on all sides and down several isles. Near the front was a big wooden table used for measurements and cutting, a hammer and scissors were set on it.

Stationed at the front entrance was a long, glass-topped counter and register. A paper coffee cup lay on its side on the wooden table, coffee pooled out of it.

Donning the protective gear, before he put his gloves on, Brogan dipped a fingertip in the bit of coffee that remained in the spilled cup. "It's cold," he commented snapping the gloves on. Very careful to avoid the vomit glommed everywhere, he dropped down to his haunches beside the doctor. "Holy hell, Doc, what do we have?" The smell of puke was god-awful.

Pete Polito lay half on his stomach, half on his side, curled up in a rigid, grotesque semblance of agony, his fingers curved like gouging claws. His face frozen in a taut grisly scream was scratched and spotted with dark shadows where bruises were starting to form before he died and blood stopped flowing, chestnut eyes bulged with explosive torment.

Sandy hair grossly mottled with the vomit Pete apparently spewed, as it was gunked on the floor under his open mouth and in nauseating globs where it had flown and landed around him. A foot away lay something rolled up in paper.

Intent on prodding around the body with gloved fingers, Martone mumbled, "Body's still warm, pretty sure he's been poisoned. Whatever it was, it took him in its grip, violently ripped and shook the hell out of him before throwing him savagely to the ground. Convulsions probably slammed his face on the floor causing

those contusions. Poison held his facial expression, after rigor comes and goes, his body will sag out of the rigid horror show."

He carefully lifted the face etched in agony, bent so his face was close to Pete's and peered into his open eyes, saw the pupils dilated, and then sniffed before setting his head back down. "Not cyanide. I can't tell you any more now, just that it wasn't a pleasant death."

Brogan muttered, "No kidding, doesn't look like he died of fun." He stood up as more forensic techs arrived to photograph the body before putting it on a gurney to take it to the morgue and then screen the shop. He bent over to get a look at the paper on the floor. It was partially wrapped around a sandwich.

"Looks like a breakfast sandwich, Doc, half eaten. Make sure the techs bag it and take it to the lab. Might be where the poison came from." He motioned to the table. "The coffee too. The cup, and the liquid spilled from it."

"Uh huh," Martone mumbled with a chuckle. "I think they know their job, Sheriff."

"Just covering all bases, Doc, I got four murders now, and no suspect. Different MO's, can't conclusively say it's a serial, but hell, they are certainly connected. No way I'm leavin' anything to chance."

Outside, Brogan took a deep breath of air that didn't smell nauseatingly like death and vomit. That whole scene was freaky. Sure, he'd been in war, saw every atrocity known to man, but, shit, the excruciating agony was so carved into the man's face, Brogan could practically feel it, made his stomach sick. Plus, he had just seen Pete a week or so ago with-

"Hey, Sheriff." Navarro came strolling with Pompeii on a leash across the sidewalk up to where Brogan was standing. In the far distance, purple tarred the blue, smudging the darkening sky, charcoal clouds descended over the mountaintops, cloaking the peaks in a disturbing omen.

Dabbing at sweat pilling his forehead with a handkerchief, the agent watched Pete's body now encased in a bag being rolled out and to the waiting ambulance. "You keep this up and you'll be out

of a job, all your citizens will be dead." Pompeii let out a soft 'woof' as if he agreed.

Brogan's bunched mouth showed he wasn't amused at Navarro's attempt at a joke. One of the deputies came over carrying a baggie, he handed it to Brogan. Brogan held it up, squinted at it, said to the deputy, "A button?"

"Yes, sir. We found it near the body. It's a pearl button, feminine. Polito wore mostly flannel according to his employee," he motioned his head towards a skinny young man with stringy red hair, acne, and a large Adam's apple joggling in his skinny throat like a swatted golf ball. Using the wall to hold his body up, terrified eyes swung wildly, erratically everywhere at once but seeing nothing.

"Kid's a mess, he found the body. Couldn't even speak to 911, just screamed. He was still screaming when the police arrived. He did blather out that the last thing he did last night was sweep up, so the button is likely new."

Brogan held the baggie so Jacks could see it then handed it back to the deputy. "Get that kid to a hospital, pronto, and take this to the station, to the lab for prints and DNA, when they're done with it see that it gets to Detective Vantarzani."

"Who?" The deputy blinked in bafflement for a few beats then smiled. "Oh, you mean Tarzan. Yes, sir," he spun and hurried off to do as ordered.

"Tarzan, Rocky, Pirate, Pup, shit, Sheriff, I feel like I've fallen into a real live yet deadly comic book," Navarro joked.

His hands resting on his hips, a short grin lifting part of his mouth, Brogan grunted, "Yeah, Jacks. That would make you everyone's toy."

A bark of loud laughter burst from Navarro. "Touché, Sheriff, teach me to have a nickname of a child's game, eh?"

"Hell, Jacks, you can call me Brogan, we seemed to be drownin' in this gruesome puzzle together."

Navarro laughed darkly. "Yeah, they told me this county was like a hive, a honeycomb clustered with sweet things, dirty secrets and deadly stings."

Brogan threw him a perturbed look with a mocking grunt. "Apt description. You ever hear of the Kissing Number?"

"No. What is it?"

Brogan glanced at him, cracked a brief grin. "Never mind, hive's better."

They started walking, Navarro asked, "So, what's next?"

Brogan headed for his truck. "I don't know about you but I'm fixin' to stop by and see my filly for a minute while I wait for my reports to come in." At Jacks' grin, the sheriff long-legged it across the walk and jumped in behind the wheel.

Jacks and Pompeii turned back to wait until the CSI were done then the dog could sniff around.

The sheriff was surprised to see a Rolls Royce parked in Coli's driveway when he pulled up. Leaving the Stetson in his truck, his boots crunched over the gravel as he strode up the drive. When he reached the house, the porch door opened onto the verandah and Kip popped out. His grin joyful, the teen hopped down the steps and trotted right to Brogan.

"Mr. Sheriff!" he practically yelled.

A seldom seen smile softened Brogan's hard face, pulled in the dimple on one side. "Hey there, Kip. What's goin' on?"

Kip grinned at him, tucked his fingers in his back pockets and dug the toe of his boot in the gravel, snickered. "Nuthin'."

Brogan looked off to the house. "Uh huh, call me Brogan. You and Coli got some company, boy?"

Kip's grin turned to a grimace. "No, just my mama and granma, Grandfather Auston and some guy."

"A guy?" Brogan felt a tightness grip his chest, did Coli have a beau visiting? "Is he, ah, here to see your Aunt Coli?"

"Dunno, just some guy." Losing interest, Kip proclaimed, "Hey, you wanna see the garden I'm digging for Cotty?"

Not sure if he should stay or go, Brogan stared up at the Victorian. A sign attached over the verandah brought a small smile to his hard face.

Coli had put up a sign, it read, *Colipatra's Inn* with curlicues around the words. Hell, he would have to see for himself

if some other guy usurped his claim on her. "How 'bout a little later, Kip. Can you take me inside?" He started walking towards the house.

Kip bounded up next to him. "They prolly know you're here, Mr. Sheriff, 'cause we're way out we can hear when a car comes. That's cool, huh?"

"Yeah, that's cool, Kip." Brogan asked Kip to bring him inside, but he took one step over the three wooden steps to the verandah ahead of him, his boots thumping over the blue-planked floor, and he opened the screen door, Kip had left the big door open.

Brogan tramped inside then stopped a few feet in. "Can you go get your aunt for me, Kip?" He didn't feel right traipsing through her home.

"Okay," Kip chirped from behind him and scurried through the foyer and disappeared into a hallway.

His hands on his hips, Brogan gazed around admiring the work Coli had done on the house since the last time he was there. She'd had gilded lamps with warm golden glows attached to the walls making the blush and champagne colored open foyer soft yet vibrant and welcoming.

"So, you must be the officer Kip rambled on about whilst Silina and her sister were outside." The deep, cool, accented voice came from another arched doorway. Except for his white shirt, the man was dressed in all black, suit coat, slacks, pointed toed boots, even his hair and eyes were like oily onyx.

Brogan turned slowly towards him and the two males appraised each other. Brogan with a rigid jaw and hooded eyes; the man with an upward bend of one side of his full, sharply carved mouth in a slight smirk. When Brogan didn't respond, the smirk deepened.

"I am Ricardo Bastile," he announced and waited with an arched black brow, but the sheriff remained silent, looking through the man as if he wasn't there. The brow lowered in aloof annoyance at Brogan's rudeness.

"Brogan!" Coli's happy voice called out as she entered the foyer. She started to walk quickly to him, but then her ingrained shyness slowed her step with self-consciousness.

The dimple nicked in with his smile that flashed then faded. His low voice soft he greeted her, "Hey Cubbie-doll," his gaze flicked in question to Ricardo and back to her.

She frowned at Ricardo's smirk, her forehead knit, sounding unsure, serious, she asked Brogan, "Are you here to see me, or…for something else."

The half-smile returned bringing the dimple, he said, "For you, baby, only for you."

A smile like the sun brought out her brilliant beauty. He held his arms out, and she hurried across the floor and into them. Wrapping his big arms around her in an embrace, he pushed his nose into her hair and breathed in her honeysuckle fragrance.

Coli's hands rode up his chest to curl around his neck. Oblivious to Ricardo's presence, Brogan cupped the side of her face and seized her mouth like he was a drowning man and she was vital air.

Slanting his head, Brogan clamped their lips, lashed and whipped his tongue over every lush inch of her mouth then went after her tongue and sucking it he crushed her against him, her breasts soft pillows smashed into his hard chest, and he smiled inwardly at her breathy moan.

"Oh for fuck's sake, what a slut. Get a room," Silina jeered. She sidled up to Ricardo and tried to worm under his arm. On her toes, she tipped her head back in hopes of Ricardo kissing her like Brogan kissed Coli, with screaming needy, dying passion. But he stiffened and stuck his hand inside his suit coat and took out a pack of cigarettes.

"I'll be outside, I need some air," he grumbled and trod to the door, the screen door squeaked and slammed behind him.

Brogan pulled his mouth from Coli, but his eyes stayed on hers, his hands clasped around her waist, holding her close.

"Really, Coli, what kind of disgusting lewd behavior is that?" Goldie joined the party. She wore a leopard print clingy blouse with yoga pants stretched across her broad beam. "And you, Sheriff," she chastised Brogan, "such indecent conduct for an upright lawman to display."

Coli pushed to release Brogan's embrace, but he held her close, smiled down at her. "Don't let them dictate your feelings, Cubbie. Forget them, they're nothing." Her body trembled in his arms, but she raised her head and gave him her beautiful smile. He murmured, "Who's the creep?"

She turned her head. "Oh, you mean Grandfather Auston? He's the-"

"No baby," he said, "Ricardo priss-pants," he nipped her lips. He was chill now, the guy couldn't mean anything to her if she kissed Brogan like she did in front of him. If the situation was reversed, Brogan would have smashed the dickwad's nose in.

"Oh." She smiled against his lips. "He's Silina's new boyfriend."

"Hmm, that was a quick mourning period for her fiancé." Still holding her, he set her back a bit with a frown. "Why are they here?"

Her features stiffened, eyes lowered. "They came for, you know, I told you they were coming for a visit. It's just," she sighed, "sooner than I expected."

His fingers slid up then around the back of her neck, he raised her chin with his thumb. "I stopped by, I just had to see you, but I gotta go to work, honey, but, if you need me, for anything, anytime, you don't hesitate to call me, you got that, yeah?"

She nodded, he brought his mouth down on hers and captured her lips, her tongue, her breath, her body turned to molten gold, melting against him. After a minute he lifted his head with a smile. "I gotta go now before I toss you over my shoulder and haul you up the stairs to your bedroom."

A shy grin raised her pink cheeks. "I don't know if I'd try to stop you, Brogan." Her fingers stroked the back of his neck, caressed his hair.

Finally, she was into him, her touch was maddening, like body blasting dynamite, he wanted her to never stop. His chuckle deep and low, Brogan whispered, "When those...guests of yours are gone, you're on, baby, you're on." He kissed her again, then took her hand, and deaf to Silina and Goldie's relentless disparaging

226

comments, he pulled her outside with him. When he stepped off the porch something squeaked.

Looking down, he saw Douggie's rabbit toy under his foot. And next to the toy was a rubber bone with a plaid bow tied around an end. Apparently the puppy dude dug plaid.

The rabbit wore a chewed red and blue plaid suit, the bone's bow was green and blue. Rubbing the shadow of whiskers on his tough jaw, he said with a grin, "Those were not there before, that dog does that shit on purpose."

Coli laughed, bent and tossed the toys up on the verandah.

"Listen, ah, Coli…" he didn't want to break the mood, but it wouldn't be right for her to hear about Polito on the news. She smiled so prettily up at him for a second he forgot what he was going to say. "Uh, Pete Polito," he said and she nodded with mild puzzlement. He continued, "He was found dead today, ah, murdered."

Her mouth dropped, lashes flew up to her hairline. "What? No!" Shaking her head, blonde curls flew across her back in denial. "It can't be, I just saw him what, a week or two ago?"

He lifted his hand and palmed the back of her head, stroked down the length of her hair. "Yeah, baby, it's true."

Blinking in confusion, she whispered, "Brogan, what's going on? Who is doing all this- this horror?"

He smiled calmly at her. "It's nothing for you to worry about, Cubbie-doll, we're pretty sure it all has to do with criminal activity. Some folks have gotten involved with the wrong people and paid the price." He kept out the part about her and Silina's father, Thorne Arabat's involvement.

Arabat had been sick for a long time when he lived out of the country, but his boat, which the deceased Ellery Delian had confiscated, had been used to transport the guns. Pirate had studied the GPS on the boat and was able to track it from where it picked up the guns in Singapore and brought them to Builu.

There was no indication that the Arabat women had knowledge of any part of the gun trafficking. The grandfather's involvement is still iffy, they're still looking into him.

"But Pete? I can't believe he would-"

"I know, yeah, he seemed kinda, passive. But," he shrugged his big shoulders, "you never know who gets involved in heavy stuff when money is the treat. Let's stow this crap for now, it doesn't affect you, or any other upstanding citizen, okay?"

At her uncertain smile, he couldn't resist and pecked her nose, her cheek, her lips.

Forcing himself to step away from her, Brogan tilted his head back and squinted at the dark indigo clouds rumbling, thickening, and shrouding the mountain peaks. "Storm's a'brewin', day or so off I'd guess. Looks like it's gonna be a big one. Maybe a dangerous one."

Coli followed his gaze, her pupils enlarged in dismay at the sight of the bruising sky. "Wow, it looks fearsome. Silina told us about these apocalyptic storms that come when it's really hot and dry. But I suppose we don't need to worry, it's still spring, it's not hot enough for one of those dreadful storms."

His eyes back on her, he clasped her hand and said, "The heat has been scorching the last two days, it's dry and airless, with the storm hitting the heat, it's ripe for tornadoes. Make sure when the storm grows close, you and Kip stay inside, in a windowless room. Preferably the basement. You understand?"

Joy beautified the smile she aimed up at him, she squeezed his hand. Seeing her not taking his warning seriously, he frowned, "Listen, Coli, I'm serious. These storms are nothing to sneeze at. They can be deadly. Don't make me have to worry about you guys out here. Promise me at the first raindrop you and Kip seek shelter, right?" He drew their clasped hands up and kissed her knuckles.

A grin split her face. "Of course, Brogan, I would never let Kip be in danger. Please don't worry about us."

At his truck, he cupped her face, kissed her hard then gentle, and climbed in his truck. Through the open window he said, "Remember, don't let the bastards get you down, Coli, let it stream off your back. Seek shelter when the storm nears. If you need me, call me, I'll be here, okay?"

Her smile sweet, she whispered, "Okay. Be safe, Brogan."

He backed down the drive, his tires spitting gravel.

When he took off to hit the highway miles away, he stuck his hand out the window in a wave.

CHAPTER TWENTY-FOUR

When Brogan woke a day later, as had been happening daily now, his thoughts, his hot steaming dreams were of Coli. He wondered how she was doing with those fishwife relatives of hers. Every time he called her and asked her how things were going she had just mumbled, "Fine" and asked him how the investigation was moving.

Sitting up in bed with a yawn, he tried to push Coli out of his brain, he had murders to solve, dammit. But her pretty face kept wandering back in.

He grabbed a coffee and an egg and sausage biscuit on the way to the station. After he parked, he scanned the distant mountains, it appeared they were being eaten up by thunderclouds. With the storm skulking closer, the cloying air seared like an electric blanket, it was like sucking down scorched sand.

Once he was inside, he sucked in the cool AC and hung his hat on the rack by the door. Giving a wave of greeting to Minnie then a few deputies he made his way to his office.

Elbow deep in paperwork, Brogan didn't hear the knock. When a chair scraped the floor, he looked up, and sat back. Setting his pen down, he quirked a brief grin at the FBI agent. "Hey, whatsup?"

Jacks lowered his muscled body to the chair and leaned back. Resting an ankle across a knee, he shifted his suit coat out from under his butt and rearranged his tie that had gone askew when he

sat down. "You had your dispatch call me, you tell me whatsup." He grinned back.

"Oh, you're gonna like this, Navarro," Brogan goaded.

Resting his forearms on the arms of the chair, Jacks cocked his head at the sheriff. "I hadn't pegged you as a teasing kind of guy, Sheriff. Spill it."

Brogan set his elbows on his desk and threaded his fingers, smugly smirking behind them. "Remember we appropriated Ellery Delian's phone and both home and office computers?"

Jacks nodded faintly. "Yes, your hacker said he couldn't find anything on them." His dark brows twitched in curiosity.

"That's right. But one of his co-workers had reported that he thought he'd seen Delian hauling around another laptop, but we could never locate, or confirm it. We sent Dam in to further question staff about anything to do with Delian, had they seen any strangers around, had Delian seem nervous, any changes at work, all the regular inquiries."

Impatiently, Jacks said, "I got it, the person who said they'd seen the other computer blabbed more. What happened?"

His grin widening, Brogan sat back and picked up his pen. Rolling it through his fingers, he said, "My my, don't they teach you patience at FBI school? You're supposed to mutely stare me down until I anxiously cough up all I know."

"You can be a real bastard, Sheriff, you know?" Navarro bantered with a matching, mocking grin.

"Yeah, been told. Anyway, Dam is dynamite getting information from the females, and he intimidates the males. They end up telling him all their deepest darkest secrets, things that have nothing to do with the investigations."

Jacks waved his hand up at him to speed it up.

With a chuckle, Brogan told him, "Okay, what a baby," he rolled his eyes with a smirk. "The one guy pointed the finger at another associate and he broke down under Dam's grilling and about puked with nerves as he came clean.

"The skell admitted that when he heard Delian was murdered, he stole his laptop thinking he could get Delian's client list and all

their information, and then take them all over instead of them being evenly disbursed amongst the other associates. He found his password in his date book."

"But the executive directors would know who his clients were. What was the point?"

"Yeah, they would know the clients but not their specifics. Apparently there is a ton of data, numbers, accounts, personal information, bunch of shit that string like cobwebs between Delian and his clients. No one would know all that except Delian.

"This thief thought he could just step into Delian's murdered shoes and carry on with his clientele, tell their boss he should have the accounts because he knew very specific details about them. He would lie and tell the boss Delian gave him the info, keep under wraps Delian's notes and records so no one else but him would have access to them."

Jacks narrowed his eyes at his new friend. "All right, somehow I'm thinking there's more, something that would interest *me*. Out with it."

His laugh like a clap surprised both of them, Brogan grinned. "Oh yeah, son, oh yeah. Little did the thief know that there was nothing on the computer about his clients. It was all emails and notes, names and accounts of people he was involved in with gun trafficking. And talk about specific details such as dates and places, photos of meets, you name it, it's there."

Navarro sat up in his chair and shifted to the edge of it, eyes bright and eager. "Oh, fuck what? Give it to me."

Brogan nodded keenly, enthusiasm filling his face and voice, he said, "Yeah, bro, it's all there. A guy, Thorne Arabat, you know, you've heard us talk about those shrews, Silina and Goldie Arabat?"

He made a face. "Yes. Other than walking Pompeii through their home when they were kept outside, I'm damned glad I wasn't involved with having to question those bitches."

"Huh," Brogan snorted in agreement. "You called that one right. The associate that had the laptop was terrified to let anyone know he had it. Both because he would get fired and also because he feared the traffickers would come after him.

"Anyway, so, Delian recorded that this Arabat purchased, and apparently smuggled the weapons into the country, Singapore was the latest he shipped from. That big boat we thought at first was Delian's we learned it was really Arabat's, and that was how they brought them here. Delian had worked with Arabat, that's why he knew he was dying and that he'd leave his fortune to one of the daughters.

"He had assumed incorrectly at first that it was the youngest that would inherit it all because Thorne had spoken with affection about her to Ellery. And he went after her."

Brogan's brows daggered down in a scowl at the hell Ellery Delian had put Coli through until he realized Silina would get the bulk of the estate. Thank God her father left the money to Silina, it got Coli away from the abusive bastard. Arabat was quite clever, it's likely he did it all on purpose.

"Thing is," Brogan's grin crookedly evil, he said, "when Goldie and Silina find out all of the ill-gotten money Thorne and Delian procured, and they inherited, will be taken by the government, you're gonna want to duck that explosion of female wrath, yeah?

"I think it was a last laugh on Arabat's part to Goldie and Silina. He knew eventually the law would figure it all out. He's sitting there in hell, laughing his ass off that God giveth and God taketh away. Sweet revenge on a woman and daughter he despised." Coli's house would be safe, it had been passed down in the family for generations. He chuckled. "That dang dog of yours was right, the guns had been on the boat."

"Yes," Jacks agreed, smiling smugly with pride for his dog. "I hope you added to the warrant that Pompeii detected a positive when I took him around the exterior of Palumbo's restaurant?"

Brogan nodded with a short laugh. "Oh yeah. Judge refused to sign the warrant even with all our information. The K-9 indicating the positive scent of gun powder pulled the judge over the edge for probable cause and he signed with a twitching mouth and shake of his head."

"That's my fella, I told you he was good," Jacks said proudly. "And I bet Pompeii was right about the gallery too?"

Brogan grinned large. "Yep. According to Delian's notes the guns were stored in Delian's love shack and the gallery, then they were transported to Palumbo's restaurant basement where they were, are, eventually dispersed, trafficked. He kept concise records so there would be no confusion in what went where and who got paid what."

Navarro jumped to his feet. "Damn, all that on his computer? What a stupid loser. If he was still alive, Palumbo would have him killed for putting it all at risk."

Nodding with a sly smile, Brogan pushed a paper across the desk to the agent. "We don't have the proof yet, but yeah, it's all pointing to Palumbo. Rex Reno and Dane Zachary were up to their necks with Palumbo and the guns, and I think maybe they caught Kandy-Marie snoopin' around the gallery's basement when she found the guns and knocked her off to keep her quiet.

"I had a rush on the blood and nail DNA we found, and I got a text a while ago from our lab, it was verified as we had assumed, it was Kandy-Marie's. That Poppy girl probably knows more than she let on, that's why she ran, she figured she'd be next."

"And Palumbo ordered Delian's hit. The other girl, Blanco," Navarro mused, "you think she was killed because she knew too much as well?"

"Likely." Brogan shrugged. "Palumbo's dickhead son flashed his guns to every chick that came within his radius thinking they made him look badass, dangerous, and therefore hot."

"I need to go to Palumbo's, Sheriff." Jacks picked the paper up off the desk and read it. "Hell, you've already sent the swat teams on it." He tossed the paper on the desk. "I'm going there, this is my bust, Brogan."

"It is. They're waiting for you, on your order to hit the raid." Brogan stood up, his phone rang. He waved Navarro on, told him, "Go on, I'll meet you there."

Jacks hurried to the door, over his shoulder he grinned. "I owe you, man, first drink's on me!"

Laughing, Brogan reached for his phone answering, "Yeah, Dillon here."

A young voice came through the phone, "Hi Sheriff Dillon, I'm a tech in the lab, Porsha Reyes, how are you?"

A groan rumbled in his chest, pleasantries made him so impatient. "Yes, hello there Ms. Reyes, what can I do for you?"

"Um, well, we ran those hairs that were found on the victim Ellery Delian, and there were more, Dr. Martone told the CSI to bag at the Polito scene. We ran 'em through the multiplex PCR system. You know, it amplifies DNA sequences that-"

"Miss, uh, Reyes, skip the techno jabber and tell me straight out. What did you find?"

She was quiet. Another groan rumbled, he had hurt her feelings. Women. So thin-skinned. Men were so much easier, you can curse, and piss and insult and, "Miss-"

"Yes, sir," she said stiffly, "they were definitely animal hairs."

He waited, they already figured that. When she didn't go on, he cleared his throat and said, "Miss Reyes, continue. Please."

A not subtle sniff, and she said, "They were dog hairs."

He waited, again. When she didn't go on he urged her, "Miss Reyes, I have things to do, just tell me everything you discovered, quickly, please."

This time her huff came through. "Fine. Geez, I'm just doing my job." He was about to rip her a new one when she said, "Through more forensic applications we were able to identify the breed of the dog." Before he could bark at her to go on, she rushed, "Specifically bulldog. More precisely, French bulldog." After her dramatic revelation, the tech waited eagerly for the sheriff's praise, instead, he disconnected.

Brogan stumbled backwards, his butt hitting his desk. Too stunned to take it in. French bulldog. "How many damned French bulldogs can there be in Builu County, that were both near Delian and Polito?" His palm slapped against his forehead, his head was spinning. No wait, Delian and Polito both had been near Coli, the dog hairs could have easily transferred.

Before he could accept what he was just told, he heard a commotion. Winnie's voice was loud, she was almost shouting. He

moved to the door to see what was going on and came up short when Silina Arabat blew into his office.

"Miss Arabat," he set his hands on his hips asking, "what the hell is going on?" He needed to talk to Coli, he didn't need her sister's shit now.

Silina took a moment to run her eyes up and down his body not bothering to conceal her blatant interest. She held a bag in her hand. Wiping her face clear of the vampy ogle, a solemn sadness took over, she said, "I hate to have to do this, Sheriff, but…"

God save him from melodramatic teeth pulling females. "Ms. Arabat, please, I have to be somewhere."

"Okay, slow down big boy. I," she took a huge shaky breath, let it out, "I really hate to do this, I mean," her eyes dipped down, so sad, so regretful, "she is my sister after all."

"Coli? Has something happened to Coli?" He almost grabbed her arm in frightened aggravation. The thoughts that suddenly plagued him scared the hell out of him. His Cubbie-doll in trouble? Danger?

Silina pulled him out of his horrible ponderings. "Here," she reached in the bag and pulled out a can. She held it out to him, stated, "I found this in Coli's trash."

Brogan stared at the can of varnish in her hand. "What the hell is that?" Anger and fear chomped at his gut, he had to go see her.

"It's varnish, Sheriff. The news said that that girl, Camille something was poisoned with it."

Blinking blankly at the can, he muttered, "What are you giving it to me for?"

The sadness and regret flared to fierce anger, streaks of livid red speared her thin cheeks in her rapidly darkening face. Clenching the can in her fist, the other fist she raised and shook as she bellowed, "She killed my fiancé!"

Brogan took a step back. "Miss-"

Her face screwed up with rage, she leaned into him and screamed, "She murdered my beloved fiancé! I-" Some of the strength deflated from her wrath, she drank in a heaving breath. "I mean, I love my sister, but- but," the rage boiled over again, she

threw the can at his desk shrieking, "she killed the only man I ever loved and she shouldn't get away with it!"

The can clanked on the wood then clattered rolling across it to come to a stop against a thick file. Brogan couldn't think straight, his angel, he pictured Coli's soft face, her shy smile, the tenderness in her caress when he lay shattered on the road that day, the gentle way she treats Kip. "No, she couldn't-"

Silina snapped, "Yes she could, and she did. It's not like she hasn't tried to kill before," she stroked the pads of her fingertips over her stiff yellow hair and sniffed. "She went to prison, you remember, a felon convicted of attempted murder."

Her eyes closed to mere slits, she sneered, "Yeah, my- uh brother almost died because of her jealousy. And now," she sniffed harder and wiped the drip off the end of her pointy nose with the back of her hand. "She's done it again, only this time she actually killed people. That girl, and Ellery, my poor, poor sweetheart," sobs suddenly hacked in her chest.

"Ah." Scrubbing his nails down his face, Brogan moaned, then said coldly to Silina, "Kip is your son, Ms. Arabat."

Her head shot up. Blinking a tear back at his ire Silina denied it, "No, he's- he's, never mind," she shook her head exasperated. "You have to do something, Sheriff, before she hurts another person!"

She reached out and clutched his shirt with both hands. "Listen to me, the news said that paint store guy, Peter- Peter Polito is dead. She dated him! When Kip ran into my boyfriend Ricardo in the library he told him that Ricardo better not hurt Coli like that other guy, that Pete guy did or he'd be taken care of. You see? She's a black widow, Sheriff, you have to do something! What if we're next! We're not safe in our beds!"

He pried her grabby fingers off his shirt, and said coolly, "That's easy to fix, just get the hell out of her house and go home to yours and lock your doors. I gotta go," he about threw her hands away from him.

Silina glared at him, astounded that he would speak to her like that. The tip of her nose shaped like a flathead screwdriver turned

neon pink. Her jaw worked side to side, eyes slit to glowering yellowish peas. "Fine," Crossing her arms, her chin in the air she announced, "Mark my words, you'll fuck her and she'll stab you while you sleep!"

Dark red raged up the back of his neck, he bent and set his knuckles on his desk, shoulders hunched, and leaned towards her. Voice deep, calm, he said quietly, "You need to leave, Ms. Arabat, now."

She was smart enough to see she'd pushed the edge of the envelope. Sheriff Dillon looked fit to be tied, his eyes disappeared under furious lids, mouth a grit line. Silina shut her mouth and stood stock still.

"*Now*!" he snarled through his teeth with blistering wrath.

Not wanting sheriff fury detonating all over her, Silina backed away. She didn't dare say another word, but letting out a peeved huff she scurried out of his office.

Brogan took a few minutes to clamp his rage, gnaw back the curses in his clenched throat he wanted to fling at her fleeing big butt. His hands still on the desk, he let his head fall forward while he sucked in deep breaths.

When he felt he was back in calm control, Brogan lifted the landline and called a lab tech.

The lab was next door, it took five minutes for the tech to arrive. A pretty young woman with caramel skin knocked lightly on the doorframe then entered his office with a polite, "You called for a CSI, sir?" Her hair was styled short with wide wavy spikes on top and cut shorter on the sides. Her perky grin split wide and friendly.

Still fighting his anger he had to work to ease the tension in his face and soften his voice. "Yes." He pointed to the can on his desk. "Bag that and take it to the lab, I want chemical makeup and fingerprints, DNA if there is any. Priority, got it?"

Her wide mouth settled into a professional smile. "Yes, sir." She bagged the can of varnish and was gone in a blink.

He was about to leave when Pirate strolled in carrying a file folder. "Lo, what's up?" Brogan couldn't help the impatience that snapped in his tone.

It didn't bother Pirate, emotions were foreign matter to him, he simply didn't care. "Here's the dump on Ellery Delian, Kandy-Marie Birchfield, Petra Peerina and Camille Blanco's phones," he handed the file to the sheriff.

Taking it, Brogan said, "Give me the gist." He opened the file and read along as Pirate spoke.

Pirate sat a hip on the corner of the desk and crossed his arms. As usual he was all in black. He pushed his black-framed glasses up his forehead making short black locks spear up. "Okay, start with Petra Peerina. Nothing odd, just calls to and from family, a few girlfriends, numerous outgoing calls to burner phones of Rex Reno and Dane Zachary. Peerina verified they were the numbers she had for them. They increased to about fifty a day the week after your first visit there, none were incoming."

"Yeah, the men had disappeared the next day, she told me she tried relentlessly to reach them."

"We still haven't found anything on Reno and Zachary, no real phone numbers, addresses, papers. Ah, there were a ton of calls on Kandy-Marie Birchfield's phone to and from men. We tracked them down, buncha one night stands." The edge of his mouth kinked drily with a shade of disgust, he said, "And I mean a *buncha,* like hundreds, bro."

Brogan nodded. "That's about what her folks said, she liked the men."

"Understatement," Pirate muttered. "Kind of the same pattern for the Camille Blanco vic. Some girlfriends, a lot of males. I put a buncha deputies and CSA's on it, we were able to track and clear them. All of the people we questioned had alibis for both vics' murders. Blanco's phone had calls connecting with Tonto Palumbo."

Brogan's brows peaked. "Oh yeah?" He dropped onto his chair and wheeled it to the desk and set the open file down. "But, that's no surprise, we knew they dated. What about texts? We can read the data, right?"

One shoulder bumped, Pirate replied, "We did. Mostly sexts. Geesh, Brog, they texted shit back and forth that would make your

hair curl," a rare curve raised the side of his tough mouth, "and other things too."

The men shared a chuckle. Pirate sobered quickly, laughter wasn't his thing. "Anyway, nothing regarding guns or his father, no business, just their monkey business."

"Okay. What about Delian?"

The smile appeared again briefly but triumphant. "The shit's there, Brog, calls with old man Palumbo, Palumbo's men, we can prove their connection. Unfortunately there were no texts we could obtain, they were careful not to put anything in writing. Next is up to you to prove Palumbo ordered Delian's hit."

Brogan grunted. "Workin' on it. Anything else?" He thumbed through the file, flipped a paper, skimmed it, then moved to another.

Pirate slid off the desk to his feet, folded his muscled arms over his broad chest. "Blanco's stomach contents came in. Cuisses de grenouille." He smirked at the baffled look on Brogan's face. "Frog's legs. Specifically, sautéed in lemon and garlic parsley butter."

Brogan's lips twisted. "Why would anyone pay to eat something slimy that hops out of a swamp?"

Pirate's head fell back with a loud laugh. Swiping a hand over his mouth, he grinned at Brogan's grossed out expression. He said with a small snicker, "Apparently it was served with saffron rice." Then his face straightened back to its regular hard, blank mask.

"Uh, yeah, still gag." Brogan's upper lip curled. He said, "Can't be many places serving frog legs. Martone told us the vic likely died early in the morning. Who eats frog legs for breakfast?"

"Gross at any time. But," Pirate offered, "with the tequila and Triple Sec also found, I'm thinking margaritas, it's more likely after a night of drinking she probably went out for a very, very late dinner. We need to find a restaurant that stays open late and serves frog legs."

Brogan reviewed the rest of the file then closed it, leaving it on his desk. "Okay, good job. Get Dam on it." He got up and fished his truck keys from his pocket. "Keep in touch, I have to go to Palumbo's restaurant."

"I heard about the raid, at least something is jelling, eh?" Pirate walked with him until they got to the bullpen then Pirate went down a hall and Brogan out to his vehicle.

CHAPTER TWENTY-FIVE

As Brogan hustled along the street, his heart told him to go to Coli's, but his head made him drive to the swat scene. The dog hairs were explainable, and she was remodeling the Victorian, stripping wood and re-glazing so varnish would be expected. It's common, not an exotic element like cyanide. No need to jump to suspicious conclusions.

When he arrived on the scene, there was a massive jumble of police cars, vans, huge black hummers, and bomb squad trucks containing integral mesh cages. The festivities were mostly over by the time he pulled up, parked and hopped out.

A crowd of police hustled around the restaurant. Brogan could see the front doors had been plowed open with a metal ram, one was hanging by one hinge. People teeming in the street shrieking in excitement were corralled, held back by police and ropes.

Double lines of officers flanked the main walk leading up to the restaurant, and men were being shepherded out of the building like they were walking the gauntlet. Hands cuffed behind their backs, heads down or turned away from the jeering throng, they shuffled through, dragging shoes on the stone walk. Brogan spotted Jacks, he made his way over to him.

Navarro was standing in a circle of suits like him along with uniformed officers, he looked up and grinned at Brogan's approach. Brogan muscled through the crowd to reach him. When he did, they bumped fists.

"How'd it go?" Brogan asked him while watching the men being led out of the restaurant. The thugs he'd seen the other day slunk by, trussed up and heads down. Tonto Palumbo was already being shoved into a police van.

Palumbo's barked furious complaints and curses shouted from the open doors at the back of the van. Several girls in skimpy outfits and high heels jiggled and giggled as they were trundled along.

His grin couldn't get bigger, Navarro puffed his chest out, said with the victorious pride of a hard win, "It was great, bro, they bashed the door in, wood chunks flew everywhere. Those beefy thugs came pounding out the door, then froze when they saw an army of guns aimed at them. The cops restrained them then the swat teams burst inside, you could hear the hollering and screaming all the way out here.

"I went in after the first team, we found the guns in the lead-lined basement. Stacks and stacks of crates of them, just like I knew! Palumbo plays big with other people's lives, but he's a coward. He'll roll over on his source and traffickers in a heartbeat."

Brogan nudged him with his elbow and jutted his chin towards the restaurant. Cheers and boos rose from the crowd, from other business owners, rubber-neckers as well as police.

Vitale Palumbo was being escorted out. His wrists bound behind his back, a cop on either side of him held his arms. He was cursing, and spitting, threatening and screeching, he looked up just as he was led past Brogan.

Brogan gave him a two-finger salute off the brim of his hat, and had to bite back the jolt of glee at the look on Palumbo's face. The mobster's heavy face was mottled red, flames of murderous fury torched from his ears.

As the police dragged him by, he screamed, "You motherfucking puissant! I'll get you for this! You'll pay, you hear me?" He was almost past when Jacks waggled cheery fingers at him with a huge grin and said, "Tootles, Vitale. Keep in touch, send us a note, we'd love to hear how you're loving your new life!"

Palumbo's face ballooned maroon like he was having an apoplexy, he shrieked all the way down the walk and they could still hear him when he was shoved into the back of the van.

Brogan hung around until all of the people in the restaurant had been ushered out and locked up. He brought Jacks up to date on the information Pirate had relayed.

When SWAT started bringing out the crates of guns and loading them into trucks, Brogan told Navarro he had somewhere to go. They fist bumped their victory again, made a plan to get together for drinks, and he climbed in his truck.

Aiming the truck towards the highway, Brogan put his phone in a holder, put it on speaker and told Alexa to call the lab. When someone answered, he said, "This is Sheriff Dillon, I need to speak to whoever was testing the solution that poisoned Camille Blanco."

Speeding out of the city, he hurtled past the suburbs and hit the open highway. Groves of trees paraded by before he entered the sprawling grasslands. Farms and crop fields flew past in a blur.

Someone said, "Hello? Sheriff Dillon?"

Clearing his throat, he gruffed, "Yeah. You got what killed Camille Blanco?"

"Yes, sir. It was plain varnish. It appears to be a common generic type."

He felt his heart squeeze, it was hard to draw a breath. "Okay. What about Peter Polito?"

Papers rustled, he heard computer keys tapping, then the response, "Nothing yet, sir."

Brogan thanked her and kept going towards Mal Tierre. By the time he passed the pastures of blue cornflowers and reached Wisteria Road, he had calmed down, telling himself Coli was in no way involved with any of the malevolent crap that was going on in Builu County. It was Palumbo, Rex Reno, and Ellery Delian, and whatever henchmen were in between.

Her car was in the driveway, he pulled up the gravel drive and parked behind it. Acrid heat smacked his face as he left the truck. It seemed to be even hotter here than in Lupo where the police station

was located. Maybe with Coyote Lake nearby the station it added some humidity to the steaming air.

He expected to see Kip come flying out. With the bank loan, Coli only worked at the bar two days a week and she could be more present for the teen. Thank God that scumbag SOB boss of hers was out of the country with some family issue, and she was working the catering side, not inside the saloon.

His boots hit the blue planked floor of the verandah. He noticed she had added a few more pieces of white wicker furniture and a couple of rocking chairs. The more time he spent at the Colipatra Inn, the more he really liked it. Coli had an eye to what guests would aesthetically enjoy.

The door opened and Coli greeted him with a pleased smile. "Brogan, hey, glad to see you!" She held the screen door open for him to enter the mansion.

Once inside, his instant urge was to kiss her, he fought it, and the arousal that started the second he laid eyes on her.

When he didn't kiss her, she stepped back, brows crinkled in a frown. "Are you mad at me, Brogan?"

Realizing his face reflected his harsh thoughts, he cleared the tightness from his jaw, eased the pinching around his eyes. "No, no, not at all, I just have to, ah, ask you a few questions."

Dressed in a creamy blouse and jeans, she clinched her hands in front of her, the smile wilted, turned wary. "Questions about what?"

His hands itched to touch her, he went to cross his arms over his chest but didn't, he was already so much bigger than her he didn't want to intimidate her. His hands came to rest loosely on his hips.

Glancing at the woodwork she had so laboriously stripped and stained, polished, he sighed. "The wood that you finished, the baseboards," he jutted his chin in the direction of the grand staircase, "the bannister, floors, tables," he paused, his gaze returning to her.

Clearly puzzled, she asked, "What about them?"

Drumming his fingers on his hips, he asked, "The paint stripper you used, what brand was it?"

Her forehead wrinkled. "I didn't use any chemical strippers, I sanded everything."

Glancing around again incredulous, he exclaimed, "You sanded every lick of wood in this Inn by hand?"

Fingers latched in front of her, she twisted them with a shrug. "Sure. I read that harsh stripping stuff can be toxic, I was worried about Douggie. It was good work, tired me so I didn't reflect on…things."

"You worked yourself to exhaustion so you could pass out at night without memories swimming through your head." It was a statement, not a question. He'd done the same thing himself.

She nodded reticently.

"Okay, do you still have the sandpaper, sander, whatever you used?"

Mouth firming, her head cocked. "I, yeah, sure. I keep all the supplies and equipment like that in the cellar locked in a cabinet. I don't want Kip or any guests coming in contact with them. What's this about, Brogan?" Her voice cautious, fingers twisted harder.

Not answering the question, he asked her another, "What about varnish? What brand did you use to stain the wood, or, you know, polish, shellac, whatever it is?"

Shaking her head in bewilderment, she told him, "I didn't use any, I used tung oil and buffed afterwards some by hand and some with a buffing machine. Brogan-"

The breath visibly eased from his tight lungs, a smile broadened. "Never mind, Cubbie-doll, it's nothing, just a curiosity. Where is your, and I use the term loosely, your family? Kip?"

Finally her pretty smile reappeared. "The family has gone out to dinner, I wasn't invited, and Kip is at the Gregorys'."

Wiggling his brows suggestively, he said with a side smirk, "You mean we have the house to ourselves?" At that moment his stomach growled, he spread his hand over it with an embarrassed grin.

"Okay," she laughed, "let me get you something to eat, then, perhaps we can…"

"Get to know one another better, closer, more intimately?" Brogan grasped her hands and pulled her to him. Once her breasts crushed against the slabs of chest he gripped the hair at the back of her head and pulled it, forcing her neck to arch, her lips to part, and he lowered his head and fed on her mouth. He was grinding his hips against hers when his stomach growled again making them break apart with laughter.

"Okay, big boy, come on, let's go to the kitchen." Holding his hand, she drew him to walk beside her through the corridors. She led him to the dining room and told him, "Why don't you have a seat here, I'll bring you some of the roast and potatoes I made last night."

Brogan lounged in a chair, cupped his hands behind his head and closed his eyes and sighed contentedly. His girl was not guilty of any involvement with the Palumbos or the others, she was just a sweet, brave, hardworking, engagingly gorgeous woman.

He sat up and adjusted his jeans. Hoping it wouldn't take her long to prepare the food, he wanted to get the eating out of the way and move on to better things, like her in his arms, and maybe him in her bed. With that thought making his pulse zing and pants tighten, he glanced around the room. She'd made it as pretty and feminine as her.

White lacy tablecloth over a dark pink underlay, the glasses were dark pink and the flower arrangement centerpiece added a flash of color. The sun was still up, mild yellow light streamed through drawn-back drapes of pink and white flowers. The light shone on the china cabinet against the wall. Huge cherry wood with glass doors, Brogan could see the china behind the glass.

His pupils fired, blinking, he stood up and walked over to the cabinet. A slight shake to his hand, he opened one of the doors and lifted out a glass. His gut plummeted with a sharp pang. Holding the glass, he carried it to the kitchen. As soon as he entered, his heart sank and his stomach clenched.

She heard him come in, she looked at him over her shoulder and smiled. A platter of roast and potatoes with a gravy boat beside it and a bowl of corn were on the counter in front of her. "You must

really be hungry, Brogan. It'll only be a few minutes, would you like a drink-" her eyes widened as he opened an antique cutlery case with gold filigree on the counter on the other side of the fridge.

He lifted out a knife, then set it and the glass from the cabinet on the block island. "Hell, Coli…"

She spun around, wiped her hands on her jeans, saw the glass and asked, "Oh? What would you like to drink?"

The glass was leaf etched, the rim was shiny gold. Next to the glass was the knife. It had a pearl handle with flecks of gold, stainless steel blade.

Her hand on the fridge door, she stopped at the stiffness in his face. "Brogan, what's the matter?"

Brogan scraped his fingers through his hair with a labored sigh. Staring down at the glass and knife, he asked, "Do you have a blouse that has pearl buttons?"

"I don't…understand. What is going on?"

"Do you?" His voice so rough and short, she jumped.

"I- I, yes, I do. But I don't-"

"Show it to me."

She just stood, her lips parted, eyes blinking in confusion. "But-"

He gripped her arm and turned her towards the doorway. "Now."

They didn't speak as they traipsed down a short hall to a back staircase that led upstairs. Then they moved up another staircase to the third floor. He stayed one step below her, his hand on her waist.

She brought him to her bedroom far at the end of the hall. When they stepped inside, she said to him, "Brogan, please, tell me what this is about?"

Low and quiet he growled, "Just show me, Coli." There was no flirtation or lightness in his voice.

"Okay." Growing alarmed, she walked across the white and peach rug to a polished mahogany armoire. She opened one of the decoratively curved doors and pushed back several hangers. Reaching towards the back, she pulled out a white blouse and showed it to him. "I've only worn it briefly in the past months as it's

too light for the weather. Well, except now with the heat…" she trailed off at his set face.

It had a frilly collar. Brogan picked up the front of it, his shoulders dropped. The pearls matched the one found at the Polito murder scene, and clearly one button was missing. Cursing under his breath, he set the blouse on the peach and gold comforter on the bed, and grasped her arm and forced her to turn her back to him.

"Brogan?"

He tugged the handcuffs off the back of his belt and clapped one over her wrist. Reaching down, he caught her other hand and pulled it behind her back. Her wrists were so tiny, delicate, he'd only actually ever handcuffed one other woman before, and she had nearly matched his height and weight. Coli felt so fragile in his hands, his heart sickened.

Winding his thick fingers around her slender arm, grabbing up the blouse he walked her to the door while reciting her rights. "Colipatra Cassidy, you are under arrest for suspicion of murder, you have the right to remain silent…"

She tried to halt him by digging her shoes into the rug exclaiming, "No, wait, Brogan, I don't understand, what is going on? Tell me!" He didn't respond to her cries.

Downstairs, he dropped the blouse, glass and knife into a bag and continued pulling her with him out of the house, down the steps and across the path to his truck.

Opening the back passenger door, his voice dark and low, growly as an angry bull, Brogan asked, "Where's Douggie? Do I need to have someone come and care for him? And Kip, when is he expected home?"

Her voice mired in confusion and growing fright, barely audible, she murmured, "I pay Silina to feed Douggie and let him out when I'm not here. Kip will be at the Gregorys' for a couple of nights."

He lifted her and set her in the back seat and buckled her seatbelt then climbed in the front and drove them out of Mal Tierre to Lupo.

Tears streamed down her round cheeks, she cried all the way to the jail, her aching sobs audible in the small space of the cab. She kept asking him what was going on. "Who did I murder, Brogan?" Her voice clogged with tears rose strident the more she asked and the more he remained silent. He couldn't bear to hear her lies or fake denials.

His own heart was breaking, his head spinning. Damn, she had him fooled, so sweet, tender, all an act. The superb act of a murderess, she deserved an award. He didn't, couldn't talk to her. His voice would break along with his heart.

It was a struggle to keep his eyes away from the rear view. One glimpse of her tears and he'd turn right around and take her back home. "I want you to be quiet, Coli, don't say another word until we get, uh, you get an attorney."

Straightening, Brogan cleared his throat and gripped the wheel, he was the sheriff, he couldn't let his feelings get in the way. Even though his feelings were brought upon by her trickery, he couldn't deny them, shut them off. How was he going to be able to lock her in a cell and walk away, leave her there alone, imprisoned, he was so fucked.

When he reached the station, it was almost deserted but he saw several cars in the lot, Pirate was still there burning the midnight oil. The sun was setting when he brought her to the jail behind the station. She'd stopped asking him questions, just cried quietly.

Lifting her out of the truck, he set her on her feet and gripped her arm. Clutching her rigid arm in his tight grasp, he had to actively force himself not to stroke her, comfort her. He pushed the door open and led her inside the jail. Deputy Duff Gillan had his feet up on the desk and his hat over his face, loud snores bubbled from under the hat. His fat belly rose and fell with each snort.

Brogan ushered her to one of the five cells and pulled the door open. Builu's larger jail was closer to the Barriga but on the outskirts.

"No, Brogan, please, I don't understand what's going on, why are you doing this to me?" She pushed away from him again digging

her feet into the floor with her protests. Her face and front of her blouse were wet from her tears.

He couldn't look at her, he'd break down, let her go. And he couldn't do that. There was too much evidence, the glass and knife, the dog hair, the varnish can, the button, *fuck*. Without speaking, he drew her inside, her struggles less than a feather against his hand of iron.

When she was in the cell, he turned her body around so he could remove the cuffs, shifting his eyes from the red rings around her small wrists that she unconsciously rubbed when released.

Tucking the cuffs in his belt, he stepped back from her, moved outside of the cell and closed the door with a clank. Rotating the key that was already in the lock, he turned away from her. He couldn't take it. Partially turning his head without looking at her, he warned, "Bab- ah, Coli, please don't talk to anyone until you have a lawyer."

Peripherally he could see her beautiful face was red and tear-streaked, bewilderment, fear and betrayal flushed pain in her blue eyes. Like the fulminating storm in the blue sky, it ravaged the color, destroyed the brightness, eclipsing the natural glow until the light shut off.

He stomped across the hardwood floor and shoved the deputy's boots off the desk. Duff's feet fell clunking to the floor and he sat up so fast with rattled snorts his hat flew off and he nearly fell with it. "What the fuck-" he sputtered angrily regaining his balance on the chair.

"Deputy Gillan," Brogan ground at him. First he had to arrest his girlfriend, and now he found his lazy ass deputy asleep on the job. The urge to beat him bloody with his fists was overwhelming. He controlled himself with effort. "I've put a prisoner in one of the cells."

Gillan leaned to see around Brogan, and his eyes rounded. "A broad, wow. What'd she do?" He struggled to bring his hefty body to his feet, tugged the belt up his big belly. Wide sausage fingers forked through limp, wheat colored hair, one sausage knuckle slid a swipe under a short, thick nose. His neck and jaw were also thick

and short, eyes like brown jellybeans lit up at the sight of Coli, heavy lips curled up in a glutinous crescent.

"Never mind. Just keep an eye on her. Get her water if she needs it but don't go in her cell, no one comes in back here, and she doesn't come out of the cell."

Brogan stomped close to the deputy, got right in his face and jabbed a strong finger in his flabby chest, he commanded fiercely, "I repeat, you do not go into her cell. Am I clear?" He jabbed his finger hard with emphasis into his chest with each word, "Am- I- clear?" Coli's wretched crying abysmally muffled in the background.

"Uh, yeah, yeah, sure, of course, Boss. No prob, I got this handled." Duff gripped his belt and tugged it higher over his belly, another half inch and he'd have a wedgie into tomorrow.

Brogan didn't move, he stared at the deputy, one he hated to admit he despised. He had no respect for him, he was lazy, cut corners, called in sick a lot, and the sheriff was sure he was involved in illegal activities that at some point, Brogan had plans, when all this murder shit was over, to catch him at.

Until then, he had to leave Coli alone with Gillan as her jailor. And that gave him a real jumpy feeling in his gut, real jumpy.

He got back in the deputy's face. "Anything happens to her, I'll-" He broke off. Threatening his deputy wasn't kosher, but still. "Just, keep her safe, ya hear? And stay away from her." He moved away from Gillan and started for the door. He shouldn't, but, he paused in front of the door and looked back.

She was sitting on the bunk, bowed over with her head in her hands, her small shoulders wracked with heart-wrenching sobs.

It was like a magnet pulled at him, hard, to go to her, get her the hell out of that damned- he shook it off, expelled a heavy breath and strode out the door.

Leaving the jail, Brogan stalked out of the main building and across the front of the station to the other side where the lab was stationed. He had to show ID to the guard posted inside the door even though the man knew he was the sheriff. He faintly inclined his head at the deputy's greeting.

"Hey, Sheriff, how's it goin'?" The man was probably the oldest on staff. His hair was snow white with fuzzy eyebrows to match. Make a nice Santa at Christmas with cherry cheeks and a round nose.

Brogan didn't want to be rude, but he was barely holding it together, he grunted his response. He made his way down a corridor passing offices until he reached the first lab. The lights were on, he went in and was surprised that there were several techs working. They briefly glanced up at his entrance without changing their serious countenance or stopping their work. He said, "Hey, ya'll, ya got anything for me?"

A male tech poked some buttons on a machine that started whirring. He responded with gravity, "We have the poison identified that killed Peter Polito, as well as how it was administered. It was in his coffee."

One brow arched when he didn't continue.

The tech coughed, said, "Oh, the uh poison, it was hyoscyamine, the chief alkaloid occurring in the leaves and the tops of the plant henbane." He jutted his jaw to a paper report lying on the counter.

Brogan asked, "Is this, uh, henbane a local plant?"

The tech nodded, looked at the machine in front of him and jotted down some numbers. "Yes, it's biannual in the spring, has flowers with five yellow petals."

"So, this plant is always deadly?" Picking up the report, Brogan's forehead screwed up as he read it, a picture of the plant was stapled to the back of the report.

"Yes, sir," the young man responded as he swung around on his stool and regarded the sheriff. "In low doses it can be inebriating and actually an aphrodisiac. But," he gestured to the report in Brogan's hand, "in hefty doses, it causes dilated pupils, hallucinations, coma, respiratory paralysis, really nasty convulsions and then…death."

Recalling Polito's grisly twisted body frozen in agony, vomit spewed everywhere, his face battered from slamming on the floor in

convulsions, Brogan said, "I take it Polito was doused with a heavy dose?"

His countenance grave, the tech shoved glasses with wide lenses up his nose and nodded. "Oh yes, sir. Seriously heavy. We've only tested the coffee so far, but it's likely the poison was also in the breakfast sandwich since there was so much found in his body. If it was all in the coffee the victim would have noticed such a strong, weird and likely bitter taste.

"The coffee was loaded with sugar and cream, and the sandwich smelled strongly of spices, hot turmeric and maybe cinnamon, other ingredients like cayenne that might have been added to mask the taste. There was spinach in the sandwich as well and the leaves of the henbane plant had been interspersed with the spinach leaves."

"Uh huh." Brogan set the report down, pawed at his chin and perused the other items on the laminate counter the tech worked at. He pointed at a picture of the half-eaten sandwich.

"At the scene I noticed that the paper around the sandwich was, ah, loose and crumpled, at the time I just assumed it was because the vic was eating it and when he convulsed and fell to the floor. But now…" he picked up the picture. To himself he murmured, "Yeah, it could have been loose and wrinkled because it had been doused and then re-wrapped."

Setting the picture down, he asked, "Exactly what kind of sandwich was it, I mean the ingredients, specifically?"

Pushing his glasses up on his head, the tech pressed his eye against a microscope. He leaned back and picked up the report, lifted the picture up, and read the back of the page under it, "Egg, brioche bread, spinach, horseradish mustard sauce, spicy mayo, tomato, and ozuna sausage."

Brogan rubbed his stomach with a wince, muttered, "Hell, that alone would kill me." He closed his eyes as the words rang familiar. The tech had turned back around returning to the microscope. "Hey kid, you eat much breakfast in the Barriga?"

His glasses still on top of his head while his eye was on the scope, the young man lowered them, looked to Brogan with a casual, "Yes, sure."

"Those ingredients, I'm kinda picturing an ad, a poster or something, with those words, any of it ring a bell with you?"

"Sure, Sheriff. There's a bookstore café on the same street as the paint shop of the victim. It's called Papyrus and Panini. They have photos of the sandwiches extolling their famous, secret recipe mustard sauce, and the sausage is made there by hand. It's actually pretty good if you have a cast iron stomach." He waited, but when Brogan didn't ask anything else, he shoved his glasses back up and turned his attention back to the microscope.

Brogan mumbled a vague, "Thanks." He exited the lab and trekked back to his truck. Climbing in, he pushed images of a frightened, tearful Coli from his mind as he drove off towards the Barriga. He was ten miles away when his gut hurt so bad, his heart cramped, he swung the truck around and drove back to Lupo.

On the way back, he ran the evidence through his mind. Coli never struck him as a dimwit, but shit, she had willingly let him into her home several times and hadn't even tried to hide the glasses or the knife.

She could have denied owning the blouse the pearl button came from, by the time he got a warrant she could have burnt it and buried it. That is, if she noticed the missing button and thought about where she'd lost it.

Removing his phone from his belt he plunked it in the holder and told Alexa to call the lab. When someone answered, he said, "Yeah, this is Sheriff Dillon. I had a CSI come and retrieve a can from my office earlier. Can you find out-" he broke off as the other person told him he would direct his call to the forensic agent.

She answered right away, "Janine Trampet, hello Sheriff."

"Miss, uh, Ms. Trampet, did you check out that can like I asked you to?"

"Yes, sir. Only one set of prints on the can, we've entered them into AFIS, there were no hits there. It was varnish as the can label read, and no DNA that we could pick up."

"Okay, I need you to run the prints again through AFIS and compare them to a Juvenile offender, Colipatra Cassidy. How quick can you do that?"

"Take only a few minutes, I think, sir."

"All right, you have my number, call me back as soon as you confirm." He wrapped both hands around the wheel, and stepped harder on the gas, there should have been numerous prints on the can. It was packaged, packed and shipped and placed on a store shelf, there should have been several prints, at the very least it should have had both Coli and Silina's prints on it, but the girl had said there was a single set. Of course Coli could have wiped the can, but if she was that careful why toss it right in her own trashcan?

He was pulling back into the lot when the CSI called back. He answered, and she said, "Sir, I ran the prints, had my supervisor double check, but there is no match to Ms. Cassidy. Is there anything else I can-" Brogan hung up, it was strange, but didn't abdicate the other evidence.

As he strode through the parking lot and up the back walk to the jail he argued with himself. He had no business checking on her, he wouldn't be doing himself any favors to have to see her and walk away again, yeah, he had no-

In his anxious haste, he wrenched the door open and stalked inside, and stopped dead.

CHAPTER TWENTY-SIX

They weren't audible outside the cement walls, but inside Coli was screaming her head off. In her cell, she was crushed into a corner, pressed against a wall, and she was fighting off Deputy Gillan who was crawling over her, holding her trapped with his weight while he tore at her blouse and ripped at her jeans. Coli kicked and punched and screamed bloody murder.

Gillan growled fiercely, "You shut up you little bitch and quit fightin' me or I'll gag ya and cuff your hands behind your back, ouch!" A kick landed on his thigh and he shoved her harder into the wall, grabbed her legs and jerked her down on her back while forcing more of his weight on her.

Grappling at her jeans, he ripped the button off, his own trousers were already undone. His gun belt was slung over a chair, his zipper down, the front of his pants and his underwear were pushed down.

While he scrabbled with Coli with one hand, he was pulling his penis out with the other. Under him, she screamed and punched at him even as he pushed her legs apart and maneuvered between them. "Okay," he huffed out of breath, "that's it, I'm gonna slug ya, calm ya down, cuff ya then I'll get those jeans-"

His last words chopped off as Brogan stormed into the cell and snatched the deputy's shirt and collar and wrenched the fat man off her and literally threw him in the air.

Gillan shrieked when he landed hard on the cold unforgiving tile. After the first bounce and skid Brogan was on him, his fists

pounding the deputy's fleshy face as he now screamed for his life. Gillan tried to cover his face with his arms but Brogan just bashed them out of the way, not even slowing as he heard bones cracking.

Blood hurled from Brogan's fists smashing with loud smacks as they slammed brutally into Gillan's face again and again until the deputy was no longer recognizable.

Someone heard Coli's screams when he had left the door open, a deputy raced in shouting into the radio at his shoulder. He rushed over and grabbed Brogan's arm trying to pull him off the unconscious Gillan.

"Sheriff, Sheriff!" he shouted, "shit, stop, stop man, you're killing him!" While jerking at Brogan's arm, he kept yelling for help into his radio. Within seconds, several more deputies charged in and they pulled Brogan off Gillan.

When they jerked him loose, they all staggered backwards with the force of it, freeing Brogan who now fought the deputies to get back at Gillan.

"Sheriff, stop, Brogan my brother," Pirate was there. He got behind him and wrapped his arm around his neck in a chokehold and commanded, "Everyone back off, back the fuck off." The other deputies gingerly released Brogan and cautiously moved back a step. Pirate whispered in Brogan's ear, "She needs you, Brog."

Pirate's words broke through the red rage deafening Brogan's mindless brain and he stopped fighting. His stiff body loosened slightly, the rage still grinding his words, panting hard he muttered hoarsely, "I'm good, Lo, leggo." Pirate slowly released him then patted his shoulder.

Oblivious to the other deputies standing anxiously around him, Brogan pushed through them to get to the cell. Coli was still on the cot, huddled in a corner with her arms wrapped around her knees. Her entire body shook wildly, her face was red and streaked with tears, her chest raced with frantic breaths, a cut lanced her cheek, blood slid from it.

"Oh fuck, baby," Brogan cursed a string of invectives, lurching into the cell.

Her terrified eyes wide as saucers flit around at the men then at Brogan, she scrunched up tighter, pressing into the wall, there was no escape. When Brogan reached her she ducked her head into her arms as if protecting herself from his assault. Brogan quickly sat down next to her and gathered her into his arms. She was a shivering, shuddering, weeping mess against his chest.

He wrapped her tightly in his embrace and murmured in her ear, "Baby, baby, Coli, it's okay, no one is gonna hurt you, not anymore, I swear, shh, calm down now." He pet her head, stroked her back, continued whispering comforting words, his nose in her hair, his lips pressing her ear, he kissed the side of her head.

Cuddling her close, he said to Pirate, "Lo, get that piece of shit to the hospital, secure him to a bed, when he's cleared, get him back here and lock the fucker up."

Pirate stared down at the demolished bloody slop that was Deputy Gillan, he said drolly, "That's gonna be a while before that pulpy thing gets cleared. Hell, Brog, you did some damned damage." He grinned proudly at his boss, and friend.

Brogan glared at the other gawking deputies and instructed, "A couple of you help Lo, the rest of you get the hell outta here," and he set his lips back on Coli's ear kissing gently and whispering softly.

He didn't watch as the men hustled about the jail picking up the unconscious Gillan and dragging him out, their murmurings and shuffling feet excruciatingly loud until they moved out the door and Brogan heard it shut quietly and latch.

When they were alone, he gripped Coli's upper arms and moved her back so he could look at her. Her head was down, tears still fell, lips trembled but the hellacious shaking had lightened enough her teeth stopped chattering. Strands of wet hair pasted across her face,

Brogan gently swept them back with the rough pads of his fingers. He tugged out his handkerchief and gently wiped her face.

"Baby," he murmured, sliding his hand under the side of her jaw he lifted her head up, "you're safe now, look at me." He waited, she trembled and kept her eyes lowered. "Coli, look at me."

Her damp lids fluttered, a tear hung from a few lashes, she raised her eyes but kept them pinched in case he was going to harm her. He didn't think his heart could have hurt more than it already did, she was afraid of him like she had been in the beginning, worse, and that about killed him. "Cubbie-doll, I'm gonna take you home now." She blinked in confused distrust.

"Yeah, honey, home to Colipatra's Inn." Hell, he'd release her ROR until he made sense of the whole thing. Thankfully he hadn't done an arrest report on her yet. The only way he'd keep her in the cell now was if he stayed with her, and he couldn't do that.

"Come on." He got to his feet and lifted her off the cot to stand. She gasped, her knees buckled. Brogan swept her up in his arms, said softly, "I'm so sorry, Coli, so sorry. I had no idea that fuck- uh, scumbag would attack you. I never would have left you-" She tucked her face into his shoulder with a wounded sigh.

"Okay." There wasn't anything else he could say, he couldn't take it back, make it not have happened. Cripes, his own deputy raping his prisoner, his cubbie, a shiver of fury and fright rankled through him. Gillan's lucky he still draws a breath, if the deputies hadn't come in and pulled him off, the guy would be singing with the angels now, make that burning with Satan.

When he reached his truck, he slipped her in the passenger seat. She sat rigidly unmoving like a broken statue, unblinking. He buckled her seatbelt and closed her door, and drove her home.

Pulling into her driveway, he turned the car off and twisted to face her. "Coli-"

"B- Brogan," the sob coughed out. Slowly she turned her head to look at him, brushed her tousled hair off her shoulders. "What, I mean, I just don't understand all this- this…" she faltered as her words choked in her throat.

Brogan took in her helpless, still terrified bearing, hair a mess, face red and puffy, her body still trembled, and she was still the loveliest thing he'd ever laid his eyes on, and his manhood still throbbed for her, and his heart still beat with the want of her. It was all he could do to keep his gaze away from her torn blouse, he didn't need to become more inflamed.

"Coli," he sighed at the betrayed pain in the blue eyes as she glanced at him then away. "Let me ask you straight out," he waited for her to look at him. When she did, he asked, "Did you kill Ellery Delian or have anything to do with his death?"

Her lashes flung up, she squeaked with horror, "Me? Me? You're asking me if I- if I…" her voice choked out again. She stared wide-eyed at him, but he looked back at her impassively, waiting for her answer. Flaxen brows daggered down as anger moved the fright aside. "I can't believe you would ask me- uh," she shook her head, lips bunched, she looked him in the eye.

"No. I did not k-kill Ellery, or, or have anything to do with it. How could you think that I would be capable," her jaw suddenly clenched. "Oh, yeah, I forgot, the prison time I did for hurting Kip, yeah, that sure makes me guilty of murdering everyone on the planet. Great. I can't believe you think," she shook her head again, this time with despondence, "never mind. I see there was never anything real between us, I see you never believed in me or trusted me," her shoulders slumped. She raised her head and glared at him. "Any other questions, *Sheriff*?"

Ah, back to square one. Brogan sucked in a heavy breath, let it out slowly. "Uh, yeah, did you kill Peter Polito, or have any involvement with that in any way?"

Her mouth dropped with shock. She slammed it shut and swallowed hard, choking down her anger and hurt. "No." Coli reached for the door handle. "Am I free to go, *Sheriff*? Or do you have more intention on verbally beating me up, or dragging me back to jail so more of your deputies can assault me?"

His sigh harsh, he told her, "Coli, hell, I'm the goddamned sheriff of Builu County, it's my job, I," he raked a hand through his hair. "Honey, there's…evidence that points heavily towards you. No, I've never believed you guilty of ever harming even a fly, or especially Kip, but my job, I had to ask to get the elephant out of the way. There's too much evidence, I had to take you in. Listen," he reached out to take her hand, she snatched it away and lifted the door handle.

"I am not your honey, *Sheriff*, apparently I never was, please don't call me that. I believe we're done here, with everything." She didn't look at him, kept facing forward, blinking back the tears that threatened.

He stammered, "I, uh, for now we can't, be…together, until this all sorts out, but we need to talk. I mean-"

Her voice jagged, she exclaimed wearily, "Oh, I know what you mean. Don't worry, us being anything ever again is not something you need to be concerned about. I would thank you for rescuing me tonight but," her crooked smile rueful, "you put me there, put me in that position, left me helpless, defenseless," the tears were collecting stuffing her throat.

"Shit, Coli, I didn't know that bastard was a fucking raping monster. I never would have," Brogan shook his head. He sat back with a groan. Glancing around he noticed there were no cars other than hers in the driveway. "Your family still isn't home? What about Kip?"

"Huh," she opened the door. "That is no longer any of your business. You going to chain me to my bed or can I go?"

That visual struck him right in the groin. "Uh," he pushed the image away, "yeah, you can go."

He wanted to say more, but what could he say, that he hated this whole thing, that he wanted to forget everything, the murders, his job, what he'd just put her through, and gather her up and take her to her bedroom and hold her all night? But he couldn't. Not that she'd let him.

Brogan had to sit still and watch her fumble the door open and slide out onto shaking legs and stumble to her house. He didn't think she'd make it up the steps, his hand on his door he started to go to help her, then dropped his hand. She would only rebuff his assistance and hurt them both more.

When he saw the lights come on inside, he drove off, no cheery wave this time.

CHAPTER TWENTY-SEVEN

A night of tossing and turning, when he got up, Brogan was just as tired as when he'd gone to bed last night. Of course his nightmares were of Duff Gillan ripping Coli's little body to shreds as he beat and assaulted her, and Brogan was on the outside of her locked cell as he screamed and raged unable to get to her.

The morning didn't get any better. He nicked his face shaving again, made his coffee strong to help perk him up but it was too strong, it was bitter on his tongue and fiery abrasive going down.

Setting the half-drunk coffee on the kitchen counter, he wasn't hungry, the hole in his stomach that matched the one in his heart was aching and churning.

On his way through the living room, he saw Felipé sitting in Brogan's easy chair.

"Hey buddy." Brogan started towards him to give his pet a quick pet, but the cat gave him a kitty glare then turned his head dismissively and jumped out of the chair. Tail up in the air, he sauntered away out of the room dissing Brogan.

"Huh, great," Brogan grunted, "even my pet is peeved with me for bringing emotional as well as physical harm to Coli." He grabbed his hat and keys and muttered, "Yeah, I suck dirt." *But it was my job, there was just too much evidence to ignore*, his brain whined.

When he entered the station he barely acknowledged Minnie's greeting and didn't hear her say to the female deputy she was

chatting with, "Oh no, something's up with that boy. The past few weeks there's been a bounce in his step and he was actually smiling instead of just gruffing at people, and now," the two females watched Brogan moving without his usual strong, confident stride disappear down a hall to his office. "Now he's back to dark and brooding. So sad."

He checked his messages then called Pirate. When he answered, Brogan said, "Lo, the vic Polito's breakfast sandwich and coffee were poisoned. I need you to go to the Papyrus and Panini café and ask if anyone remembers seeing anyone with him that day, and grab all the camera video in the neighborhood of the paint store."

"Sure, Brog. There won't be any customers at the shop, they closed it down since the murder but I'll find an employee, and survey the other stores in that location. Um," he paused with his question hanging.

"I took her home," Brogan replied with a rough exhale. He clarified with a depressed tone, "To her home,

"She okay?"

A few beats went by then Brogan said, "Kind of. Ain't gonna get over that kind of shit soon. I wish I coulda stayed with her, just…"

"Why didn't you?"

"Huh," he grunted scornfully, "she wants nothing to do with me. I put her in that dangerous position, and she's not gonna forgive me for it. Worse, I accused her of murder, hell, Lo, I might as well of run her over with my truck."

Pirate commiserated, "That's how it is with chicks. Blame a guy for everything and remind him of his mistakes for the rest of his life."

Brogan snorted. "I wish she would berate me the rest of my life, at least she'd be with me. As it is, she wants nothing to do with me, ever."

"Sorry, bro, I'll go get on those cameras at the Panini place."

The sheriff grumped, "Yeah. Listen, Lo, do you remember any of the news reports mentioning what the cause of death was for that girl, Camille Blanco?"

Pondering the question, Pirate answered, "Not that I recall. I'm sure they reported different things on different stations."

"Sure. Okay, I'll let you go, I have to check on some frog legs." He cringed at Pirate's blast of coarse laughter. Wow, second laugh out of Pirate that week, should record it, no one will believe it.

"Better you than me, bro," Pirate's grin came through the phone. He said, "Later," and hung up.

A brief smile pulled in his dimple, Brogan slid his cell into the holder on his belt and took off for the restaurant Quispe that Rocky had located for him. Apparently it was the only restaurant relatively near Camille Blanco's apartment that had the slimy amphibians on the menu.

Forty minutes later he parked in the lot, grabbed his hat and strode into the restaurant. Blanco's apartment was in a seedier section of the city, the restaurant was across town in the ritzier area. Big windows with blue and white striped puffy curtains made the place very bright. Round tables scattered the dining room that served lunch and dinner.

He called ahead so they'd let him in, it wasn't lunchtime yet but they'd left the door unlocked for him. Glass tabletops with blue placemats kept the lightness present, bunches of green ferns in vases graced the tables. Blue, ruffled cloth lanterns interspersed with red ones decorated along the tops of the ivory walls.

A young man, actually a lanky teenager with hair in his eyes, was placing settings on the tables, he looked up when Brogan entered. Plunking a fern in a vase he asked, "Sheriff Dillon?"

Brogan tipped his head. "Yessir, I spoke with a Ms. Vu?"

"I'll get her, Sheriff," the boy said then scurried through a swinging door.

Shortly, the door swung open and a woman strolled out. She was tall for an Asian, straight black hair arrowed down her back and whipped across her slender butt, her long red dress clung to her slight curves to just past the knee.

She moved to Brogan with graceful strides in four-inch heels, her hand out. Several gold bangles jingled on her wrist, long slim fingers grasped his hand in a surprisingly strong grip. "Sheriff

Dillon? You asked to meet with me? I am the evening hostess, Lanh Vu, I came in early regarding your call. How can I help you?" Gold hoops sparked against her inky hair.

Shaking her hand lightly, Brogan commented, "A friend of mine in New York City dated a girl, Hoa Vu, she was Vietnamese."

Lanh's laugh was a girlish tinkle. "That is your curious yet polite way of asking if I am Vietnamese?" She laughed again. "You are right, my grandparents came over after the war. So…" one brow like a thin, black magic marker slash arched.

Granting her a cockeyed smile, he said, "Yeah, Hoa was a sweetheart. What I need to know is if you remember this girl," he slipped a photo out of his breast pocket, photographs were easier for witnesses to ID than images on phones. Brogan held the picture out, she accepted it with her long slender fingers and studied it.

He said, "We believe she was here on the 15th, she had the frog legs and probably wasn't alone. It would have been either very late at night or very early in the morning that she was here. Do you remember her?"

Her bottom lip pushed up as she concentrated on the photo. "Sure, we prefer to call them cuisses de grenouille," she smiled slyly, pretty teardrop shaped eyes twinkled. "People are more apt to order a fancy foreign name than if we just say 'would you like the frog legs?' Like snails, no one wants to eat a snail, so they're called escargots."

"Yeah," he agreed, a slight shudder twitched his shoulders. "I'm not partial to chowing on slugs or amphibians that eat crickets. So, you remember her? Was she alone?"

The black hair swayed as she shook her head. "No, she came in with, oh, it was our large booth, four other women? I was going off shift as they were finishing, the four left this girl alone when they were done." She tapped the picture and said, "She was on her phone arguing with I guess her boyfriend so the check was paid and the others grew annoyed with her and left."

"I need descriptions of the other women and any information you can give me about them, credit card receipts if any?" He pulled out his notebook and handed it and a pen to her.

"No problem." She sat down and set the book on a table and wrote.

Brogan waited patiently, glancing around the pretty restaurant, colorful collages hung on the walls. Some tables had blue tablecloths, others pink. His mind drifted, he thought, *maybe Coli would like-* his throat clenched. They wouldn't be enjoying any more dinners together. Ripping his thoughts of her away, he glared at the liquor bottles behind the bar, yeah, he could use a stiff one right now, maybe ten.

Lanh handed him the notebook and pen and stood up. "Here, I can't get the credit card receipts until later when the manager comes in."

"All right, thanks." He presented a lank smile and stuffed the notebook in his pocket. "How about security cameras?"

Her mouth made a small moue, the bottom of her hair swished. "No, we have none. But I think the bank a few buildings down from here does."

He tipped his hat slightly. "Thank you, I appreciate your help. If you would contact me as soon as you have that credit card info I would be mighty obliged."

Smiling at the sheriff, Lanh's gaze rolled down his long length and back up, the smile broadened. "Any time I can help, Sheriff, please, don't hesitate to call me."

His hand on the door, Lanh called out, "Oh, Sheriff, wait. There was another woman that joined your victim a while after her friends left."

He swung around. "Yeah? Tell me about her."

Her elegant shoulders shrugged. "Nothing to tell really, I only saw the back of her, I was leaving. One of the servers or bartender might have seen her, I believe I saw her carrying two drinks to the booth your victim was in. It was all quite, vague, I wasn't paying much attention."

"Young? Old? Thin? Hair color?" Brogan questioned.

"Ah," she murmured, her tongue poked out she set a finger to her chin, "I can't really say. She wore a hat and long jacket and I only saw the back of her."

"Who waited on her?"

Lanh's face creased as she thought about the 15th. "I'll have to get a copy of the work schedule. Again, not until the manager comes in, sorry."

"It's fine, Ms. Vu. You have been very cooperative and I'm sure any information you can get me will be useful." He thanked her again, touched the brim of his hat and the door swung closed behind him.

As usual Brogan couldn't get Coli off his mind. He had to know how she was doing, he dug out his phone and dialed her landline, she didn't have a cell.

Squelching his groan at the sound of Silina's hello, he stuck his key in the ignition and turned the engine over and took a calming breath. "Is this Silina Arabat?" he asked although he knew it was her.

"Who's asking?" The snide nasal sound in her voice made Brogan's stomach ill. Coli was alone with those abominable people and there wasn't a damn thing he could do about it. Short of grabbing Coli and sequestering her at his place, that meant restraining her, and he had considered it, several times, but she'd only be more pissed at him.

Plus, they have a law against that, called kidnapping. Still, the thought kept floating through his worried skull.

"This is Sheriff Dillon, I'd like to speak with Coli," he stated brusquely. The less he spoke with the half-sister the better, he felt it was like he could get the plague from the woman over the phone.

Silina's loud snort made him jerk the phone from his ear. "She's busy. Something has upset the poor thing and she's outside walking off her angst."

Her tone went from snide to solicitous, she offered, "Maybe I can help you with something? You'd be so much safer with me than my sister the killer. And in bed? Let me tell you that I-"

"I want to talk to Coli, get her."

Shot down, Silina jeered, "You don't know what you're missing, Sheriff." Brogan thought she was going to hang up on him,

but then she asked quickly, "That paint store guy, the one Coli dated, what killed him?"

Brogan was taken aback, but it couldn't hurt to tell her. He said, "It was a poisonous plant, henbane." He heard her gasp.

"Oh! No kidding? Are you sure?"

"Why, do you know about this plant?"

"Well, I mean, I hate to snitch on her-"

Lord, he slapped his forehead. "Just tell me what you know, Ms. Arabat."

"You can call me Silina, Sheriff," she simpered.

How damned aggravating! He groaned, then demanded, "Just fucking tell me what you know."

"Okay, okay keep your lid on. Coli took me for a walk in the woods behind her house, and I remember seeing that kind of plant. I know what it was because in my horticulture class in high school we learned about poisonous plants. Coli practically dragged me out there, do you think- maybe, wait, I think she was warning me, warning me to- to-"

His sigh was loud and rough. "Ms. Arabat, what you're telling me is so damned far-fetched. I don't believe there just happens to be that plant-"

"Oh yeah? I'll show you. Wait, I'm texting you a selfie we took that day, you can see for yourself the plant is right behind us." She forwarded the pictures she took that day to his phone, and Brogan's heart plunged and hit rock bottom. The picture clearly showed the two girls and the plant he'd seen the picture of at the lab with yellow flowers was indeed, right behind them. He'd have to arrest her again. Fuck.

Tomorrow, he'd go get her tomorrow. He needed to have all his ducks in a row, yeah, he'd wait until tomorrow. His head tilted up as he drove towards home and he recoiled.

The burgeoning storm in the bruised smoky sky was moving closer, it wasn't late yet in the day but it was darkening.

Against the sooty sky, huge clouds, strangely golden, not gravel grey or black glistened and clumped, attaching to each other becoming one colossal storm. The whitish-golden cloud storm was

odd looking, eerie as hell, it brought chills to Brogan's skin that had been so terribly heated from the scorching air. He cranked the AC.

CHAPTER TWENTY-EIGHT

Coli's head was spinning, she didn't know if she was coming or going. With the Victorian came 600+ acres of land, most of it wooded. She couldn't understand why people considered the land in Mal Tierre to be so bad if trees and shrubs and wildflowers could grow in it.

Thirty acres surrounding the house were cleared grass with a few scattered trees for beauty and shade, the ground was rocky but the grass grew thick.

Since she still hadn't had trails made in the woods yet, Coli walked and walked and walked the thirty acres of grass and a short ways inside the wooded perimeter until her legs were too tired to go another step.

Back at the house she sank down on a porch step and tried to sort her thoughts. Brogan had actually arrested her. She couldn't wrap her mind around that the man she trusted and...liked a lot, could think she could ever harm another soul.

He didn't want to do it, it was written in big black ink across his rugged face, he looked like it was hurting him more than her. But nevertheless, he did cuff her and lock her up and then left her alone with that- that- pig. A deputy, a man of the law, a violent rapist.

Locked in that cell for twenty or so minutes, she could feel the deputy's eyes burning through the bars, searing lacerations of lust up and down her body. She had pulled her knees up, hugging them,

trying to disappear into a tiny ball hoping he'd lose interest and go back to his newspaper. But he didn't.

Duff Gillan had pushed his chair back and hitched his pants up, his eyes on her. The huge lecherous grin virtually dripped saliva from his incisors. The heavy man moseyed over to her cell. Coli could see the drool in the corners of his thick lips, she hugged her knees tighter and pressed against the wall, praying he would not pass through the bars.

Brogan had threatened him not to touch her, or go inside her cell. When the deputy stuck the key in the lock, slowly swung the door open and stepped inside, her body visibly started trembling.

The grin as sloppy and gargantuan as his belly, he unbuckled his weapons belt, and then his regular belt, removed them both and set them on a chair outside the cell and kept coming at her. "Hya, little honey," he said, the grin slobbered wet, he licked his lips noisily sucking in the leaking saliva.

Moving closer, he tucked his thumbs in his pants. "Oh yes, you are a sweet one, aren't you? Young, fresh, really pretty, and damned tight and juicy I bet. You're gonna love what I got for ya, honey."

He unbuttoned the top button on his slacks and tromped closer until his knees were almost against the cot. Coli squirmed away until her back smacked the corner cement wall.

"Please don't, don't touch me," she begged trying to hold back the tears of terror as they filled and clotted her throat, the deputy had a foot and at least 150 pounds on her.

Her eyes galloped around the room searching for a weapon, of course there was nothing there but a tiny water closet, bedding, and the cot and chair.

"Now, now, just stay cool, sweetie, you're tiny but you can take my big Johnson, huh? You girls are built to adapt. You stay relaxed, mebbe be a little into it and we'll have a good time, right?" Stalking to her, the panic screamed in her head, she had nowhere else to go, there was no one around to help her. He unzipped his trousers and reached out to grab her.

Coli squealed and tried to kick at him yelling, "Get away from me!"

He caught the sleeve of her blouse. "Come on, sweetie, make it easy on us both."

"No!" she screamed. "Sh- Sheriff Dillon told you not to- to harm me, you're not supposed to be inside here with me! He'll- he'll punish you if he catches you in here!" Coli frantically yanked at her arm to get him to let go of her blouse.

Gillan let her arm go and set a knee on the cot and snatched at the front of her blouse. Gripping a fistful of material he jerked her to him. Her mouth opened to scream and he grabbed the back of her hair, wrapped it around his other fist twisting it painfully and held her taut while he jammed his mouth over hers.

Slobber slathered all around their lips, Coli screamed into his mouth, punched at him, kicked anything she could reach. His mouth so much bigger than hers she couldn't stop him from forcing his kiss on her, forcing her lips to stay open.

He stabbed his tongue in and she tried to bite it, that made him pull back and he slapped her. "Bitch, don't you fucking hurt me, you little slut." He put his beefy palm on her chest and shoved her hard against the concrete wall knocking the air out of her lungs with a hack. Her head banged on the cement and Coli saw stars.

He took the opportunity of her disorientation to grip the sides of her blouse and tear it apart. When he went for her jeans, she sucked in air and screamed.

The deputy got off on her struggles. "Yeah, honey, it's kinda more exciting when you fight me." He smashed her back at the wall, and held her there with a wide meaty paw hard against her soft chest and wrenched at the buttons on her jeans.

When he couldn't get them undone and get the jeans down, he gripped her ankles, leaned away and jerked her flat on her back, again whacking the breath out of her lungs with the swift violent act.

Using his hefty weight to hold her down, he stuck his fingers in the top of her jeans to just rip them off her body. Hitting at him, Coli screamed, "Stop! Help, someone help me!"

Not able to get her jeans down, he groused, "Shit, I'm gonna slug ya, cuff ya and cut them off you-"

And Brogan had burst in and made bloody meat out of the deputy's face. Then he had brought her home. Dropping her head in her hands, Coli wept. Her entire life had been hell, she just couldn't break from being a loser victim. When she inherited the Victorian and got Kip, she had thought she was finally swimming the sweet cream of life.

Things were going so well. She and Brogan were moving towards a relationship, she had everything her heart could desire, and now, it figures. Why did she think she deserved anything good? Damaged goods everyone kept saying, good for nothing.

Even that deputy thought he had the right to put his hands on her, as if she wasn't a human, or that she had rights. Her heart lurched painfully with the realization she was going back to prison.

She thought of Kip. "Oh dear, what is going to happen to him? What will happen to Douggie?" She didn't kid herself that Silina or Goldie will take care of either of them. Silina only fed Douggie when Coli had to work and when Kip wasn't going to be around because she paid her to.

If Coli was put back in jail, Kip would get sent away, and it would be a lot worse than the group home he lived in in Ohio because the State would no longer pay for his care. It would be up to Silina, and she would spend the least amount of money she could to house him.

And Douggie? Silina would dump him so fast at the first pound she could find if she didn't drop-kick him out to the woods instead. Coli pictured his punchy, sad little puppy face crying for her to come get him, bring him home.

She would be unable to help Kip or Douggie; they would suffer because of her. She'd break her promise to Kip that she would take care of him and he was looking so forward to helping her run the Inn. The tears broke loose and poured down her face.

She sat there crying until she had nothing left. Exhausted, her body felt like an aching empty shell. Nothing to do but go to bed.

Her dreams were filled with Brogan. His husky laugh, that dimple that flashed so rarely, she wanted to say goofy things to make

him grin so she could see it. Low growly sexy things he whispered in her ear, his amazing kisses that made her toes curl. Dark smoldering eyes, massive masculine shoulders that blocked out everything else as he lowered his hard body on-

A noise startled her, an ear perked; when she heard nothing else she settled back down with a soft sigh, it was just the wind. A storm was on the way. As it continued approaching Builu, the rumbling clouds were growing to mammoth proportions, agitating and churning, tossing branches and loose things around.

Even with her lids closed, Coli was aware the morning sun was splintering around the edges of the ruffled curtain.

She didn't care. There was no reason to get up. She was going to prison for murder, this time they would never let her out, she'd never see the light of day again. Never see Kippie or Douggie, or...Brogan ever again, what would be the point of getting out of bed, taking a shower, cooking breakfast for her ungrateful family.

No, tears eked out the corners of her eyes, she would just stay in bed until they hauled her off to jail. Maybe she could starve to death and save her the agony, and everyone time and the cost of prosecuting her again for a yet another crime she didn't commit.

Creak. She heard it again, and a breath, someone was in her room! Her lashes flew up with a gasp. "Grandfather Auston, what are you-" Her eyes hopped to Ricardo standing beside him, the two men wore identical lewd smiles directed at her.

The older man said proudly, "See Ricardo, didn't I tell you how captivating she looks when first waking up?"

Ricardo nodded, they both were now standing right by the bed, not even a foot from her, goose bumps prickled up her arms. He agreed, "Yes, you told the truth, Auston, babe is a knocking fox all right, awake or asleep."

Coli was so shocked she didn't move, then she realized she was in her jams in bed with two men gawking at her like she was a luscious cool pool and they were sizzling hot and ready to jump in. Breaking out of her shock, she clutched at her blanket and pushed up to one elbow. "Grandfather Auston, you must leave immediately! You shouldn't be here in my bedroom."

Ricardo smiled at Auston and said, "You were right, she is a feisty little toy." Auston hummed in accord.

This wasn't good, Coli feared they weren't here to just chitchat with her. Pulling the blanket higher, she threw a hand out at them and demanded, "You- you two get out of here! Get out of my bedroom this minute!"

"And such a babydoll when she's angry, very hot." Ricardo grinned. He bent quickly and grasped the hand she threw out, using it to push her to lay back down. "No babe, you're staying right there, Auston and I want some playtime," he pinned her wrist to the bed.

Shades of jail! Was she put on this earth to be assaulted by men? Does she have 'rape me' written across her forehead? Forever she'll be treated as a criminal and people thinking they have the right to abuse her, that she deserves it.

"Let me go, get out of my room!" Coli ineffectively kicked at the blankets that secured her legs, her punches only made him laugh. She fought to free her wrist but Ricardo was strong and he just laughed more with amusement at her struggles.

He half turned to Auston and said over his shoulder, "She's your granddaughter, you have the honors to go first, sir. I'll hold the girl down for you so you can easily plow her."

Auston's smile was so vile Coli's body clenched in horror. The evil in his eyes that was always strictly bricked up behind those black pits of wickedness gleamed at her, and sickening memories of her childhood flooded her terrified mind.

Images of the old man touching her when she was a child whenever no one else was around. The times she stayed at his house he'd crawled into her bed, shushing her when she cried out. His hands, those gnarly hands pushing up her nightgown.

Coli screamed and thrust her body up, she had to get away, but with a grin Ricardo restrained her. He caught her other hand and pressed both to the bed above her head. Thrashing against his powerful control, her back arched, face bursting red from the strain of fighting him, "No!" she screamed, her vocal cords already sore and hoarse from the episode with Deputy Gillan.

276

"Granddad!" Silina shrieked from the doorway. Both men ignored her, Auston paused his hands but slid his knee further on the bed about to straddle Coli.

Silina's shoes stomped across the floor. "Goddammit Coli, you're doing it again." She clumped right to the bed and glared daggers down at her struggling half-sister. Slamming her hands on her bench-seat sized hips, she groused, "You bitch. You stole him away from me when you were a baby, and here you go again. I wanted his affections, I wanted all of his attention, I wanted him in my bed only, but no. You beguiled him even as a toddler."

Auston rolled his eyes, Ricardo's brows arched with incredulity. Coli's mouth hung open, she blinked crazily trying to grasp what her sister was spewing.

Silina's sneer making her frightfully ugly she spat, "He fucked me once, got me pregnant, then he went after you. It's always you. Ellery wanted my money but he wanted you back, and once again you steal *my* grandfather from me! I hate you!" she shrieked, shaking her fists at Coli.

"Silina!" Auston snapped, removing his hands from Coli's bare skin and straightening. "This is none of your concern, get out."

His granddaughter whimpered, "No, Granddad, please, take me, not her. She's just trash, you know that, jailbait, prison garbage, probably diseased. She's not good enough to lick our boots."

Still struggling against Ricardo's harsh grip, Coli uttered in dismay, "Grandfather Auston? He's Kip's father?"

Her horrified eyes jolted to the old man. "You're her grandfather, my God, you're like 40 years older than her, and- and incest, oh my God, that's- that's obscene, immoral, illegal, blasphemous!" she was wrenching her hands so hard it was hurting her arms.

Eyes bulging with rage and jealousy, face a swollen beet, Silina screamed, "Granddad was mine! I had to get rid of you." Her voice lowered, a smirk bloomed.

"Yes." The dreadful smile contorted her face. "It was me that threw that brat out of the tree-house. They answered my prayers and took you away and I thought I'd never have to see your ugly puss or

278

the brat again. Then," the smirk bowed to grief. "Daddy died and there you were, thrust back into our lives again. A visit from Ohio once in a blue moon I could take, but now, you come to live in *my* state and keep jamming Kip up my ass, and have the gall to lure *my* men away."

Bending over, keeping Coli pinned down, Ricardo twisted his head to give Silina a quizzical look. "You said the boy was your brother."

Her face screwed up in fury Silina spat at him, "Oh shut up! You see," she sneered again at Coli, said to Ricardo, "all the men want her. Grandfather, Ellery, now you." Grinding her teeth she complained, "It was bad enough Ellery was seeing all those other women, I looked the other way, but then you," she waved her hand at Coli. "He wanted you back and I had to stop it. I would have killed you instead but then I'd get stuck with Kip."

All three stared at her, Ricardo and Coli in stunned disbelief of her admitting to murder, Auston looked bored. Silina sniffed, "Yeah, I killed Ellery to keep you from having him, and framed you so they'd take you away again, this time for life."

Auston's eyes lured back to Coli's exposed body, but Ricardo and Coli gaped appalled disbelief at Silina.

Silina sniffed with pride and told her, "It was easy, I brought a bottle of cognac, his favorite, to his office, along with a couple of your crystal rock glasses and a handful of hair of that dog of yours, and I told Ellery I wanted to give him head. Of course," she scoffed a snort, "he would never turn that down. On my knees, I had him so involved, hard as a missile, I told him I needed a sip of booze to finish him and I stood up.

"He wasn't happy, but he took a sip too, and that's when I stabbed that knife into his chest. It was harder to do than I thought. Those antique knives of yours that I swiped to frame you when I brought Kip over that first night aren't quite as sturdy as they look."

"Oh God, Silina." Coli couldn't believe it. So stunned, she stopped struggling for a second, then she realized she was half naked and two, no three people were gawping at her.

Silina threw her a hideous glare. "You pissy pain in my ass, it was because of you I had to do that girl, too."

Eyes rounded in preposterous disbelief, Coli cried, "Girl? You killed *people* because of me?"

Silina said with an aggrieved snort, "Huh. Bitch Camille mocked me with it. She was screwing Ellery too, but she kept throwing it in my face that he really wanted you, because you were so much hotter than me.

"She got her rocks off making me feel like shit. Worked every one of my nerves, that girl. Paybacks are a bitch like her. So," a mild shrug of one shoulder, "I called her. She said she was out having a late dinner with friends, invited me to join them. I told her a bunch of lies about her boyfriend Tonto to keep her on the phone long enough until her friends got annoyed and left her.

"Then I went inside. I was totally in disguise with glasses and a wig, she hardly recognized me. She was half in the bag so she couldn't taste the varnish in her margarita. I was damned surprised to hear she made it home before croaking. Then there was the paint store guy," she shrugged without a shred of remorse.

Continuing on with her unbelievable, hideous story, Silina said, "He was just another frame for you, my dear dumb sister, to nail you to the wall so tight there would be no wriggling away. I found the henbane in your woods earlier and tricked you into posing in front of it wearing your frilly blouse. You didn't even notice a button was missing. I flirted with the paint store moron for a few days, then brought him breakfast.

"While he was enjoying his poisoned food, I tucked your button in his pocket. It must have fallen out when he was slamming on the floor in convulsions. But all the better, I heard it was found under his body, pretty much sealed the deal that you had killed him. I slipped the blouse from your laundry basket back in your closet so you couldn't wash off your DNA."

Ignoring Coli and Ricardo's horrified shock, she said, "So, you need to know, sweetie, I forwarded the picture of our selfie to your loverboy sheriff and tossed more dog hair on the floor of the store,

made sure some of that was in Pete's pocket too. You wonder why Sheriff Dillon arrested you? Ha!"

Her hazel eyes squinted in hate at Coli. "I created so much evidence against you I can't believe that bastard let you out of jail."

Coli regarded her sister with sickened dismay, then she snapped out of her immobilized shock renewing her writhing, thrashing struggles, grunting and crying out with her efforts to break free from Ricardo's grasp.

Auston kept his eyes on Coli's bare breasts bouncing with her thrashing. He said, "Ricardo, remove my granddaughter so I can enjoy my treat in peace and quiet."

"No, Granddad, please!" Silina cried, the end of her pointy nose wet and red. Ricardo reluctantly released Coli's wrists and turned to his girlfriend. "Come along, hon." He circled his long fingers around her arm.

"No!" Silina screamed. "Don't throw me out, Granddad, please! I'll be quiet, I won't interfere, I'll just watch, maybe I can help- join in, please!"

"Ricardo," Auston growled. The young man tightened his grip and hauled Silina from the room.

With everyone moving, Coli managed to pull her shirt down and cover herself.

Shifting one knee back on the bed, Auston threw his other leg over to straddle her, he shook his head, tut-tutted, "Coli girl, don't fight me, I won't allow it. If I must manacle you to gain your cooperation, I-" Coli had worked her legs free from the sheet and blanket and she rammed her knee into his groin as hard as she could.

A heaving sound choked out, Auston bent double, cupped his groin and retching, stumbled back from the bed. Coli scrambled to her knees then leaped off the bed. She made it to the door, but bent over yet still on his feet, Auston grabbed at her pajama pants to hold her from fleeing.

Coli hit at his hand and yanked at the pants, but he held on, while regaining his strength. Managing to get his other arm around her, he tugged her to him then slung an arm around her waist, and clamped his hand across her throat cutting off her air.

"When you run out of air, Colipatra," he wheezed in her ear, "you'll settle down." Holding her tight to his body so she couldn't hit or kick him, he dragged her back inside the bedroom.

His feet moving awkwardly without the support of his cane, he carefully lifted one foot behind, and- out of nowhere- Douggie barraged into the room barking furiously.

He flew under Auston's foot unbalancing the old man. Auston let go of Coli, floundering to catch himself from falling, Douggie pushed his body under Auston's other foot and the old man tumbled to the floor with a howl.

"Oh, Douggie, good dog!" Coli squealed. "Come on, boy," she shouted, taking a step to the door but Auston stretched out his arm and grasped her leg. "No! Let go!" She kicked wildly at him but he held on and was jerking at her leg to pull her down to the floor with him.

Douggie bounded up and down barking then he sank his teeth into Auston's ankle and the old man wailed and let go of Coli's leg. Seeing Auston shake the puppy off Coli ran to the door and out to the hall. She knew she couldn't scream for help, everyone in the house wanted to hurt her.

She ran to the stairs but she heard Auston clomping after her, his cane rapidly striking the floor in his haste. Douggie didn't bark anymore, she prayed Auston hadn't hurt him.

Just as she reached the staircase, Auston grabbed her again, his cane clanking to the ground so he could hold her with both hands. He jerked her back from the stairs so hard Coli stumbled backwards falling to her knees.

Moving around to get in front of her, breathing hard, Auston snarled, "You will pay for that, Colipatra, now you get your little ass up and back into the bedroom and I will have full compliance out of you. You're getting a whipping from my belt for that crap you just pulled." He stared down at her thinking he'd cowed her and she would quietly do as he said.

"Okay," she said meekly and moved from her knees to a crouch.

He smirked down at her. "Hurry up, you've already made me wait," he rubbed his crotch and winced, he still hurt from her kick.

Still stooping, Coli said breathlessly, "Okay, but I think I sprained my knee when I fell."

Impatiently, Auston strode to the stairs and called out, "Ricardo! Get up here, I need your help!" He pivoted and started back towards Coli grumbling, "More trouble than you're worth, little girl, I'm going to make you very sorry for this aggravation you're putting me through."

Staying low, Coli grabbed up his cane and suddenly snapped it out between his ankles causing him to trip.

He was close to the stairs, he squawked, "*Ack! Coli!*" and tottered backwards towards the staircase. His heel hit the edge of the top step, flailing his arms uselessly, he screamed as he toppled over the step, and bounced and banged and thumped, his screams stunted as he cartwheeled down the entire staircase until he crash-landed splayed out on the floor at the bottom.

He didn't move. Coli didn't hesitate, she spun and raced to the other staircase at the end of the hall. Rushing down the steps, her bare feet thumping on the carpet she exited the stairs near the kitchen. Her breaths fast and shallow, heart slamming at her ribs, she ran as fast as she could to the side door.

If she could get to her car, she could get away. The thought of where she could go flickered briefly as she ran breathlessly, she didn't want to go to the police station, they'd only lock her up.

Snatching her spare keys off a hook by the kitchen entrance, she sprinted to the side door, she would go to Brogan.

He had brought her home, as despicably as he'd treated her, she knew he would protect her, she believed he cared about her, even if he thought the very worst of her. That she was a cold-blooded killer, no, she huffed skidding around the corner before the door, that was her sister.

Nauseous with the sordid disbelief of vile perversion and profane evil that has infected her entire life made Coli's legs weak. It was too much to take in, her own sister killed Ellery and an innocent man and woman. And, without a dot of remorse, Silina had flung her own child to what she'd hoped would be his death.

She had to tell Brogan it was Silina, others would be in danger if she continued unleashing her jealousy and homicidal wrath. Bare feet slapping the tiled floor like a rubber band snapping fiercely, she dashed over the cold tile and hit the door and kept running as it flew open.

Stumbling across the wooden porch, she skittered down the steps and bit back a cry when her foot struck gravel. Ignoring the pain, she was sure she would be dead if she stayed at the house, sprinting, arms pumping hard Coli sped to her car.

Stones cutting and digging into the soles of her feet, she held her breath as she fumbled with the key. Letting out a sigh of relief when she jabbed it in and wrenched the door open. She would drive straight to the station, she'd ask for Brogan when she got there-

Wham!

Pain exploded, radiating from the blow to her head- the hit so hard it blinded Coli as she sank to the ground. She felt the gravel scrape her face as she fell forward, and everything went black.

It had to be only seconds later, her brain a stinging fog, she lay paralyzed, breaths rushed shallowly from her chest. Head aching in agony, her eyes pained and glued closed, she struggled to open them, voices rumbled hazily above her.

"Damn, Goldie, you have one helluva swing, woman." Ricardo sounded impressed.

Still holding the iron skillet she slammed into the back of Coli's skull, Goldie preened in his praise. Staring down at Coli, Ricardo said, "What do we do now? I didn't get what you promised me, Auston. I hope Goldie hasn't killed her, I still want to bang that girl."

Leaning heavily, weakly on his cane, Auston's face was scratched and bleeding, he sighed with irritation. "She's still breathing. The little bitch hurt the fuck out of me. You and Silina take her out to the vacant prairies, do what you want to her then dispose of her. No one will miss her, we can take over the mansion and sell it."

"It's in her name," Goldie reminded him.

Auston brushed lint off his shoulder and leaned more heavily on the lion-topped cane. "Silina can act as her, no one will know the difference. There's enough of a resemblance with her driver's license to fool anyone who doesn't know her, the realtors and bank, whatever."

"Okay, this is great." Silina beamed. "Now I can have you back, Granddad."

Ricardo's eyes slanted sideways to her with disgust. "You people are sick. Grandfather fucking granddaughter, you," he lifted his chin to Goldie, "knew all about the incest, that the boy is Silina's. You knew the girl was a killing machine, not that I mind that so much, it has its place and time, but, hell, you freaks take the cake."

Goldie squinted an eye at him. "Sure, and you are dating my daughter but was upstairs eagerly about to rape her sister. Last week you were in my bed, so, you are just as nasty as we are, sonny."

"What?" Silina shrieked. Turning on her mother, her neck and entire face rushed dark red, she spouted, "Mother! You slept with my fiancé and now my boyfriend? You are so repulsive, how could you-"

"Oh get over yourself, Silina, you stole your sister's fiancé out from under her, you have no honor with men or family," Goldie sniffed at her.

Silina retorted angrily, "No, you-"

"Girls, come on, we don't have time for this." Ashton gestured with his head to the bickering females. "She'll be coming around, toss her in the trunk and get her out of here. Find a secure place to bury her. Go before the storm hits. It's not a thunderstorm, it's a haboob, a perilous dust storm," he tilted his head to look up at the sky.

The golden white clouds had deepened to orange and had moved past the mountains making the mountains all but invisible. Shrouding them in an orange-gold fog that appeared to be breathing, puffing bigger and bigger with each swirling breath. A dry acrid wind streaked across the open fields whipping heat that burnt skin, and flinging around anything not tied down.

Feeling the heat and wind blasting her cheek, Coli knew she needed to fight for her life, but her limbs were limp, they ignored her mind's screeching fuzzy orders to move. She felt hands on her, arms sliding under her legs and back, her head draped back, hair brushed the sharp gravel, she felt strands get pulled out. Someone, it had to be Ricardo, lifted her off the ground in his arms, he ordered, "Open the trunk."

She heard shuffling and scraping, shoes crunching on the gravel, heard the old rusted trunk creak open. Coli tried to open her mouth, tried to force words of pleading out, but only inaudible croaks gutted up her arched throat.

Feeling him lower her, her back settling against the hard surface of the inside of the car, she tried again to cry for help but only soft whimpers scratched out. Her eyes were stuck closed but she could still tell when the lid lowered blocking out the light, then, the snick as the trunk latched.

Outside the car she could detect the rumbles of their voices, she couldn't make out what they were saying, her brain ached, ears clouded, the excruciating pain in the back of her head let her know she was still alive.

Only a minute or so, and the car rocked as someone climbed in, she heard two doors bang shut and the ignition fire up.

She rolled as the car swayed down the drive and turned onto the street.

CHAPTER TWENTY-NINE

Another sleepless night, Brogan sat up with a groan. He couldn't get her off his mind. There was no way his Coli was guilty of Ellery or Polito's murder, and he was positive she wasn't the one who harmed Kip when he was a baby.

After the very first time meeting Silina, a feeling had niggled in the back of his brain about Coli's innocence. Silina denying her own child, her hatred for Coli had made Brogan suspicious right off the bat.

He'd thought about it then, that it was Silina that had done the dastardly act that damaged Kip, and took all those years of Coli's young life. But, there was no evidence, it was a long time ago. Coli herself didn't know what had actually happened.

It had also entered his mind that Silina had done Delian in, but with Palumbo so involved with Delian it seemed more feasible that it was the gangster that had him hit. Pete Polito must have somehow been involved with Palumbo. Yet, his name was not in Delian's phone or computer, there was zero mention of him, no connection to the other players, except to Coli.

But then, all the evidence for Delian, with the gold-rimmed glasses and the knife, and the pearl button under Polito, not forgetting the henbane, the dog hairs, even Camille with the varnish poisoning pointed like a gigantic arrow to Coli. It was all too pat and obvious. Either Palumbo had ordered all the hits, or someone was framing Coli.

His chuckle derisive, the evidence was so overkill, it had to be a frame. However, that still left Kandy-Marie and the disappearance of Rex Reno and Dane Zachary hanging out there. Brogan needed to dissect the damned evidence if he had any hope of exonerating Coli.

His insides cringed at remembering cuffing her delicate wrists, her small hands trembling in his grasp. Piercing blades of his betrayal striking from her gorgeous blues, the heart-wrenching sobs that had torn him up as he left her there with that depraved cockroach, Gillan.

Brogan showered and dressed, not taking time for coffee or breakfast, he just grabbed his keys and strode to his truck, oblivious to the severely dry, snapping angry wind and furious golden sky. Widely breaking the speed limit, he headed for the highway that would take him to Mal Tierre.

Sitting at a long traffic light before the entrance to the expressway, Brogan unhitched his phone, swiped it on, maybe there was news about Palumbo confessing his sins. Thoughts spun of Silina bringing him that can of varnish, and the oddity that the only prints on it were hers.

Silina could have picked up the dog hairs and planted them. She had access to Coli's knives and glassware and could have easily stolen them.

Sure, he'd been suspicious of the bitch, but then all the items belonged to Coli. The cop in him needed to play by the rules. Arrest the suspect, Coli, and sort the rest out after. Aw hell, Brogan rubbed the back of his neck harshly as another recollection struck him. How stupid was he, how blind. He scrolled to his texts and found the one from Silina. The picture of the girls in the woods behind the Victorian.

Something, it had bothered him then, it bothered him more now, nagging, a feather tickling the back of his neck, he rubbed it again. "Ah," his eyes narrowed at the picture and a shiver rolled up his spine, "there, that's it." He quickly dialed Tarzan.

"Yo, Brog," the detective answered breezily.

"Tarzan, take Rocky and go to the Arabats' residence in Beyth Aven. Arrest Silina Arabat, the mother, Goldie too, if they're there, they might not be."

"What's up?" Tarzan's voice was instantly serious.

"Silina Arabat sent me a picture of her and Coli in the woods behind Coli's house. She had indicated the plants behind them, it was henbane. That's the poison that killed Pete Polito."

"Oh, hell, I'm sorry, Brog, your girl did do it? Not Palumbo?"

The light turned green, shaking his head, Brogan roared up the ramp to the expressway and zoomed into the ongoing traffic. "No, not Palumbo and not Coli Cassidy. Silina Arabat. I was so busy looking at the plants, and Coli, I didn't give Silina a thought. Now, I see."

"See what?" Tarzan interjected at his pause.

"Silina Arabat killed Delian and Polito. The blouse. That pearl button that was found under Pete Polito's body. Coli was wearing that blouse in the photo. It was already missing a pearl button. Long before Pete Polito was killed.

"On the report of the scene and evidence, there were zero prints on the button. If it had torn off while Coli was killing Polito and she was aware, she would have picked it up. If she was unaware, her prints would be on it. However, if you were planting evidence you'd ensure your prints weren't on it, so you'd wipe it.

"The bitch took Coli's blouse, tore the button off to frame Coli, somehow talked Coli into wearing it then she put the blouse back, I have it in evidence. I'm positive they'll find Silina's DNA on it. I have a feeling Silina snuck it back into Coli's closet without it being washed to keep Coli from noticing the missing button. Arabat will claim since they're sisters she'd borrowed the blouse, but, I'll get it all pinned down to where there is no reasonable doubt that bitch did Polito and probably Delian too."

"But Palumbo-"

"Palumbo is guilty of the gun trafficking, and likely a lot of other illegal shit. But, in this case, I don't think he ordered any of the hits. And, I'm thinking Rex Reno and or Dane Zachary did Kandy-Marie. Reno was stowing the guns in the basement of the

gallery. I think he caught Kandy-Marie snooping and bumped her off, dumped her out at Andy Caper's farm. That girl, Poppy, Kandy-Marie must have confided in her about her suspicions.

"When Kandy-Marie was murdered, Poppy feared she'd be next and she beat hell out of Dodge. We already know Reno and Zachary were up to criminal activity with the gallery as a front. There was no income coming in, but the bills were paid, electric and stuff. Pirate said the bills were paid in cash or money orders. They split, high-tailed it out of there as soon as Royce came back for more questions."

"What about Ellery Delian? Why would Silina kill him?"

"Dunno, although I'm sure it has something to do with jealousy. She stole the abusive bully from her sister. No doubt she did in Blanco as well because she was sleeping with Delian and Silina knew about it."

"Pete Polito? Delian, and Camille Blanco? You saying this woman killed all those people, not Vitale Palumbo?"

"I'm not positive, we'll find out when we bring Silina in. Hell, Tarz, I'm pretty sure when she was 13 she tossed her own baby out of a tree to kill him, she clearly didn't want to be hindered by a child, and she could get Coli out of her hair too, two birds one stone, and now again for the second time.

"We couldn't figure Polito's involvement in the gun trafficking. There was no evidence at all against him. I think Silina killed him to throw more shade on Coli. She was framing her for Delian and Polito's murders. The girl, Blanco, other than jealousy who knows why that crazy bitch would kill her.

"But, I'm almost 100% that the perp is Silina Arabat. I don't think it's gonna be all that hard to prove, yeah? She had easy access to Coli's house to steal the knife and glass, the hairs and the blouse. I believe we have two killers.

"I mean, hell, she brought me the can of varnish and threw her sister right under the bus claiming she found it in her trash, and, that was *before* it came out that Blanco died from that sort of poison. Then she just happens to know about the henbane plant, and happens to know it grows on Coli's land, and happens to get a selfie of them

in front of the plant and with Coli wearing the blouse the button found under Polito came from. The button torn off way before Polito was killed.

"Way, way, way too much evidence, it screams frame up. And if Silina is framing Coli with the evidence, then, shit, it points to her as the killer, right?"

Tarzan considered everything his friend was saying, paused, then asked, "What about that frog restaurant, could anyone ID Arabat? No one else was caught on video around Camille's apartment, she had to have been poisoned at the frog place."

Tarzan's calling the restaurant the frog place brought a smile to Brogan, then he sobered. "No. The servers and bartender paid no attention to the woman who had bought a drink and sat with Camille. Their vague description didn't match any of the players. Dark hair and glasses. Actually, sunglasses." Brogan blinked. "Yeah. It was nighttime, she went in disguise, clever girl. I bet dollars to donuts that she wore a damned wig."

"A lot to unravel, Brog. Okay, I'm on my way to the Arabats', where you going?"

"I'm goin' to Coli Cassidy's. I fear she might be in danger. If Silina and Goldie Arabat are there, I'll bring them in and call you. If you get 'em, buzz me. Later."

A dozen miles down the road and his phone rang. "Dillon," he answered.

"Me, Brog."

"Whatcha got, Lo?"

"Dam located cameras near the frog restaurant. I found a female in a video, not blonde, a brunette, wearing a pretty obvious and ugly wig, and she wore sunglasses but she bears a slight resemblance to your girl, Coli Cassidy, going into the restaurant the same time Blanco was there."

A beat, then, "How do you know about Coli? What she looks like?"

Pirate snorted, "Son, I know everything about everyone. Your girl is smoking hot. This babe in the video, like I said, there's a slight resemblance to Coli, she's got a sister, right?"

Brogan grunted. "Yeah, real bitch. For the record, she doesn't look a thing like Coli, nothing."

Pirate chuckled at the possessive insistence in the sheriff's harsh voice. "Okay. Like I said, your babe is smoking hot, the sister not so much, has a really big caboose and a sharp nose on her. I don't think the action she has going on up front is real, by the way."

Grunting again, Brogan said, "No doubt. Send me the pic. And, listen, the Polito killing, forensics checked the coffee cup for prints and found none except Polito's. Shoulda had at least the clerk's at the shop so that means it was wiped clean before given to Polito. She probably held a napkin around it before she handed it to Polito to keep her prints off.

"If they haven't, tell them to dust the bag the egg sandwich came in, and the wrapper around the sandwich. That broad is cunning but not that smart. For sure her prints will be on the bag or the wrapper. I bet we get more pictures of her goin' into the paint store with a bag from the Panini place."

"Will do."

They both disconnected. He heard it ping, but he didn't look at his phone until he came to a stop sign at the corner of Cornflower Lane and Wisteria Road.

Running his finger over the swipe, the photo downloaded immediately, confirming his suspicions. A crystal clear picture of Silina Arabat in a dark wig and sunglasses entering Quispe's of the infamous frog legs, the time stamp reflected a few hours before Camille Blanco was found dead.

A bad feeling made him feel queasy, it wasn't going to ease until he had Coli safe in his arms.

****

"Uh, Coli moaned. Every bump bounced her head on the hard floor of the trunk. Dizzy from her head wound, she managed to pry her eyes open.

Curled in a fetal position, she shifted her legs, then her arms, they were weak but thank goodness Ricardo hadn't tied her hands behind her or gagged her.

Carefully drawing in long breaths to stabilize the woozy disorientation and weakness, she didn't move for a minute. But, she couldn't just lie there and wait for them to park somewhere then come and get her and kill her; she must do something.

Gulping down the nausea that threatened with her every movement, she forced herself up to brace on a forearm so she could pat all around the trunk. There were levers in some cars designed especially for when people, mainly children accidentally got locked in car trunks. But, unfortunately her vehicle was as old as the hills, she was lucky she had electric windows.

The smallness of the trunk, the oppressive heat, no fresh air, Coli felt the walls closing in, claustrophobia was biting at her brain stealing her breath. She needed to calm herself, if she freaked out she'd die. Stuffing the panic climbing up her throat, she needed to slow down her racing pounding heart to think.

She had to get out of there, their voices had been muffled through her hazy pained ears, but as Ricardo put her in the trunk, she heard them talking about how after Ricardo had his way with her, they were going to kill her, bury her out in the prairies where her body would never be found.

The car was moving, screaming wouldn't do her any good. She remembered seeing on TV when a woman was abducted she kicked out the backlights and that brought attention to the car.

Hands shaking like an earthquake roiled in them, she brushed her palms along the rough carpet around her, yelped when the car hit a pothole and her head banged on the roof. Seeing stars again, Coli sucked in a quivering breath to suppress the nausea the bang raised.

She squirmed to her back, located one of the taillights, pulled her knee back and kicked the light as hard as she could. Nothing happened except now there was a shooting pain in her leg.

Shifting to her side, her elbow hit something. Coli felt around and exclaimed, "Oh my gosh," she grasped the wooden handle of a

hammer. "Thank you, God," she nearly wept, "and thank you for not letting any of the sociopathic trio see it."

It took ten whacks before she was able to break the plastic molding and glass. Rolling back, her chest billowing with heavy panting, she thought, *now what?* The car jostled and rocked, bumped and rattled over the dirt road that she assumed was Cornflower Lane. At the end of the long road it split into a fork at the end of the street, the road went in two opposite directions.

Maybe if she stuck her arm out the light hole someone would see it, she wriggled to the light. Her arm was too short, it wouldn't be seen unless they were stopped, and she knew they weren't stopping until they parked the car to kill her. Her heart pumped with wicked palpitations. "Okay, okay, Coli," she told herself, "calm down, take deep breaths. You panic and you're dead."

Lying still, sweat streamed down her face, her pajama top was soaked, she drew in measured deep breaths until her racing pulse diminished enough she could think. She moved her arm to get more comfortable, and it pushed into something that was in the corner side of the light. She missed it when she was feeling around.

Rolling to her stomach, Coli reached for the item, grabbed it and pulled it to her so she could make out what it was in the dark trunk. She couldn't see it, but she could feel it. It was Douggie's chew toy. A smile sifted even as terrified as she was.

The pup had left his toys outside, and she had tossed them in the trunk because she was planning to take Douggie to the Gregorys' so the two boys could play with him. She felt around some more and clasped the rubber bone. The smile fell, what good would a couple of dog toys do her?

Feeling the car slow, she assumed they had reached the fork. Her body rolled to the right when the car turned to the left, the way to the prairies. Quickly she shoved the chew toy out the broken light. But she knew it was hopeless, no one would see it or understand why it was lying in the dusty road.

Another couple miles and they came to another turnoff, she pushed the bone out the light, then laid back and closed her eyes to garner her strength.

Already fighting the relentless dragging down feeling of fainting, the rocking car lolled her. Coli blinked the drowsiness from her eyes, how long had it been? How far out to the plains had they gone?

As scared as she was knowing what was going to happen when the car stopped, she welcomed the ending of the nauseating rocking. The jostling only added to her queasiness, worsened the throbbing pain in her head, and lying there curled up in the small boiling hot trunk in the dark, waiting… was unbearable.

The Victorian was located in the rocky area with forests on the edge of the grasslands, past the lusher grass the partial desert began.

Coli had no idea how far they'd gone when she felt the car bump over clumpy grass then smoother packed dirt, and…it rolled to a stop.

Her heart pounded out of her chest, she was so frightened she could barely draw a breath, sweat prickled down her spine.

CHAPTER THIRTY

Brogan's heart sank when he saw that Coli's car was not at her house. There were other vehicles there though, so he parked and strode to the Victorian taking the porch steps two at a time, his boots thumped loudly over the planked verandah.

Banging his fist hard on the door, he put his finger on the bell and pressed, not letting up. He could hear the musical tinkle melody Coli had chosen ringing inside.

Keeping his finger glued to the bell he pounded on the door, no one came. What. The. Hell. The bastards weren't gonna answer the fucking door.

Furiously, he raced around the house trying to peer into windows. But either drapes were drawn, or glass was tinted and he couldn't get a good look inside. He tried every door he reached, they were all solidly locked.

Brogan stood back and glared at the house searching for any movement. What he wanted to do was throw a rock through a window and get inside. He couldn't, he felt something was wrong but he had no probable cause to break in.

"Damn," he cursed, looked up to the sky, and grimaced. The storm wasn't a thunder-rain storm, it was a full blown haboob. Strong turbulent winds whipped up a wall of dust and dirt a thousand feet thick and 100 feet high, it could completely envelope an entire town at once.

Visibility was already dimming as was the sunlight as the monstrous storm crept from the mountains over the dry hot plains and headed straight for Mal Tierre.

Staring at the bright orange, massive cloud wall coming at him, he worried, "What if Coli was out driving in this?" He ran to his truck, he had to find her.

A few feet from his truck and something bumped his boot. Expecting a branch or some shit bouncing over his foot, he looked down and Douggie's maw was on his boot. "Hey boy," he said, crouching to give him a pet, "where's your mommy? She- what the hell?" His hand was wet, he looked at it, blood smeared his fingers.

"Douggie," he muttered, bending to examine the dog to determine if it was Douggie that was injured or he carried someone else's blood, like Coli's. His fingers sifted over the dog, when they roamed the back of his head Douggie whimpered.

Brogan leaned in for a closer look. "Ah, okay boy, you got a good gash in your head. You need a vet, come on." When he went to scoop him up the dog whimpered again and shoved his nose into the gravel.

Puzzled, Brogan murmured, "What pup, what are you trying to tell me-" Then he saw what the dog was trying to bring to his attention.

Long strands of blonde hair were tangled in the gravel. Some bits of gravel and hair had smears of...blood on them. A few drops of oil near the hair told Brogan it was where Coli normally parked her car.

Now that the hair caught his attention, he studied the area carefully. Glancing all over, he noticed that the gravel was gouged up and disturbed, many footprints of all sizes in a bunch had stomped the grass by and on the oil spot, the gravel was all shoved around in patches, like there had been excessive activity.

Between the hair, the blood, the messed up gravel, the injured dog, and Coli's car gone, spindles of icy fear lifted up the hairs on the back of his neck, sweat dotted his hairline. Something bad had happened here.

Brogan picked the dog up and started for his truck. "Okay boy, we're gonna go find your mama then take you to the vet, you okay with that?" Douggie gave a tiny woof, then closed his eyes. Brogan set him carefully on the passenger seat and climbed behind the wheel.

He drove down Wisteria Road as it was the only way that led in and out of the Victorian's location. Turning off Wisteria he followed Cornflower Lane all the way to the end where it forked into two totally opposite directions. He stopped at the stop sign, what to do now?

****

Coli heard the two car doors open but not close. Of course not, her sister was a lazy slug and Ricardo was apparently a kindred spirit. Just as evil and just as lazy. She braced, listening to their footsteps shuffling on the dirt come around from both sides of the car getting louder as they reached the back.

She could hear them talking but couldn't make out what they were saying, but they didn't sound happy. Silina's nasally voice was angry and whining, nothing new there. Coli held her breath, she was going to pretend she was still out of it.

The key scraped into the keyhole, creaked in its turn to unlock, and the trunk lid was lifted.

Silina was still grousing, "No, I don't see why you have to fuck her. It was different when it was going to be you and Granddad. I couldn't argue with Granddad, he wouldn't allow it, I'd be sore for a week. But now, Granddad isn't here, let's just kill her and bury her like he said."

"Shut the hell up, Silina, for once for God's sake would you zip it?" Ricardo rattled off a string of harsh Spanish words that were likely curses. "Just get the shovel and go wait inside the car if you don't want to watch me."

Still holding her breath, Coli was appalled at their total lack of a conscience, discussing raping and killing her like they were talking about a grocery list. Under her body, her fist tightened its hold, her

heart was pounding, she had to stay perfectly still, even out her breathing.

As the trunk lid opened, Ricardo's voice came closer. "Broad is still out cold, boy, your mother can sure pack a wallop with that cast iron pan." He leaned in and listened, then said, "She's still breathing, Goldie didn't kill her. There's a blanket in the back seat, spread it out there under that tree," he instructed.

Coli could hear Silina's harrumph of irritation at being ordered around. Ricardo bent and slid his hands under Coli and lifted her out of the trunk.

Holding her tight to his chest, she bumped slightly as he carried her to where Silina was bitching a wild streak while laying out the blanket. Ricardo was so intent on what he was planning to do to her, he didn't notice Coli kept one hand tucked in the small of her back.

"Seriously, Ricardo, the storm is almost upon us, do you have to do this? Just break her neck and leave her, they'll assume it was the storm that killed her. Wild animals might take off with her body parts and that will be that. Save us the trouble of having to dig a damned hole." Silina's mouth was slurry as sandy dirt swooped into it with the swirling hot wind.

Spitting the dirt out and wiping her tongue with her palm, Silina went on, "I mean, geez, look, Ricardo," Silina pointed at the hundred-foot high massive wall of the sparkling orange, gusting cloud that was approaching.

Dust, dirt, and sand twirled, rushing around inside the mass as it grew bigger and fiercer. It was the plains but there were pockets of trees, yet everything between the three people to the horizon was disappearing into the blinding white-orange tempest.

"It's only going to take a few minutes, I might want to do it twice, quit complaining. If you can't shut up go sit in the car," Ricardo told her. He dropped to one knee and laid Coli on the blanket.

"Okay, sweets," he said and lightly slapped Coli's cheek. "I need you to wake up, won't be as much fun with you unconscious. However," he chuckled, "that won't stop me from getting what I want. I wish we could keep you for a while, I'm sure a couple of

times inside you won't be enough to satisfy me. But," he sighed, "I can't take the chance of you escaping and turning me in. So, let's make our limited time together spectacular, shall we?"

Coli lay still as a board until she felt Ricardo's fingers grasp her pajama bottoms and she suddenly swung her arm from behind her back and slammed the hammer into Ricardo's temple.

Grunting a small 'oof' he collapsed on the blanket. Coli jumped to her feet, swayed as the dizziness struck her, she had to take a second to steady herself-

Whack-

Silina slung the shovel into Coli's back, Coli dropped to her knees, almost face-planting.

"Damn you, Coli, always screwing things up for me you cow. This ends now." Silina pulled the shovel back to hit Coli again, aiming for her head this time. She swung the shovel and Coli rolled as it whizzed past her head causing Silina to stumble off balance and topple forward tumbling to her knees.

Coli staggered to her feet and started running.

Silina gathered her wits, pushed off the ground, clutching the shovel, she ran after her smaller half-sister.

Left behind, Ricardo lay stretched out on the blanket, the hammer resting next to his limbs that were twitching with seizures.

****

Brogan sat at the fork, the two roads going in opposite directions, if he went the wrong way, heck, he didn't even know if she was out there. She might have gone shopping for all he knew. But, a brow sloped up as he probed the catastrophic sky, she would be too smart to go out into that thunderous hell rampaging straight at them.

Beside him, Douggie uttered a weak woof as if he heard and agreed with Brogan's thoughts.

Then he saw it, something was in the middle of the left side of the forked road. It looked like a rubber rabbit wearing a plaid outfit. "Oh baby," he smiled, praising Coli, "you are the smartest."

He turned to the left fork. Brogan had to force himself to drive relatively slowly, he felt the urgency to find her, but he didn't want to miss another breadcrumb by speeding past it.

The urgency intensified as the storm inched closer, the wind rattled the truck hurling sand and ripped branches, whirling clumps of dirt pinged at the metal body and crackled against the glass windshield. Visibility was so bad now it was like driving through a dense yet moving malignant fog.

Face at the windshield, squinting through the billowing dust storm, Brogan could just make out that up ahead the road was ending, cut off by a rare grove of trees, his hammering heart fell again. He'd chosen the wrong turn.

"Ah, shit, boy," he muttered to the sleeping dog as he gripped the wheel about to spin it to turn around when he caught the plaid material whipping in the wind a few feet in front of the truck.

"Douggie, my man," he crowed, "that's yours too!" He drove past the rubber bone, his body slanted forward, nose almost pressed against the windshield so he could see through the engrossing cloud.

He hadn't gone far past the thicket of trees when he spotted Coli's little red car, and his body agitated eagerly. "Calm down, you don't have her yet," he warned himself. The fact that her car was parked out in the middle of nowhere did not bode well.

Sand and dirt ground under the tires as he cautiously approached the car. Stopping a few feet from it, he glanced around first, but there was little to see but the orange heaving wall pressing down on him. The wind whipped his hair and clothes, particles flung stinging his exposed skin.

Carefully sliding out of the truck, he closed the door to keep Douggie protected. The wind slashed his skin and slapped his hair, dirt stung as it struck. Tromping cautiously to the car, he peered in a window, it was empty. The lid to the trunk was up revealing it too was empty. A taillight was broken completely out, *ah hell, she'd been in the trunk*. That's how the toys got on the road.

Squinting against the flying dust, he glanced around but could see nothing except a blanket shoved up against a tree. Appeared that the wind had tossed it there. "Come on, Coli, girl, where the hell are

you?" he asked the raging cloud while struggling to see ten feet ahead.

At the last second he heard a grunt behind him and he ducked, raising his elbow up to block whatever might be coming at him, good thing, as Ricardo swung a hammer at Brogan's skull. The hammer caught a glancing blow off Brogan's shoulder knocking him forward, he lurched awkwardly to catch himself from falling, behind him Ricardo let out a slew of venomous curses and came after him.

Brogan sought to gain his balance and Ricardo barreled at him launching the hammer, slicing it rapidly back and forth like a sword at his head. Brogan stumbled backwards ducking left then right, he heard the hammer whiz by it was so close to his ear.

He saw a line of blood trailing from Ricardo's temple, he hoped that was Coli's doing. Then his stomach cramped, Ricardo was here but Coli wasn't, was he too late?

Brogan leaped and crouched, twisted and ducked as Ricardo kept swinging the damned hammer trying his damndest to bash his brains in.

Sweating and huffing like a stuck pig, Ricardo grunted with every swing and miss, he swung faster, harder- "Goddammit!" he roared narrowly missing Brogan's cheek as the sheriff jumped back from a vicious swing.

"You bastard!" Screaming his fury, he lunged at Brogan heaving the hammer with all his might- Brogan sidestepped and grabbed the hammer as it rocketed past his head, and pulled it using his weight forcing Ricardo to keep hurtling forward with the momentum.

Ricardo belly-flopped slamming his face into the ground. Tossing the hammer, Brogan jumped on him, flipped him over on his back, and battered the man with his fists until the ground ran red and Ricardo no longer moved.

His big chest heaving with rushing breaths, Brogan sat back on his heels and wiped the back of his hand across his sweating forehead. Seeing the blood on his hands he had no doubt it was all

over his face and clothes. But he couldn't worry about that now. "Damn, I lost control, I needed the guy to tell me where Coli is."

Huffing, he stared down at the prone man. Ricardo's chest still rose and fell but only very slightly, his face was a gruesome mash of blood and tissue and shattered bone.

Brogan rolled him over on his stomach and cuffed his hands behind his back, not that he was going to be able to be moving much too soon. Still breathing hard, Brogan struggled to his feet. Wiping his hands on his jeans he bent over and grabbing Ricardo's shoulders he dragged him to Coli's car.

After getting the man inside, Brogan stood, scrutinizing the area the best he could, he just felt, *knew* Coli was out there somewhere. His head down, he fought the storm to search around the area. The wind slapped his hair and clothes harder as the storm continued its journey swallowing everything in its path.

He kept an arm over the tops of his eyes to keep the dust and sand out. It was hopeless to see where she went, he might as well just try a direction-

There, footprints in the hard-packed dirt heading south, he followed them in a sprint even as the wind was sweeping them away. The haboob, stories tall, clouds blended into the sky until they became one writhing mushrooming orange mass descending to cover as far as the eye could see.

The sun still shone above it making the orange and white particles in the dust storm sparkle and twinkle, a killer fairytale that blacked out illumination to the rest of the countryside.

Fighting his way through the storm, it knocked him sideways and backwards, he fought onward with his head down, lids half closed to keep the particles out of his eyes, he was breathing hard but had to keep his mouth closed.

Lifting the hem of his shirt he pressed it over his mouth and nose and trudged on.

Brogan tried to listen for voices, movement, but he heard nothing but the roiling storm and saw nothing but orange dust engulfing him. He was losing hope he would find her, and thinking

about seeking shelter when he heard it. A thin scream barely perceptible sifting through on the wind.

He turned towards it and pushed through the storm praying to hear it again or he'd never find her. There, again, a slight wail through the walled cloud, he pressed on in the direction of the scream. Up ahead, the land rolled into high jagged hills, the mountains millions of years ago had left enormous boulders scattered behind.

His heart stopped. Up a steep hill, he saw Coli and her sister locked in combat. Silina's hands were around Coli's throat and she was strangling her. Silina was much bigger and heavier than Coli, and Coli seemed to be losing the battle. The screams were coming from Silina, she was shrieking her rage.

Brogan cupped his hands around his mouth and yelled, "Coli! Coli!" The wind smacked his words away. He started running-

Coli was on her knees, bent backwards and Silina hovered over her, forcing her to arch back further and further, her hands clutched around Coli's neck she was squeezing and shaking it-

Brogan ran faster, shouting Coli's name. Right before his eyes, Silina pushed too hard and she toppled over Coli knocking them both to the ground, and as one, they rolled off the side of the steep rugged hill, must be a cliff because Brogan couldn't see them, they were gone.

He roared, "No- no- no- *Coli*!"

CHAPTER THIRTY-ONE

The sheriff stood in horrified shock, blinking tears whipped out from the blasting wind and striking sand. Wiping his eyes, he pushed through the buffeting storm to the steep rocky hill.

He climbed with his knees bent, hands grabbing the ground, keeping his sight on where he'd seen Coli disappear. It took forever fighting the force of the storm when he finally reached the spot where the girls had been fighting.

Brogan dropped down further to this hands and knees and crawled to the edge with the storm trying to pound him into the ground. His heart jumping out of his throat, he peered over the edge terrified of seeing Coli's broken body lying on the rocks at the bottom of the hill.

A few yards down, his relief about took his breath away, Coli was alive, but, instead of climbing down the sloping side to safety, she was inching sideways. Her little fingers clutching to the jagged rocks, her head bowed to the storm.

Brogan's gut clenched when her foot slipped and she had to grapple hard and fast to stop from tumbling to her death down the side of the precipitous hill.

"Coli!" Brogan called out, his voice lifting over the surging currents of the haboob.

She didn't look up, he put his hands around his mouth and shouted, "Coli! Coli!"

Her body stilled, head cocked, she tilted her head keeping her eyes half-closed from the flying sand, her mouth dropped at the sight of him.

"Stay there, baby, I'm comin' for you, don't move!" Brogan shouted then carefully climbed over the edge of the cliff, and slowly hand over hand, one foot moving at a time, he made his way to her.

Coli clung to the rocks, the wind spanking her pajamas, hair flinging around her head, watching him fight to get to her.

Moving painstakingly slowly, Brogan scuttled down and over to her. His stomach loosened its clench with a shudder when he reached her. "Baby," he shouted, grabbing her arm. "C'mere," and pulled her into his deft embrace.

Coli stiffened at first. "Brogan!" Gulping hard her throat was so dry, she asked, "What are you doing here?"

"I came for you, and when I get you safely home I'm gonna tan that little hide of yours. What the hell are you doing? We need to get down, why were you-"

Huddled against his chest, Coli pointed.

Brogan followed her motion and saw Silina lying far below but way to the side with the ground pitched steep and deadly under her, and corkscrewing jagged rocks around and above.

She lay prone on a few rocks that jutted from the hillside that must have caught her plunging somersaulting body on the way down. She wasn't moving, her arms and legs lay crookedly on the rocks.

It didn't break his heart to see the murdering sociopath lying broken on the boulders. Brogan tightened his arm around Coli and said, "Come on, we need to find shelter," he started to draw her down the easier, sloping side of the hill, but Coli shook her head, pulled back from him.

His brow furrowed, he shouted quizzically, "What? We need to go, baby, there's a wicked thunderstorm pushing behind the haboob." He pulled her tight to his side.

"No." She pushed at him but he didn't loosen his grip on her. "I have to get Silina!"

The storm blustering around and between them tried to wrench Coli from his arms. "What? Why? She tried to kill you, she's more than likely dead, you are not risking your life to get to her." Even in the shimmering yet darkening storm he saw Coli's face blanch.

"I can't leave her there, Brogan, she may be hurt, she needs help, I have to-"

"You don't to have to do shit, babe, you're getting somewhere safe." He started dragging her away and down the hill. She fought him, shouting, "No! Brogan, I can't leave her there!"

Cursing a blue streak, ignoring her struggles to get free, Brogan continued hauling her down the steep hill, "Let me get you safe and I'll go get her."

"Brogan-"

"I'll get her, I promise, come on." He about lifted her off her feet to keep her moving once they hit the flat ground. Tucking her tight against his side, he hustled her towards the grouping of boulders back near her car.

The boulders formed a tiny cave. With a huff, he shoved her in as far as he could and slid in after her.

The big rocks sheltered them from the brunt of the storm, their heavy breathing filled the small area. Catching her breath, Coli said, "Brogan, I can't leave her there." She tried to scramble around him, he blocked her in.

"No, baby, you stay here. I said I would get her." He dragged his sleeve across his eyes and forehead, lifted the hem of his shirt to wipe his mouth. On his hands and knees, he wrapped his hand around the back of her head, pulled her forward and planted his mouth on hers.

Twisting his head to fit more tightly, he ground their mouths furiously together in his frantic fright for Coli's life, and fury at what had happened to her, and angry fear of her trying to put her delicate little body back out in the broiling storm to go save her murdering sister.

Her fingers caught in his shirt at his chest, she clutched the material in her fists, and gave as good as she got. He hated to break

away, hated to leave her, *hell*. Leaning back, he gasped, sucking in big gulping breaths he said, "Stay tuned for part two of that, baby."

Setting her back from him, he stuck a finger in her face. "Okay, I'm goin' out there, you do not move from this spot. There's a killer thunderstorm raging behind the haboob pushing the dust storm more fiercely and making it all more deadly than usual. Please, baby," he cupped her chin and said, "don't make me have to come back here then go back out there to find you. Okay?"

Her lips pressed, she nodded. "Okay. Be careful, Brogan. I'll do as you say. Just," she took a deep breath, "try to get her, but don't risk your life."

His brow lifted, it was risking his life leaving the protection of the boulders. Her cheeks blushed. "I, I know, I mean, if it's too treacherous to get her, then…" her sigh a groan, "leave her. I'd rather lose her than you."

That brought a smile to his harsh face, he bent and kissed her gently, chucked her chin, and crawled out of the rocky shelter. He turned at the entrance and said, "Stay there, Coli, please." It sounded like he was asking her but the tone of his voice was a threat if she moved.

Outside was a cauldron of blind raging wind and flying debris, a regurgitating blend of dust, sand, dirt and anything the storm could pick up along the way to join the party.

Not able to really see where he was going, he followed their footprints that were rapidly being blown away back to the hill. He checked his phone for bars, but there were none.

It was harder to get up the hill on the other side, the rocks jagged out, dangerous and cutting, but he had to go up where Silina lay rather the way he had originally gone up. It would be too hard to climb down those sharp rocks from the top, so he went up from the bottom.

He found her quickly.

CHAPTER THIRTY-TWO

Kneeling beside Silina, Brogan set two fingers to her neck. She had a weak pulse. When he touched her, her arms twitched, then her legs. Her back, neck weren't broken.

He should leave her there for experienced paramedics to retrieve so they could secure her, protect her neck and spine, but the storm could finish the job the fall caused and kill her. He had to chance it.

Brogan slowly, carefully lifted Silina, groans retched out of her limp body as he picked her up. He was going to have to get back down the treacherous hill and to the boulders without dropping her and breaking his own neck, so he gingerly maneuvered her over his shoulder and carried her fireman style back to the shelter of boulders.

Once there, he let her slide from his shoulder to his arms, still, it was difficult to stoop and hold the girl but he managed to get them both inside. He carried her as far inside the cave-like shelter he could get then gently laid her on her back.

Coli crawled over but stopped before she reached her sister, she looked up at Brogan. "Is she…"

"She's alive, baby." He moved nearer to her and sat down with a tired sigh. "But she's hurt pretty badly." Crossing his legs, he brushed sand and crap out of his hair and off his clothes.

Creeping close to Brogan, Coli slung her arms around him and laid her head on his shoulder. "Thank you, Brogan. I'm so glad

you're okay, I was petrified while you were gone, I never should have had you go get Silina."

The fear lessened from her voice fraught with worry, turned abashed. "As horrible as it sounds, I cared more that you survived than her, but I was panicked, hysterical with- with everything that happened, so scared I couldn't think. I pictured her alive and the storm carrying her off and snapping her in two- and-" she broke off with a sob.

"Baby," Brogan sighed, and lifted her to sit on his lap and slipped his arms around to cuddle her.

His nose in her hair, he said, "It's okay, once I had you safe in here I was going back for her anyway. Like you, I would have chosen your life over hers, but I couldn't leave her there either."

Coli arched her neck to peer up at him. He brushed her dusty snarled hair from her equally dusty face. He bent to bring their lips together but she stopped him and asked, "Why?"

His brow wrinkled. "Why what, Cubbie-doll?"

She stroked his rough cheek with trembling fingertips. "You arrested me, locked me up, believe I am guilty of murder. Why are you here?" Her voice held confusion and sadness.

Brogan wriggled back to lean his back against a boulder and snuggled her, kissed her temple. "Maybe for a fleeting half a second because of the damned evidence I believed you were guilty of murder, Coli, but I know you aren't capable of hurting even an ant.

"But, with all that evidence, I'm the law, I had to do my job, I would have appeared biased, corrupt if I had looked the other way. I came back to the jail that day because as I drove away I couldn't bear to leave you there in that cell. It killed me, baby, to put you there," he combed his fingers through her tousled tresses.

He took a hard breath before going on, "When I returned and saw that animal assaulting you, shit, I would have killed him if Pirate and the deputies hadn't pulled me off him. I," he forked his fingers through his own hair, "decided I had to take you home, leave you there while I figured out what the hell was going on. I needed to refute the evidence. The more I thought about it, I became suspicious

of your sister, but we had all assumed the mobster Vitale Palumbo was at the root of the murders."

"But Silina was guilty," Coli murmured, and nestled more comfortably in his arms.

He blinked down at her. "You know?"

Her head brushed his shoulder with her nod. Then she looked up. "She bragged about it before they took me. How did you know it was her?"

Cradling her in the crook of his arm, he webbed her face with his broad hand. "Things started coming through my thick skull. Hers but not your fingerprints were on the can of varnish she brought me claiming you used it to poison Camille Blanco.

"Why would you take the time to wipe your prints off then toss it right in your own front yard? I think Silina wiped it clean so you would look suspicious for covering your own trail. Also, we couldn't pin it down for sure, but I didn't think the cause of Camille's death had been released to the news yet Silina knew about it.

"Then the fact that I believed you were too smart to use your own cutlery and glasses to leave at the scene of the crime, and then leave them out in the open for me to see knowing I would visit you. And, there was the photo of you and Silina in your back woods with the picture of henbane behind you."

"Henbane? Picture?"

A wry chuckle, he traced her lips with a fingertip. "Yeah. She sent me a picture of you and her standing in front of a henbane plant. It can be toxic, she used it to kill Peter Polito, to frame you further. The thing was," he shook his head, smiled without humor, "she was stupid. She deliberately took the picture making sure you were wearing that blouse with the pearl buttons, the one I took from your armoire. She had left a button from it under Pete's body and put the blouse back for me to find."

"Oh. I remember that day. She insisted we go outside for walk and went into the woods even when I kept warning her it was too tangled and dangerous, the trails were all overgrown." She frowned

thoughtfully. "She also insisted I wear that blouse, said my t-shirt was ugly."

Her lips bunched wryly. "I should have known better when she said she wanted to put a photo of me on their mantle at home. Gosh," she lowered her head, shook it with chagrin, "I am so gullible." Coli glanced over at her unconscious sister.

"She hates me, has always hated me. I've always known it, she never bothered to hide it. I had hoped when we grew up, living apart she might someday at least maybe tolerate me, but she held her hate cell deep, every atom of her raged to hurt me. I just don't get it, Brogan, I don't know why."

"Pure jealousy, baby. Everyone loved you, you're gorgeous and sweet and loving and caring, everything she isn't. She wanted to destroy you so she would no longer compare herself to your beautiful soul. She thought if she got rid of you then all your beauty would transfer to her and everyone would love her, want her."

Shyly, Coli said, "I still don't get why you're here. How on earth did you find me?"

"Ah, darlin'," he murmured, bent and kissed her, caressing her face with his thumb. He gazed at her, his eyes travelled her face, lips, eyes, his pupils enlarged, covering the irises completely radiating his desire for her.

"I had a bad feeling, I had to get to you. I was afraid, so afraid, I felt you were in trouble. Douggie showed me the messed up gravel, strands of your hair caught in it. I took off after you."

His mouth quirked in a proud smile. "I found Douggie's toys and followed your trail. Like I always said, baby, you are the smartest person I know, well, maybe except Pirate," he grinned. "So, tell me what happened at the house, how did you end up out here?"

Her lashes lowered covering her eyes, they splayed on her dusty round cheeks. "Um," she paused, it was too embarrassing to say. Two attempted rapes in as many days. What was she, a magnet to heinous people? Was there a light flashing over her head that said 'easy victim, come do as you please with me?'

A hoarse snivel erupted from the back of their shelter. Hate filled with poisonous jealousy, Silina snarled, "As usual," she

groaned in pain, "my sister the whore displayed herself naked on her bed and enticed, *invited* my grandfather and my boyfriend to fuck her any which way they wanted." A slight shuffle sounded then a cry out, "Ow, ow, help me, it hurts," she whined.

Ignoring her, Brogan cupped Coli's jaw to make her look at him. "Baby, what the hell is she talking about? I know you wouldn't do that." His eyes narrowed at her. "They didn't, did they hurt you?" His fingers tightened in her soft skin as he questioned her.

"Tell him," Silina croaked out a sneer. "Tell him how you pushed Granddad down the stairs, and hit Ricardo with," she gasped a breath of pain, "a- a hammer, you bitch." Thunder crashed suddenly making them all jump. It grew so dark Brogan and Coli couldn't see Silina lying further back, but her groans and cries of pain reached them.

Coli's anger showed as she said, "They were going to kill me, was I to just stand there with a foolish smile and say 'have at it'?"

"Baby," Brogan said with concern, yet happy she defended herself and hurt the bastards. "I am so proud of you, but are you hurt?"

"Who gives a shit about her! I'm the one that's injured!" Silina's scream rasped with pain. "I think my legs, my arms are broken. You have to help me! Sheriff, take me to the car. Leave that whore here and get me to a *fucking hospital*," the end of her words shook off with a gasp and cry of pain.

Coli saw Brogan's bloody knuckles, she grasped his hand. "Brogan, what happened?" She knew he'd cut them up when he attacked Deputy Gillan but this was fresh blood.

Brogan casually wiped both knuckles on his jeans. "Ricardo came after me with a hammer." Because Brogan was present and Ricardo wasn't, he left the implication of what happened afterwards hang.

"It was my hammer!" Coli announced. The rain came then, in roaring sheets. Thunder crashed, the only light was from the long jagged flashes of lightning. Tucked in the refuge of the boulders, like a cave, it was pitch black.

"Who cares!" Silina shrieked then howled with pain. "Sheriff, take me to the car, right now!"

Brogan cuddled Coli and settled back against the boulder wall. He had checked his phone again and still no bars. The thick storms would block satellite connection. "No. We're way off the road, it'd be too dangerous to try to walk or drive in that shit. We'll chill for now."

Squeezing Coli against him, he said, "We'll hash it all out when we're home safe and sound."

"Noooo," Silina wailed, "help me! Take me outta here!"

Coli threaded her fingers together, twisted and tugged on them until Brogan set his hand over them to still their fretting. "Baby, what is it?" he asked, his head close to hers.

"Oh, it's Douggie. He saved me, Brogan. I wouldn't be here now if he hadn't attacked Grandfather Auston when he was assaulting me. Their plan was to...uh, rape...me and then kill me. Bury me out here where I would never be found."

Her tired smile broadened with pride. "But my brave puppy foiled Grandfather, it was because of him I got away the first time. I heard him yelping then go silent as I fled. I've been so worried Grandfather hurt him, even..." she couldn't say the word kill, she was too scared that it had happened.

Then her face lifted with relief. "You said he showed you my hair in the gravel, does that mean he's all right?"

Brogan wound his arm to pull her close. "Yeah, baby. He's hurt, but he's okay, he's in my truck, we'll take him to the vet on the way home."

"Oh, Brogan," she sighed with contentment. Her smile beautiful, she wrapped her hands around his neck and pulled him down for a kiss of gratitude, and more.

With Silina's moans and cries and pleas, and cursing that she would see them tortured and dead when she was healed, and the thunder booming in a baleful background, Brogan lowered his head with a smile, the pair made out to the tune of booming and whining. Even the harrowing sound of a freight train roaring by didn't distract them.

314

By the time the storms diminished, Brogan and Coli were entwined, lying drowsy on the hard ground. Brogan had maneuvered Coli so she was mostly lying on top of him, their breaths and heartbeats in sync. At the back of the cave Silina had passed out from the excruciating pain.

Holding Coli against him, Brogan shifted to sit up. Petting her hair, her head resting on his chest, he murmured, "The storms have passed, Cubbie-doll. I'm gonna go out and see if I can get a signal. Stay here until I come for you. Hear me?"

She smiled sleepily up at him. "Yes, Boss, whatever you say."

"Hmm," he grunted, cradling her jaw he nipped her lips. "I'm thinkin' some sassy little girl is lookin' for a certain sheriff to discipline her, yeah?"

At the shocked, apprehensive look on her face he laughed loud. "I'm thinkin' it's gonna be fun disciplinin' you, baby."

Her expression nonplussed with half fear, half-arousal, he laughed again, kissed her and settled her to sit back against the boulder wall and got up.

At the entrance he reminded her, "Stay put, baby. And don't go near Silina. Yeah, she's severely injured but she can't be trusted, that one's a cunning, slippery skunk." His bulk blocked the reining sunlight that now pushed through the remnants of the dust and storm clouds.

When he moved, the light streamed inside brightening their rocky hovel.

Brogan got a signal and called Tarzan giving him directions to where they were, and instructions to call for a couple of ambulances.

He and Coli walked back to where her car and his truck were parked, and they were stunned at the sight that beheld them.

Coli's little red car had apparently met a tornado judging by the dents all around it, and it was upside down, and not where it had been left. *Uh oh*, the thought frizzed through Brogan, he'd left Ricardo in the car. Boots splatting in puddles, he ran over to the vehicle. Coli hesitated then followed him.

Crouching, mindful of the broken glass sprinkled like salt over the dark wet earth, Brogan peered inside the car, it was empty. "Huh," he grunted. "Where-" a spot of color in his peripheral, he turned to see Ricardo lying bent under a tree. The tree was black and splintered, looked like it had been struck by lightning. "Stay here, baby," *Ricardo might not be a pretty sight.*

He hustled over, lowered to his haunches. Ricardo was on his side, wrists still cuffed. His dark hair and clothes were singed, skin sooty, the damage Brogan had inflicted to his face still prevalent under burn marks and soot.

Brogan thought he'd be safe from the storm when he left him in the car, who knew a damned tornado would come spinning by? Must have been the loud train roar they'd heard while tucked in the shelter of the cave.

Ricardo appeared to have been electrocuted by the lightning. He must have crawled out of the crumpled car after it got tossed by the tornado and made his way to the tree thinking he would be protected under it.

Brogan touched the pulse at his neck, it was shallow but it was there.

Coli was tiptoeing towards them, Brogan stood and moved her away to another cluster of boulders. "We can wait here, baby," he pulled her into his arms.

By the time Tarzan, Rocky and Dam arrived with wailing sirens, Brogan and Coli were leaning against the boulders in an embrace, mouths plastered together.

Tarzan hopped out of one of the cruisers and jogged to Brogan with a confused yet broad grin. "Brog, man, what the hell?" He reached the couple that reluctantly broke apart at his approach. His eye caught their hands twined and the soft blush of desire on their faces.

Brogan kissed the tip of Coli's nose. "BRB, baby." He tapped Tarzan's arm for the detective to follow him. The men trod over to the police cruiser, the ambulances' sirens grew louder as they neared.

Rocky climbed from the driver's side of a second cruiser, Dam hopped out of the passenger side. Curiosity on the three men's faces didn't ebb the cheesy grins at seeing Brogan and Coli in a clutch when they arrived.

"I take it you've cleared the hot babe, Brog." Rocky grinned at the shy blush that pinked Coli's cheeks aware they were talking about her.

"Uh huh." Brogan grasped their arms, turning them to face away from Coli. "I still think Rex Reno and probably Dane Zachary killed Kandy-Marie. The guns were stowed in his gallery's basement and her blood and torn nail were there.

"As soon as we started questioning them, they disappeared leaving no paper trail comin' or goin' makin' 'em look guilty as sin. But Silina Arabat was the one that murdered Ellery Delian, Camille Blanco and Peter Polito." The corner of his lip rose crookedly at their shocked expressions.

"We knew about Blanco from the video of Silina's presence at the restaurant, and the staff confirmed Silina was alone with Blanco inside," Rocky said.

"We picked up more video of her entering Polito's store with a cup of coffee and white bag with the café's Papyrus and Panini on it right before he died, so that was a given. Staff there also confirmed she'd bought that egg and sausage sandwich and a cup of coffee. Her prints will clinch it. But Delian? I thought that was Palumbo?"

Brogan shrugged, glanced over at Coli. She was staring off towards where the storm was now wreaking havoc in the next town over in the distance. The huge, black whirling dervish was faintly visible. "True, Delian was involved in the gun trafficking and smuggling, but Silina was jealous of his desire for her sister and killed him to end it, and framed her sister."

"Uh," Dam gulped, and said, "that'll do it. A bit severe though."

"Yeah," Brogan agreed. "Bitch is cold, no conscience whatsoever. Wanted to make her sister suffer back in prison again. Total sociopath. She was injured in the storm, she's over there in those boulders," he indicated the direction of the cave they'd used

for shelter. "Hey, Rocky, get me your jacket," he motioned to the cruiser with his chin.

Confused, Rocky did as he said, got his jacket and gave it to Brogan. Brogan trod over to Coli. She was standing barefoot in her pajamas, the top exposed a sliver of her flat belly every time she moved, and the material was thin enough it showed how the cool breeze that picked up was affecting her. She crossed her arms over her breasts.

Brogan helped her into Rocky's jacket and buttoned it up. Gave her a kiss and then lifted her in his arms.

"Brogan!" she gasped.

"Your feet have taken enough punishment, baby." He carried her to his truck and settled her in.

"Douggie!" she squealed with relieved delight. Grabbing up the dog, she hugged him to her chest. "You're okay, puppy, I was so worried Grandfather Auston had hurt you."

Brogan leaned in the truck and patted the dog's back. "Careful, babe, he is hurt. He's okay but like I said, we're gonna stop at the vet's on the way home."

The ambulances appeared from around a crop of trees and came to a stop near them. Paramedics jumped out. Brogan advised them of Silina, where she was and her injuries, and he pointed to where Ricardo still lay on his side, his wrists cuffed at his back.

Avoiding muddy puddles left from the downpour, half of the paramedics hurried to the cave with a collapsible cloth gurney, the other half jogged to Ricardo.

Leaving Coli in the truck, Brogan rejoined his team. The four lawmen stood near a tree, the wind had lessened as the storm blew off down the plains, but it tickled the leaves making occasional drops of rain fly over and plink on the men.

Watching the paramedics working on Ricardo, Rocky asked, "What happened to that guy? He doesn't look too good."

Brogan didn't look over at Ricardo, he crossed his arms and said flatly, "He and a tornado and a strike of lightning had a party."

"And Silina Arabat?" Tarzan asked.

One big shoulder bumped, Brogan said just as matter-of-factly, "She took a tumble down a very steep jagged hill. They both tried to kill Coli."

"Shit, Brog, you got a story to tell." Tarzan grinned.

Brogan nodded, squinted over to where Coli was waiting, a shade of a smile drew that dimple in. "Yeah, later."

Dam said, "Crackers, Brog, what a wild scene. Murder and mayhem, and that female killed three people? Two grown men and a woman?"

"Coli and I chatted while waiting for you. Coli told me Silina also admitted that she was the one guilty of throwing her baby out of a tree house trying to kill him. Her purpose was to get rid of him and frame her half-sister at the same time. It worked.

"The boy was brain damaged and sent to live in a group home, and her sister was locked up in juvenile prison for most of her childhood for a crime she didn't commit. Silina confessed that she killed Delian because of jealousy, and she did Blanco because he ragged on Silina that he preferred her sister to her."

"What about the paint store owner?" Rocky asked.

Brogan's face twitched with his repulsion. "She murdered an innocent man purely just to tie more evidence against her sister. She wanted Coli gone for good this time. She planted Coli's crystal goblets, the antique knife, her pearl button, and her dog's hairs, and added a can of varnish and a photo.

"She didn't know Coli hadn't used paint stripper or varnish, she sanded the wood in her house and stained everything with tung oil. Silina brought me a can of varnish she said she found in Coli's trash. There wasn't another can anywhere, not in the house or the trash."

"Diabolical black widow," Dam commented, the others nodded their agreement with his description.

"Yeah, well, she was scheming but just not that smart. When I found the knives and glasses in plain sight at Coli's house, I was aware that Silina, and Silina's mother Goldie, and the sick bastard grandfather all had access to them too. Not counting getting caught on video near two murder scenes at the times of the crimes, Silina

messed up by taking the photo of Coli wearing the blouse with the button missing before Polito was killed."

Tarzan said wryly, "Typical dumb criminal."

They watched the paramedics wheel Ricardo to an ambulance and get him inside. Tarzan asked, "What's up with that one? How's he figure in?"

Brogan's face darkened. He told them, "Ricardo Bastile, filthy pig. He's Silina's new boyfriend. He was going to rape Coli along with her sick bastard grandfather. They brought her out here to kill her and bury the body. Coli fought back," his proudness of her clear in the light in his eyes, the softening of his mouth.

"Her grandfather was going to rape her? Condones her murder?" Dam was appalled.

"Yeah, the fuckers. He wasn't her blood grandfather. The mother was in on it too. Apparently the old geezer assaulted Coli when she was a toddler, a child. Deranged sicko got his own real granddaughter, Silina, pregnant with his child when she was only twelve years old."

"The poor thing."

Brogan scowled at the sympathy in Dam's voice. "He didn't force her, she wanted it, wanted him. Another reason she wanted Coli out of the picture was because the perverted grandfather still desired Coli, and Silina was a jealous bitch." They quieted as the paramedics carried Silina out on the collapsible gurney. When they placed her in the other ambulance, one of the paramedics came over to speak with Brogan.

"The male is in pretty bad shape. Took a helluva beating looks like by fists." All eyes shifted to Brogan, his expression remained bland.

"It appears the poor guy was struck by lightning. The entire side of his face was scorched. It's blistered, he's never going to look the same again. We think he was electrocuted so there'll possibly be brain damage. People," the man said blithely, "we tell them again and again, don't go under trees when there's a lightning storm."

Shaking his head, the paramedic glanced over at Coli sitting in the truck. The passenger door was open, her legs hung out, Douggie was cuddled on her lap, she watched the proceedings.

"That little girl, ah, young woman," he nodded towards Coli, wearing Rocky's jacket and said, "she's in her pajamas, bare footed. I thought I saw injuries to her arms and face, and likely her feet. We have room in this ambulance, we can take her too."

"No," Brogan said flatly. "She stays with me, I'll take her to the Urgent Care. Need to get the pup to the vet." After all that had happened, he wasn't letting Coli out of his sight.

"Sure bro," the paramedic replied. He dipped his head to the men and tramped back to the ambulance heedless of his boots plopping in muddy puddles along the way.

"All right." Brogan rubbed the back of his neck, his eyes on Coli. "I'm taking her to the clinic, then stopping at the vet's, then I'm taking her home. Her grandfather, I mean," his lips twisted in disgust, "the old pedophile, and Silina's mother Goldie may still be at the house. I want them gone before we get there. Arrest them both for attempted rape and attempted murder. First degree."

"Attempted rape?" Dam asked, his gaze flicked to Coli.

A growl came deep in Brogan's throat. "Don't question me, boy." His scowl lightened as pride for Coli came back into his voice. "That little girl fought off the old man, Goldie, Silina, and that strong stud they just put in the ambulance."

He said, "Okay, we're outta here, go take out the trash at the Inn." He made his way to his truck. Waited for Coli to move her legs inside and he closed the door.

CHAPTER THIRTY-THREE

Douggie was examined and cleared by the vet after his wound was cleaned, stitched and bandaged. At the Urgent Care, Coli's cuts were bandaged up as well and cleared to go home. On the way, Pirate called Brogan.

"Yeah, Lo," Brogan answered.

"Got some info, Brog, you're gonna dig, lotsa stuff," mischief and actual mild elation laced his deep, normally hard blank voice.

Brogan's hand on Coli's knee squeezed. "I have all the good news I need right here with me, Lo." She smiled up at him, covered his hand with hers.

"Uh, okay. I'll tell ya anyway. First police business. The old man, Auston Augustine, he didn't make it. After the haboob passed, he and the woman, Goldie Arabat tried to make a run for it to their car, they were nervous the cops might show up. Ha, they did, Goldie must have ESP."

"Lo," Brog groaned, "get on with it."

"Hmm, impatient, son. Aaanywaay, they misjudged the strength and lethal wrath of the storm that chased behind the haboob. From the powerful pairing of the squally lightning storm and the windswept haboob, devastating tornados ignited all over parts of Builu County.

"According to Mrs. Arabat, a tornado rampaged across the lawn and scooped up the old man, whirlpooled him around and around

carrying him way off down the road where it eventually launched him at a wrought-iron fence that surrounded a farmhouse.

"Kinda grisly, bro, but it suddenly dropped him, he landed on a spire of the iron fence, poor guy was impaled. I met Doc Martone at the hospital, he didn't think he died right away, might of suffered a bit before passing. Kinda like a pinned fly." Pirate didn't look the least disturbed at the gruesome picture he drew.

He went on, "The woman was dragged by the tornado, her feet in the air, face planted on the ground, and, shit Bro, saw her myself, it was nasty. Face scraped up beyond recognition. Tore off deep hunks and chunks of skin down to the bone all over her body."

Brogan grunted. "Okay, that is, ah, interesting news."

"Got better, Brog."

"Yeah?" He'd relay that info to Coli in a more vague description of what happened to Goldie and the Old Man Incestuous Raping, Murdering Asshat.

He heard Pirate take a deep breath before he spoke. "Yeah," Pirate parroted his friend. "Someone has come forward, Brog, from Iraq."

Brogan's body stiffened, tingles raced up his arms at the word Iraq, his smile disappeared. "And?"

"Ah, this person was there during it all, man, everything. He has immigrated here and his cousin is a cop in Oregon, and an ex-marine, like us. The guy confessed to his cousin that he was there that day, hiding, afraid he was going to die. He will tell our ex-Command that he saw not you, but Gunnar shoot Davey."

His breath stopped, pulse raced, Brogan's voice caught in his throat.

Pirate took a beat, then said, "They always claimed friendly fire killed Davey, American bullets were retrieved from his body. You were the only one inside when he was shot. You remember in that pandemonium hell that day, there were guns lying around everywhere from our comrades that fell.

"Gunnar testified that he saw you and Davey go into that building alone. He said the building was vacant, no one else could have shot Davey. There was no proof that you shot Davey, but there

wasn't anything proving you didn't, ergo the General Discharge."
He paused.

Brogan stared blindly out the windshield, his hand crushing the wheel.

"He's credible, Brog, he was an Iraqi soldier. His squad was after the same group we were. His men were all killed, he hid. There was chaos, blood, smoke, he ran away when you and I carried Davey out. He told his captain what happened when he returned to his base, but they said it wasn't their business. He had always been curious about what he had seen. He wanted to know what happened that day after the firestorm.

"When he finally landed here in the States his cousin helped him google it. When he learned of your General Discharge, he told his cousin what he witnessed, and they went to the local Marine base and made a statement. "

"He stated he saw Gunnar shoot Davey just before you entered the second room of the building behind him. You remember, all of us were scattered all over in the crazy bedlam, no one could say where anyone else was. Gunnar was in the building before you and Davey entered."

"But why? Why would Gunnar kill Davey?"

"Well, the transcript I read," *hacked,* "said that apparently Gunnar and Davey were distant cousins and lived in the same town. Gunnar was looking to borrow an extra pair of socks in Davey's duffle and he found a letter. Gunnar's fiancée had been cheating on him with Davey. Her letter said when the guys got home she was leaving Gunnar for Davey."

He paused before saying with feeling, "Brog, man, you're gonna be cleared, you hear me? You're gonna get your life back. Brog?"

Brogan's hand holding the phone dropped in his lap, Pirate's voice still coming from it. Seeing his face frozen, eyes wide and unstaring, Coli took the phone from his hand and said, "Hello? This is Coli Cassidy, something, something's upset Brogan. Can you-"

A chuckle rolled from the cell, Pirate told her, "Yes ma'am, something happened for sure. Something good, monumental. Make

him tell you about it. He knows all your dark shit, make him tell you his. Tell him to call Pirate when it sinks in." He hung up.

Coli held the phone in her lap and turned to Brogan. His Adam's apple was jogging up and down with his rapid swallows, beads of sweat trickled down his temples, he still stared blankly at the road, one hand squeezing the wheel, the other Coli's knee. "Um, Brogan, you're kind of hurting me," she told him.

"Huh?" He glanced down, his fingers were digging into her knee. "Oh, ah, sorry." He loosened his grip but kept this hand there.

"It's okay. Can you, um, tell me about the phone call? I spoke with Mr. Pirate, he said to ask you about the call, and when you, I guess, have time to reflect on what he said to give him a call back."

"Hmm." Brogan drove from the Urgent Care and through the business section of Mal Tierre.

"He, uh, said to ask you to tell me about what he told you. So," she watched his brow quirk, lip twitch, he blinked and seemed to clear his head.

"Okay, baby, but I'm starvin', I'll tell you over lunch. That all right with you? If you're feelin' up to it."

"No, I'm fine. The doctor gave me something for my headache, I'll survive my cuts and bruises." She half-turned to look in the back.

Douggie was curled up in a box stuffed with cushioning on the seat. Brogan had wrapped the box up in the seat belt. He was sound asleep from the anesthesia the vet gave him while he stitched his wound.

"Douggie should be fine for an hour." She swung around and smiled at Brogan. "Yes, I could eat a horse!" Her eyes flicked to the back seat. "Not that I would of course."

"Of course." Brogan chuckled. Driving down Tres Calle, he asked, "There's not much in Mal Tierre except bars and diners, but there're two nicer restaurants, not five star, maybe two star. Violet Petals and Helio-chompers. Violet Petals is a soup and salad bar. Helio-chompers is more burgers, hoagies, gyros, calzones. Which would you prefer?"

Coli's gaze swept back and forth checking out the city street. The buildings were designed in western style. Lots of wood and

brick, wagon wheels out front, barrels and wooden fences, haystacks, steer horns posted over doors. The storm had missed most of the downtown area. "Oh Helio-chompers, sounds more exciting tasting."

"Helio's it is." Brogan drove down the street and parked in front of a cowboy restaurant. It had a one-beam log fence out front to tie a horse to. He parked and hurried around to open Coli's door.

Entering the restaurant, they passed through a door designed to look like saloon swinging doors, with giant, green ceramic cacti on either side of the entrance.

They ordered subs, Rueben with slaw inside it for him, Philly cheesesteak for her. They both had root beer and shared the fries and onion rings.

Coli took a sip of her soda then bit the end of a fry dipped in ketchup and said, "Okay, spill, big boy."

A bark of a short laugh erupted from Brogan. Grinning at her, he crunched an onion ring. "A little action and my baby comes out of her shy shell. All right, Cubbie-doll."

Picking up his sub, he sobered somewhat. Taking a bite, he chewed and swallowed before speaking. "The first part of the news was that, ah, I had sent the police to your house. They took Goldie to the hospital."

Her brows rose, fry paused at her open mouth. "Oh? Is she all right?"

He squeezed mustard on his sandwich.

"Gee, Brogan, it already has thousand-island dressing, coleslaw and a bunch of other condiments…" she grinned at his sandwich.

"Yep." He took a huge bite and chewed thoughtfully. "Goldie was pretty banged up in the storm. Instead of stayin' safely inside the house, they ran for their car and, well, a tornado raced through there too. There was no damage, baby, to the Victorian, but Goldie was hurt pretty badly. She'll be sort of okay. It'll be a while for her rehab before she can stand trial."

Dabbing at her lips with her napkin, Coli reached for an onion ring. "She wanted me dead, but, still, I'd feel horrible if she had died

in the storm. What about Grandfather Auston?" Revulsion and a hint of fear of the old man were in her voice.

Brogan watched her. He was damned glad the old bastard died, and painfully after what he'd put her through, as a child and as an adult. All three of the Arabats sent Coli away to prison taking away her childhood for something she didn't do, and the old bastard had molested her when she was little and defenseless. Then the bastards had tried to kill her.

Brogan tried to keep the gladness out of his tone when he told her, he said carefully, "He didn't make it, Coli, I'm sorry." He wasn't sorry the creep died, he was sorry Coli would feel bad even after what he put her through.

She set her sub down. "Oh dear. How did it happen?"

"He was swept up in a tornado and," he didn't want to tell her he had been skewered, she's the softy kind that would have nightmares over that. "He just, didn't survive his injuries."

"Wow." Her eyes watered, she sniffed the tears back.

"Baby." Brogan clasped her hand. "Don't feel sorry for some sick perverted asshole that wasn't your blood. He'll be dancin' with the devil and get his real due then. Don't waste your sympathy on the likes of him."

Her eyes rolled down to her sub, she tore off a piece of shredded beef and slid it in her mouth. "I guess."

Brogan patted her hand then picked up his Rueben. "So," Coli cocked her head at him. "Mr. Pirate said you had a…history to share with me. I'm listening."

His shoulders humped as slaw slipped out of the side of his sandwich, he turned it to lick the escaping slaw. Brogan debated whether or not to tell her about his past, but, he planned on them having a life together, a family, children, their relationship should start out with no secrets.

She repeated gently, "I'm listening. No judgments here, Brogan."

Relief and suffering poured out in his sigh. "Yeah, babe. Well, I was a Marine. Pirate, Tarzan and Rocky were in my unit. We were in Iraq, it was…bad over there. Our squad was sent deep, our task

was to take out a gang of vicious insurgents. They slaughtered everything in their path, and took full brute joy in everyone they sadistically destroyed.

"We saw unspeakable horrors. One time we came across a pyramid. When we got close we realized it was made up of human parts. Hands, feet, legs, heads, young, old, male, female, babies."

"Oh, Brogan, what you had to endure, I'm so sorry, for all of you."

He sat back, crossed an ankle over a knee and fiddled with a knife. "Yeah. Anyway, we were deep in a jungle, more like a forest. We'd taken out pockets of insurgents when we came upon a ramshackle building. The forest had almost grown over the structure, it was that old. Then, we were hit by gunfire.

"We hunkered down, shot back. It only took less than an hour for five of our unit and all of the rebels to be killed. The dust settled, we cleared the perimeter, but not the house.

"One of our guys, Davey Morrison and I were gonna search the structure while the rest of the team held down the perimeter. I didn't know where everyone was, our men were scattered. Some were hauling our deceased to a central location so we could take 'em home with us." The agony he experienced lined his eyes and mouth, his skin flushed with pain at the memories.

"So," he took a deep breath, let it out slowly. "Davey and I went in, there were several rooms, we separated to search them. Suddenly, there was gunfire, inside the house. I felt the sting of a bullet hit my shoulder, the force of it spun me, slammed me into a wall. Davey raced out of a room screaming, 'Go! Go! Go!' So I ran. I was dozens of yards away and near our troop when I realized Davey wasn't with me. I had to go back in."

Blue eyes wide as balloons, Coli cried, "No, you didn't!"

He nodded. "Yeah, of course I did. But Pirate went with me. Tarzan and Rocky were part of the unit that gave us fire cover while we raced across the dirt and leaves and, we had to slow at the doorway for possible ambush. When we got inside, ah," his voice hitched, he lowered his head in his hands.

Coli placed her hand on his arm but stayed silent, let him get his grief under control.

A few heavy, shuddering breaths, he continued, "Davey was down. Pirate watched my back while I checked on him. He was...dead. I dropped my weapon when I knelt to make sure. Hell," he shook his head, "half his head was blown off, there was no doubt he was gone. We checked the rest of the building, it was vacated. Pirate and I got under Davey's arms and hauled him the hell out of there." He stopped, eyes blank with the dreadful memory.

Waiting patiently, after a few minutes, Coli prompted him, "Then what happened, Brogan?"

His body did a full shake, and he blinked, turning his pained gaze to her. When his eyes lit on Coli, some of the strain rolled off his tensed shoulders, eased the lines in his face. He stroked the side of her face, smiled briefly. "You ease my pain, baby."

She squeezed his arm, he went on, "Yeah, so, when we got back to base, after the medic stitched me up is when another in the unit, Gunnar Galfston claimed that I had shot Davey."

Coli's brows hopped up. "You? You would never-"

"Damned right, I would never." His chest lowered with a heavy exhalation. "I'll skip the middle of the cheery story. They couldn't prove or disprove I did it. It was one of our bullets in his head, and while getting Davey out, I inadvertently left my gun in the building, we never went back there so they couldn't compare ballistics. But, they couldn't disregard what happened, so I ended up with a General Discharge."

"That was unfair, Brogan!" Coli protested.

"Yeah, it was. Afterwards, I managed to get this job as sheriff here. Shortly after I got hired, Pirate, disgusted with the fallout of the events, left the Marines, Tarzan followed, and then Rocky. I got Tarzan and Rocky jobs here, Pirate wanted nothing to do with any kind of institution, he didn't trust them. He went independent. Although he does work with us on occasion."

"Mr. Pirate seemed to indicate there was...news about that?"

He chuckled. "It's just Pirate, no mister, baby. Yeah, great, fantastic, unbelievable news. There was an Iraqi soldier at the scene.

He hid during the gunfight, but he saw Gunnar shoot Davey. He's immigrated to the States and he's at Command as we speak, clearing my name."

A broad grin pulled that dimple in. He exclaimed with disbelief, "Goddamn, baby, I'm cleared. I'll get benefits and pension, but the only thing that really matters is that my name is cleared, I'll get my life back."

Coli's smile was big, but it didn't fill her eyes.

He saw it. "What, honey? What's wrong?"

"Oh, nothing, um, you'll go back into the Marines, I can totally understand it. Maybe, you'll…" the smile quivered, "send me a postcard, and email once in a while?"

Brogan's eyes popped in confusion, then he understood. Smiling, he reached over, curled his hand around her neck, pulled her towards him and lodged a long, hard kiss on her lips.

When he released her, her eyes were dusted with desire, matching his. "Cubbie-doll, all I care about is getting my name cleared. I like my life here. I've made my home here amongst my loyal friends, I like my job, and," he leaned in giving her another wild kiss, "I love you."

Her lips froze under his, she pulled her head back, brows wrinkled. "You- you what?"

"You heard me, Cubbie, I love you. When I was at your house and grasped something bad had happened to you, my insides died. I've never been so terrified in my life. I don't want to live without you, baby, I realized then that I loved you. I want there to always be an us. I want to spend the rest of my life proving to you how much I love you."

A tiny gasp, pink stained her cheeks, a stunned Coli blinked at him. "You- you do?"

He kissed the tip of her nose. "You bet, baby. Hell, I can't wait to move into that Victorian mansion of yours. There's a rocking chair with my name on it on that verandah. And," he winked, "I hear the owner is a helluva cook."

He sat back and picked up his sub. "Eat up, baby, Kip's out at the Gregorys', your family is…gone, let's go have us some alone

time. I wanna show you what real lovemaking is like, baby, not violent brutal rape. You with me?"

Sucking on her straw, Coli smiled shyly, nodded. "Brogan."

"Yeah, baby?"

"Thank you for coming for me, for saving me."

"Cubbie-doll, you saved yourself. You got away all on your own. I don't know that you could have gotten yourself and Silina down the hill, but you're smart and resourceful, I'm sure you would have found shelter and waited out the storm."

"Maybe, but I would have more than likely broken my neck as you're always harping on me, and don't forget Ricardo was there waiting, prepared with the hammer. He would have ambushed me, no, you are my hero, Brogan."

She beamed at him. He reflected the beam back at her. "Yeah, and you're my beautiful, brave heroine."

On the way to the Victorian, Brogan's cell rang. He pulled it out, swiped and put it on speaker then stuck it in the phone holder on the dash. Without looking at it he answered, "Dillon."

"Bro," came the response.

"Lo, hey man, we'll talk, but right now Coli and I-"

"Only a second, bro, just another bit of info. Petra Peerina came by with a picture she found on her phone. There had been an event, cheese and paintings or whatever at the art gallery. There was a photograph of Rex Reno, it came up on facial recognition. We just got the full data now. His name isn't really Rex Reno, it's Ronan Roarke. He was a deputy on some resort island or some such."

There was a pause as if Pirate was looking up the name of the resort. He said, "Here it is, Isle of Orainn. Some island out in the Northwest."

Another pause and he went on, "I spoke with the sheriff there. Roarke was a rogue, a corrupt son-of-a-bitch that used his job to violate women, he committed blackmail and some other crimes they're digging up. Apparently the shit hit the fan and the guy blew.

"Thing was, the Coast Guard or something tracked the helicopter he escaped in, said they saw it crash and burn. They found the wreckage but no body. They weren't sure if he walked outta

there, it was dead winter and he landed out in the middle of nowhere with no supplies."

"They're sure Reno is this guy?"

"Yep. Sheriff on the island scanned a pic of Roarke and your BFF, Jacks Navarro confirmed it was him. But, dude's in the wind. No trace of him or Dane Zachary."

Brogan said, "We still got a guy lookin' for that girl, Poppy? Reno, Roarke, whatever, may go after her. She could be a witness to Kandy-Marie Birchfield's murder, she could be in danger."

"Royce is on it. Anybody can find her, that bro can," Pirate told him.

"Okay, hell, son, good news all day, all around." He smiled at Coli who was glowing at him. Hell, she always glowed, from the inside out.

"I'll holler at ya later, son, I got me a big date, waitin'."

CHAPTER THIRTY-FOUR

One Year Later

Coli stood at the window in her bedroom, a soft smile adorning her face. It was all worth it, all the fire and damnation she'd gone through. The prison, the assaults, her despicable family, the trial.

The trial, ah, her head fell back, she gazed at the ceiling. It had been terrible. Silina fought it until the very end, but the evidence, she was on the videotape at Pete Polito's, the Panini guy recognized her as buying the breakfast sandwich.

She had been smart enough to wipe her prints from the coffee cup, but stupid enough to leave them on the bag and the wrapper of the sandwich. Her DNA was even found on the henbane leaves she'd stuffed in the sandwich.

She was seen with Camille Blanco right before she died. She had access to Coli's cutlery and glasses and her blouse, and the dog hair.

Brogan had been right, her DNA was also on the blouse, which her attorney said they were sisters, and sisters borrowed clothes. But it just piled on top of all the other evidence.

Heavens, she'd killed three people, kidnapped Coli and was assisting in her sexual assault and planned murder. She'd flung her own baby into the air hoping he'd die. Unfortunately, they couldn't

prosecute her for that, there was no evidence and Silina wasn't about to confess to anyone else.

The trial went on for weeks, it was ridiculous since a blind deaf person could see she was guilty as sin. Plus, she'd confessed to Coli and Brogan. But, Silina thought when she limped in every day the jury would pity her and let her off.

She suffered permanent damage to her arms and legs in the fall off the cliff. Her limbs had been pretty much crushed, her arms hung funny and she had a pronounced limp in her right foot. Even her face was a bit off from a crushed cheek.

But, the jury didn't care, apparently they felt she'd made her own trouble and sentenced her to 25 to life. Maybe she did get off lightly after all for three first degree murders.

After seeing Silina found guilty, Goldie and Ricardo took pleas. They confirmed Silina's guilt, clamping a closure lid on her professions of innocence. They'll never be the same either.

Goldie's face was beyond repair, chunks of it were gouged out and mauled when she was dragged by the tornado. She kind of looks Frankenstein-ish now.

And poor Ricardo. He was worse off than Kip. Face badly burned and partially brain damaged from the lightning strike he could barely follow the court's proceedings. They both received 20 years, and since they were in jail pending their trials, Coli and Brogan were the only ones that attended Grandfather Auston's funeral.

Brogan was angry that Coli wanted to go, after what the old man had done to her, but, he would never refuse her anything, and he would never let her go alone. It was a brief funeral, and now Coli could close that chapter and get on with her life.

Coli lowered her head to look out the window, the ache in her heart receded as she gazed out at the backyard. The gardens were chock full of different squashes, lettuce, broccoli, beans, peas, carrots, tomatoes, potatoes and on and on. They'll also reap a winter harvest as well.

She'd proven everyone wrong that nothing would grow on her rocky land. They had layered and lavished the soil with fertilizer and love.

The garden fully supplied the Inn's vegetable needs. Which, her smile widened at the sight of guests wandering the grounds, was packed to the gills.

Word of mouth spread like wildfire. Finally most of the trails in the woods were groomed and ready for horseback riding. Coli had made a deal with a ranch up the road for horses until she could get her own barn and stables built.

The only blight on their happiness was Brogan's military case hadn't yet been instigated. He had a lawyer but was told cases were backed up possibly for years.

Brogan was okay with that though, now he knew others knew he was innocent of the charge that he'd killed his friend.

He had love and his new created family, and friends, and a good job. He told Coli daily he was so fulfilled it overflowed from his long time, turned-to-stone heart that had revived with Coli's love.

"Cotty." Kip tramped into the room, his face shone with happiness and health. He was flourishing at the Inn. The guests loved him and he loved taking care of them. He learned from each guest, he learned about their state, their histories.

He soaked it all up like a sponge, he gained new knowledge every day enhancing his brain power. He could only enhance it so far due to the damage, but he was ten times better, and happier than he'd been when she had first brought him home.

She pivoted to face him, the smile almost hurt her face she was so happy. "Hey, Kippie."

"Cotty, Marky wants to see the punkin' patch, is that okay?"

Kip loved his pumpkin patch. He was in charge of it, and it was rolling in enormous round, orange gourds. Guests were starting to ask for some. Halloween will be especially cool with the pumpkins and scarecrows already staked in the back grounds.

She couldn't wait to decorate with bales of hay scattered and ghosties hanging around the porch. "Sure, honey, but remember,

you need to get dressed. Do you know where Mr. and Mrs. Gregory are?"

He nodded briskly. "Yeah. They're showing some guests the stuff in the carriage house. Some of Mrs. Gregory's paintings are for sale you know, and Mr. Gregory gets all braggy about them. He likes to show them off."

Also a success. Coli had turned the carriage house into the local amateur artisan gallery, and it was doing fantastic. Locals bought from neighbors, and guests from around the country flocked to it, again by word of mouth.

"Mrs. Gregory said she was coming to help you get dressed, Cotty." He headed for the door, his grin infectious.

"Kip, find Douggie and **Felipé** and put them in your room. You know how they manage to somehow trip the guests, and today of all days I don't want to have anything mar the occasion. Okay?"

"K, Cotty." He disappeared through the arched doorway.

Coli called out after him, "Don't get dirty, Kip, and don't forget to come up and get dressed!" When Mrs. Gregory came to help her dress she'd ask her to make sure Kip cleaned up and dressed.

The sun gleamed through the window striking her ring. She lifted her hand to admire it, her smile so full of love.

Only a month after they opened the Colipatra Inn and received their first guests, on the verandah, the paddles twirling gently above, the flowers sprightly in baskets, Brogan got down on one knee and took a tiny case out of his pocket.

He'd had it custom made for her. A ruby in the center because they had each other's heart, surrounded by spears of colorful gems, sapphires, emeralds, amethyst and topaz, intermingled with diamonds between each spear of jewel.

He'd told her he wanted to give her the moon and the stars and the sun, but for now he'd give her a rainbow.

"It is so very lovely, my dear, just like you." Mrs. Gregory stood in the doorway with a big cheerful smile.

An hour later, Coli trod gracefully down the sapphire staircase and met Kip. His face was red with nerves, but still he grinned ear-

to-ear. She slipped her hand in his arm and said, "You look so dashing in your tux, Kippie."

The tips of his ears turned red as they strolled through the Victorian and to the back. "You mean like James Bond?"

She laughed. "Yes, just like James Bond. You have the rings, right?"

Frantically he patted every pocket until he pulled them out. They were tied to a tiny satin pillow. "Mr. Gregory put them in my coat pocket so I wouldn't forget." He grinned at her. "You look really pretty, Cotty, like a fairy princess."

"Thank you," she said with a sweet, loving smile. Her gown was satin with shimmering cap sleeves and bodice, a short veil topped her shining golden ringlets. She lifted part of the skirt so she wouldn't trip over the long train with the white stilettoes.

The back of the Inn was huge with glass French doors and they were wide open. Coli took in the scene laid out in front of her. The vegetable gardens way off to the left of the grounds, the pumpkin patch off to the far right.

In the middle, the amazing rose garden thrived, so delicate and colorful, the fragrance of the blossoms permeated everywhere drawing guests to their beautiful bounty. She was able to put bouquets on all the tables in the Victorian.

White chairs with pink bows lined both sides of the garden, vases of calla lilies and pink peonies led the way to where Pirate, Tarzan, Rocky, and even Jacks Navarro stood flanking Brogan.

All the men wore gigantic grins. But, Brogan's eyes heated as soon as they lit on her. Rocky and Jacks were her groomsmen, and Pirate and Tarzan stood for Brogan. Pink and white rose petals carpeted the aisle.

The music started, Deputy Lenita Pupatelli, lovely in a pink organza gown sang Ava Maria beautifully as Kip walked Coli down the aisle.

The guests, staff at the police station, and the O'Riordan's employees minus the manager, Winston Luzzini who wasn't invited, also special returning guests at the Inn, all rose as Coli and Kip trod slowly over the carpet of rose petals.

Coli's eyes rounded and then she shook her head with a grin.

Up at the makeshift altar, under a trellis of pink and white roses, down by Brogan's feet lay Douggie and **Felipé**. Douggie appeared to be asleep as usual, **Felipé** looking bored was licking his white paw. They both wore black bow ties. She assumed that was Brogan's doing.

Kip brought Coli to Brogan then stepped back as they'd practiced.

Pirate, looking like a pirate in a tux, moved discretely to Kip and held his hand out with a whisper. Kip blushed, then giggled as he handed the rings to Pirate. While he did that, Brogan took a few steps forward to meet Coli, his eyes aglow.

Sliding her hand in the crook of his arm, he murmured, "So beautiful, Cubbie-doll. No flower could ever come close to your exquisite beauty, baby, you take my damned breath away."

"And you, Brogan," she whispered shyly even though they'd spent a lot of quality time getting acquainted with each other's bodies the past months, and Brogan had indeed taught her what real lovemaking was like. It was making love, gently, vigorously, edgy, always thrilling and satiating.

Brogan worshipped her body and cherished her, and he made it crystal clear how much he loved her. "You are so handsome in your tux you bring delicious tingles to my…" she ducked her head slightly in embarrassment.

He caught her chin and lifted it, he had pushed her to speak what she wanted without fear of judgment or criticizing. "Your…" he said with an arched brow.

Giggles feathered her throat, she stood on tiptoes to whisper in his ear, "You make my lady parts tingle."

He couldn't help it, Brogan barked out a laugh. The groomsmen tittered, Kip laughed with them although he didn't know what was funny, and that made the audience chuckle.

The minister tried to frown at them all, but the corners of his mouth nicked up.

Father Barker waited until everyone quieted again then he said his words, then Coli and Brogan said their vows. Coli stifled a giggle

when Douggie had laid his maw on Brogan's foot, and **Felipé** was rubbing his white furry face against Coli's leg.

Brogan grinned big and whispered to Coli, "I guess they're tellin' us we've all been accepted into the family."

He bent closer and said in her ear, "Speaking of family, as soon as the reception is over how 'bout we start workin' on that, Cubbie?" And he enjoyed the blush that filled her gorgeous face. The works were already in for Coli to become Kip's legal guardian, and for Brogan to adopt him as his own.

The reception was wild and joyful with dancing and food and drink and heavy partying. Copious pictures were taken, it was a happy wonderful event. But, Brogan waited impatiently towards the end of the night for the guests to leave.

Kip was staying the night with the Gregorys. Brogan and Coli would have the house to themselves as for the few days they hadn't had any guests so they could concentrate on the wedding.

They planned to leave for Hawaii in a few days, but Brogan had big plans for consummating the wedding tonight. Coli's dress was gorgeous and he couldn't wait to get her out of it.

They said goodbye to the guests who tossed wildflower seeds and rose petals over their heads. Then they saw Kip off in the Gregorys' car, Douggie and **Felipé** disappeared as usual. The newly married couple stood in the foyer.

Brogan smiled at Coli. "Well, Mrs. Dillon, are you ready for," he wriggled his brows at the staircase.

"Oh yes, Mr. Sheriff, always ready for you, my husband." She slid her hands up around his neck and pressed her lips against his, then squeaked when he lifted her up in his arms. "What are you doing, Brogan?"

His broad laugh trailing them, he strode for the sapphire staircase. "You're my Scarlett, baby, and I'm your Rhett, I'm gonna show you how a husband makes love to his bride. Yeah?"

"Yeah," she grinned, and he swooped her up the stairs.

THE END

The Kissing Number

Louise Furley